All That I Am has won more awards than
any other book in Australian history.

Winner, Miles Franklin Literary Award 2012

Winner, Barbara Jefferis Award

Winner, Australian Independent Bookseller Award for Best Debut Fiction

Winner, Indie Book of the Year 2012

Winner, Australian Book Industry Award, Best Literary Fiction

Winner, Australian Book Industry Award, Book of the Year 2012

Winner, Nielsen BookData Booksellers Choice Award 2012

Winner, Western Australian Premier's Book Award 2012

Short-listed, Prime Minister's Literary Award 2012

Finalist, Victorian Premier's Literary Award 2012

ALL THAT I AM

"You will have suffered a couple of blows to the heart and the solar plexus by the time you finish *All That I Am*, a book that hits a nerve and jangles the body, for it speaks to the times we are living in RIGHT NOW. Courage, it seems, is a constant, is a precious element of humankind in times of upheaval and terror. The need for truth, yearning, and the connection of one human to the next— as Anna Funder writes it—is so tangible it popped my head apart some." —Tom Hanks

"History, like hope, is not something to be solved, but to be carried. Anna Funder has written an essential novel about how we carry the bricks of history on our backs, and how we continually build new homes from the material of the past. *All That I Am* is an intimate exploration of human connection and our responsibility to one another. Funder breathes life into Kundera's aperçu that the struggle of man against power is the struggle of memory against forgetting." —Colum McCann

"The subtlety of Anna Funder's novel is in the elegance of her precise prose, and in her painstaking portrait of an ordinary woman swept up in extraordinary events. . . . The result is a strong and impressively humane novel." —*Times Literary Supplement* (London)

"A seamless and powerful tale . . . a narrative of individual endeavor and survival that examines universal themes. Above all, this is a book with a strong moral compass. . . . Dora and Ruth, especially, convey a sense of truthfulness and decency that transcends their time and should inspire us, even now, to expose injustice and tyranny." —*Independent on Sunday* (London)

"Anna Funder proved herself a first-rate reporter with *Stasiland*—now she appears as a compelling novelist in a dark story of German émigrés in the 1930s, struggling to warn the indifferent English against the Nazis."   —Claire Tomalin

"Absorbing . . . by alternating between Ernst and Ruth, Funder leaps through time with alacrity. She adds an integral perspective on a shopworn subject by invoking the lives of Nazi dissidents whose attempts to alert the world to the growing menace of Nazism were ignored until it was too late."
                                                  —*Publishers Weekly*

"A murder mystery now more than three generations old becomes a catalyst for a deeper, richer story about two perennial but inexhaustible themes, love and loyalty. Rarely has a novel been filled with such intelligent, inquisitive, introspective characters."   —*Canberra Times*

"A superb novel. . . . This book is a wonder. Do, please, read it. . . . It is a novel about confronting grievous loss, and the horror of realizing, as history closes over you, that you will never be understood."
                                                  —*Spectator* (London)

"A beautiful ensemble novel of Graham Greene–esque proportions in terms of suspense and moral scope. . . . Elegantly illuminates the bloom and emaciation of love under extreme pressure."
                                              —*Weekendavisen* (Denmark)

"A gripping story of love and betrayal. Dora is the most attractive fictional heroine in a long time."   —*New Statesman* (London)

"A pacy and exciting read. Captures perfectly the sense of her characters' deprived and dangerous lives." —*Daily Mail* (London)

"A remarkable story told with clarity and precision, along with moments of insight and literary grace." —*The Guardian* (London)

"With its story of Europe's huddled outcasts of the Third Reich, *All That I Am* should be compared to such novels as Erich Maria Remarque's *Arch of Triumph* and Lillian Hellman's *Pentimento*."
                                                    —*Politiken* (Denmark)

"Funder's political and moral intelligence shine even more brightly than in *Stasiland*; the compassionate but unsentimental truthfulness toward her characters is even more moving for being interwoven into a narrative of such complexity."   —Australian Books of the Year

"A literary work as suspenseful as the best thrillers, Funder's extraordinary first novel is an unflinching portrait of courage in devastating circumstances."   —*Library Journal*

"Superb. . . . Funder writes beautifully, with an understated lyricism that never gets in the way of the gripping story. Deeply moving and highly readable."   —*Irish Times*

"Funder is a sophisticated, psychologically subtle writer. . . . *All That I Am* is, unquestionably, about people and issues that matter. It is provocative, imaginative, sometimes fierce, and always humane. I loved it."   —*Sydney Morning Herald*

ALL THAT I AM

ALSO BY ANNA FUNDER

Stasiland: Stories from Behind the Berlin Wall

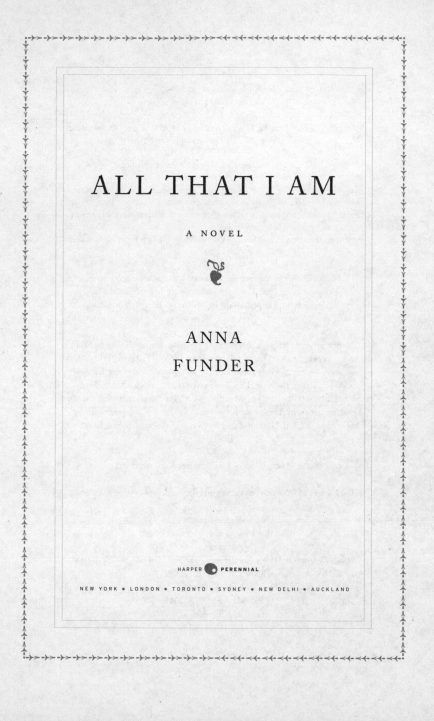

ALL THAT I AM

A NOVEL

ANNA
FUNDER

HARPER PERENNIAL

NEW YORK • LONDON • TORONTO • SYDNEY • NEW DELHI • AUCKLAND

HARPER ● PERENNIAL

First published by Penguin Group (Australia) in 2011. First U.S. hardcover published in 2012 by HarperCollins Publishers.

P.S.™ is a trademark of HarperCollins Publishers.

ALL THAT I AM. Copyright © 2011 by Anna Funder. All rights reserved. Printed in the United States of America. No part of this book may be used or reproduced in any manner whatsoever without written permission except in the case of brief quotations embodied in critical articles and reviews. For information address HarperCollins Publishers, 10 East 53rd Street, New York, NY 10022.

HarperCollins books may be purchased for educational, business, or sales promotional use. For information please write: Special Markets Department, HarperCollins Publishers, 10 East 53rd Street, New York, NY 10022.

The first epigraph on page ix is from 'In Memory of Ernst Toller' by W. H. Auden, copyright © 1976, 1991, by the Estate of W. H. Auden. Both it and the quote on page 155 are reproduced by kind permission of the Estate of W. H. Auden. The second epigraph on page ix is reproduced by kind permission of Nick Cave and Mute Song Ltd. The third epigraph is Simon Leys' translation of Antoine de Rivarol in *Other People's Thoughts*, Black Inc., Melbourne, 2007, p. 11, reproduced by kind permission of Simon Leys and Black Inc.

FIRST HARPER PERENNIAL EDITION PUBLISHED 2013.

The Library of Congress has catalogued the hardcover edition as follows:

Funder, Anna.
All that I am : a novel / Anna Funder.
p. cm.
ISBN 978-0-06-207756-1 (hardcover)—ISBN 978-0-06-207757-8 (trade pbk.)—ISBN 978-0-06-207758-5 (e-book)
I. Title.
PR9619.4.F86A78 2011
823'.92—dc23
2011028168

13 14 15 16 17   OFF/RRD   10 9 8 7 6 5 4 3 2 1

In memory of
Ruth Blatt (née Koplowitz)

Dear Ernst, lie shadowless at last among
The other war-horses who existed till they'd done
Something that was an example to the young.

W. H. Auden, 'In Memory of Ernst Toller',
May 1939

Outside my window the world has gone to war
Are you the one that I've been waiting for?

Nick Cave, '(Are You) the One That
I've Been Waiting For?'

The most civilized nations are as close to barbarity
as the most polished iron is close to rust. Nations,
like metals, shine only on the surface.

Antoine de Rivarol

ALL THAT I AM

When Hitler came to power I was in the bath. Our apartment was on the Schiffbauerdamm near the river, right in the middle of Berlin. From its windows we could see the dome of the parliament building. The wireless in the living room was turned up loud so Hans could hear it in the kitchen, but all that drifted down to me were waves of happy cheering, like a football match. It was Monday afternoon.

Hans was juicing limes and making sugar syrup with the dedicated attention of a chemist, trying not to burn it to caramel. He'd bought a special Latin American cocktail pestle that morning from the KaDeWe department store. The shopgirl had lips pencilled into a purple bow. I'd laughed at us, embarrassed at buying such frippery, this wooden shaft with its rounded head that probably cost what the girl earnt in a day.

'It's crazy,' I said, 'to have an implement solely for mojitos!'

Hans put his arm around my shoulders and kissed me on the forehead. 'It's not crazy.' He winked at the girl, who was folding the thing carefully into gold tissue, listening close. 'It's called ci-vi-li-sation.'

For an instant I saw him through her eyes: a magnificent man with hair slicked back off his forehead, Prussian-blue eyes and the straightest of straight noses. A man who had probably fought in the trenches for his country and who deserved, now, any small luxuries life might offer. The girl was breathing through her mouth. Such a man could make your life beautiful in every detail, right down to a Latin American lime pestle.

We'd gone to bed that afternoon and were getting up for the night when the broadcast began. Between the cheers, I could hear Hans pounding the lime skins, a rhythm like the beat of his blood. My body floated, loose from spent pleasure.

He appeared at the bathroom door, a lock of hair in his face and his hands wet by his sides. 'Hindenburg's done it. They've got a coalition together and sworn him in over the lot of them. Hitler's Chancellor!' He dashed back down the corridor to hear more.

It seemed so improbable. I grabbed my robe and trailed water into the living room. The announcer's voice teetered with excitement. 'We're told the new Chancellor will be making an appearance this very afternoon, that he is inside the building as we speak! The crowd is waiting. It is beginning to snow lightly, but people here show no signs of leaving . . .' I could hear the pulse of the chanting on the streets outside our building and the words of it from the wireless behind me. 'We – want – the Chancellor! We – want – the Chancellor!' The announcer went on: '. . . the door on the balcony is opening – no – it's only an attendant – but yes! He's bringing a microphone to the railing . . . just listen to that crowd . . .'

I moved to the windows. The whole south side of the apartment was a curved wall of double casements facing in the direction of the river. I opened a set of windows. Air rushed in – sharp with cold and full of roaring. I looked at the dome of the Reichstag. The din was coming from the Chancellery, behind it.

'Ruth?' Hans said from the middle of the room. 'It is *snowing*.'

'I want to hear this for myself.'

He moved in behind me and I drew his hands, clammy and acidic, across my stomach. An advance party of snowflakes whirled in front of us, revealing unseen eddies in the air. Searchlights stroked the underbelly of clouds. Footsteps, below us. Four men were racing down our street, holding high their torches and trailing fire. I smelt kerosene.

'We – want – the Chancellor!' The mass out there, chanting to be saved. Behind us on the sideboard the response echoed from the box, tinny and tamed and on a three-second delay.

Then a huge cheer. It was the voice of their leader, bellowing. 'The task which faces us. Is the hardest which has fallen. To German statesmen within the memory of man. Every class and every individual must help us. To form. The new Reich. Germany must not, Germany will not, go under in the chaos of communism.'

'No,' I said, my cheek to Hans's shoulder. 'We'll go under with a healthy folk mentality and in an orderly manner instead.'

'We won't go under, Ruthie,' he said in my ear. 'Hitler won't be able to do a thing. The nationalists and the cabinet will keep a tight rein. They just want him as a figurehead.'

Young men were pooling in the streets below, many of them uniformed: brown for the party's own troops, the SA, black for Hitler's personal guard, the SS. Others were lay enthusiasts, in street clothes with black armbands. A couple of boys had homemade ones, with the swastika back to front. They were carrying flags, singing, *'Deutschland, Deutschland über alles'*. I heard the cry, 'The Republic is shit,' and made out from its intonation the old schoolyard taunt – 'Rip the Jew's skirt in two/the skirt is ripped/the Jew did a shit.' Kerosene fumes buckled the air. Across the street they were setting up a stand where the young men could exchange their guttering torches for new-lit ones.

Hans returned to the kitchen, but I couldn't tear myself away.

After half an hour I saw the wonky homemade armbands back at the stand.

'They're sending them around in circles!' I cried. 'To make their number look bigger.'

'Come inside,' Hans called over his shoulder from the kitchen.

'Can you believe that?'

'Honestly, Ruthie.' He leant on the doorjamb, smiling. 'An audience only encourages them.'

'In a minute.' I went to the closet in the hall, which I'd converted into a darkroom. It still had some brooms and other long things – skis, a university banner – in one corner. I took out the red flag of the left movement and walked back.

'You're not serious?' Hans put his hands to his face in mock horror as I unfurled it.

I hung it out the window. It was only a small one.

PART I

RUTH

'I'm afraid, Mrs Becker, the news is not altogether comforting.'

I am in a posh private clinic in Bondi Junction with harbour views. Professor Melnikoff has silver hair and half-glasses, a sky-blue silk tie, and long hands clasped together on his desk. His thumbs play drily with one another. I wonder whether this man has been trained to deal with the people *around* the body part of interest to him, in this case, my brain. Probably not. Melnikoff, in his quietness, has the manner of one who appreciates having a large white nuclear tomb between him and another person.

And he has seen inside my mind; he is preparing to tell me the shape and weight and creeping betrayals of it. Last week they loaded me into the MRI machine, horizontal in one of those *verdammten* gowns that do not close at the back: designed to remind one of the fragility of human dignity, to ensure obedience to instruction, and as a guarantee against last-minute flight. Loud ticking noises as the rays penetrated my skull. I left my wig on.

'It's *Doctor* Becker actually,' I say. Outside of the school, I never used to insist on the title. But I have found, with increasing age, that humility suits me less. Ten years ago I decided I didn't like being treated like an old woman, so I resumed full and fierce use of the honorific. And comfort, after all, is not what I'm here for. I want the news.

Melnikoff smiles and gets up and places the transparencies of my brain, black-and-white photo-slices of me, under clips on a lightboard. I notice a real Miró – not a print – on his wall. They socialised the health system here long ago, and he can still afford that? There was nothing to be afraid of, then, was there?

'Well, Dr Becker,' he says, 'these bluish areas denote the beginnings of plaquing.'

'I'm a doctor of letters,' I say. 'In English. If you don't mind.'

'You're really not doing too badly. For your age.'

I make my face as blank as I can manage. A neurologist should know, at the very least, that age does not make one grateful for small mercies. I feel sane enough – young enough – to experience loss as loss. Then again, nothing and no one has been able to kill me yet.

Melnikoff returns my gaze mildly, his fingertips together. He has a soft unhurriedness in his dealings with me. Perhaps he likes me? The thought comes as a small shock.

'It's the beginning of deficit accumulation – aphasia, short-term memory loss, perhaps damage to some aspects of spatial awareness, to judge from the location of the plaquing.' He points to soupy areas at the upper front part of my brain. 'Possibly some effect on your sight, but let's hope not at this stage.'

On his desk sits a wheel calendar, an object from an era in which the days flipped over one another without end. Behind him the harbour shifts and sparkles, the great green lung of this city.

'Actually, Professor, I am remembering more, not less.'

He removes his half-glasses. His eyes are small and watery, the irises seeming not to sit flush with the whites. He is older than I thought. 'You are?'

'Things that happened. Clear as day.'

A whiff of kerosene, unmistakable. Though that can't be right.

Melnikoff holds his chin between thumb and forefinger, examining me.

'There may be a clinical explanation,' he says. 'Some research suggests that more vivid long-term recollections are thrown up as the short-term memory deteriorates. Occasionally, intense epiphenomena may be experienced by people who are in danger of losing their sight. These are hypotheses, no more.'

'You can't help me then.'

He smiles his mild smile. 'You need help?'

I leave with an appointment in six months' time, for February 2002. They don't make them so close together as to be dispiriting for us old people, but they don't make them too far apart, either.

Afterwards, I take the bus to hydrotherapy. It is a kneeling bus, one which tilts its forecorner to the ground for the lame, like me. I ride it from the pink medical towers of Bondi Junction along the ridge above the water into town. Out the window a rosella feasts from a flame tree, sneakers hang-dance on an electric wire. Behind them the earth folds into hills that slope down to kiss that harbour, lazy and alive.

In danger of losing their sight. I had very good eyes once. Though it's another thing to say what I saw. In my experience, it is entirely possible to watch something happen and not to see it at all.

The hydrotherapy class is at the fancy new swimming pool in town. Like most things, hydrotherapy only works if you believe in it.

The water is warm, the temperature finely gauged so as not to upset the diabetics and heart fibrillators among us. I have a patch I stick on my chest each day. It sends an electrical current to my heart to spur it on if it flags. From previous, quietly death-defying experiments, I know it stays on underwater.

We are seven in the pool today, four women and three men. Two of the men are brought down the ramp into the water on wheelchairs, like the launching of ships. Their attendants hover around them, the wheels of the things ungainly in the water. I am at the back, behind a woman in an ancient yellow bathing cap with astonishing rubber flowers sprouting off it. We raise our hands obediently. I watch our swinging arm-flesh. The aging body seems to me to get a head start on decomposition, melting quietly inside its own casing.

'Arms over heads – breathing in – now bringing them down – breathing out – pushing till they're straight behind you – breathe IN!'

We need, apparently, to be reminded to inhale.

The young instructor on the pool edge has a crescent of spiky white hair around her head and a microphone coming down in front of her mouth. We look up to her as to someone saved. She is pleasant and respectful, but she is clearly an emissary bearing tidings – rather belatedly for us – that physical wellbeing may lead to eternal life.

I am trying to believe in hydrotherapy, though Lord knows I failed at believing in God. When I was young, during the First World War, my brother Oskar would hide a novel – *The Idiot* or *Buddenbrooks* – under the prayer book at synagogue so Father would not notice. Eventually I declared, with embarrassing thirteen-year-old certainty, 'Forced love hurts God,' and refused to go. Looking back on it I was, even then, arguing on His terms; how can you hurt something that doesn't exist?

And now, eons later, if I am not careful I find myself thinking, Why did God save me and not all those other people? The believers? Deep down, my strength and luck only make sense if I am one of the Chosen People. Undeserving, but Chosen still; I am long-living proof of His irrationality. Neither God nor I, when you think about it, deserves to exist.

'Now we're concentrating on legs, so just use your arms as you like, for balance,' the girl says. Jody? Mandy? My hearing aid is in the change rooms. I wonder if it is picking all this up, broadcasting it to the mothers wrestling their children out of wet costumes, to the mould and pubic hair and mysterious sods of unused toilet paper on the floor.

'We're putting the left one out, and turning circles from the knee.'

A siren sounds, bleating on and off. Over at the big pool, the waves are going to start. Children walk-run through the water with their hands up, keen to be at the front where the waves will be biggest. Teen girls subtly check that their bikini tops will hold; mothers hip their babies and walk in too, for the fun. A little boy with red goggles darts in up to his chin. Behind him a slight young woman with hair falling in a soft bob on her cheeks walks calmly forward, shoulderblades moving under her skin like intimations of wings. My heart lurches: Dora!

It is not her, of course – my cousin would be even older than me – but no matter. Almost every day, my mind finds some way to bring her to me. What would Professor Melnikoff have to say about that, I wonder?

The wave comes and goggle-boy slides up its side, tilting his mouth to the ceiling for air, but it swallows him entire. After it passes he's nowhere. Then, further down the pool, he surfaces, gulping and ecstatic.

'Dr Becker?' The girl's voice from above. 'It's time to leave.'

The others are already over near the steps, waiting for the wheelchair men to be positioned on the ramp. I look up at her and see she's smiling. Perhaps that microphone gives her a direct line to God.

'There's ten minutes till the next class but,' she says. 'So no hurry.'

Someone is meting out time in unequal allotments. Why not choose a white-haired messenger, lisping and benign?

Bev has left me a small pot of shepherd's pie in the fridge, covered tight in plastic wrap. It has a sprinkling of pepper on the mashed-potato topping, and it also has, in its perfectly measured single-serve isolation, a compulsory look about it. So I thaw a piece of frozen cheesecake for dinner – one of the advantages of living alone – then fizz a Berocca in a tall glass to make up for it. I'll have to explain myself to Bev when she comes tomorrow.

In bed the cicadas outside keep me company – it's still early. Their chorus coaxes the night into coming, as if without their encouragement it would not venture into this bright place. *What a ni-ight!* they seem to chirrup, *what a ni-ight!* And then we are quiet together.

TOLLER

Two quick knocks at the door – Clara and I maintain formalities because formalities are required between a man and a woman who work alone in a hotel room, as between a doctor and a patient in the most personal procedure. Our formalities transform this place of rumpled dreams – the sod-green curtains, the breakfast tray uncleared, the bed I hastily made – into a place of work.

'Good morning.' An open smile on her red-painted lips, lips that look suddenly intimate. It is the smile of a young woman whose flame is undiminished by racial exile; who has possibly been loved this morning.

'Good morning, Clara.'

Today she wears an apricot faux-silk shirt with lavish sleeves and three-button cuffs – a cheap copy of luxury that lasts but a season and may just be the essence of democracy. 'Peachy', as they'd say here in America, although in English I can't tell poetry from a pun. She brings with her morning air, new-minted for this day, the 16th of May 1939.

Clara looks around the room, assessing the damage of the

night. She knows I do not sleep. Her gaze comes to rest on me, in the armchair. I'm fiddling with a tasselled cord. Its green and gold threads catch the light.

'I'll do it,' she says, springing forward. She takes the cord and ties back the drapes.

But the cord is not from the drapes. It is from my wife Christiane's dressing gown. When she left me, six weeks ago, I took it as a keepsake. Or an act of sabotage.

'No mail?'

Clara collects it each day from the postbox on her way in.

'No,' she says, her face averted at the window. She takes a deep breath, turns, and walks purposefully to the table. Then she rummages in her bag, still standing, for her steno pad. 'Shall we finish the letter to Mrs Roosevelt?' she asks.

'Not now. Maybe later.'

Today I have other plans. I reach over and pick up my auto-biography from the table. My American publisher wants to bring it out in English. He thinks that after the success of my plays in Britain, and my American lecture tour, it should sell. He is trying, God love him, to help me, since I gave away all my money to the starving children of Spain.

I don't need money any more, but I do need to set the record straight. As sure as I sit here today, Hitler will soon have his war. (Not that anyone in this country seems to care – his open-ing salvo, the invasion of Czechoslovakia just weeks ago, has slid down to page thirteen in the *New York Times*.) But what people don't realise is that his war has been on against us for years. There have been casualties already. Someone needs to write their names.

Clara is staring out the window at Central Park, waiting for me to gather my thoughts. While her back is still turned I ask, 'Have you read *I Was a German*?'

'No. No, I haven't.' She swivels, placing a stray curl of dark hair behind her ear.

'Good. Good, good.'

She laughs – Clara has a PhD from Frankfurt and a fine mind and can afford lavish self-deprecation. 'It's *not* good!'

'No, it is.'

She tilts her face to me, the freckles strewn across it as random and perfect as a constellation.

'Because I'm going to be making some changes.'

She waits.

'It's incomplete.'

'I should hope so.'

'No. Not updates. Someone I left out.'

My memoir is subtly, shamefully self-aggrandising. I put myself at the centre of everything; I never admitted any doubts or fear. (I was cunning, though, telling of isolated childhood cruelties and adult rashness, to give the illusion – not least to myself – of full disclosure.) I left my love out, and now she is nowhere. I want to see whether, at this late stage of the game, honesty is possible for me.

When I open the book in my lap its pages stand up like a fan, held tight to a midpoint. The National Socialists took my diaries – probably burnt them on their pyres as well. I must work from memory.

The girl sits down at the table, side-on to me. Clara Bergdorf has been working with me for five weeks. She is a rare soul, with whom silences of whole minutes are calm. The time is neither empty, nor full of anticipatory pressure. It expands. It makes room for things to return, to fill my empty heart.

I light a cigar and leave it smoking in the ashtray. 'We'll start with the introduction. Add this dedication at the end.' I clear my throat. 'I call to mind a woman, to whose courageous act I owe the saving of these manuscripts.' I breathe deeply and look out at the sky, today a soft, undecided colour.

'When in January, 1933, the Dictator of Braunau was given power against the German People, Dora Fabian, whose life has ended —'

And then I break off. Clara thinks I am paralysed by grief, but it is not so. I simply do not know how to describe that ending. In the park the wind toys with the trees, shifting leaves and branches a fraction every which way – as if the music has stopped but they cannot, for the sheer life of them, keep absolutely still. Clara risks a glance in my direction. She is relieved to see I am not weeping. (I have form in that department.)

'Sorry.' I turn back to her. 'Where was I?'

'"Dora Fabian,"' she reads back, '"whose life has ended."'

'Thank you.' I look out again and find my word. 'Sorrowfully,' I say, which is the plainest truth there is. 'Whose life has ended sorrowfully in exile, went to my flat and brought away to safety two trunk-loads of manuscripts.'

Clara doesn't look up. Her hand moves steadily across the page, coming to rest only moments after I stop speaking.

'The police got to know of what she had done and sent her to prison. She said that the papers had been destroyed. After she was released from prison she fled from Germany, and, shortly before her death, she got the papers out of Germany with the assistance of a disillusioned Nazi. Full stop.'

Clara puts down her pencil.

That is all? I close my eyes.

Dora's editorial trace is all over my book: the sharp focus, the humour. At the end of our lives it is our loves we remember most, because they are what shaped us. We have grown to be who we are around them, as around a stake.

And when the stake is gone?

'All right, then?' Clara asks softly after a few minutes. She thinks I've drifted off, taken advantage of her sweet presence and gone to sleep. She touches the edges of the pad in front of her.

'Yes, yes.' I sit up properly again.

I will tell it all. I will bring Dora back, and I will make her live in this room.

RUTH

The doorbell is ringing.

I ignore it. Without opening my eyes, I can tell it's morning.

Ring ring ring ring ring ring ring . . .

Verdammtes bell. Fuh-ken bell, as they say here. The thing has aged along with me and it sticks. I move my bad leg with the other one over the side of the bed, and slide my feet, gnarled as mallee roots, into the sheepskin shoes – one built up, the other plastic-soled. I leave my wig on the dresser.

Ring ring . . .

I open the door. The van speeds off – I can just make out, in purple writing on its side, 'The World on Time'. It's seven o'clock in the morning! A tad *early*, if you ask me.

A FedEx package on the mat. I stoop to get it with my stiff leg sticking out – I am a bald giraffe in an unreliable dressing gown and I feel sorry for any passers-by who might see me, mangy-minged and inglorious. This gives me a wicked thrill, till I imagine they might include children, whom I have, in general, no desire to horrify.

I move into the front room, my favourite room. It smells of furniture wax – Bev must have done it while I was out yesterday. She uses the wax – along with her Vicks VapoRub and her copper bracelets – as part of an arsenal against decay and time, suffocating the world with a layer of polyvinyls to make it shiny and preserve it forever like the plastic food in Japanese restaurant windows. She sprays the glass-fronted bookcases, the wooden arms of the chairs, even – I have witnessed this – the leaves of the rubber plant. One day I will sit too long and she will spray me as well, preserving me for all time as an exhibit: 'European Refugee from Mid-Twentieth Century'. Not that I need preserving. *Unkraut vergeht nicht,* my mother used to say: you can't kill a weed.

The other side of the package reads 'Columbia University New York, Department of Germanic Languages'. Here in Sydney, the events of the world wash up later as story, smoothed and blurred as fragments of glass on the sand. And now?

Dear Dr Becker,

            We refer to previous correspondence in this matter. As you are aware, the Mayflower Hotel is to be demolished at the end of 2001. The building is being emptied in preparation for this.

Um Gottes willen! How would I be aware? Sitting here in Bondi? And what 'previous correspondence'? Then again, it might have slipped my mind.

The enclosed documents, belonging to Mr Ernst Toller, were found in a safe in the basement. The material consists of a first edition of Mr Toller's autobiography, *I Was a German*, together with sheets of typed amendments to it. A handwritten note with the words 'For Ruth Wesemann' was found on top of them. The

German Restitutions Authority has confirmed that you were formerly known as Ruth Wesemann.

Should you so decide, the Butler Library of our university would be honoured to house this material for future generations. We already hold first editions of all of Toller's plays, and his correspondence from his time in the United States. We have taken the liberty of making copies for safekeeping.

If I or any member of the university faculty can be of assistance to you, we would welcome the opportunity.

Yours sincerely,
Mary E. Cunniliffe
Brooke Russell Astor Director for Special Collections

Toller!

His book is brittle as old skin, or a pile of leaves. The spine is broken, sprung loose from the cloth cover because of the sheets of paper thrust between its pages. Something from him to me: it can only be about her.

I reach to put it for a moment on the coffee table but my hands are shaking and some of the papers fall out onto the glass, then slip off to the floor. Inside me a sharpness – my hand moves to check the patch over my heart.

In his presence, and hers, I am returned to my core self. All my wry defences, my hard-won caustic shell, are as nothing. I was once so open to the world it hurts. The room blurs.

When I pick the book up again, it falls open at the first, typed insertion:

I call to mind a woman, to whose courageous act I owe the saving of these manuscripts. When in January, 1933, the Dictator of Braunau was given power against the German People, Dora

Fabian, whose life has ended sorrowfully in exile, went to my flat and brought away to safety two trunk-loads of manuscripts. The police got to know of what she had done and sent her to prison. She said that the papers had been destroyed. After she was released from prison she fled from Germany, and, shortly before her death, she got the papers out of Germany with the assistance of a disillusioned Nazi.

Ernst Toller
New York, May 1939

Toller was always a master of compression.

I pull a rug over my knees. I'd like to crawl back inside the night, perhaps to dream of her. But one can control dreams less than anything in life, which is to say, not at all.

TOLLER

I am so settled here I might never leave this room. The Mayflower Hotel, Central Park West, is quite a good hotel – not the best, by any means. Still, if I am honest, better than I can afford. But honesty is so hard. If I look too closely at the truth I might be unhinged by regret and lose hope in the world.

Then again, I may be well and truly unhinged already. Last week on the subway, a man hanging absent-mindedly onto the leather hand-strap stared at me a little long. Without thinking I flashed him what Dora called my 'famous person's smile'. The poor fellow turned away as if ignoring a tic.

I fled Europe for the land of the free, but I didn't quite count on invisibility. In Berlin or Paris, in London or Moscow or Dubrovnik, I couldn't take two steps without wading into autograph hunters. Once in a tender moment, Dora said it was good for me to know my work was appreciated. But I had been famous a long time; I was on first-name terms with the phantom-Toller the press had made. Though I needed applause like oxygen, I never believed the love and plaudits were for the real me, who, because of my black times, I kept well hidden.

Clara has gone to get coffee. We are in a hiatus; the hotel knows I can't pay the bill but is not throwing me out. Out of gratitude, we don't push the limits by using room service.

I love Central Park. There's a man out there now on a soapbox gesturing to passers-by, trying to attract and keep them like papers in the wind. I know that feeling: eyes screaming that the world belongs to you and you can reveal it all, if people will only stop, and listen. It is this prospect, of something freshly imagined, some new possibility of belief, that America holds out to all comers.

The book is in my lap. What *chutzpah*, to write my life story at forty! Or a bad omen. Perhaps, having written it down, I now feel the life is done. Dora would have made me snap out of it. There are some people just the thought of whom makes us behave better.

It is six years ago now, that we worked on this book. In Berlin, in my narrow little study on Wilmersdorfer Strasse. Dora's desk was behind the door, practically obscured if anyone opened it. She would sit there in the shadow, stockinged feet resting on two dictionaries stacked on the floor. My desk was bigger, under the window. She took down my words, pulling me up and putting me to rights if I veered off course. Dora thought I left the bitterest and most basic emotions out of the book, in favour of, as she put it, 'all that derring-do'. I didn't want to write about what went on inside me.

Our worst fight happened when I was writing about my – how should I say? – my collapse, after I was discharged from the front. When Dora wanted to interrupt me she used to put the steno pad down in her lap. When she had something serious to say, she'd swivel around to the desk, place pad and pencil down carefully there, and turn to me empty-handed. This was an empty-handed time.

She clasped her palms together between her thighs. 'I think . . .' she said, and stopped. She ran both hands through her dark, bobbed hair, which fell straight back into her face. She started again. 'You've just written here so powerfully about the horrors of the trenches.

And trying to save your men.' Her voice, airy and deep, got deeper. 'We need to see what that courage cost you.'

My heart beat slower. 'Read it back?'

She took the pad from the desk and read: '"I fell ill. Heart and stomach both broke down, and I was sent back to a hospital in Strasbourg. In a quiet Franciscan monastery kind and silent monks looked after me. After many weeks I was discharged – unfit for further service." And that's it.' She held out one blunt-bitten hand. 'That's all.'

I crossed my arms. 'I had thirteen months on the Western Front,' I said. 'And all of six weeks in the sanatorium. It was a black time. There's nothing to say about it.'

She rubbed her hands over her face. 'Let's leave it for now, then.' She turned back to the desk.

If I could see her now, even just to fight with me, to swivel her bony back away from me, I would give it all.

'So.' Clara's voice breaks the air. She places two cardboard cups down on the table in front of me, smiling as if to signal a new, better beginning to whatever is going on in this room. 'Guess what's so special about this?'

It takes me a moment to register her question. 'The magic of putting liquid into paper?' I have loved this kind of discovery since I got here, the sheer, left-field, practical ingeniousness of America.

'No.' She shakes her head. 'These cups are *endless*.' She uses the English word. 'Infinite cups! We can go back and they will refill them, forever.'

I must seem unconvinced, or not quite adequately enthralled.

'Or maybe not.' She shrugs and laughs a little, sits down. 'I'll have to find out how that works.'

Clara flicks through her steno pad, happier now after her contact with the outside world, her discovery of the bottomless cup. Clara is not even my secretary, but Sidney Kaufman's, from MGM's New

York office. Sid felt sorry for me after my scripts went nowhere (not enough 'happy ends', said Hollywood), so he's lent her to me.

She finds her place.

But I am frozen. Caricatures I can do. Types in a play – the Widow, the Veteran, the Industrialist – but not someone so huge to me. What if my only talent is for reduction?

'To understand her,' I say, 'you have to understand what she was trying to do. Dora was . . . a verb.'

Clara smiles.

'It all came out of the war. Our pacifist party, the Independents. And, I am sorry to say, Hitler and this war he is now making.'

I look through the book in my lap to find the passage about my breakdown. It is extraordinary to me now, the deceit of words, how in saying everything one can reveal nothing at all. I will start by doing as Dora said.

'Ready?'

'Yep.' Clara picks up her pencil.

'Okay. The heading is "Sanatorium".' And then I continue, at dictation pace.

It is practically a boy who stands to sing. Blond down on his cheeks, and some thicker, unruly hairs on his chin. Seeing him in this state of transformation – neither boy nor man – feels an act of intimacy that should not be allowed. Outside of here he would have started to shave. With a movement of his shoulders he pulls his wrists into his cassock, as if they're too tender to be seen. But he cannot stop his hands from gesturing with the notes, which move out from him to fill the room and soar inside us.

There was a boy his age at Bois-le-Prêtre, sitting in the ditch with tears and snot running down his face. His uniform didn't fit and he failed to salute me.

'What is it, Private?'

'My friend,' he blubbered. Behind him lay a boy in the grass, also sixteen or seventeen. His eyes were still open. The back of his skull and left ear were blown off. The flies had started to come for the meat.

'What are you doing here alone?' I asked the boy. I knew the cruelty of my question: until the shelling twenty minutes ago he was not alone. Now he was trying not to leave his friend. He was trying not to be left.

'I . . . I . . .'

'Get back to camp.'

The boy got up and started to move down the unsealed road, between two rows of thin poplars.

'Private!'

'Sir?' He turned around.

'You forgot to take his boots.'

He gave me a look of hatred so pure I knew he could keep fighting.

Such brutality we had taken inside of us.

In the sanatorium we sit at a long table, the monks in brown robes at the head of it, soldiers down the end. We patients wear remnants of uniforms – the greatcoats are especially prized – or a mishmash of civilian clothes if relatives have managed to send some. The only sound is the leather of the novitiates' sandals slapping the stone as they bring in the meal. All is calm, apart from the Christ hanging at the end of the room, naked and dying. He looks familiar – like a relative? So far as I can tell, he and I are the only Jews here. A row of high windows lets in light that striates the room, illuminating the air in all its minute, flying particles.

I have not spoken for seven and a half weeks. In the military hospital at Verdun they put electrodes on my tongue to spark it, as though the failure were mechanical. When I cried out they determined there was nothing wrong with my body, so they sent me here, where time, shunted only by slow bells, stretches out to heal.

The silence was a relief.

Lipp nods as he sits down next to me, tucking a napkin into his collar and spreading it out wide over his chest. He is a medical doctor in fancy clothes, but also a socialist – he insists on living in a stone cell just like everyone else here. Lipp is chatty, assiduous in his care of us. Nothing shocks him. During the day, I watch him move among the men as though doing the rounds of a normal hospital, speaking quietly, pulling on his goatee. He addresses me without waiting for an answer, as if to be mute were an entirely appropriate reaction to this world.

In the summer of 1914 everyone had wanted war, me included. We were told there had been French attacks already, that the Russians were massing on our border. The Kaiser called on us all to defend the nation, whatever our politics or religion. He said, 'I know no parties, only Germans . . .' And then he said, 'My dear Jews . . .' My dear Jews! We were bowled over by our personal invitation to war. War seemed holy and heroic, just as they had taught us at school – something to give our lives meaning and make us pure.

What could we have done, ever, to need such purification as that?

Dr Lipp bows his head and closes his eyes, then crosses himself and addresses his attention to his bowl, where barley and pieces of carrot float in a pale broth. Unusually for a socialist, he is also a fervent Catholic. He is convinced all things are part of a plan, even if we mortals cannot know it.

Some of the veterans have horrendous wounds, mended as best as possible at field hospitals before the men came here to be tended for other, unseen damage. Four are missing legs, or parts of them. Each is entitled to two prosthetic legs from the War Ministry in

Berlin, but they have not come. The fellow opposite us has lost both arms, one from the shoulder, the other from the elbow. His prostheses have arrived. They are made of metal and attach around his chest on the side where there is no arm, and to the remnants of the other arm by leather straps with metal buckles, the same as on a school satchel. He must need help to put them on in the mornings. As he sat down, I noticed his fly buttons were left open – is this an oversight, or a necessity? In a world without arms, dignity is hard to maintain. Can he handle his prick with the hook?

His neighbour reaches across for the man's spoon and without asking starts to feed him. Before, when I passed returned men on the streets of Munich or Berlin, the legless wheeling themselves along on boards, their cloth-bound hands pushing the ground, or sitting on their stumps on grey army-issue blankets selling matches, or the hundreds and hundreds of 'storkmen' on crutches, I thought them adept. I permitted myself the fantasy that, because of the cripple's skill with the board or crutch or cane, he had come to terms with his situation. Here, we fall off crutches and out of chairs, soiling ourselves and weeping with rage. This, too, is a transition stage that should be hidden. And it is being hidden, here.

It's a good broth today – chicken. The monks raise their own, and are not required to send them in for the war effort, just the bones afterwards for stock-meal, like everyone else. Theo on my left used to be an apprentice waiter at Aschinger's restaurant in Berlin. His nose and top jaw have been knocked out by a grenade; he wears a dark cloth patch that covers the centre of his face. Beneath it is a reddish hole his breath goes in and out of. The patch has no practical value; he wears it to spare others the sight of him. His eyes are pale blue above it, and hard to look at too.

Theo starts to feed himself, putting the spoon to the back of his throat and swallowing as best he can. The noise is disgusting. He will never kiss a girl. He will never work. He cannot speak.

Outside, the dead are honoured as heroes, but in here the maimed are ashamed.

Lipp turns to him and nods his approval. 'Good man,' he says, 'that's the way.'

The next course is matjes and potatoes. Theo mashes the oily fish into pieces of potato and does his best.

At the end of lunch, they ring another bell. We set down our spoons, traces of apricot syrup a bright filigree in the bowls. Talk resumes on the way out. Men light cigarettes. I walk behind Lipp, who is telling Theo of a metal prosthetic jaw, 'ingeniously screwed into the remaining bone'. They have taken Theo's sheets away.

When Lipp moves on to another inmate, Theo falls in with me. He raises his eyebrows and the little cloth puffs out a snort. He's brave, but he has the look, like many of us here: This cannot possibly be my life; there must be some mistake.

I think Theo likes our mutual silence. He knows as well as I do that the government doctors are not coming to give him a mechanical jaw – or if so, only in passing. They are coming to assess whether he, Theo Poepke, can return to civilian life, or whether he will be sent for the foreseeable future to one of the secret military hospitals. This is not a health issue. It is one of morale: the authorities do not want the horrifically wounded to sabotage support for the war, to frighten women on trams.

Just as Theo has settled into my cell to read, Dr Lipp runs in brandishing the newspaper.

'The tide is turning!' he shouts, then louder: 'The end is near!'

Theo raises his eyebrows at me good-naturedly. We are mute, not deaf.

White bubbles of spittle have collected in the corners of Lipp's mouth and the pale pink lining of his trouser pocket hangs loose from his hip.

'The Social Democrats have split! A group of them are voting to end the war! Block the funding! They're founding a new anti-war party, the . . .' He squints his left eye for better grip on his monocle. '"Independent Social Democratic Party". This is it, boys —'. He slaps the paper loudly with the back of his hand.

'Show me that,' I say.

'— and they're not locking them up this time!' Lipp finishes. Then stops, a wet grin splitting his face. 'He speaks,' he says.

Theo looks at me, his eyes going up at the corners. It could be a smile.

Once I started talking, they soon let me out. At first I was aimless. It was 1917, and although the end of the war might have been nearer than the beginning, it was still too far off. I went to Munich and enrolled at the university; I had a love affair with a girl whose sweetheart was at the front. When he was killed she lost interest in me.

My friends kept dying, throughout that year and the next. I had been saved but I did not feel worthy of it. Then I joined the new party – the Independents – and we campaigned for peace. My strength started to return. The authorities called us traitors, saboteurs of the war effort. They broke up our meetings and took us into custody. But we were as prepared to die for our country as they were; some of us already had. We just wanted to save it first.

In the monastery I thought the atoms had realigned to form me again, moved into place by notes of song and invisible grace. But now I see that the solid thing was outside of me; I had hitched my hopes to history.

The revolution came in Russia, and we waited for our own.

Clara moves her shoulders, her neck from side to side. It is as if we have both been back in the monastery with the wounded and the monks.

'Are you all right?' she asks.

'I haven't thought of those people for a long time.' My voice is hoarse.

There's a line between her brows and her eyes are searching. It is a face ravaged with puzzlement, sympathy brimming close to the surface. She blinks it away. 'How about I go get us some sandwiches?'

'Thank you.'

She puts her hands into the small of her back and arches, catlike, then pushes out her chair. She moves to the door for her jacket, but turns to face me before she gets there.

'After lunch, I thought, we could work in the park for a bit.' She opens her arms, gesturing at the abandoned world. 'I mean, for some air. See what's left of the cherry bl—'

I shake my head. I will stay in this room. I have always worked best in captivity.

She slips on her jacket.

'Why don't you have yours in the park?'

She is uncertain, then relieved. 'Okay . . .' She shoulders her bag.

'Actually, take the afternoon off. We've done enough for one day.'

She looks at me sceptically. It is inconceivable to her that someone would voluntarily stay in a room day and night when right outside this grand city shimmers and beckons like an amusement park, a lucky dip for grown-ups. Also, she suspects I'll not eat.

'I'll bring you a sandwich first.'

'No need.'

'The usual?' Clara has a way of ignoring me that is tender, not brusque. She is a ringmaster in a room with a tired old lion. She needs no chair or whip, the tone of voice will do.

'Thank you.'

'Capers?'

'Please.' I smile up at her. 'And thank you, Clara.'

RUTH

I take the milk out of the fridge and sniff it. It's okay. I boil the kettle and take care to pour the water into the cup, *not* the tin of International Roast. Last week, in a minuscule moment of steaming absent-mindedness, I ended up with an overflowing coffee tin. I wedge a packet of Scotch Finger biscuits under my armpit and take the cup down the hall to the front room. Most old people, I am convinced, live on Scotch Finger biscuits.

When I sit back down in front of Toller I spray crumbs everywhere – it's the Big Bang of biscuits! There are more crumbs than there ever was biscuit, and the thing will remain forever inexplicable. Bev is coming later on to clean. Of course she is cross when the place is not already clean. Long ago I decided to treat her huffing and puffing, her toxic, airborne reproaches as a game, as something that bonded us. She can sneer at my slovenliness (but I gave up the cigarillos!) while I feign gratitude for her ministrations. By this ritual we silently acknowledge that her virtue is superior to mine, though I, by happenstance and in no way that speaks to my merit, am superior in money.

So Toller had been in a sanatorium. I find it hard to think of such a firebrand mute. Dora never mentioned it – maybe she didn't know much about it. Though she did tell me other things about his war, things he would not speak about publicly. He'd volunteered, she said, because he'd wanted to 'prove with his life' his love of Germany. His physical courage had frightened those around him. Once, when a soldier lay wounded in no man's land, Toller ran out to pull him in but was forced back into the trench by a hail of artillery fire. For three days and nights the boy called them by name, at first loud and desperate, and then weaker and sadder. By the time he died Toller's enthusiasm for the war had curdled into a suicidal recklessness in the protection of his men. Dora said he felt responsible for the mess they were in, as if it were, somehow, all his fault.

Dearest Toller. Why is it famous people are so much shorter in real life? The first time Dora brought him to my studio in Berlin – I was at Nollendorf Platz, so that makes it 1926 or '7 – I opened the door and looked down and saw only two huge-horned gramophones, a pair of legs under each. Dora's voice came from behind one.

'He bought six of them, would you believe. For friends. One for you.'

'But we've never met!' I was embarrassed as soon as the words left my mouth, as if I'd said them in front of royalty. But I was shocked at the extravagance.

'Don't be so literal, Ruthie,' Dora's voice said. 'You going to let us in?'

They put them down on a table. Toller turned to me, smiling. For an instant I was in the presence of a piece of fiction, someone come to life from the pages of the Munich Revolution, from a WANTED poster, from theatre playbills. And then he was just there: a youngish man in a rumpled silk shirt, with wild, grey-streaked hair streaming off his forehead, pumping my hand. He held my eyes with his.

Toller had no small talk, no register for *Bekannten* – acquaintances. He would fix you with those dark eyes, for slightly too long. His only mode, with everyone, was intimacy. Women loved him for it. He bypassed all the agonising repartee, the uncertain negotiations of flirtation, and spoke as if he knew them, had already been inside them. Who wouldn't give themselves, wholly and fully, to a man who might at any minute sacrifice himself to save the world?

He was still smiling, holding my hand. 'I'd be able to look you in the eye,' he let go and gestured loosely to his bandy legs, 'if these damn things were straight.'

I laughed.

'Dora's told me all about you.'

'Really?' It seemed unlikely to me. Dora was over at my lighttable, looking at some negatives. I could tell by her stillness, though, that she was listening. Just as everything he said to me was intended for her.

Dora turned around, suppressing a smile. 'He's exaggerating,' she said, her eyes on him. 'I barely said a thing.'

'She told you I needed a gramophone?' I looked from one to the other. They laughed. 'It's very kind but I can't —'

'Please,' the great man said, showing me both palms, 'I couldn't resist. I really would like you to have it.' He started to cough, raising a fist to his mouth.

I saw then that to make a fuss would be to imply there was something abnormal about buying six gramophones on a whim, at least one of them for someone you'd never met.

'Well,' I said. 'Thank you.'

He looked relieved. The coughing stopped. 'Sorry.' He lowered the fist to his chest. 'An old lung problem.'

Dora let out a chuckle. 'That was your generation's *malaise du jour*, wasn't it?' she said. 'The problem on the lung.' She was a straight talker, though utterly without malice. People rarely took offence, but I saw Toller start. My cousin had been working for him for all of two weeks.

'And yours would be?'

'Oh, well . . .' She was thinking quickly. 'Ours would be – a complex of some kind. Father complex, mother complex, insecurity complex, authority complex . . .'

'Got all those too,' Toller smiled. 'They just don't make me cough. And anyway, I'm not even ten years older than you.'

Dora nodded as if to say *touché*, and turned back to my light-table. There was a tension between them I could almost see, like a string across the room, taut and loose and taut again. I realised they were lovers.

I pointed Toller to a stool. 'Shall we get started?'

Dora had arranged for me to take his photograph for a poster promoting *Wotan Unchained*, his new play. She'd told me how biting it was – a comedy about a megalomaniac barber called Wotan who wants, through a deft combination of demagoguery and butchery, to save post-war Germany from communists and Jews. (To think of that now! Terrible for Toller, really, to be able to see so clearly what was coming.)

I touched his shoulders lightly, to square him to me. The cyclorama behind him was white as his shirt; it would be beautiful to have that great dark head coming out of brightness.

'Just be yourself,' I said, moving back to my camera.

'Easy for you to say.' He eyed the camera on its tripod. 'You get to hide behind that thing.'

I stopped winding the film on. He was smiling at me in such a way that I felt suddenly, and absolutely, seen.

I turned back to my work.

'"Act natural",' he continued, 'is the worst thing you can say to an actor. They simply forget how to be. They get a kind of slow swagger.' He readjusted himself on the stool. When I looked up again he was posing, fist to chin and frowning, like Rodin's *Thinker*.

'Stop impersonating yourself,' Dora called from the other side of the room.

'Told you it's too hard,' he said softly to me, and then he started fooling about, forming pose after pose, thinker to boxer to a gorilla scratching his sides, like an actor warming up, or someone looking for his character. This wasn't working at all.

'Dee, can you give me a hand here?' I called.

She came over. I gave her a light meter to hold, behind me. It was a useless task: I needed her in his line of vision, to steady him.

The photograph became famous. It was used on all the playbills for his productions from then on, and sometimes by the news-papers too. It's a close-up, dominated by the eyes. They are large and kind and, somehow, naked. His mouth, full and curved, is closed. His brow is a little furrowed; there's a matching cleft in his chin. He looks as if he's just asked you, a beloved, to join him in one of his causes – feeding the starving Russians or repealing the censorship laws or freeing political prisoners. He is the poster boy for the new, post-war world, and though he knows the price you might pay, he wants *you*. He sits in a halo of light fragile as glass, as a bubble.

The sun, streaming through my front window, appears to have cleared a patch on my head: oh, the thermal advantages of female pattern baldness! I wasn't always so spare up there. But I must say it has been, in general, a boon not to have been a beautiful woman. Because I was barely looked at, I was free to do the looking.

Toller's book is on the table. Some of his amendments are still wedged into it, where he wanted them to go. I bend forward to collect the ones that have scattered.

Outside, a construction truck beeps into the neighbour's, blindarsing into a park. The clouds are retreating over the street and the front garden, away from me in my dressing gown in my house, out to sea. In Sydney's spring they perform each morning, rolling back from us like a tin-lid on sardines. The birdcall is intense. I choose to believe it is joy at the new day, but I know they're checking to see who has made it through the night.

From this angle in my chair, those clouds will snag on the frangipani in the yard, its branches naked as a gigantic coral, probing the air. If the tree doesn't stop them the clouds will go on to smother the two electric wires tethering this house to the pole in the street. *Water and electricity do not mix.* Voices come back to me, or sometimes just injunctions.

The mind is an interesting organ. Spooling and unspooling of its own accord. Or is the brain the organ, and the mind something else altogether, an effect of it, a *Scheinbild*? Professor Melnikoff tells me that Alzheimer's patients regress in their memories until the first things they learnt are the last things they forget: 'please' and 'thank you', the residual civilities of the human, hardwired into the hippocampus. One will become un-toilet-trained, but politely. *Thank you for wiping.*

But Alzheimer's, *Gott sei Dank*, is not what I've got. It's just that occasionally, as on the edge of sleep, an obscure memory pops up, like a slide in a carousel. My friends and the other people slip off it and into the room, they breathe and fidget and open their mouths.

Some memories may not even be my own. I heard the stories so often I took them into me, burnished and smothered them as an oyster a piece of grit, and now, mine or not, they are my shiniest self.

*   *   *

Nineteen-seventeen was the year that I, too, first came across the Independent Social Democratic Party. When Toller was in the sanatorium I was eleven, and in treatment of my own. But it isn't so much the illness as the recovery that has stuck in my mind. That was when I lived at Dora's, and my life began, as observer, audience. And as cousin.

That year, scarlet fever swept through our town in far-flung Silesia. Four children died. The proper doctors were all at the front, with my father. Father had volunteered, like so many Jews. He hadn't been allowed to study law – no Jews permitted till his younger brother Hugo's time – but the war welcomed them with open maw. In my child's mind I imagined no harm could come to him, what with all those doctors there.

When I had been sweating for three days, my mother sent Marta for the *Sanitätsrat*, the town's first-aid officer. He was a retired butcher with huge hands and yeasty breath. From his trade he had a certain confidence in jointing; he put his thumbs directly into my shoulder, ankle, knee, hip – till I yelped.

'Here!' he declared, pointing to the small tent of skin over my hipbone. 'The fever has lodged here!'

The man opened a case like one for a musical instrument, removing a long glass cylinder. He screwed the needle into it while they held me down – Marta and Mother at my shoulders, Cook at my feet. The *Sanitätsrat* put his hand on my upper thigh. Cook's mouth disappeared into a line.

When he finished I saw the full syringe marbling red and yellow-green.

'We must string up the leg,' the *Sanitätsrat* said. He went away and brought back a frame from his shop. It still had meat hooks jangling on it from a triangle of metal. He connected my bandaged foot to a pulley-and-weight system over the frame. This was meant to stretch the infected leg, lest it grow shorter than the other.

I stayed in bed for two months, and have since walked with a shift in my gait that has never bothered me once.

My father came home soon afterwards. He had a crippled arm, a wound he was as proud of as he would have been of duelling scars from a university fraternity. He had to learn to do everything with his left hand. Once, at lunch, my mother thought I was mocking his clumsiness and pulled me up sharply.

'What is the matter with you? Cat stole your manners? Half your soup falls back into the bowl.'

My mouth would only open part way. The pus had lodged in my jaw too, and locked it.

'So much for our Loquax,' Mother said. 'You seem to have worn out the mechanism.'

The family irony: they called the quiet one Loquax. Mother had certain areas of tenderness and whimsy – care of sick animals, silly operetta lyrics, expensive gifts for the servants, elaborate hat trimmings (I remember a toy bird, and – can this be right? – a miniature but entire three-masted ship) – but she was a Spartan at heart. My brother and I were undeserving of our wealth and health, but for our misfortunes we were personally responsible. (This, I have found, is a difficult life bargain.)

In Beuthen a local doctor offered to operate on my cheeks, to snip the tendon and release the jaw.

'But she will be scarred for life!' my father cried. In the trap on the way home he worried aloud. 'We can't have her scarred as well.' He meant as well as limping.

In Berlin Uncle Hugo, Dora's father, found a surgeon with an idea. He would cut me from behind the ears, where the scars could not be seen.

After the operation my parents left me for six weeks at Uncle Hugo and Aunt Else's, so the professor could visit his handiwork. It was the first time I had stayed away from home on my own.

My head was shaved and wrapped in gauze bandages, over the crown and taut under my chin. The professor had left gaps for my eyes, nostrils, mouth and ears. People ignored me, as though I were a deaf person or a pet: intimacies and arguments were carried on in my hearing.

Children are the only people who can see adults from inside their lives, permitted to observe every small thing, as if their forming minds are incapable of judging what they see, or as if it does not lodge there, somewhere, permanently.

I saw Paula, the housemaid with the strawberry mark on her face, kissing a wooden spoon for practice, long and with longing, her eyes shut. When Dora was at school I touched the mysterious suspenders and clasps she used when she bled, left hanging over the back of a chair. I watched Cook hoard eggs over five days to make a cake for her son's nineteenth birthday, even though her Michael had died the year before on the Somme.

The apartment at Chamissoplatz was large, and the three of them – Hugo, Else and Dora – seemed to live independent adult lives there, connected by bonds of rational affection and mutual regard, rather than the rule of blood. As far as I saw, they never slept. I could wander the corridors at any time of day or night and no one would reprimand me or send me back to bed; they fully expected that reason and nature would take me there, eventually.

If I came across Else in her study she would turn to me, her hair escaping its bun, floaty and alive, and show me one of her chemical equations. She would explain the beauty of the letters and brackets and numbers, of elements obeying laws. I could watch Hugo pace his room, mouthing an address for court the next day – or was it parliament by that stage? – then stop mid-sentence and move to the lectern to correct it. If he glimpsed me in the doorway he would call, '*Just* who I wanted to see!' and invite me in to pack his pipe, or play with Kit, the dim and feathery red setter who slept away his days in there. Hugo had no special voice for children. When he spoke to you he made you into your best self.

Hugo and Dora left early, so in the mornings I went in to Else. I sat in her room while Paula helped her dress, one covered button at a time up her spine. I remember once, she turned her head to me, heavy as a flower on a stalk. Paula kept working.

'Impractical, don't you think?' Else's voice was deep, unexpected, like Dora's. 'They should be at the front.'

I nodded. When Paula was gone she leant in to me. 'Those buttons,' she raised her eyebrows at the silly world, 'are a sign to others that I keep a maid.'

I nodded again.

'Come on, chatterbox, you need your egg.'

After breakfast Else would leave for the university laboratory and I would moon about. Sometimes I made pictures.

Dora had been given a Schulprämie box camera for topping her year. It sat on a high shelf in her room. She had no interest in it, but it fascinated me: a box with an eye. I held it to my chest and looked down into the small glass. Everything was contained there in rounded miniature: her steel-framed bed and white counterpane, a tottery pile of books on the floor next to it. I sensed the instant layer of protection between me and the world; I could be looking down but seeing straight ahead. Most of all I liked the way it gave me a reason to be looking. Dora let me use it while I was staying.

At first I made pictures of still things. Rhomboids of light thrown onto the carpet by the afternoon. The timpani of copper pans hanging in the kitchen, and their shadow-twins on the chalky wall. Myself in the mirror, the mummy-like head bent over the box, dark lashes fringing the bandages. The camera's shutter was a lever at the side of the box. It made a long, soft, metal sound, the sound of capture and theft. I owned these moments when I owned nothing at all.

Later I was bolder, asking my subject to hold still. I got Cook's floury hands on the ceramic mixing bowl and, once, Dora's face so close I caught the flickering mahogany lights of her iris. A pigeon on my window ledge turned into a grey blur of speed on the print.

When she came home for lunch Dora and I would eat together, just the two of us at table. Every day I had broth and rice pudding through a straw. After a couple of weeks I couldn't face it any more.

'Come on, Ruthie, just a little,' Dora said. 'It's not for much longer.'

I looked at her plate. A crumbed cutlet with fried potatoes and kale.

'Who needs to open their mouth so wide anyway?' she mused, chewing. 'It's probably just a residual thing. Like an appendix. A development from before knives,' she waved her knife, 'when people had to bite off huge chunks of antelope. Or whatever.'

Dora had no interest in food. She would much rather talk until her dinner went cold, then abandon it, justifiably, as congealed and inedible on the plate.

'I can't eat this mush any more,' I said.

She glanced at me. I was looking down at her meal. She picked up her plate and marched off to the kitchen, returning with a bowl of broth for herself.

'You smiling, Loquax?'

I nodded. She looked doubtful. Then, suddenly, full of mischief. 'Let me show you something.' She stood up again, placed one elbow on the table and made a fist. I thought she was about to show me a new kind of arm wrestle.

'Watch this.'

She opened her mouth wide and lowered it over her hand. Staring at me, she put her lips around the little finger, then, one by one, the other knuckles went in. She stopped at the thumb. Took in more air through her nose. It hurt to watch, but her eyes held me the whole time. A twist, an ugly grunt, and the thumb was in.

I was horrified, entranced. Here was my cousin, a woman but not quite, her black eyes full of pain, with a fist, a whole fist, in her mouth.

'Uugh!' She ducked and it slid out like a wet ball. Her lips had white stripes on them where they'd stretched.

'See?' She laughed, rubbing her mouth. 'Who needs such a jaw! Why on earth would anyone in their right mind do that?'

I was eleven years old and I'd never wanted to do anything more in my life.

One afternoon she didn't come home. It was April. I sat on the window-seat, watching the street. The trees held tight their secret green, unconvinced of spring. The doors to the next room were open. Through them came the murmur of men's voices, a pipe-tap on a shoe. I wasn't listening. Hugo was there with his friend Erwin Thomas, a colleague from the Ministry of Justice. I watched the street: tram cars shunting along their tracks, and the shifting patterns of hats.

When Dora finally came in I could see her through the gap between the doors, rosy from cold. I didn't go in to them, but moved back to the divan in the shadows of the room. Like all children, I knew that adult conversation was better if I wasn't there. Dora held leaflets in her left hand that flipped and fanned.

'Uncle Erwin!' She shook his hand. 'Papa.'

Hugo held her by the shoulders a moment. 'How did you go?' He turned to Erwin. 'Dora has been at the Krupp factory. Leafleting the women.'

Dora had joined the Young Socialists at fourteen, and now the brand-new anti-war party, the Independent Social Democrats. She and Hugo had spent each afternoon that week drafting the leaflet, and I had hung around in the background, listening to them debate every word and idea behind it. I understood little, but enjoyed the warmth of purpose between them. Hugo's speciality, honed from defending unionists, was criminal procedure. 'It's legal,' he had said over the draft, 'but I'm afraid that's no guarantee.'

I caught the seriousness in his voice. 'What do you mean?' I asked.

'Being legal is no guarantee against arrest these days.' The war was still on, Hugo explained, so protesting against it could be sedition, no matter how carefully worded the leaflet. Protesting against it at a munitions factory would, at the very least, provoke the authorities. Still, both Hugo and Dora felt it had to be done.

Here she was, though, home again safely, standing on the red rug in her lace-up shoes, looking from her father to Uncle Erwin and back.

'May I?' Uncle Erwin asked, extending his hand for a leaflet. He wore a ring with a crest on his little finger.

Uncle Erwin held out the leaflet with straight arms and read aloud: '"When the time comes for an end to this criminal war . . . count on your support as workers united in international solidarity . . . in the cause of peace . . ."' He looked up, bewildered. 'You're calling for them to strike?' He turned to face Hugo. 'Krupp is a Paragraph 172 essential industry. Such a protest is illegal!'

Erwin was not a real uncle, but a family friend. His father Max, a Nobel Prize-winning chemist, had been Else's teacher at university. The tips of Uncle Erwin's sandy moustaches were waxed to dangerous, magnificent points. I often wondered how he slept with them. I believe, thinking about it now, that he was a man who felt it was important to do 'the done thing'. He skied at St Moritz and summered at the family estate in Prussia; he read the current books, precisely because they were current. For Uncle Erwin there was a curriculum for living in which the things to do had been set down by others. The satisfactions and pleasures of life consisted less in doing them than in having ticked them off the list. He sometimes wore a black, astrakhan-collared coat that fascinated me – a man dressed in the soft-coiled underbelly of a lamb.

That day, he had on a tight grey flannel waistcoat, with a heavy fob-chain disappearing into its right pocket. His face was red.

Hugo said nothing and sat down. He had a quality of listening that could turn into a force of silence. Erwin switched to Dora.

'In a practical, let's say "materialist", sense, my dear' – he stroked the flat part of his moustaches with one hand – 'you are asking these women to vote themselves out of a job.' He looked again at the thin cyclostyled paper. '"You are at the heart of the industrial machine,"' he read, '"you have the power to reverse the lever of destruction —"'

'The union will support them while they are off,' Dora interrupted. 'We're looking at the broader issue here.'

'If you're doing that, then, my dear,' he eyed her, 'you must know that a vote for peace is hardly a vote for industry.'

Dora was shifting her weight from one foot to the other. 'I believe,' she said, 'you just admitted our economy depends on making machines for war.'

She was seventeen. I had never heard someone so young speak to an adult like this. It wasn't just talking back to him, it was the confidence to be calm doing it.

In Erwin's cheek I watched a bulge rise where his jawbone flexed under the skin. He turned to Hugo. 'You checked this?' He held the leaflet out as if it were a contaminated thing.

'I did. It's legal. Which is not, of course,' he smiled at his daughter, 'to take anything away from her courage in distributing them.'

'The law's a fig leaf over power,' Dora quipped softly.

Hugo unhooked his glasses from each ear and began to clean

them. 'My friend,' he said, 'I can see why you might have been swept up in 1914. But you must now be brave enough to change your mind. It is time to call for an end to this terrible war.'

Uncle Erwin's shoulders were high and tight. 'Our men are out there.' He thrust his arm towards the window, as though the soldiers were right outside. 'They are at Passchendaele and Verdun and the Eastern Front. They are dying, and you would make it for nothing!'

Hugo checked his glasses in the light. 'No,' he said softly. 'I would make it stop.'

Uncle Erwin was coming in and out of my line of vision through the gap between the doors. Dora moved to take the leaflet from his hand but he snatched it away. She glimpsed me but made no sign.

When Uncle Erwin spoke again it was to Hugo. His voice was pained. 'Do you believe in nothing?'

'I believe,' Hugo said evenly, 'that we are squandering the good name of Germany, along with her blood. The fact that the nation has gone to war does not make those who opposed it at the beginning, and those who oppose it now, traitors.'

'I am . . . behind . . . my country.'

'And my country,' Hugo said, 'is wrong.'

The hand with the ring consumed the leaflet. And through his cheek I watched his jawbone, locking and unlocking.

After Uncle Erwin left I started to cry. I don't know why – perhaps a reaction to adult anger. Dora and Hugo followed the sniffling and found me. They joked about the built-in handkerchief of bandages on my face, but I have always been ashamed of crying.

When it was time for me to go home to Silesia, Dora took her prize camera down from the shelf.

'Of course take this with you.'

I couldn't believe the casualness of her generosity; how light she could be with something so valuable to me.

I am now near enough to one hundred years old, which means it is only twenty times my little span since Christ walked the earth. That is not so long. Apart from the past coming up much closer, being old makes you privy to other people's endings. Hugo died of a heart attack less than two years later. He keeled over on a small bridge at a lily pond in the Tiergarten while walking Kit. He was found by two lady cyclists, Kit exercising his distress back and forth. Hugo was fifty-six years old and the revolution he and Dora had wished for was in full swing. Grief is the extension of love, and I believe Dora, at eighteen, took what she felt for her father into politics.

TOLLER

That hotel bed, with its thick white sheets and green-and-gold cover, looks innocent enough now, but it is a place of torment. When I can't sleep my childhood crimes return to haunt me. At three a.m. a siren along West 61st Street can unravel my early life, revealing it to be nothing but a string of unpardonable incidents. My father brings me a soft brown puppy. I call him Tobias. But he will not obey me. And we must all obey! I put him in a bucket to teach him a lesson; I dunk him under the water again and again, till he is a sodden, lifeless handful of fur. My heart shrinks to a black ball.

On his deathbed my father, riddled with cancer, beckons me to lean in. His voice is terrible; he cannot suck enough breath. All that remains is anger. I bend my ear to his mouth. 'It's – all – your – fault,' he stammers. Apropos nothing and everything. Then the black-winged reproaches come beating the air above my chest and trying to put out my eyes. At three a.m. nothing is more certain than that I deserve it, I deserve all of it, I deserve worse than this.

In the daytime when Clara is here, the creatures of my shame slither their filthy bodies back under the bathroom door, or so I think. I can see the puppy story for what it is: the violence of obedience, re-enacted by a child as it was done to him. We revolutionaries wished to rout this brutal authoritarianism, this terrible subservience, from German culture. I wanted to rout it from me.

My father's deathbed (and his lifelong) aggression created in me a strange pathology of responsibility. Aside from the privileges of class, that is how I came to feel it was up to me to fix things. Because otherwise, it *was* all my fault.

And, with our revolution, we tried. But as I flick through the book on my lap I see the odd, impersonal way I've described the events of it. I am always right in the middle of them, though I don't seem to make anything happen. Like a man pedalling hard on a bike with no chain.

'No mail.' Clara is standing in the tiny tiled foyer to this room, closing the door behind her. She wears a creamy dress, belted at the waist. I check quickly – I am dressed too.

What she means is, there is no news. We are both waiting, each day, for news. I have written three times to my sister Hertha in Germany, with no response. I know in my bones they have taken her away, and her husband and my nephew Harry, who is seventeen. Clara's parents have managed to get the money together to put her younger brother Paul – but not themselves – on the *St Louis*, a ship full of Jews escaping Europe for Cuba. And then, we hope, for here. The *St Louis* is due in Havana next week.

Clara brings the other letters over to the table and I look up at her clear, open face. I do not doubt that some part of her is racked with worry for her parents. But she can, like most people, contain it.

But when she sits and I look closer, I see that Clara is biting her bottom lip. Small, grey-blue shadows have appeared under her eyes and she seems thinner, cheekbones sharper. I get a sudden sense of what she will be like at forty, her life half led: fully, first-generation American, with perfect-toothed children and a past that includes once, long ago, listening to a washed-up old revolutionary from another world settling the account of his life.

I wish there were something I could do to help her parents, but there is nothing. From here, all I can do is try to explain.

'It is not possible to understand Hitler,' I say, 'unless you understand his hatred. And that began with us.' I light the first cigar of the day, inhale its black heat. 'What he is doing now will obliterate the memory of progressive Germany for a century. And, I am quite sure, of me along with it.'

Clara reddens. 'I started your book last night. I can't understand how I haven't read it before.'

'It wasn't on any curriculum.'

It is not her fault she knows nothing of the revolution. Though it was only twenty years ago, it never made it into history classes. Our revolution was a brief, post-war flirtation with the utopian left that was bloodily put down and then, with a parallel violence of the spirit, erased from national memory.

For the young, though, twenty years is a lifetime. The war she was born into is almost unimaginable, as is the sense we had so powerfully that things could have turned out differently. The young, for this reason, always have hindsight on their side.

'There's no need to take this down,' I say. She sits back, hands folded in her lap, and listens.

'At the end of the war, when we'd clearly lost, the generals ordered the naval fleet in the North Sea into one last, do-or-die attack on the English. The sailors recognised it as a suicide mission and refused to go. What began as a mutiny spread into a revolution – unbelievable in our nation of the obdurately obedient. Workers' and soldiers' councils sprang up right through Germany – in Hanover, Hamburg, the Rhineland and Munich, taking over the administration of local government, the repatri-ation of the wounded from the front. Though its leaders were mostly from our Independents party – journalists and pacifists – we hadn't instigated the uprising, we merely attached ourselves to the workers and soldiers who had. The Russians had had their communist revolution over eighteen months earlier. Ours was utterly home-grown.

'Lenin did telegraph us from Moscow at one point,' I tell Clara, 'but his view was that Germans were incapable of a revolution.' Her head tilts in a question. 'Because we could not storm a train without first queuing for tickets.'

She laughs, small teeth in perfect rows.

'But truth be told it was our pacifism, more than the dreaded German orderliness, that was our undoing.'

The revolution! They were heady days in Munich. I felt more than recovered from my breakdown. I stuffed wads of folded newsprint in the heels of my shoes for two extra centimetres and set off to address the women in munitions factories. I distributed my poems, and read from the play about the war I was working on. I found I could bring myself to tears with my own words, tears I'd then see reflected six hundred times in the eyes of the women below me. 'They dress it up as a fight for ideals,' I cried from chairs in factory canteens or beer halls or from the backs of trucks, 'but they sent us to die for oil, for gold, for land.'

Our revolution would change autocratic, warmongering Germany forever: extend the vote to all, remove the military and the aristocracy's control over government, socialise industry, make education free and available to everyone. It would be a new, just world and there would be no more war.

The Kaiser fled to Holland leaving us in charge, soldiers and workers and writers. We had wanted peace, but suddenly we had power. We had no idea how to keep it. 'Poets are the unacknowledged legislators of the world!' I cried, as if poetry, and not a standing army, could enforce the changes we wanted. Our leader, the revered journalist Kurt Eisner, refused on principle to censor

ANNA FUNDER

the press, or to distribute weapons to the people. When our representatives visited the Princess in Potsdam, she thought of the grim fate of the Russian royal family and was frightened for her life. Instead, our men heel-clicked and asked if there was anything she or her children wanted for! None of us had the killer instinct, in any appropriate sense, for politics. Not because we hadn't killed before, but precisely because we had.

And then a young aristocrat gunned Eisner down in the street. I found myself pushed to the helm of the revolution. Did I say helm? I led it as much as a piece of flotsam leads a wave. I was twenty-five years old. My opponents jeered: 'Who does he think he is, the King of Bavaria?' But the people knew that I, like Eisner before me, was prepared to throw away my life for them. In those strange days, that seemed enough of a qualification.

In Munich I convened the Revolutionary Council in the former bedroom of the Queen, workmen's boots clanking across the parquetry. It was a people's revolution: every utopian and mad crank bustled in to see me with his or her personal solution for the liberation of the human race, having identified the root of all evil as cooked food, unhygienic underwear, birth control, or the use in water closets of newspaper instead of natural moss.

By comparison, I thought I kept my head. Though there I sat, enthroned on Her Majesty's blue-silk-upholstered dressing chair, issuing proclamation after proclamation. As if in some writer's dream, simply by declaring something to be true it would become so: 'Socialisation of the Press!' 'Requisitioning of Housing!' 'Against the Adulteration of Milk!'

Up in Berlin the Social Democrats had taken over after the Kaiser fled. They hated our revolution – called it anarchic, anti-democratic, and of course they did not want to cede control of Bavaria.

So, they started rounding up men who had come out of the war on the other side: disaffected veterans failing to find their way back to civilian life, and the Free Corps, those early Nazis who could not accept that the war was lost. Berlin sent them in their tens of thousands to mass on our border. These were the Whites. They wanted to blockade us and starve us out.

I needed someone I could trust to conduct the desperate diplomacy with Berlin. Relieved to see a familiar face one day, I appointed Dr Lipp Minister for Foreign Affairs. But instead of negotiating with the enemy, he appealed to a higher power: Lipp wired the Pope our every move. 'The pernicious lazy monarch,' he confided to His Holiness, 'who clearly spent his days playing boats in the bath, has, to top it off, absconded with the key to my lavatory.'

It turned out Lipp had been an inmate at the sanatorium, not a doctor at all. When my deputy Felix Fechenbach found him, Lipp was waltzing through the typing pool with a basket on his arm, distributing a red carnation to every girl. Presented with the resignation I had drafted for him to sign, he took a comb from his pocket, ran it through his beard and declared, 'This, too, will I do for the revolution.'

Uneasiness spread inside me in a way I could tell no one about. Was I so close to crazy I couldn't see it? It didn't matter. I was the leader, and I needed to keep leading.

I was desperate for a peaceful solution. I couldn't bear to see the birth of a pacifist, socialist state in a bloodbath. Rumours of the attack came while I was speaking at an inn close to the border. I would stop it at any price. I commandeered a horse from a boy. His younger brother insisted on riding with me. As we got closer to Dachau my companion was shot dead, clear off his mount. I rode on in the direction the bullets had come from, a riderless horse at my side.

At Dachau I managed to negotiate a ceasefire with the forces from Berlin. But that same afternoon, from over on our side, a saboteur started firing. That gave the Whites their excuse. One hundred thousand of them stormed into Munich against us. Our rag-tag troops, half armed and slipshod and hungry, numbered at most a fifth of that. It was May 1919, and the blood ran in the streets. Most of our leaders were slaughtered. I would have been too, but friends persuaded me to hide in their homes.

And for this I first became famous: Red Toller rides into battle against the Whites! But I was never a communist, I was an Independent, and I was not riding into battle, but to sue for peace. Like all the reasons for my fame, it does not quite square with the truth. From the minute I put those wads in my shoes I have never been able to get the public Toller to sit faithfully on the facts of the private one.

The WANTED poster of me was up on bollards and lampposts and train stations all over Bavaria, plastered over my proclamations. My supporters defaced it. I pitched in and defaced myself, growing a beard and dyeing my hair red with peroxide so I no longer matched it. When I caught myself reflected in a shop window I saw a crazed John the Baptist and averted my eyes.

An artist offered me sanctuary. I spent three weeks in a cupboard behind a false wall at his house in Schwabing while the Berlin forces continued murdering our leaders. In my head everything that had happened, that was still happening outside, whistled and whirred. Some poor detective had the misfortune to resemble me. When he rang the bell at a flat looking for me the owner shot him dead on the spot. Newspapers reported my demise – my driver identified my corpse at the mortuary. When my mother read of it in Samotschin she sat for three days on a low stool, surrounded by shrouded mirrors, and mourned.

In the end they came to the artist's house, knocked on its walls and found me. But those three weeks saved my life. I got a trial; Albert Einstein, Thomas Mann and Theodor Lessing came to vouch for the honourable motives of the revolution, and for my integrity, if not my political acumen. I was sentenced to five years.

Clara has been sitting quietly in the other comfortable chair.

'What we couldn't know back then,' I continue, 'is that on the night right back at the beginning of it all when the workers and soldiers elected Eisner our leader in the huge Mathäserbräu beer hall, the night that he proclaimed the Republic of Bavaria, if we had looked closely among the faces on the bench seats we would have seen in a corner an undistinguished, jowly returned corporal, not drinking but watching.' I tell her how this man seethed at Germany's defeat, denied the Kaiser's responsibility for the war and its loss. Instead he blamed progressive Jews, pacifists and intellectuals for bringing Germany to her knees – we who had been left to clean up the mess when the government responsible for it fled.

'In 1923, while I was in prison, this man, Hitler, tried to take over Bavaria by force. He was given a lenient sentence with privileges. Actually, you might take this down.'

She readies her pencil. I clear my throat.

'It is a revolving-door system in Germany; the prisons of the twentieth century connect one regime or revolution with the one that follows and crushes it. Leftists and rightists have intimate knowledge of the same cells, mop up each other's blood. We could leave generations of graffiti messages scratched into the limewash, argument and counter-argument, and maybe in a thousand years an answer would be there for all to read.'

I watch Clara's lips silently shape the words I have just spoken, as she takes them down in her strange, curly marks.

'Now,' I tell her, 'Hitler is rekindling the war. He wants the victory he felt we took from him. He's made a list, and he is working through it.'

She puts a hand up to her mouth, then removes it. Her wrists are slender, somehow familiar. 'So,' she says, 'you are on the front line. Again.'

I look out the window. In the park there's a hot-dog cart with balloons attached to it, and rainbow whirligigs for the children. 'Hardly.'

There is still light in the sky, but it's time for Clara to go. She and her husband Joseph are living with his cousin, in a small place on the Lower East Side. Joseph was second violinist in the Cologne orchestra but he has not found work yet, and he waits each day for her to come home.

And then I know. I get up so fast the chair behind me tips back onto the carpet. 'I need to go home!'

Clara looks stricken.

'I mean England – not home, of course. Can you book me a passage. Tomorrow?'

She is waiting, hoping I'll make more sense, come back to her.

'Not to *go* tomorrow! For, say, next Friday. Yes – that gives us a week. If you book we can pay in a couple of days. I'll find some money, somewhere.'

'All right,' she says slowly. This is not how she thought things would go here. But I am now galvanised with purpose. Her green eyes follow me around the room.

'You should come tonight, then. To say farewell.' Clara says this in a measured voice, the voice of someone aware that their efforts, though appreciated, will likely come to nothing. 'They would love to see you –' she closes her bag and looks up at me – 'before you go.'

Since Christiane left me, Clara has been trying to get me 'out of myself'. I'm not being very cooperative. (Though if I believed this were literally possible, I'd do anything she said.) Lately, her efforts have taken the form of urging me to meet with my refugee friends – George Grosz, Klaus and Erika Mann, Kurt Rosenfeld – at their Thursday gatherings at Epstein's restaurant downtown.

'Good idea,' I say, rubbing my hands together and smiling.

RUTH

This day has decided to be full-throated and beautiful. Shadows are sharp on the road out front; everything throwing its shape around. Workmen in blue singlets and Blundstone boots traipse in and out of next door.

In 1952, when I bought this house, Bondi Junction was cheap, a place of lazy Californian bungalows, cars in side driveways and street cricket. Now all around me homes are being bulldozed on million-dollar blocks; new glazed bunkers for peering at the ocean over steel-rimmed balconies are being erected to the boundaries, dwarfing me in my house like a relic from another time. Bejewelled real-estate vultures circle about in BMWs, put cards and letters in my box. They are waiting to match my death notice to their title search, to whip out the Deceased Estate signs they have pre-prepared in the boot and plant them, triumphant, all over my lawn. Get your piece of *Lebensraum*! they might as well cry. A *Platz an der Sonne* going for a song!

But they will not win. The beauty of this city is too elemental, too fecund and raw, to be tamed by mere money. Though the financiers and bankers and dot.com millionaires hug the shoreline, their topiary palaces and towered developments will never conquer this landscape. Bougainvillea and wisteria, ficus and monstera treat it all just as food and trellis and will, if unchecked, devour the lot. And there, smack in the middle, the sparkling, billowing harbour – the earth is alive here. This beauty is a force, and it will never lose.

I have always been seduced by beauty. Seduced and consoled, and then betrayed. Then seduced and consoled again.

The cat's at the door! Who let him outside the flat? Scratch, scratch.

Mein Gott, is my *Arsch* sore from sitting. I don't have a cat. It's a key in the latch. Someone is letting themselves in.

Bev stands over me. She looks unhappy. No doubt I am responsible. Although, as I examine her face, I see that there are other possibilities: the bottle-coloured hair a pinky-orange unknown to nature and her bad eye a bit twitchy today. Or, possibly, her thieving daughter Sheena, an ex-nurse with a heroin addiction whose sadness is the one and only terrible thing, I've discovered over the years, it gives Bev no satisfaction to talk about.

'Well,' she huffs. 'Sitting around like a bottle of milk, are we?'

Mrs Allworth in Bloomsbury called me ma'am. 'If you'd like, ma'am,' she would say, 'I could do the windows. From the inside only, mind.' When she said 'If ma'am would prefer' I knew she was cross. I didn't like 'ma'am', but this Australian 'we' is worse – it makes me feel like a Greek chorus, all the parts of me breathing and heaving together like some ancient, static, sore-arsed monster.

'I've been down at the village with the oldies –' Bev doesn't bother waiting for a response – 'giving hand massages. Poor old ducks.'

Eastlakes Village is a retirement home and Bev must be nearly as old as the inmates. I think she goes there to 'halp' them so as to create a more definite distinction between her and them. She also goes to the Red Cross, partly because she wishes to be as good-hearted as she can muster, and partly, I believe, for the talismanic properties of 'halping'. 'There's always someone more unfortunate than you,' she likes to say, and she wishes to keep it that way. Bev brings me stories from both places and elsewhere, usually of cancers and deaths. Her expressions of sympathy involve ghoulish detail: the prostate 'big as a rockmelon', the hole in the throat where you 'put the voice box straight in – so *practical*'. She prefers the death of someone she knows, or once knew, or at least someone who knew someone she knew. The closer the death is to her, the more it is a sign of a cosmic reprieve: she has been passed over. 'There but for the grace of God,' she says with a small shiver, and feels blessed.

Is to be passed over the same as being blessed? I do not feel blessed.

But today it is not illness, it is her neighbours in the council unit next to hers.

'Those people next door,' Bev says, 'you wouldn't believe it. It's still goin on.'

Are they Portuguese? Pacific Islander? I can't remember, but am still lucid enough to know I ought to remember, that this conversation has probably been going on for some weeks in instalments between us, and that she would break from me, internally, if I asked. I realise suddenly that I don't want her to break from me, that I, Ruth Becker/Wesemann/Becker, with my thousands of lost photographs and my ostensible bravery, now have a need for company that surmounts both principle and distaste.

'*Those* people,' Bev is saying, 'they put all their rubbish out in the lane on a Tuesday. They know the collection is not till Thursday. It's *disgusting*. I've told er!'

Her bad eye is now uncontrollable. To be able to summon up righteous anger at will is, I think, a psychological skill more cathartic than meditation, or breathing into a paper bag. It is also quite entertaining to watch.

Bev sniffs the air and her bosom expands like a pigeon's. 'She knows I'm watchin er too. From my winda.' She collects a couch cushion. 'So do you know what she does?'

I say nothing; nothing from me is required.

'She sends one of them *children* out with the bin.' Bev punches the cushion. '*Disgusting*. Won't dare do it herself now.' She throws the cushion back and spies the half-eaten packet of biscuits on the table. I am suddenly aware of the spray of crumbs on my jumper – I am probably disgusting too. I check my teeth with my tongue for mashed Scotch Finger. But Bev goes on, '*So* many children. I think there are *five*. *Disgusting*. Like rabbits.'

So they're Catholic. Portuguese then? Still, I don't think I'll risk it. Last week we nearly parted ways over Bev's conviction that Aboriginals are born liars.

It strikes me that Bev must be lonely too, which might be why she rings the council to complain about her neighbour's rubbish. They haven't yet computerised the service and she gets some poor person on the other end whose every conversation is recorded as a guard against irascibility and other human responses. For Bev, it is as good as a friend.

'You stayin here?' she asks.

I nod.

'I'll start out the back then.'

She plods down the corridor to the laundry. Her bustling and banging out there gives me an odd reassurance. I am strongly enough in the present that I can go back.

I could still find my way around the villa I grew up in with my eyes closed, if I needed to. I could slide my way down the four flights of the banister, I could trail my feet in socks over the parquetry, opening the double doors from room to room. I remember each of the eighteenth-century enamels – landscapes of the seasons – set into the magnificently tiled, floor-to-ceiling heaters. Ours was the grandest house in Königsdorf, a smallish coalmining town in Upper Silesia where my father owned the lumber mill. It was a German town until I was twelve, when the war ended, and then the area was ceded to Poland. The new border ran four kilometres away from the villa, and I kept on catching the tram every day to school, which happened, now, to be in another country. We stayed completely German.

Because Dora was an only child, our families had encouraged us to think of each other more as sisters than cousins. After my operation, almost every school break I went up to Berlin, so the two of us grew up with holiday intimacy and reprieves during term in between. I had an inkling of the luck of this arrangement even as a child: the time apart allowed us to escape the friction of siblings. I suspected I would have been annoying to her, full time.

Still, I shadowed her. I joined the Independents in Königsdorf at sixteen. By eighteen, when I finished school, I was desperate to get to where the action was. It was spring 1923 when I went to visit Dora at Munich University.

Dora had finished her PhD on the economics of the German colonies, and was staying on at the university to teach for a year. She had written to me about the campaign for Toller's release she was running from her room on campus. Though Dora had never met Toller – he'd been in prison since 1919 – he was our party's most famous member. From his cell he'd sent four plays into the world – searing works about the human price of war and the need for peaceful revolution, freedom and justice. One of them had played for more than a hundred days. Ernst Toller was the wunderkind of German theatre and the conscience of the republic. As long as he was locked up, we considered the new Weimar Germany to be as bad as the Kaiser's old, warmongering one.

Dora couldn't make it to the station in Munich to meet me, but she'd given me directions to a café. As I walked through the Englischer Garten, I watched a brother and sister flying a kite papered with green scales. When I got closer I saw they were banknotes. In her letters Dora had described women running from factories to bakeries with their pay in wheelbarrows, hoping to buy a loaf of bread before the prices inflated. I knew the hyperinflation was caused by the government simply printing more currency to pay off its war debt, but it was still a shock to see the money worthless in front of me, dipping and tugging at the air.

Dora wasn't at the café yet. I ordered a coffee for 5000 Reichsmarks. When she opened the door I saw her first, as she scanned the room. Her hair had been cut short, and she wore a pale-blue collarless shirt and trousers. As she pulled out a chair she apologised for not having met the train. She didn't offer a reason.

'Was it hard to convince your parents to let you come?' Dora smiled, taking out a tobacco pouch and starting to roll a cigarette.

I nodded. 'They think I'm here to lose my virginity, though they can't bring themselves to say it.'

She laughed. 'Well, you *are* here for the cause. And you *are* a materialist like the rest of us.' She removed a stray piece of tobacco from her bottom lip, her smile wide as a plate. 'We would say it's silly to value something for its non-use.'

We laughed so hard that Dora started coughing and people stared.

When the bill came it was for 14 000 RM – Dora's coffee had cost 9000 RM. The waitress shrugged. 'If you want the same price, ladies,' she said, as if explaining a natural phenomenon to children, 'you need to order at the same time.'

Dora took me back to her room. I could stay there with her. Over the bed hung the WANTED poster of Toller I knew from her bedroom at home. She'd glued the top over a rod and tied a string to each end. She told me it was forbidden to put more hooks in the walls, so she'd taken down the crucifix that had been there and used its pin. I supposed she'd put the Christ away in a drawer.

I read the police description: 'Toller is slightly built, about 1.65 to 1.68 metres tall; has a thin, pale face, clean-shaven; large brown eyes, piercing gaze, closes his eyes when thinking; has dark, almost black, wavy hair; speaks standard German.' I looked at the photo on the poster. An intense young man stared through the camera as if to somewhere else. He didn't look like a dangerous revolutionary to me. He looked like someone riding backwards on a horse.

Dora slid her arms around me from behind and gave me a squeeze. Her cheek came up to my shoulder. 'We're getting there,' she said. 'Thomas Mann and Albert Einstein have both written to the newspaper in support of the campaign.' She let go and turned away to her desk, feeding a piece of paper into the typewriter. 'Glad you're here, by the way.'

I started to unpack. My things were strewn all over the bed when there he was at the door. A tall man with blue eyes and a full mouth. He wore an open white shirt belted at the waist in the latest style, like an urban pirate. He had a newspaper rolled up in one hand.

'Am I i-interrupting?' he smiled. The voice was big, lazy, deliberate.

'Not at all,' Dora said. 'This is my cousin Ruth.' She gestured loosely. 'Ruthie, this is Hans.'

He nodded at the bed. 'Nice underwear,' he said. '"Koenig's, when only the best will do."'

Dora rolled her eyes and laughed. 'This is *not* normal, Ruthie,' she said, 'a man who can tell the brand of silk at fifteen paces.'

Hans chuckled. 'It can be a useful thing to know,' he said, looking at me squarely.

I wasn't affronted, or even embarrassed. I wanted to get into this adult realm, the new world they were making where intimacies might be public and desire stated plainly. I felt the thrill of it in my stomach.

I cleared a space and sat down on the bed. Hans sat on the floor and leant against it, opening out his newspaper. He had come to show Dora an article about another Independent. I heard their words, but I wasn't taking them in.

'Bertie's really taking it up to the government now,' Hans said.

A man called Berthold Jacob had publicly accused the government of assassinating a pacifist. I saw over Hans's shoulder a picture of the dead pacifist, his head leaking blackness onto the cobblestones, and next to him one of Berthold Jacob, a thin-faced fellow with round glasses and a goatee. Hans's fingers, long and smooth, held the paper apart.

'If Minister von Seeckt only talks about it in parliament but doesn't lay any charges against Bertie, it's proof that he's right.'

'I'm sure he is,' said Dora, turning and leaning over her chair back, chin on her hand. 'They're trying to stamp out the last embers of the revolution.'

'Bertie's moving to Munich, you know. Next month. Wants to come to our meetings.'

'Really?' Dora's eyes lit up. She took the pencil she was chewing out of her mouth. 'That's great.'

The two of them spoke of Bertie as one might a famous person, or a shared, important secret. I had never heard of him. I noticed a rivalry in their admiration, a ratcheting up of the details each of them knew about this man, ostensibly in order to tell me, but really as a game with one another.

Hans said, 'He's taken an apartment in Schwabing.' Dora countered, 'He works twenty hours a day, they say, summer and winter.' Hans, whose friendship with Bertie went back to the war, had deeper sources. He parried: 'He was gassed at Mons, you know.' They became absorbed, sparring and laughing. I stopped listening.

I watched Hans's chest moving under his shirt, the soft sheen of his skin. I forced my gaze away to his feet but my eyes travelled back up over his legs, long and splayed, and I wondered how he was made.

When Hans was leaving I stood to shake hands, but he pulled me in. 'Welcome, Comrade Becker,' he smiled, and gave me a kiss.

The door closed behind him. I touched my cheek. 'Who *was* that?'

'Hans Wesemann.' Dora had already started to type something.

'From the paper? *The* Hans Wes—?'

'M-hm.'

I fell back on the bed. I knew Hans from his 'Despatches from the Front', which had appeared every week or two in our newspaper at home. I knew he'd been leading a platoon near enemy lines when he stopped 'ostentatiously' (he'd admitted it himself) to light a cigarette, and a piece of Tommy's shell tore through his neck and pierced his windpipe. He coughed and hacked till it came up again, and then pocketed it as a souvenir. I knew that other times, when the smoke from his pipe got in his eyes as he took aim, he'd put the whole thing in his pocket alight, to save on matches. And I knew he'd helped carry his mate Friders, killed six minutes before the armistice took effect, back to Germany in a zinc bathtub. I saw in Hans's pieces a heroism and anti-heroism combined, a willingness to do the deed but a reticence about taking the glory that was seductive beyond all measure. I know it's possible to fall in love with someone by falling in love with their writing, because I already had.

'But he's so young,' I said.

'Went to war at nineteen.' Dora didn't look up. 'Lots of veterans are young. Toller's the same.'

In this way I was swept up at eighteen into Hans and into the party at the same time. If Stockholm Syndrome describes a prisoner falling in love with her jailer, there should be a name for how a cause cements two people, masks their differences as secondary to the purpose at hand. We were all of us subsumed into an aphrodisiac atmosphere of self-sacrifice. So many of our generation had lost their lives for Germany that now, though we did not fully know it, the stake for our commitment to stopping it happening again was our lives.

I stayed in Munich for two months. When all the local members of the Independents met, we used a hall at the university. There were probably fifty of us. But more often a few, a sort of unofficial leadership, would get together in Dora's room. It felt like being at the centre of the world. We drafted leaflets, arguing over the wording. We worked the cyclostyle to print them and made pails of lumpy grey glue. We went out nights pasting them up all around town, making sure to put plenty around the electoral offices of local members. We addressed student meetings in smoky rooms and crowds in the quadrangle. Half our energy came from the cause, the other half from each other.

As the weeks went by, I was infected by the others' excitement about Berthold Jacob coming. Bertie, I learnt, had served on both the eastern and the western fronts with distinction, but after he was gassed his life developed a single, pacifist focus that, Hans said, 'borders, quite sanely, on mania'. Bertie had become celebrated by progressives all over the country when he uncovered documents that proved Germany's responsibility for starting the war. This made a lie of the government's claims of a defensive war.

Since I'd joined the Independents I had become used to talk about opposing government measures and proposing new ones, but it was an entirely novel notion to me that the government would lie to the people, even in the most serious of matters, such as sending men to war. I can remember the shock of this awareness, the feeling of radical aloneness: if we couldn't trust the authorities, who could we trust? The answer was: us.

Bertie was now, Hans told me, on a mission to stop the new war this government was planning. He had turned his energies to revealing the secret, illegal build-up of the Black Army, and the manufacture and stockpiling of weapons to furnish it. His method was ingenious. Bertie sought out information already on the public record – in military bulletins, official government publications, the conservative press – information that most people did not know how to interpret. He monitored the personal columns in the local papers of hamlets, looking for sudden increases in population – more weddings, births – and would find, when he visited, young men on the football field being drilled twice a week in 'gymnastics', with batons standing in for weapons. Alone in his attic Bertie had calculated, from the huge number of men on its official payroll alone, that the German military was in a position to take command of one million troops. And they were not, as Hans put it, 'training for nothing'. Bertie's mission left him no time for formal study, but in our circles his articles brought him the respect of a zealot, or a savant.

The morning he arrived he stood just inside Dora's room and put a hand on his chest. 'Berthold Jacob,' he said, as if the rest of us might not know, as if we hadn't been waiting for weeks.

Hans sprang up. 'Bertie!'

I watched Hans shake his friend's hand, holding him at the elbow. Bertie was not what I expected a famous, fearless radical pacifist to be. He had hunched shoulders and a neck that bent forward. His small brown eyes looked at us from behind round, rimless glasses. A goatee only partly covered his gas burns, nasty things that reached like pink and hairless stains down under his collar. (Wasn't the gas so cruel? Always attacking the tender bits: lips, groin, ears.) His hair rose in tufts in all directions and he wore too many clothes, like someone insensible to heat and cold, or someone wearing all he owned. His voice was high, friendly, uncertain.

'You must be Ruth,' he said, blinking and extending his hand. 'Hans has told me all about you.' I held his small hand and nodded. I thought, for some reason, of a ferret.

And that, I suppose, was where the five of us became joined – a five-pointed constellation, held together by forces we could not see – Dora, Toller, Hans, Bertie and me.

'Sit down, everybody,' Dora said, brisk as usual. The personal matters, for her, could wait.

Perhaps it was because she was the most brilliant speaker in the party, or perhaps it was simply because we met in her room that Dora had assumed the leader's role. I don't think Hans wanted it for himself, but it didn't sit too well with him either. He motioned Bertie to the armchair and pulled Dora's desk chair to one side for himself. I was on the bed. Dora remained standing, her hands on the back of a bentwood chair, shifting her weight from hip to hip.

She began by listing the activities in our campaign to release Toller: letters, meetings, posters, speeches. Before she'd finished, Hans's knee was jigging up and down, out of his control. Like many returned men, he had a need for action in his blood; if he sat still too long, things could come into his mind he did not want there. But that wasn't it. I looked at him and I felt it too. In the same room as Bertie, our efforts seemed suddenly amateurish, undergraduate. By the time it was Hans's turn to speak he'd subtly switched from being part of our campaign to being its critic. He complained about our nightly sorties gluing up leaflets, 'only to make work for the police who rip them down'.

'Any suggestions then, maestro?' Dora asked, her voice cool. Suggestions, of course, should have come before we were in such illustrious company.

Hans leant his chair back on two legs against the wall, practising moving a pencil over his knuckles. He glanced at Bertie. 'Why don't we get Toller's own views on his situation, and put them in the paper?' he said. 'Let the man speak for himself.'

Dora flicked her head sideways, a practical gesture to push back her hair that doubled as a sign of impatience. 'I hardly think the prison authorities are about to let him campaign for his own release,' she said.

'He's allowed visitors, isn't he?' In one swift movement Hans righted his chair and collected the pencil from the floor. 'An interview might just do the trick.'

I looked from Hans to Dora and opened my hands, warding off dissention. 'Perhaps Toller could write to the newspaper himself?' I said.

Bertie cleared his throat. The bickering stopped. 'I don't think,' he said slowly, 'that would work.' He pushed his glasses back up the bridge of his nose with his forefinger. 'The prison censors wouldn't let him say anything important, and even if he did, the newspapers wouldn't print it.' He paused. 'Perhaps Hans's idea isn't such a bad one.'

I don't think there had ever been anything between Dora and Hans; I never asked. This was another kind of sparring. Dora suspected Hans of egotism, of putting himself at the centre of everything – starting with his war reporting. I argued with her that Hans had simply been using his own experiences to show the stupidity of battle and the honour of the men in the face of it. 'Still,' Dora had said, 'if you look closely, Ruthie, it's all about him.' That, I suppose, was something I didn't mind.

'Why don't I give it a shot?' Hans continued in his unruffled way. 'Can't do any harm, can it?'

I looked at Bertie, who was silent, then back to Dora.

She put her cigarette down in the ashtray and turned away, picked up a stack of leaflets from her desk. 'I suppose not,' she said eventually. 'We'll save you a bucket and a pile of these –' she swivelled sharply around, slapping the leaflets against her hand – 'for when you return.'

Hans never really returned, I would say now. Or not as part of our group. The next day he borrowed someone's motorbike for the ride through the countryside to the prison where Toller was being held. He sweet-talked his way past the governor and, flanked by guards, walked through six sets of doors that were laboriously, idiotically unlocked before him and then relocked behind him, before he got to the famous prisoner. Toller was seated in a wicker chair under a horsehair blanket, his whitewashed cell lined with books. Swallows had built a nest between the bars of the high window. Our hero was still in his twenties but his hair was turning grey.

Back in his room Hans worked hard on his piece. He reported to the nation on its great hope, whose soul, he declared, 'soars above captivity and loneliness'. Toller's time in solitary confinement, he wrote, 'has focused his poetry upon his only free companions, the swallows'. He ended: 'I walked out of there a free man but the beating heart of Germany remains inside.'

The interview was a sensation. Under huge public pressure the authorities gave in and offered Toller early release. Hans's star rose too: two major national newspapers wanted him to write for them.

But the victory was hollow. Toller refused his freedom. And he did so in a letter to the newspaper. 'So long as my companions arrested with me are still in here,' he wrote, 'liberty has no meaning.' Toller went so far as to dissociate himself from the campaign for his freedom, 'if it is intended for me alone'.

The next time we met it was just the three of us; Bertie was on one of his fact-gathering trips. Dora could not bring herself to congratulate Hans.

'Worked out well for you,' she muttered.

'That's unfair, Dee.' She ignored me.

'How could I know he'd be offered release?' Hans shifted his shoulders.

'That *was* the aim, wasn't it?' We looked at her, shocked by the bitterness in her voice.

'Well . . .' Hans opened up his hands. 'I – we didn't know he'd refuse it.'

None of us had foreseen Toller's solidarity with the other prisoners. Dora's eyes moved involuntarily to the WANTED poster then blinked quickly away. Her voice was small. 'Back to work then,' she said.

A week later Hitler and his National Socialists tried to take Munich in a coup. Hitler ended up in the same fortress as Toller, but of course for a much shorter time. The authorities were always more lenient on coups from the right.

Not long afterwards, I left with Hans for Berlin. He took a room in a shared flat; I stayed with Aunt Else. I worried that Dora would think it some kind of betrayal of her for me to be with Hans. I told myself this couldn't be right, there was no logic in that. But the heart has its own logic, fierce and undeniable.

Before I left Munich she held my arms, an ironic smile playing on her lips. 'The one thing I'd say you haven't developed here,' she said, smoothing a stray curl off my forehead, 'is an adequate distrust of flattery.'

'I suppose I've not had the practice,' I replied. I did not see her for a while after that.

The next time we were together was the spring of the following year, when Dora moved to Berlin to work in the office of the parliamentarian Mathilde Wurm. I had started studying French and history and literature at the University Unter den Linden, and Dora leased a flat of her own not far from there, near the Reichstag.

By then she had a boyfriend too – Walter Fabian, the editor of a union journal in Dresden. Dora had sent me letters about him, describing him as charismatic and funny, and 'always the best-connected man in the room'. She had been writing for his publication, which he ran, she said, 'like a wily king runs a country'. Walter kept a dossier of compromising information on government officials, which meant he could often publish articles others would not have dared. I hoped that her being in love meant she would have forgiven me for whatever disappointment I'd caused by going off with Hans.

When I entered her flat Walter was there on the couch, sleeves rolled up, sorting papers. He had a round, clean-shaven face, a fine, domed forehead under a receding hairline, and piercing, sky-blue eyes. He sprang up, adopting Dora's easy intimacy with me too, as if I were a little sister. 'Hello Ruthie,' he said, hugging me close.

At some point I can't remember the two of them slipped off to the registry office in Dresden, with a typist from the journal as witness. I don't think either of them was set on marrying – it had something to do with the residency requirements in Dresden, given that Dora wanted to keep her flat in Berlin too. They loved each other but at the same time they insisted that marriage would change nothing. It didn't. Walter was serially unfaithful (he had, I believe, four wives in the end). Dora made light of it, saying the marriage withered after a year from inattention, 'like a houseplant'. But I knew marriage was something she did not want to try again.

That first time I met Walter at her flat was just after Toller had been released. He had served out his full term. When I accidentally smashed a glass in the kitchen I went to the cupboard for a broom. Something slapped against the door as I opened it. Hanging on the inside was the WANTED poster. Not on display, but not quite put away either.

TOLLER

'They were asking after you at Epstein's last night, Joseph said.'

Today Clara is late, because she went first to the shipping office. She wears a deep-pink blouse, open at the neck. I wonder if a secretary is to a writer as a model is to an artist: a muse, a breathing presence to make us feel our blood, a small piece of the beauty of the world we wish to rise to. Her thigh presses into the table.

'I . . .' I look up at her sideways. 'I had some reading to do.'

Clara knows this is not true, that I didn't do any reading.

'Also some packing?' I venture, as back-up. Two half-packed suitcases lie open on the bed.

'Good then,' she says. She wants to believe in that version. Now that I have a departure date, we are nothing but to the point with one another. She has the steno pad out already.

'I've been wondering,' she says, that crease between her eyebrows again, 'why, when you talk about the war, or the revolution, you use the present tense?' Her voice is gentle, but she has clearly prepared this question for me and she will go through with it. 'Is it still going on in your mind?'

'No.'

How can I explain to her that what I have written down has often become all that I remember? I threw a skein of ink on the page to catch the truth, but made only a sieve and it slipped through. I need the present tense like magic, I want Dora's voice in my ear and her scent in my face. I need for her to live on, outside the limitations of my scribbling.

'It's because,' I say, 'I do not wish to spend these coming days . . . I just can't bear to say "she *was*" all the time.' I feel red heat in my face as soon as the words are out.

'I see.' Clara nods as if this were perfectly understandable. She chews the inside of one cheek. 'Still. If we are going to put these new parts into the book, the past tense would be less confusing.'

'Yes,' I find myself saying. 'You're probably right. It's just . . .'

My own life was always raw material for something else. It was never as real as when I remade it, into a play, a book. For this reason I fear I never gave the world its due. My psychiatrist said guilt towards the world is the black-winged rustle of my disease. But that does not stop my sick thought from also being true: my life and everyone in it were grist for my mill. And the greatest irony, the mother of all ironies, is not lost on me. Though I fed the world and those I loved into my work, it never, quite, lifted away from the circumstances of its birth – the war, the revolution, my imprisonment – into something eternal. Audiences loved the plays because they showed them the chaos of their times, but they are barely performed these days. I have lived on in the gap between my ambition and my talent, like a critic. I do not wish to write Dora into a poor version of herself.

'. . . it's just that I do not wish to write Dora into a poor version of herself.'

Clara is sitting with her hands together, under her chin. Her voice is soft. 'There's no version now. Nothing.'

I nod. She picks up the pad and starts to take it down.

*   *   *

The morning of my release, prison guards escorted me to the Bavarian border. I took a train to Leipzig, where that evening my play *Masses and Man* was opening. I walked the streets like a ghost awoken from a five-year sleep. Women were wearing their clothes looser and their hair shorter. Better-fed children indulged a yo-yo craze, and telephones in cabinets had appeared on the pavements.

In prison I suffered as men suffer, but I was able to write as I have never written since. In five years I wrote four plays and a book of poems. Since writing was forbidden, I did it after the lights were turned off, with a candle under a blanket, on toilet tissue that was smuggled out by visiting friends. And there my life unfolded further into its contradictions. My play *Hinkemann* is about a man who returns emasculated from the war, but it made women want to heal me, love me, take me home. I became famous and fêted all over Germany while I was the most solitary man alive.

In Berlin *Masses and Man* had been shut down on the opening night, after clashes between nationalist anti-Semites and socialists threatened to turn the theatre into a bloodbath. Actually, a bloodbath crossed with a pigsty – the nationalists came armed with rotting vegetables and chewed bones. The revolution was over, but it seemed I'd managed to resurrect the violence of it and bring it right inside the theatre. The woman in my play believes revolution can be accomplished without violence; her tragedy is it cannot, and then we all – pacifists and nationalists alike – have blood on our hands. Meanwhile the bankers stimulate the war effort by setting up brothels behind the lines. True of course, but unmentionable, and it drove the right-wingers insane. In Leipzig, the Union Repertory was daring to put the play on because its members could stand guard against any brawlers.

I slipped into the theatre after the lights went down and found my seat. Then I panicked – what if someone recognised me? What if my presence made the violence I expected worse? And what if the production was awful? I sank deep in my seat. Then, slowly, I relaxed, as the audience gasped, applauded – recognising themselves in the costumes of soldiers, of prisoners, in shrouds. It was exhilarating. I risked a glance at the rows of faces behind me, all turned up to the light. I felt the same thrill I'd felt speaking to the masses in Munich from the back of a truck. It was the power, if I am honest, of a dictator. Of finding, catching, twisting something inside them.

When the bankers started dancing to the music of chinking coins around the stock-exchange table, the heckling started from the back seats. 'Traitor! Saboteur!'

People turned their heads. Rowdies were standing up in the last five rows, wielding batons and pelting things at the stage. Something splattered in the aisle right next to me. Then the mob began moving down the aisle towards the stage, but union guards ran in with truncheons and forced them out. All the while the actors bravely kept going.

Halfway through the second act, a murmuring set up in the audience. My neighbour whispered to me, 'They say Toller's out – he's here!'

'He is?' I sank my head into my chest. The whisper grew into a chant. 'Toll-er! Toll-er! Show us, Toll-er!' It was all so strange, so soon. A spotlight leapt off the stage and roved over the audience. It found me. I was pulled up, moving on a sea of arms; I thought they would quarter me. I could see nothing outside the circle of light. Then I saw they were smiling and it was madness, like a wedding. They passed me hand over hand till I was set down on the stage. By now the audience was stamping its feet. The actors made room for me as if I were a bomb, a miracle, as if I needed more space than they. In the front row a woman keened and pulled at her clothes.

I held up my hands.

The room quietened.

'Apologies for the interruption,' I said. The place exploded into laughter. 'I am very moved,' I continued, and suddenly I was. 'This play was written in isolation, in a kind of death. It is you,' I gestured to the cast, and out to the audience, 'who bring it life. Thank you.'

I walked off into the side curtains, expecting the players to take up where they had left off. But it started again, the banging and the calls. 'Toll-er! Toll-er!' I went back out. Things were being thrown on stage, but not vegetables this time – there were scarves and gloves and corsages and God knows what. I raised my hands again. 'All I can say is, the spirit of justice is alive and well here tonight, in Leipzig, in Germany. I thank you.'

Backstage I was in darkness, alone. The chanting continued, but my knees felt unreliable. I couldn't go out there again. I put a cigarette in my mouth and went to light it but both my hands were shaking and the matchbook was stuck together. I couldn't get it open, and when I did I couldn't control the flame. I put one hand under the other to steady it but together they shook even more.

Out of the corner of my eye I saw something move. A girl, watching me. A woman.

'Well done.' Her voice was low, matter-of-fact. She took two steps and placed her hands around mine, slipped the matches from them and struck one.

'I'm Dora,' she said, the flame between us lighting our faces.

'Ernst.'

She laughed, bright and big. 'I know.'

I hadn't been this close to a woman in five years. She was small and fine. Her eyes were calm, as if she knew me.

She touched me lightly on the arm. 'Stay right here.' Then she walked out onto the stage, hands held high into the light.

A stagehand sidled up behind me. 'Who's that?' He pointed with his chin.

'Her name is Dora.'

'And she is . . . ?'

I turned to him. 'You don't know?'

He shrugged.

We both looked on. When she had subdued the crowd the woman announced, 'We have been honoured here tonight by the presence of the greatest playwright of our generation.' They erupted again. The woman smiled, opened out her hands. 'And now,' she spoke over them and they hushed, 'what he wishes is for the play to go on.'

Then she was at my side again. 'I'm sure you want to see it,' she said. 'Come.' She led me around the back of the theatre, through the empty corridors, up to the lighting box. When the technician saw me he stood up, smiling and bowing, shuffled over to make room.

After a time I learned to be the person they thought I was. I was needed everywhere to speak, to sit on committees, to lend my name to causes, to interpret the times. I dined in the best restaurants, bought fine clothes. But I knew there were two parts of me, the public man and the private being, and they would not, ever, quite fit back together.

RUTH

It gives me a kind of vertigo, to be inside Toller, looking at Dora. I see her, and I see at the same time the effect she had on men. Dora was sincere and straightforward and practical; she never flirted. Because she played no games, men felt most fully themselves with her, as though there were no difference between their inner and outer lives.

I remember her going to Leipzig to see the premiere of *Masses and Man*. She told me she had managed to meet Toller afterwards, but she would never have painted the scene like that. Though she later shared so many things with me, back then she would have considered it the betrayal of an intimacy that she fully expected to have.

Intimacy. The first time Hans and I made love we went to a hotel by one of the Berlin lakes. We had bought cheap rings at a flea market.

'Shall we go down to tea?' Hans asked.

We stood on our room's balcony, overlooking the terrace. The wind had set everything in motion; the lake was roiling, alive. Hans moved behind me, took my hips in his hands. Below us, white-gloved staff wheeled gleaming, chrome-hooped trolleys of cakes between the tables, their cloths ballooning like sails. Drinks waiters stood stiff as pins, as if to hold the whole scene down, scratching orders onto paper. Somewhere we couldn't see, a band played, the wind snatching away most of the notes, throwing back only the odd, undersized bar. I looked down on the shining plates, the sun-caught forks, the wheeling, turning chrome. Right below me, a gust ruffled a man's dark hair against the grain, from nape to crown, like the parting of fur. Next to him, a jewelled hand emerged from under a white, wide-brimmed hat, brushed a crumb from a child's cheek. I wished I'd brought my camera.

'I don't feel like tea,' I said. I turned around to him and he moved backwards, into our room. I was suddenly caught in a play of muslin and wind. I unwound myself, fighting and laughing, from the attentions of the slip-curtain.

Hans was standing there, tall and soft-skinned, his blue eyes just looking. Hands loose by his sides. I knew there had been experimenting with boys – why would there not be? It was much like experimenting with yourself, and we believed in freedom of choice of all kinds. Now, though, we had chosen each other.

'It's like a scene in a Brueghel painting down there,' I said. 'After a village wedding. All feasting and chatter and music.'

'You think so?' He shook the hair out of his eyes, relieved, I think now, that the time had not quite come. His physical shyness was unexpected, and it made me love him more. 'I don't. Brueghel painted ordinary people. This is more like the upper deck of that English *Titanic*. All the privileged ones ignoring what they're sailing into.'

I slipped off my shoes.

'I mean,' he stepped backwards again, 'it simply can't go on that a privileged class totters about here having coffee to music when those waiters live hand to mouth. What bothers me –' I started to unbutton my blouse – 'what bothers me m-most, is that those waiters will organise their whole lives so as to appear clean and pressed and healthy here and not upset the clientele!' He held out his hands, fingers splayed. 'The real conditions of their life are probably shared rooms and bedbugs, carbuncles below the collar-line and hot meals only once a week! This is the kind of workers' complicity in their own m-misery that must be stopped.'

'Not right this minute it doesn't,' I said, and I took his hands.

In the night I woke. The moon, reflected off the surface of the lake, played on the ceiling, where a large plasterwork vine curled around itself in graceful, overplayed whorls of leaves and tendrils, bearing at unnaturally regular intervals fat bunches of grapes. Hans slept. I counted the bunches (eleven), traced my eyes over the vine, finding the beginning and the end, then the end and the beginning.

I put on a robe and went downstairs, across the empty terrace with its cleared tables, across the promenade, down the stone steps to the lake. The black water opened in silver ripples to let me in. It was cool, but it was the consistency of silk, water with moon in it. It wrapped around my new body, to my chin. I was liberated now, from preciousness and sniggered mystery. I was a known quantity to myself, free to do with that whatever I liked.

When Hans and I decided to marry we spent a long weekend with my parents at the villa in Königsdorf. My mother was suspicious at first. What could this beautiful man possibly see in me, she thought, apart from my money? She was fine and blond and I had thrown to the sire: thick-lipped and dark. When she saw Hans she had no faith that such a man could love me either.

I watched her watching him with her small, pale-blue eyes, noticing how carefully he was dressed – the blue and yellow argyle sweater, two-tone shoes. She made the whole weekend a test. When artichokes were served Hans said, 'Delicious!' though I doubt he'd seen one before. Mother waited till he picked up his knife and fork then intoned, 'Art-i-chokes,' ostentatiously peeling a petal with two fingers to show how it was done. When Hans took the tongs and bent to retrieve a coal that had fallen from the fireplace she said, 'No,' as if he were Chinese or a dog she was training, and rang for the maid. While he smarted the ember burnt a hole through the carpet, suffusing the room with the bitter smell of singeing wool.

One morning after breakfast Mother said to me, 'What lashes the boy has. One would think he was wearing kohl.'

I said nothing, so as not to give her the satisfaction. At some level, the cruelty of a parent to their child – for her disdain of him was a strike at me – is shameful to the child. We wish our mother to be kind not just because it hurts us when she is not, but because the deviation from motherliness is abnormal, something to be hidden. Hans had grown up in a small house in Nienburg, where his father was the local pastor. What Mother condemned as nouveau riche tastelessness I saw as the best effort of a young man to free himself from dour origins. Mother wanted it both ways: while I was unworthy of him, he was unworthy of our family.

In my family no one performed manual tasks of any kind, ever. Nor did we practise any religion. My father worked hard in his lumber concern, but as its owner and lord; my mother's idleness was proof of his success. We were Germany's Enlightenment Jews, secular, educated, and more Prussian than the Prussians. I wanted to get away from the repressed cruelty of it, the deafening amounts of denial.

In Hans's family, while his mother cooked and mended, his father wrote sermons about the day of reckoning and the end of the world. 'What does it profit a man,' Pastor Wesemann would thunder, 'that he build up his house in this world . . .' while Mrs

Wesemann stewed fruit, pickled cucumbers, covered a broken window with brown paper until they could afford a glazier. Hans's life had been shaped on the one hand by the honest, practical necessity of manual labour, and on the other by its utter pointless- ness when faced with the coming apocalypse. This mortal veil, he used to joke, was ripped up by his father every Sunday and darned by his mother on the Monday. Later, after Hitler came to power, Pastor Wesemann found that the National Socialist ideas about the coming of the thousand-year Reich dovetailed nicely with his own millenarian beliefs, and he installed a maroon Bakelite swastika on his altar as sign of his double devotion. Hans had at least as much to run from as I did.

He tried hard, but towards the end of our visit Hans came to feel like the parvenu Mother saw him as. 'She hates m-me,' he mut- tered in the garden. By the Sunday he had started to pause heavily at the beginning of a sentence, like a gramophone record stuck in a groove. Mother waited for each utterance with an expression of sympathetic victory, as if the delay were the confession of falsehood she had been awaiting since Friday.

My father was kinder. He would have liked for me to marry a Jew, but this boy – though a pacifist – was a war veteran, and of good heart, and Father did not see so many reasons why I might not be loved.

When it was over we caught the train back to Berlin. I'd always felt that even the geography of my family's part of the world – the rumpled mountains dense with coal and riddled with tunnels – was darkly complicated. Once back in northern Germany, the earth smoothed out, grew flat and free and calm, a sea of clear green right up to the coast.

In the dining car I tried to coax Hans out of his funk with an impersonation of my mother. 'Oh, I am a Prussian of infinite control and reason.' I held my nose up and my neck long. 'Which is why

I am per-fec-tly willing to burn a hole in my Persian carpet for the sheer pleasure of teaching you your place.'

Hans was slumped back in his seat, turning a pack of cards over and over on the table with one hand. He stared out the window. He was beautiful – the picture, in fact, of what I would have thought my mother wanted for me. Excepting only, perhaps, that the effort showed a little: his cravat too neatly tied, trousers a bit flashy. Sometimes the imitation is brighter than the real. That didn't bother me since I'd loved him even before I'd laid eyes on him. I wasn't sure if my mocking my mother would ease his humiliation or rub it in. But when he looked back at me he was smiling. Hans was always careful not to denigrate my parents directly to me.

'Nous allons épater les bourgeois,' he said, 'but we've got to eat first.' He picked up the menu. 'Artichokes, anyone?'

I grinned. In Hans I had found an ally who would help me scorn the values of duty and obedience as well as the privilege I had been born into. He watched it all more closely than I.

Our wedding reception was at the best hotel in Breslau, the nearest big town. All our friends came, Dora with Walter, Bertie and the others. On the steps of the town hall they threw confetti and petals and shouted our party's slogan, 'A threefold Red Front!' It wasn't perhaps the most romantic hurrah, but it was the alliance we most craved: between the Social Democrats, the Communists and us.

Hans and I moved into the apartment in Berlin. My father paid for it as part of the wedding settlement, along with our steel and chrome chairs, cornflower-blue carpets and sleek wedding bed.

In the big city Hans's journalistic career went from strength to strength. Still, though he never spoke of it, I knew he felt it was tainted by the Toller episode. He had asked a man to betray his co-prisoners and accept release. None of us had thought of that beforehand, but Hans had been the one whose career got a boost. Dora's criticism lodged deep in him.

Hans tried to make it up in his columns. They started off humorously, but the closer the Nazis came to power, the more bitter and baiting they became. And the more brave.

When General Ludendorff, who had run the war – along with the country, as a supply store for it – claimed in his memoirs that he 'won the war' Hans quipped, 'He did win it too; only the German people lost it because they were so careless as to starve to death before victory was achieved.' Hans reported on the Berlin lavatory attendant who was arrested because she'd replaced her regular supply of toilet paper with a stack of left-wing newspapers for the enlightenment of her clientele. He made friends with the famous bachelor actor Edgar Reiz and with him took on the challenge from an English publication to determine whether Berlin was, as the paper claimed, the most 'depraved and vicious' city on the Continent.

'For research purposes only,' Hans wrote, he and Edgar trawled through girl-bars, boy-bars, gin palaces, cabarets, the foyers of fancy hotels. Early in the morning they found themselves at Magnus Hirschfeld's esteemed Institute for Sexology near the Tiergarten, where the great man himself, portly and feminine behind his cravat and his little round glasses, explained 'in his caressing lisp' that 'there is no such thing as depravity'. 'Something,' Hans noted with relish, 'the English have well known all along.'

In 1928 he went to hear Hitler – then a leader of an opposition party – and wrote one of his most notorious pieces. As a boy, Hans had overcome the worst of his stutter by watching closely how people's lips moved, and pre-thinking each of his own sentences to the end before he began them. This had trained him to notice things others didn't, which was useful for a reporter. Hans told his readers how, at the Sportpalast, the microphone had failed. After some halting and repeating himself, Hitler, furious, threw the thing to one side. 'And there was born,' as Hans put it, 'The Great Adolf's famous bellowing technique. "The bastardisation of peoples has begun!" Herr Hitler cried. "The negroidisation of culture, of customs – not only of blood – strides forward."' Hans wrote that the crowd murmured its agreement, feeling itself as one with the Leader against these unseen, viral enemies.

He then recounted how he had attended the reception for Hitler held after the event in a private apartment. 'We were searched for weapons on entry,' he wrote. In the salon, he found the Leader holding forth on 'this rotten parliamentarianism! This cancer of the German people.' And railing against Berlin for the 'terrible promiscuity of its semi-Slavic population'.

Standing at the back of the crowd, Hans coughed politely. 'And are you married, Herr Hitler?' he inquired. The air turned to ice. The acolytes glared. Hans backed away. 'I saluted at the door with my raised arm and energetically said "*Heil*" and "*Sieg*",' he wrote, 'and only realised when it was too late that I had raised my left instead of my right arm. And as I put on my coat in the hallway, I could hear Adolf say, "What an unpleasant person! Who was that anyway?" No one was able to tell him, and I hurried away before they tried to ask me personally.'

The Nazi Party sued for libel.

There was some confusion at *Die Welt am Montag*. Hans's editor swore that the piece had been submitted as a factual report. He had not been told, he said, that it was a hoax.

'It was ridiculous enough,' Hans scoffed to me. 'I didn't think I needed to spell it out.' Reality was becoming so silly, we thought, that intelligent people could no longer tell the difference between a report and a satire.

Fortunately, the Nazi Party lost the case and had to pay costs.

Some of Hans's more pedestrian colleagues grumbled about journalistic ethics – even fraud! But to others he was a hero: he'd taken on the Nazis and he'd won.

From then on he felt protected.

Although Hans directed his satire broadly at Hitler it was Goebbels who inspired in him a particular, personal vitriol. The Propaganda Minister he baited like a bear. Perhaps it was their shared small-town heritage, or the fact that for both men it was their skill with words that had lifted them out of it. Hans became Goebbels' public nemesis, never referring to him by name, only as 'that distinctly Semitic-looking male', who 'under normal circumstances would have been an energetic teacher at the girls' school in Euskirchen'. Goebbels had written a novel called *Michael*, which Hans only ever and always called *Michael the Ignored*.

In one infamous piece, Hans invented a visit to Goebbels' godmother in his hometown of Rheydt on the Rhine. Surrounded by pots of artificial flowers, he listened to the old woman reminisce:

> Oh, dear sir . . . I don't know what the boy's problem is with the Jews. He used to play so nicely with the Katz children, whose father, a butcher, lived right around the corner . . . But he could never keep his mouth shut. The boy always had to have the last word.

Goebbels lost his cool. He hit back in the Nazi Party's paper, *Der Angriff,* at 'a certain Galician, Hans Wesemann', who, when he was refused an interview with Adolf Hitler, 'composed one with his dirty paws. Now,' Goebbels wrote, 'this noble scribbler is fouling the provinces with the excrement of his sick brain.'

'Not bad,' Hans said over eggs at breakfast, '"excrement of his sick brain".' We looked at each other across the top of our newspapers. 'But then again,' we said together, 'he is, of course, a *novelist*.'

The more famous Hans became, the more outrageous his pieces, and the more the Nazis hated him.

A construction vehicle is delivering long pieces of timber up the next-door driveway, a red cloth tied around their ends as a caution to traffic.

I can see myself clearly at the window of our Berlin flat, way back on the evening Hitler took control, with my red flag out. The boys and the torches and the wonky swastikas were frightening, but they were also ridiculous. We had not thought through what it meant that these rednecks had made their lists; that they had individuals in their cross-hairs, and that those individuals were us.

While Hans became famous in Berlin I completed my studies at the university. Over time, I wrote a dissertation on Goethe's love poetry for my PhD so I would be qualified to teach. But mostly I spent the days behind my camera. I discovered that a photograph might reveal qualities of objects I had not seen when I snapped it. It was as if the sheer physical heft of my subject, its weight and beauty in the world, overcame me in its presence, allowing it to keep its allusive properties to itself. I photographed matches in close-up, heavy-headed and scattered like chance. A stairwell from below, curving back on itself like a concertinaed fan. My own feet on a bed, the shorter leg crossed over the other. I photographed a hand-written note on a bollard – 'HUNGER!' with a postbox number for donations. I snapped a woman in our yard holding a half-naked infant on her hip, fingers pressing his fat thigh like luxury. I caught Hans, eyes closed, neck stretched back over the rim of the bathtub, shadows revealing the architecture of his face.

In the darkroom the pictures swam clearer and clearer towards me through the solution, as if, finally, to open and settle on an answer.

Once, I went with Dora to a Hitler rally, to photograph what went on there. Dora was working for Toller by then, but still for the parliamentarian Mathilde Wurm too. She and Mathilde were investigating the irrational, passionate attraction Hitler held for women. Mathilde was in her fifties, portly and sensible, with the soft black eyes of a Labrador and the faintest of moustaches on her top lip. Widowed and well off, she was an effective politician, particularly on women's issues, though at the same time she was so mild, so level-headed, that any new idea that issued from her lips – from getting hot dinners into schools, to establishing training colleges for young women, to free contraceptive clinics – felt like something that should already have been done. Mathilde hadn't been able to have children, Dora said, which sadness she had transmuted into a mothering energy directed at the whole world. Dora was very fond of Mathilde as a political mentor, but also, I believe, as a stalking horse for her own, more radical ideas.

Hitler was appearing at an event solely for women at the Berlin Lustgarten. As he passed us, on a path strewn with flowers, women held up chapped and worn hands, as for a blessing. Some wept in ecstasy, rocking and saluting. The woman in front of us hoisted her baby up in the air towards him; I photographed the little fellow red-faced and wriggling.

Beside me Dora shook her head, half sympathetic and half disgusted. 'Some kind of chiliastic enchantment,' she whispered. 'As if he alone could save them.'

We'd arrived late and were standing at the back. By the time Hitler reached the podium I could still just make him out between the heads in front of me, but Dora was too small to see over anyone's shoulder. Behind her stood an SS guard. He glanced down. No doubt he saw the Independents badge on Dora's lapel, but she simply shrugged good-naturedly up at him, as if to say, Who would be so short?

The man looked around, then said, 'Come on, comrade, you want to see the Leader as much as anyone.' He bent his knees and put out his hands.

Dora didn't hesitate. She took them and stepped backwards onto the SS man. He moved his grip to her waist and held her there aloft, like the figurehead on a ship.

I want to see her.

For all the thousands of photographs I took in my life before exile, I have ended up with only two albums. The pictures in them seem more valuable than anything that came after.

I slide open a glass bookcase and take one of the albums down. The pages are black and there is tissue paper between each. The photos are all black-and-white contact prints, small as the negatives they came from. They are tucked into the pages at their corners. There are three here of Dora, none of them from that day at the rally. One is of the two of us, teenagers, our heads through a board at a fair that made us into Romulus and Remus. Another is a family group at my wedding, and the third, my favourite, is a portrait I made of her. Her face is turned at a three-quarter angle, her lips are closed and her gaze is slightly down, away from the camera. The set of her eyes is gentle, questioning. Her hair, bobbed short as a man's at the back, sits forward on her cheek. She wore no make-up, left her eyebrows alone. She looks as contemporary as now.

I study these pictures as if they might yield something of her up to me, or at least a new memory. The sound of her laughing, the flash of white teeth – left incisor crossed over the others. But if I close my eyes to concentrate, her face blurs. My mind is a skittish thing; it will not open if asked too directly. I must be more cunning, approach sideways at the edge of sleep, to get it to surrender something new. After all, everything in it does belong to me.

TOLLER

Clara has gone to meet her husband at the Museum of Modern Art for lunch. Today is their second wedding anniversary. This city is so full of wonders; it keeps a roving eye out for the treasures of the world, snaffles them up and puts them, democratically, on display. Picasso, at the moment. I've ordered room service, as a treat.

After the premiere of *Masses and Man*, Dora called me. The next time I saw her she was addressing a crowd from a podium. I close my eyes.

I am on the speakers' platform at an anti-Paragraph 218 rally in Berlin's Tiergarten. It is 1925. We are the generation back from the war and we are remaking the world – fairer, freer – so it can never happen again. Dora, slight, with her cap of dark hair, mounts the stairs to speak. As she walks she pushes her sleeves up her forearms. A fine gold watch loose on a narrow wrist, but no other jewellery. When she reaches the microphone, her face is partially obscured by its metal halo. She leans forward on her toes. Her black eyes stare over the rim, out at the people. She has no notes.

A ripple of insecurity runs through the crowd, which breathes in and shifts its feet on the gravel. I feel a stab of remorse: how could we have asked any woman to do this, let alone this slip of a thing? Paragraph 218 outlawed abortion, and we had decided to protest against that, and to demand sexual liberation of all kinds – for women, homosexuals, prisoners. I'd been on the organising committee for the rally, along with Einstein and other celebrities, and we had asked for women 'in secure stations in life' to speak about their own experiences of abortion. 'Self-denunciation for the cause', we called it. Given the criminal penalties and social stigma attached to abortion, no one should have volunteered, and no one did. Until she rang me. 'Dora,' she said, 'from the theatre. In Leipzig.' As if I might have forgotten.

'A law . . .' Her first words to the crowd don't come out right. She bows her head, moves a fist to her lips. The audience is very quiet, part politeness, part anxiety. She starts again. 'A law which turns eight hundred thousand women into criminals every year –' her voice, surprisingly calm, is gaining – 'is no longer a law.' She eyes them. 'You are looking,' she says, 'at the face of an outlaw.'

There is a gap in time. And then applause starts.

'No man,' the girl continues over them, 'can understand the agony of a woman who is carrying a child she cannot feed. What's more, to force any woman to have a child is to stymie her activity in economic and public life.' The people go wild, raising fists and hooting. She clasps the microphone stand in one hand and bends it to her mouth. 'Your body,' she continues, 'belongs to you.'

Then, over the din, she stretches out one arm, acknowledging the crowd. I catch my breath. In that moment I see in Dora something I know in myself – the sense of holding one's life in one's palm, to do with as one likes.

On the battlefield I had nearly thrown away my life many times – or had it taken from me. I felt its cheapness and its value like a heavy coin, or a pain. But where did Dora have this from? So much of love is curiosity, a search inside the other for some little piece of self; emerging from the bear cave of them with your birthday candle and a filament of ore: the same as that I'm made of!

Pa-pada-pa, pum pum. The waiter must be feeling friendly.

'Come in,' I call, expecting to see the trolley. Instead it's a hand, followed by a soft-faced young man with a flop of hair on his forehead. Auden!

'*There* you are,' he smiles, coming in sideways. He is in a suit jacket and worsted tie, which look, as always, as if they've been slept in. I am purely happy.

In my years in England I watched Wystan's star rise as a poet – he's the best this century, they are saying – at the same time as he worked with me. He translated my plays and wrote some glorious, original lyrics for them. We would sit in my garden in Hampstead batting words and sense around (his German is good) to see how much equivalent beauty we could wring from each tongue. It is an intimate relationship, when someone is inside your work. They see you better than you can.

'I've searched every crack and cranny of New York City for you, old fellow.' He is puffing as if he's only just stopped turning over the rocks. 'My *wife* –' he smiles; he married the lesbian refugee Erika Mann to give her an English passport, and she is now in New York too – 'told me I'd run into you at Epstein's. When that didn't happen,' he opens out his hands, 'I started a manhunt.'

'Thank you.' Wystan is the only one, apart from Dora, I told of my thrice-weekly visits to the psychiatrist in London. Partly because we had to work around them, and partly because he is a firm believer in neurosis (up to a point) as a stimulus for art. I can see from how he looks at me, and then around the room, that he is gauging whether mine is working for me now or eating me alive.

'Ish – Christopher – has left me,' he says, jacket off, sitting down heavily in Clara's chair. 'Gone to California.'

'I'm sorry.'

'I wonder,' he lights a cigarette, 'whether any kind of marriage at all is possible for us queers.'

'For anyone,' I say. 'Christiane has left me too.'

'My turn to be sorry.' There's a gentle sibilance on his 's', as if he can't quite be bothered sounding it out fully. 'Must be this place.' He gestures around. 'Land of the too bloody free.'

Wystan rubs his forehead, smudging it generously with newsprint ink from his thumb. A cylinder of ash floats from his cigarette down onto the carpet. What I most like about him, I see now, is the ability to deflect emotion with a wave of the hand onto the real world, at the same time as he can nail it, in words, like no one else.

'Christopher said that all my best feelings go into my work, and he got only the residue. Which may, rather horribly, be true.' Wystan's eyes are kind, hooded like a puppy's. He flicks the pages of one of Clara's stenography pads.

'What's going on here, then?'

'Trying to get my best feelings into my work.'

He laughs through his nose.

'Actually, it's true. I'm trying to write about Dora.'

He looks up. 'Brave Dora,' he says. He always liked her, and she him. 'You haven't written about her?'

'I didn't want to use her.'

This is a conversation we've had before – about the temptation of art, like fire, to use people as fuel.

'Yes. Quite.'

I am so relieved to be understood that the words tumble out. 'But now I have nothing. Not her,' there's a thickness in my throat, 'and no portrait either.'

The waiter interrupts with a trolley, on which a large silver tureen stands, a basket of white and brown rolls, butter in curls, and two bowls. They must have assumed I was ordering for Clara too. As the young man, a neat blond fellow of about nineteen, busies himself setting the table, Wystan tucks a large napkin into his collar, which I know for a fact will mysteriously fail to prevent stains from blossoming down his front. The waiter starts to ladle the chowder and Wystan smiles, confident that the world – so thoughtful of it, really – has anticipated him. Then he reaches into his pocket for his billfold and tips the man generously.

'Thank you, sir,' the waiter says with a small nod, and then he turns. Wystan's pale eyes follow the boy till he's gone.

'This country,' he raises his eyebrows and cracks open a roll with his fingers, 'is going to be good for me. I can feel it. And not just that.' He tosses his head towards the door.

I place both wrists on the table. 'I'm going back to Europe.'

Wystan puts the bread down.

'I am useless here. No one is listening. Europe will fall.'

He nods, slowly. 'I know,' he says. 'I can't do the speeches any more. I simply don't believe that man's better nature can win. Our liberal scruples make us blind – the fascists are too seductive, and too strong.'

'What will you do here?' I don't know why I ask; I know what he will do. He will write poems that will be read in two hundred years, he will fall in love, he will come out the other side.

'Write,' he says, as if it were a small thing. 'While you go back into the fray. As usual.'

I know that he considers me, despite the underside he is aware of, a brave man. This is more a testament to his kindness than his judgement, but it means I can tell him anything.

'It's a strange pathology, don't you think,' I say, 'to want to be something other than what you are?'

Wystan leans forward, places a hand on mine. He has seen my need and he will never shame me for showing it to him. 'It's the same old thing, isn't it?' he says. 'All that we are not stares back at all that we are.'

He picks up his spoon and smiles as if to say *Guten Appetit*. But sees I am stricken by what he has said. 'Not to look at that too closely, old fellow,' he adds. 'Do what you have to. And do not discount it.' He shakes his head a little, lowering his spoon into the soup. 'Poetry makes nothing happen.'

After he leaves, the happiness of his company persists in the room. I lay my head over the chair back and close my eyes again.

I am slouching, head back on the leather car seat. Dora and I are in a cathedral of trees; from each side of the road poplars arch above us to touch. The dapples of light they admit rush over the bonnet and the windscreen and over our bodies, so we can feel our speed. Dora drives; I never learnt. Her arms are bare but she wears cream kid gloves that fasten across the back of her wrists, and she talks and talks, eyes ahead as the ribbon of road flattens under the car. She is counting votes for something – her politics were much more practical than mine – but I have stopped listening. The wind plays with her hair.

Yesterday afternoon we signed in as man and wife at the Schloss Eckberg in Dresden. As her hand moved across the register I reached into her hair, casually as I could, and removed some grass stalks. Smiling mildly all the while to the concierge. By Dresden on the banks of the Elbe the reeds grow to chest height. Dora had dragged me off the path and deep into them, laughing and pushing me down till the world was a patch of sky in a blurring green frame. In the morning she had three cups of coffee and toyed with her egg before she could smoke, this woman who was all appetite.

I have never felt so wanted. I reach across to hold her neck in my hand.

'You hungry?' she interrupts her stream of talk. 'They packed us some food.'

There's a basket at my feet under the dash. In it I find a magnificent pear. When she bites, the juice drips down.

'Damn,' she laughs. I grab my handkerchief and start dabbing in her lap and she shoots me a look, swiping her chin with the back of one leathered hand. The other hand then slipping on the wheel and the wheel spinning through it, the pear airborne past my nose and the car screeching, failing to match the turn in the road. Her feet pump the pedal but it's no use and we go, slower than is possible, to the end, which comes in a metal scream against one of the poplars.

Steam hisses from the bonnet. Dora pulls herself back from the steering wheel and sees that I am all right. A man runs towards us who turns out to be the town policeman. After he checks that we are unharmed, he shakes his head, looking up and down the empty road on this blue-sky day and wondering aloud how such a thing could happen.

'Officer,' Dora offers, as if in full and final explanation, 'I was eating a pear.'

I've left a cigarette burning in the ashtray on the other side of the room. I move to it and put it to my lips. Clara is back, sitting quietly. She doesn't swivel her head to look at me, or ask a prompting question; she lets the spell persist. As I exhale, my eyes caress the tousled crown of her dark head and it feels like old times.

She picks up her pencil and pad. I am emptying myself out in pieces here. Then trying to see what shape they make when put back together.

'Ready?' I ask.

She nods.

When Dora came to work for me she graduated from secretary to sounding-board to collaborator, and then, during the split from her husband Walter, lover. The two of them had had an amicable, even comradely marriage, the freedoms of which had, on his side, simply involved too many other people. Dora vowed never to marry again, as if somehow it had been the institution of marriage, rather than the infidelity – to which she also had a right – that had caused her pain.

Dora had a sense of purpose so profound that when I was with her it was impossible to feel lost. Her presence reduced my demons to pathetic things, impractical and bad company, which would go away if I ignored them and focused instead on the task at hand: the book or play, the speech or cause or trip. She would say, 'It's not about you, remember, it's about the work.' Dora thought I clung to my self-doubt, my edge-of-despair insights, as if they were the outward signs of deep artistic integrity – confidence and equanimity, after all, not being characteristics of genius. It stung a little, but I was grateful to be saved by her. At least half of what we call hope, I believe, is simply the sense that something can be done.

Once, on the beach at Rügen, we lay on our sides in sand so pure it squeaked. Dora had found a beautiful white stone, large as a dog's head. She closed her eyes and moved her hands over it, as over a crystal ball, mimicking to perfection the deadpan voice of a medium. 'Your fears for your sanity, kind sir, are grossly exaggerated . . .' I lay back laughing, watching her through my lashes.

Mostly I could tell when an episode was coming. I would find myself alone, reading and rereading a paragraph that no longer made sense, even though I had written it the day before. Each subordinate clause felt too heavy, literally, to move or change. But impossible – wrong! – to leave where it lay. As long as this page was stuck, so too was all other life. Making a phone call was too much effort, the company of others futile. When imagination fails, one is caught in a solecism as big as the world: the universe is reduced to a reflection of ourselves from which we cannot escape, narrow and already known. The cynic sees only cynicism, the depressive can taint creation with one glance.

When I sensed an attack coming on I would seek Dora out. In the company of someone so honest, so intelligent and so practical, doubt felt unworthy. She had her own demons to control, like the morphine she'd used since the abortion, but she always seemed stronger than me. If I left it too late and the inertia got me, I would be too ashamed to find her. I would put the word out I was abroad and spend the days – sometimes weeks – of the black time in my flat, mostly in bed. Waiting without hope for hope to come back in its own goddamn time.

Once, she did catch me like this. She had been in Britain for a week, attending a Trades Union Congress at Weymouth. By the time she got back I wasn't answering the phone, or the door. She let herself in.

'Are you unwell?' she called. I heard her shoes slap down in the entry. She padded down the hall into my bedroom and stood in the doorway.

'Your cardigan is inside out.'

'Thanks.' She started to take it off. It was soft grey marl, with buttons made from the insides of shells. 'You all right?' she asked again. She picked up a ball of paper that had landed in my sock drawer.

I hadn't shaved in a few days. The bed – a teak four-poster from the Spice Islands that my mother hadn't been able to sell in her furniture shop – had become my ark. Beyond it was chaos. On every horizontal surface were coffee cups and bowls with food caked on them and fork handles sticking out. I'd been eating mostly pork and lentils from tins; the room was muggy with it.

Screwed-up pieces of paper lay all over the floor; a pile of frag-mented thoughts sat on the bedside table, scribbled things that withered to banalities in the light of day. Next to me was a large green glass ashtray, full.

'Been living it up, I see.' She smiled, leant over and kissed my forehead. Then she sat down on the bed. Though she dealt with my demons by trivialising them, she never pretended the work was easy.

'I'm a little tired.'

'Been working late?'

'No,' I said. 'Too busy exhausting myself. By not sleeping.'

She laughed, and threw the paper ball into the wastepaper basket. 'Bullseye.'

Dora lit a cigarette and told me about an extraordinary Englishman she'd met, Fenner Brockway, who was a friend of Jawaharlal Nehru's. 'The very best kind of Englishman,' she said, 'one who appears to take it all lightly, so he can debate in a civilised manner – not like the screaming matches at our congresses. But underneath, there's a real passion for justice.'

'Probably for you too.' I looked at her sideways.

'Probably,' she said, exhaling a stream of smoke. It was a condi-tion of seeing Dora that it was not exclusive, that she was 'free'. I was, of course, 'free' too.

I don't know, now, how much freedom the heart can bear. The heart, too, likes containment.

She kissed me again. 'If I get dressed properly, will you? We can just do corrections, if nothing else.'

Clara puts her pencil down. What can it be like for her to sit there while I relate my love for her predecessor? Her legs are crossed, she runs her thumb across the spiral binding of her steno pad. When she looks up her pupils readjust from the page to me, the irises kalei-doscoping green and golden-brown. Her mouth is slightly open. It is a look that says, I see now where you are going. And it says – or so I believe – I am with you.

'Sometimes . . .' Her voice is caught, she clears her throat. '. . . just to do corrections is the perfect response.' Clara takes a deep breath. 'We should probably finish up the correspondence today. Starting with the letter to Mrs Roosevelt?'

I am writing to thank the First Lady for hosting a fundraiser for the starving children of Spain, and to insist that despite Spain having fallen now to the fascists, the funds still be handed over. Franco might use the money to buy guns, but he might, just might, use it to feed people.

Three months ago I was high. When I arrived here this room was filled with reporters, flowers, press photographers snapping on their knees. Telegrams came and went. An earnest post-graduate student would pipe up with a long question whenever he could get one in; someone took a pillowcase off the bed for me to autograph. I ordered room service for everyone, Christiane sighing as she signed for it. At that time I could do anything, I could do everything, and all at once. With the First Lady I raised a million dollars.

But I come with a switch. I sent them all away. Now it's just me, and Clara.

'Yes,' I say, 'let's start with that one.'

RUTH

I remember that grey marl cardigan of hers. Strange, isn't it, what adheres to the flypaper mind?

Much later I heard about it, but I never saw Toller depressed. The couple of times I went to his flat to collect her, he was talking as fast as you could listen, ideas spilling from him more rapidly than he – or Dora – could get them down. He buzzed about the tiny room like Superman in a trap, lighting cigarettes and putting them down, forgetting and lighting new ones. He'd set four, sometimes five, plumes of smoke going and keep moving between the ashtrays. He once told Dora he'd written *Masses and Man* in three days and nights, right through without sleeping. He wasn't boasting, she said. He was baffled.

It is true that she loved Fenner Brockway. In those days we believed in freedoms of every kind. So many boys had died in the war that we knew life was short, and cheap. There was no point not loving when the occasion arose. Those hippies of the '60s and '70s seemed so tame and vain to me, so derivative. They marched for peace but had never really known war; they confused the freedom simply to have sex with the freedom for one's sex not to matter. Dora thought sex should be something freely given, not part of a brideprice in a transaction for a woman. She was living for now.

But Dora was never confused about Toller. When he left my studio after I took his portrait that day, she placed a jazz record she'd brought on the gramophone and wound the handle. She swung me around and around till we were laughing and dizzy. Her eyes shone. 'That self-conscious, lung-afflicted fellow,' she said, 'is the grandest man I will ever know.'

Hanging the red flag out our window in Berlin had no immediate consequence. What followed were the mojito weeks, a time of false calm and cocktails. God alone knows where all those limes were flown in from – what decadence!

As soon as he was appointed, Hitler called an election for five weeks' time. But the newspapers weren't banned straight away, so Hans wrote a few more columns, typing them at the dining table and delivering them in the evenings on his bicycle. His last piece had The Great Adolf as a failed minor politician in 1942, about to undertake a lecture tour to his dwindling support base of crackpots in the United States. 'We sat down in his modest, twelve-room house in the Bavarian mountains,' Hans wrote, 'and for a time we exchanged pleasantries. I noticed immediately that the Leader was no longer sporting his famous moustache. He observed my surprise. "Germany has lost a lot of hair in the past decade," he said, "so I thought I should set a symbolic example."'

I spent those strange weeks going to meetings in people's flats all around Berlin. Our little party had changed its name from the Independent Social Democrats to the Socialist Workers Party, try-ing even harder to be a bridge between the Social Democrats and the Communists. Those larger parties had hated each other ever since the Social Democrats sent in the troops to quash the Munich Revolution in 1919. We desperately wanted them to align now so as not to split the vote against the Nazis in the coming election. We argued and drafted leaflets and assigned each other tasks: distributing them, going to speak to the unions, recruiting new members. We felt our work was real and urgent. So did the Stormtroopers.

They started breaking up our meetings, arresting members on the street, searching our satchels. One friend who was putting up notices on a lamppost was bashed in broad daylight; another disappeared for two days into custody. Our goal of a united front against Hitler was sensible, but the level of mistrust between the parties was too deep, and their understanding of the Nazi threat to them – to all of us – too shallow. We didn't stand a chance.

One evening at the end of February Hans and I went, as we often did, to the Romanisches Café, and then to the TicTacToe club on Lehniner Platz. We needed to obliterate the arguments in our heads, to live a little. The mojitos at home and the *Sekt* at the café had hollowed us out; we were full of bubbles and smoke and, now, unlikely to eat. Dora was meeting us at the TicTacToe.

On Kurfürstenstrasse women, some alone, some in small groups, stood around in deliberate idleness, moving in and out of the streetlights, making their cigarettes last. Darkness hid the sorrow of their cheap finery, granting them instead the dignity of honesty: here is a body-bargain, tenderness at market price.

We were mysteriously immune to the cold. Hans's scarf was loose; my eyes were level with the scar on his throat. Drink made him generous with secret knowledge.

'Look.' He nodded towards a woman on his left. 'That's a Racehorse – she offers herself to be whipped.' The woman had red hair under a hat at a vertiginous angle, and shiny, pine-green boots. 'And yellow,' he gestured discreetly at a motherly creature blooming out of golden boots like risen dough, 'means cripples are welcome.'

The women ignored us, shaking their legs a little in the cold. Hans was revelling in showing me his night city.

'Over there are Telephone Girls, who can be booked discreetly through the hotel. They dress as movie stars, so you can order up a Garbo or a Dietrich to the room.' I looked at them, but couldn't really tell which was which. 'And those young ones,' he indicated further down the street, 'are from good families in Charlottenburg and Grunewald. They're out for a fling and pocket money.' These last were tall and slight; one of them dandled a tennis racquet.

A slim-hipped woman in a veil stood apart, watching us closely. She held a white umbrella and her dress was fastened across her abdomen by a sequined butterfly. Hans bent his mouth to my ear, tossing his butt into the gutter. 'And that, my lovely, is a man.'

'And how do you know all this?' I asked in mock suspicion.

'Edgar.'

Since they had debunked the notion of depravity for the British newspaper together, 'Edgar' or 'with Edgar' had become the answer to many questions. Sometimes I joked that Edgar was like an invisible childhood friend, the one who did all the naughty things so that Hans came out, always and in every circumstance, clean.

Hans bent and kissed me, long and hard on the mouth. When I opened my eyes the butterfly boy was still watching us.

'Come on,' I said, and we walked to the club.

The doors of the TicTacToe opened into a floor-length leather curtain drawn against the cold. We parted it. The entry level was on a mezzanine; below us lay a vast, ornate room hollowed out into the earth. I moved to the balcony rail. Pools of light shone on a hundred tables, bright circles into which hands moved, gloved or ungloved, for a drink, to ash a cigarette, touch an arm. The air was filled with trumpet notes and smoke, the chinking sounds of cutlery, laughter, something smashing at the upper bar. At my shoulder a vase of lilies breathed, open-tongued.

While Hans found the maître d' I scanned for Dora through the chandeliers and the chrome-tubed vacuum system that linked the tables like celestial plumbing. Mirrored balls hung in the space too, taking the light and smashing it into diamond pieces that slid over the walls and the curtains of booths. I gripped the rail to hold me down, steady this spinning hour.

Suddenly, from here, in the sea of heads and limbs, under these orbs of metal and glass hanging below the pavement, all humans seemed the same – vulnerable and chittering, their movements staccato in this fractured light. They were insects – we were insects – the females with small bobbed heads, bodies sheathed in short silk and translucent dresses, beaded and open-backed and showing glimmering curves and points under skin. They trailed scarves or trains or boas in apricot, teal, gold, sky-blue. One creature wielded an outsize fan of ostrich feathers dyed puce, dark tendrils under her arm hidden and revealed, hidden and revealed as she fanned. The males were wingless, sleek and still. Except for the waiters weaving about in tails, trays at the shoulder bearing silver cocoons.

'Table 36.' Hans cupped my elbow and steered me down the stairs, then through the crowd. We passed Michelangelo's *David* on a podium, knuckles resting on one thigh and his eyes averted modestly. His chest rose and fell. I glanced around to see the other living statues for this night. Naked Justice stood not far away, dimple-thighed and blindfolded and holding a scale. As we reached our table a woman in a baroque wig and satin shoes stood staring into the middle distance. She wore only three bows, one around her waist and one just above each knee. Her skin and pubis were powdered, like something under ash.

'Bo *Peep*?' Hans cocked an eyebrow as he pulled the chair out for me.

'Does she call for you, my lamb?' I smiled.

He chuckled. We had taken to using the tongue-in-cheek

repartee of a married couple going through the motions of love when we were out. In public, it felt real. In private it felt like a running joke we could get serious from at any time, if we chose. (I feel, now, that it was a mistake to conceal intimacy under shared jokes. As if we had, already, run out of real things to say, or as if intimacy can survive untended.)

'I'm not lost at all.' Hans kissed my hand. 'The others have asked not to be disturbed, apparently. The waiter will let them know we're here.'

'Others?'

'Bert's here too. A surprise visit – I just heard today.'

'Bertie!' I hadn't seen him since he'd left for France the year before. 'What a treat.'

Hans looked up at Bo Peep. 'If she moves, you know, she breaks the law.'

I tapped a cigarette on my case. 'I know how she feels.'

The law had given rise to these living statues: it forbade full nudity if there was the slightest movement. But for me the statues were not titillation. They signalled something else: in here you could shed yourself. You could be anyone, have your heart tickled and your body moved to screams. In the morning you would climb out of here into an unchanged world, but for what happened between now and then no apologies would be owed.

Hans had just lit a cigar when he was on his feet again. I looked up to see him pumping Rudi Formis's hand. Rudi then took mine and bowed his head, mousy-brown hair brilliantined down on either side of a part neat as a furrow, and his glasses hooked behind his ears.

Rudolf Formis was one of the few people we associated with who had once been in the Nazi Party. He'd left when he felt it had cosied up to big business and no longer represented the ordinary man. Rudi was a brilliant radio technician, small and fine-fingered and sincere. He had a slight lisp, as if his tongue were fractionally too big for his mouth. If you asked him a question, there was no limit to the amount of detail he would go into to answer it, but he always had the good grace, afterwards, to shrug shyly, as much as to say, Sorry, but you asked. He'd served in Palestine during the war, where he developed a genius for short-wave radio transmitters, inventing one of the first of their kind. I used to think that fixing the finest filigree of wires to make words fly had honed his brain for detail, something he could not now unthread.

Hans was congratulating Rudi on his recent promotion to technical director of the largest radio station in the state.

'Thanks,' Rudi glowed. 'Actually, there's something I can tell you now. Do you remember your brilliant piece about Hitler at the Sportpalast?'

Hans rolled his eyes. 'I got into a lot of trouble for that one,' he said.

'I know. But you got the detail so perfectly right.' Rudi bent his head to Hans. 'Even about the microphones failing.'

'Yes,' Hans said, 'but that wasn't what —'

Rudi leant in further, included me in his gaze. 'That was me.' He tapped himself on the chest.

'What? How . . . ?' I started to smile.

Rudi was fingering his earlobe, eyes on the table. 'I, ah, pulled the plug.' We stared at him for a beat, so he added, 'Out of the socket.'

I laughed, incredulous.

'Priceless,' Hans said.

'You can't use that,' Rudi added quickly. 'I'd lose my job.'

'Sure,' Hans soothed. 'I wouldn't.'

'Oh Rudi.' I touched his arm and he flushed.

We watched him disappear into the crowd and smiled at each other. One would never have guessed it from his sober, combed-down appearance, but Rudi's parents had been vaudevillians. In their signature act, Rudi's father sat on his mother's lap and she used her arms as if they were his – to comb his hair, raise a cup of tea to his lips. Rudi had spent his childhood at the back of fairgrounds, dismantling household appliances and putting them carefully back together, as if the adult world were too unreliable. I suppose the Nazis had seemed reliable to him. He hated them now with the passion of a man atoning for his past.

A waiter put our Manhattans on the table, between the silver prong with the number on it and the telephone. The band was coming on stage: five men in top hats and skeleton suits, their faces painted black and their teeth white as bones. The singer carried a toy cannon under his arm, stuffed with paper money. 'Democracy – for – sale!' he bellowed, then the music started up. He sprang off stage and moved among the diners, an X-ray flinging fistfuls of fake currency over us. 'Democracy for sale!' The money twisted and floated in and out of the dappled light. Hans plucked a note from the air and held it to the candle. He relit his cigar then placed the bill, curling and flaming, in the ashtray.

A small thud in the vacuum chute. The compartment hissed as I slid it open. Inside was a leather cigar case with the grid insignia of the TicTacToe. I raised my eyebrows in a question.

'Not from me,' Hans said.

'An unseen admirer then.'

I opened it with two thumbs. A glass vial lay on green velvet. I pulled the cork stopper with its tiny sniffer spoon attached. Offered the cocaine to Hans.

The light on the phone flashed. I picked it up.

'A little something for quick thinking,' she said.

'Thanks.'

'We're in booth 27.'

Hans pocketed the vial. We picked up our drinks and went over. When we opened the curtain Dora and Bert weren't drinking.

Instead, laid out before them were ordnance maps, a compass, several regional newspapers, open notebooks. There was a porcelain pâté pot with a laughing pig for a handle, a dish wiped clean in front of Bertie, and another with a half-eaten fish.

'Bert!' I cried. 'I'm so glad. How did you —?'

'Pull it to,' Dora ordered.

I closed the curtain. She was rolling up the maps, a cigarette on her bottom lip and one eye squinted against the smoke.

Bert and Hans hugged, then Hans held Bert a long moment by the shoulders, towering over his little friend.

'How well you look,' he said.

Bert did not look well. He looked thinner, older, sallower. His spectacles were held together at the right-hand hinge with a knot of gauze that had turned brown from fingering. His goatee was already more silver than black – though Bert was only thirty-four – and the hair on his head sat sparse and feathery off his skull. He beamed.

After our university days, Bert had done time in prison. When eighty-one young men died in a 'practice manoeuvre' at Veltheim an der Weser, Bert had become suspicious. He studied the death notices in the local papers and visited the cemeteries and bereaved families, cross-checking the dead under their fresh mounds against official military rolls. He proved that at least eleven of the boys had been illegal 'volunteers' in 'work Kommandos' of the Black Army. The Chancellor denied any knowledge of them, as did the Defence Minister. For publication of this truth, Bert was convicted of attempted treason – violation of the State Secrets Act – and served eight months' hard labour in Gollnow prison. After he was released he crossed the border to Strasbourg and kept up his investigations, publishing a bulletin he called the *Independent Press Service*. Though it was still illegal, Dora was helping him distribute it in Germany.

Prison had no doubt been terrible, but it had also transformed Bertie, whether he wanted it or not, into the living embodiment of a cause. Nationwide fame sat oddly on those narrow shoulders. It hadn't made him grander, more statesmanlike. Instead, Bertie seemed to have developed a sense of himself as a phenomenon apart, a one-man reckoning. He maintained the habits of obscurity, introducing himself to people who knew full well who he was, failing to smile at well-meaning passers-by.

'How did you get back in?' Hans was asking.

'With parliament prorogued before the election, I thought they mightn't have clear instructions any more.' Bertie was scratching the back of his neck. 'On who to keep out at the border.'

Prorogued. Like all autodidacts, Bert always used the biggest word he could find.

Dora shook her head. 'It's not as if just because we're going to the polls the gates are open for all the old political crims to come in,' she laughed, looking fondly at Bert. 'I told you: you just got lucky.'

Bert coughed into his hand. He was congenitally unsuited to luck; luck would have upset his sense of himself.

Afterwards, Berthold Jacob was dubbed the Man Who Tried to Stop the Second World War. But at that time, so long before, although people admired his doggedness, behind his back they said, *He exaggerates, all the same.* It was as if he *knew no measure.* He had let his cause swamp his life, and this constituted, even in our committed circle of friends, a certain lack of form. Despite all he had done he was still *poor Bertie*: self-righteous, argumentative, and scrounging meals, his ears sticking out like questions and his pockets rustling with newspapers. Hans admired and loved him, but to me he called him 'living proof that being right is no consolation'.

I loved him more simply, and so, I think, did Dora. Measure was not, after all, what the times required.

The bench seats of the TicTacToe were cool, olive-green leather. The four of us sank into them, into the pleasure of our velvet-walled, candlelit cave. Outside, applause rose and ebbed between the acts.

'What are you two up to?' I nodded at the documents.

'Bert's showing me some of our burgeoning new towns in the backblocks of Brandenburg,' Dora said, 'and their brand-spanking-new electrical works.'

'A wireless for every hearth?' Hans asked. In practically his opening address, Hitler had promised every household a wireless.

'No,' Dora said. 'Components for fighter planes. Disguised as railway switches.'

Hans leaned back, with an arm around me along the seat-top. I caught a wave of his piny cologne. 'You know what they're going to call them?' he asked.

'The planes or the wirelesses?' Dora shot back.

'The wireless,' Hans sallied calmly. 'It's called the *Volksempfänger*, or VE 301 – after the day he came to power, 30/1.' He offered Dora the vial and she took it, raised the bitter spoon to her nostril.

'It's not like they're hiding anything, is it?' he continued. 'They should just call it the Hitler-Hearer.' We all laughed.

'They're not hiding it well, anyway,' Bert said, who wasn't much into jokes.

'Speaking of wirelesses,' I said, 'we just ran into Rudi.'

Dora smiled. 'Did you hear what he did?'

'Yes,' I said. 'Magnificent, wasn't it?'

'I hope he's being careful now,' Bert muttered. Then he turned to me. '*Et tu*, Ruthie? What are you up to?'

I told him how yesterday the Communist headquarters had been raided by Röhm's brown-shirted SA. They stole the entire membership list of four thousand people.

'It's getting harder,' I said. 'They killed the mayor of a town in Thuringia.'

'I heard,' Bert said.

'What about you?' I put a hand on his arm. Hans had picked up the phone to order from the bar; Dora was stuffing the maps and notebooks away in her bag.

'Fine. Bit of a problem with my waterworks actually.' He gestured dismissively to his lap. 'Doctor said it was gout. I said, "How can I have gout on one meal a day?"' Bert laughed, then started to cough again. In the too-soon offering of intimacy I saw all four corners of his lonely life.

A waiter opened our curtain. I glimpsed the stage behind him, empty now but for a bathtub. Then the players came on and took up their instruments again. They began a steady Greek dirge: *ta-la-la-la, TA-la-la-la, TA-la-la-la*. The music of anticipation, of slowly rising madness. A pair of wet hands rose from the tub, reached for a rope. They pulled up a man in a full suit and tie, his body held horizontal, sheeting water. He wound one ankle into the rope and started to spin. Then he clipped a noose to the rope and put his head in. A fine arc of droplets sprayed from his body onto the crowd.

When I turned back, Dora had taken off her jacket. She wore only a slip underneath – she never 'dressed' for anything. Without trying, she was now a creature of this place, apricot and brown, wings and skin and points under silk. She had her elbows on the table. 'I wonder why we bother, really,' she was saying. 'This election is a veneer. It can't save us even if we win.'

'Why not?' I said.

'The Nazis dislike parliamentary democracy as much as the Communists do. They won't accept defeat.'

'Why not just take over, then?'

'May I?' Bert was pointing at Dora's half-eaten fish. He started to slide the plate towards him, then stopped, cleared his throat and touched his glasses. 'Hitler needs it to look legal,' he said. 'He wants a two-thirds majority so he can pass his Enabling Act, then forget about parliament altogether and rule by decree. That way he can keep the military and industry onside. I'm told I.G. Farben and

Krupp and others are going to give him three million Reichsmarks, which they wouldn't do after a putsch.'

'Democracy for sale,' Dora said.

'How do you know all this?' Hans goaded Bert. 'Got a "source" now, have you?'

Bert never had inside information because he was massively indiscreet, about everyone and anything he thought people should know. He was so used to divining secrets from publicly available information that confidentiality was inconceivable to him. I found him open, brave; others found him hideously unreliable.

I watched Bertie's lips pull back over mottled teeth, as he bided his time thinking of a riposte. In those excruciating seconds I wondered what righteous rabbi of his childhood had taught him that truth was a defence; that if one was right, one needn't be liked. As if being liked were a trivial thing, like pleasure, or heating. Or functioning waterworks. A round of applause rose and fell for the spinning man.

Finally Bert said, 'I don't *need* a source, Johannes.'

Hans smiled a crooked drunken smile. He started to clap, slowly. 'Quite so, my friend,' he said. 'Quite so.' I felt my love pivot and wobble. I spoke over his mocking applause.

'But he won't get a two-thirds majority,' I said. 'That's what we're counting on.'

Hans stopped clapping and poured himself another schnapps from a little jug. 'There are rumours,' he said, 'that they might stage their own assassination attempt on The Great Adolf. Then use that as an excuse to crack down on all the opposition.'

Unlike Bertie, Hans thrived on rumours, on having sources, on being in the know with his 'ear to the ground'. He didn't have the patience to scrutinise government announcements or read pay lists from the public service. Although he secretly admired Bertie's capacity for work and his courage to publish and go to prison for it, admiration was a difficult thing for Hans – there was always the risk he might compare badly in his own mind. He managed this fear by teasing Bert for pernicketiness.

Bert, in turn, envied Hans his extravagant charm, his ability to wring so much pleasure from life. He watched Hans over the top of the beer Hans had ordered for him.

'Where did you hear that about an assassination?' I asked Hans. He turned his head to me but said nothing.

'It doesn't matter,' Dora said. 'The gist of it is true, rumour or not. It'll be like 1914, when they said the French had attacked us. They need an emergency to save us from.'

'He *is* the emergency,' I said. Dora laughed.

'You might be right,' Bert said slowly.

'Thanks,' I said.

'No, I mean Dora.'

'Might I?' She smiled. Bert had no tact, but I could never take offence. He picked up a pen and started colouring in the squares of the TicTacToe grid on the coaster. Dora offered him the cocaine but he shook his head.

'No!' He dropped the pen and slapped the table. 'That's it! Hitler needs the emergency *before* the election. Then he can rule by emergency decree, "in times of terror", shut down the press and stop us campaigning altogether. With the polls as they are, that's the only way he can get his majority.' Bert put both hands to the sides of his head, as if reproving it for not coming up with this sooner. 'Then, after the election, he'll pass his Enabling Act and do whatever he wants.'

There was a moment at the table in which the thought sat there and became solid, self-evident.

Bert looked at Dora. 'Where's Toller?'

'In Switzerland. Lecture tour.'

'Wire him to stay there.'

Dora frowned. 'You'll have to leave too,' Bert continued. 'You'll be high on their list.' He turned to Hans and me. 'You two as well.'

'I think we should stay and fight it out here,' I said. 'Nothing's happened yet.'

'Don't be a fool,' Bert said. His predictions were so often right he took doubt as a personal affront. 'It's clear. They're making *lists*. Or stealing them. I'll leave tomorrow myself.'

'I agree,' Hans said, suddenly sober. 'We're no good to anyone locked up.'

There was a pause.

'I'll have to get his things out then,' Dora said, to no one in particular.

Bert slid Dora's plate the rest of the way towards him and picked up his fork. While he ate, no one spoke. The evening, for Dora and Bert, was over: there was work to do. They left as soon as he'd finished.

But Hans and I stayed. In the early hours a woman came on stage in a red rubber dress with long sleeves, tight as skin. The band began a slow strip tune: she pulled a handkerchief from her sleeve. People laughed. Then one from the other sleeve. She bent down to her shoe and found one there. She patted her thighs, then tentatively reached up into the dark under her dress. Felt about. Her hand came out empty. People laughed a little more. She patted her pubic bone: a drum beat once. Another pat: twice. More laughter. She stretched her knees apart and reached up between them again – *Aha!* With one palm she stopped the laughter. Her head tilted slowly in astonishment.

With her hips canted forward just a little, she started to pull. Out came a bright piece of yellow silk, like a puppet's thread. A soft drum roll began. Hand over hand, the red rubber woman pulled, delicately, curiously. Each handkerchief was knotted to another, this one green, then blue then orange, purple, aqua, red. They came and they came – she was made of silk inside! She was empty but for silk, she was turning herself inside out for us. And at the end before we realised it was all over, there hung a tiny bell, like you might put on a cat to stop it catching birds.

I went home to sleep after that, but Hans found some friends from the paper and stayed on.

'You got any more rubber gloves? These've got holes in.' Bev is standing in the doorway, holding up her hands to show me the offending pink rubber articles. She does most of my shopping and knows full well that I have no idea about the current rubber glove situation. She is asking me so I'll acknowledge that I have ceded control over this house to her and pay due homage.

'Look under the sink,' I say, because, in the scheme of things, my domestic incapacities are really the least of it.

'Hmmph.' She turns on her heel.

Dora went straight from the TicTacToe to Toller's apartment. The stairwell was pale pink, like skin, and had flowers and field plants painted on it, fennel and nettles with tender stems stretching up the wall. She had the keys. She had every right. She would say she was delivering a parcel. Strange, how quickly we know what is forbidden. Is it the part of us that is like them which tells us?

Later, they sealed off his apartment with planks screwed into the doorjamb where the locks had been smashed, and put up a notice from the Ministry of Justice: 'Contaminated Area. Entry Prohibited'. The place stayed empty for the six and a half years up until the war and then for all the six years of war. A trophy, or a trap.

She had the keys, but because he'd gone away Toller had snibbed the top lock as well. Dora had to get both tongues to stay out at the same time. The metal teeth jangled on their ring; so loud – why, now, so loud?

She opened the lower one and held the handle with her left hand, while turning the key above her head in the top lock, scratching and slipping, looking for traction. The stairwell light timed out. She had to let go. Before she reached the switch on the wall it came on again by itself. She jumped backwards. Footsteps, and a scuffling, dragging sound up the stairs. She had every right.

He rounded the banister. Herr Benesch from the flat above, and his dachshund Willi dragging its stomach up each step, claws scratching the wood.

'Good evening,' Benesch nodded. He was a retired civil servant of some kind. 'Midnight call of nature,' he said, gesturing to the dog with a gloved hand.

'Of course.'

'Herr Toller back, then?'

'No,' Dora said, 'not yet.'

Toller never did come back to Germany. In a few weeks' time they would take his books from shops and libraries and burn them.

'I'm just dropping off some books,' she said. Her bag was on the floor.

'Need a hand?'

'Thanks. I'm fine.'

He moved past her to go up the stairs. Then, over his shoulder, 'They've been here, you know.'

She nodded. Turned back to the door.

When he was out of sight she looked at the space where he had been. You could never know if someone was giving you a warning out of kindness, or enacting some kind of self-exculpation. Was Benesch warning her before making himself safe by calling them back?

In the flat she kept the lights off. She moved from the hall past

the little bookshelf where they took off their shoes to the first of
the three rooms facing the street. Her eyes adjusted to the dimness;
she could make out the divan on the left against the wall, with the
silk sari draped over it, the little square reading table in the middle of the room. The windows were unseeing panes of black. She
crouched to below the level of the balcony and pulled the curtains
across, moving sideways like a monkey. She hoped it was too dark
to notice the fabric swaying from outside.

Her mouth was dry. In the kitchen she turned on a light.
Scratched her forearms. Ashtrays sat unemptied and a rose in the
neck of a bottle was turning to paper. She took a glass from the
shelf. The tap sputtered, plumbing juddering in the wall.

Back into the hall, where the ceiling was high and the walls lined
with bookshelves, all the way down. The books that were published
could never be exterminated completely; somewhere a copy would
survive, the fossil imprint on the world of that particular soul at
that particular time. The floor creaked and groaned as she walked
down. At the end was the grand corner room – windows on two
sides to the street. So many times she had waited for him, working
in this bed as he paced out his nights, that the creak-and-groan of
the corridor when he came down to her had the same effect as the
chink of his belt buckle undoing. She was unsentimental, practical,
hedonistic about sex. Very beautiful play, she called it. Toller had
been shocked.

But now the empty bed unmoored her heart. This heart with
a life of its own. He closed his eyes when they made love.

The men were never the same, he said, after they came out
of prison. Inside, some turned into girls, wearing ribbons and
mincing; swapping sex for protection from rape, sex for cigarettes.
They all masturbated like boys; some made vaginas out of bread
rolls. There was a traffic in matchboxes of semen from the men
to the women prisoners; pubic hair back. Talismans of longing,

the body's own need for another. The men's dreams of women were whittled and honed to slick and practical things, and when they came out living women did not match them. She knew he felt this as a loss, another way that he could not, now, get back inside his life.

'Why do you keep your eyes closed?' she asked once, afterwards. She was so slight that, hunched, her vertebrae made a ladder of bone, from nape to tail.

'You know why,' he said.

'You close your eyes to be in prison when we make love?'

Part of the thrill of Dora was that she trained her intellect, impartially, on everyone. Just sometimes, it could be you.

'Not in prison,' he said quietly.

'Well,' she leant back against the pillows, a cigarette between two fingers, 'in a prison dream then.'

He sat up and placed his feet carefully on the floor. Walked to the study and pulled the door closed. Again and again she would push for truth and end up four seconds later in a room all alone. Correct, but alone.

He must have taken the kidskin case with him. She reached up and found two others – one leather and one cardboard – on top of the wardrobe. She carried them across the hall to the study at the rear of the apartment.

The narrow little room faced the yard, her own desk tucked behind the door. He would sit with his back to the window, the day-curtain always drawn against the headaches that sometimes came in the afternoons. Dora sat in shadow, stockinged feet on some books or the rung of her chair, while he dictated, or they discussed corrections. One mind feeding into the other until their concentration collapsed under its own intensity and they would go across the hallway to bed.

She looked at the study window. The pale linen hung from its curtain rings, as always. If they came for her, she could jump to the yard from here.

She worked quickly. The most important thing was the story of his life. A first draft was nearly finished, the manuscript in two cardboard boxes with spring fasteners on the shelf nearest her desk. She opened the top one: 'I Was a German' where she had typed it.

The snap fastening caught and bit her skin as it closed, leaving a thin smudge of red on the page. She sucked her finger. She put the boxes into one of the suitcases, then turned to the correspondence, taking down the alphabetically labelled binders and putting them on the carpet. She sprang them open. She could fit more paper into the cases if it was loose.

From where she sat she saw the diaries on the bottom shelf. He'd written a lot from them. *Look Through the Bars*, as well as the autobiography. She had not read them, but she knew when he was lost he would pick one up and open it, looking to find himself inside. Some were leather-bound, some paper. The smallest was a tiny, cracked calfskin thing that had buckled to the shape of his body in the trenches. They wouldn't all fit in the cases. She'd have to come back with another case.

Photos! She returned to the bedroom with her own bag and grabbed the one from the bedside table of his mother and sister smiling in front of the house in Samotschin. Scraps of paper underneath it fell to the floor. They were covered with writing at all different angles, scrawls he'd done without bothering to turn the light on. She gathered them up too, then opened the dresser for the other photos, loose in the drawer: Toller in uniform in 1914; with the actress Tilla Durieux in Munich before the revolution; at the Berlin premiere of *Hoppla, We're Alive!* There were newspaper clippings, reviews. At the bottom of the drawer her fingers hit something hard – a coin? A medal? No, the tag from his puppy: 'Toby'. She put it in too.

Her body reacted first. The skull contracting and a bird in her chest, trying to get out.

The telephone. Just the telephone.

But everyone knew he wasn't here. Was it the neighbour Benesch, warning her? Or was it them?

She moved to the doorway and looked at the thing on his desk, ringing and ringing, black in its cradle. Fourteen rings. It stopped. She waited till her pulse faded.

Dora slung her bag with the photos in it over her shoulder, strapped the cases and tried to lift them. Paper is a trick of physics, words heavy as gold. She turned back to the phone.

'Don't come in,' she told me. 'Wait in the cab outside. And bring all your keys.'

Hans was still out so I dressed and went alone. It was raining. The cab idled outside Toller's building, its headlights making twin yellow streaks on the road. Dora carried the cases down one at a time, holding them sideways in front of her.

'Bornholmer Strasse allotments,' Dora told the driver.

When we got to the gardens the driver kept the motor running. We took a case each and struggled out of the cab.

'Night gardening, comrades?' He smiled, cutting the engine. 'Let me help.' He looked kind, in his cap. He looked like one of us.

But Dora said, 'We can manage. Thanks.'

'At least let me wait for you.'

We sent him away. A high, inaudible whistle of alarm had sounded. We didn't trust anyone.

We waited for his tail-lights to disappear, then started along the path through the garden plots near the train line. We made our way without a torch, the cases slapping against our legs and mud sucking our shoes. We could distinguish the little fences dividing each allotment. These had once been places of leisure – people grilling meat in summer, workers sitting on garden furniture with their shirts off, gap-toothed children larking on board-and-rope swings. But since the stock-market crash most people grew food here.

Hans and I had never used our plot, either for leisure or necessity: it came with the apartment. We went through the gate to the shed. Dora lit match after match while I worked the rusted padlock.

'This is just for now,' she said. 'Till I can get them out of the country.'

The lock twisted and sprang open. 'You can keep these.' I handed her the keys. 'I don't need them.' I tilted my head to look at her, her hair plastered to her cheeks, eyelashes wet. 'When are you going?'

'I'm not going anywhere, Ruthie. I have things to do here.'

'But Bert said —'

'I'll go underground. Don't worry. I'll have someone else get these out.'

'Who?'

'I don't know yet.'

'Where will you stay, then?'

She pushed the door open for me with one arm, gestured inside grandly like a valet. 'Ta-da.'

'You're joking.' The shed was dark and smelt like wet concrete.

'Not very funny, is it?' She smiled.

'No.'

Inside, Hans and I had stacked things we didn't want in the apartment – boxes of papers, a horrible Biedermeyer sofa we'd been given as a wedding present. We hid the two cases behind the sofa and covered them with some coarse grey removalist's blankets. Then we made her a bed out of a couple more. I left her with two packets of matches.

They wouldn't be coming after me; I could go home. The

underground trains had stopped running. I walked with my face to the rain as if some small suffering of mine might mitigate someone else's – the old crazy bargain with the universe.

As I rounded the corner to our apartment I smelt smoke. Hans still wasn't home. From the living-room window there was no fire to be seen, so I went to bed. Whatever it was, it would be dealt with by morning.

TOLLER

I have been walking the room while we work through the letters: apart from Mrs Roosevelt, I have to respond to Grosz, Spender and the IRS. The light is fading gently over the park, turning everything into its silhouette. I hear the click as Clara turns on the lamp by her chair over at the little typewriter table. When I sit down and face her I see she has one bloodshot eye and a nasty graze high on her forehead.

'What happened?' I cry. Good Christ, does it really take a physical injury for me to pay attention to someone?

'It's nothing,' she says, though I see she has singed the hair at her forehead as well. 'We were trying to reheat the dinner on the Primus and it blew up.'

'Did you go to the doctor?'

'No, no. Really, it's not serious.'

Of course, they don't have the money for a doctor. 'I'm sorry, have I . . . ?' I feel a queasiness in my stomach. 'Have I forgotten to pay you? These things, sometimes I just don't think —'

'*No* – stop!' She has her hands up, laughing. The stoicism

of women has astounded me all my life. 'MGM is paying me, remember?'

My head is nodding for yes, but I still feel it in the pit of my stomach. A shadow rustles at the edge of my vision. If I turn my head quickly to confront it, it slips out of sight like a floater in my eye. Clara turns back and starts typing.

I once forgot to give my wife, a girl in a foreign land, any money to live on.

When I think of Christiane I feel the blackness coming; my nostrils fill with a stink which is not human but is not sulphur. It is burnt flesh, as in the trenches. I look to the bathroom and this time I catch the last dirty feathers scraping back under the door, dropping filth in their wake. They barely fit behind there.

Six weeks ago, Christiane left me for a doctor on East 61st Street, also a refugee. I do not blame her one iota.

Christiane Grautoff was fifteen years old when I first laid eyes on her, the child star of the German stage. For two years I courted her virtually without touching her, the thing between us remaining pristine and unreal, like a perfect future. She was a slender, energetic, blond-mopped person with slanted green eyes, unphilosophical and self-reliant. She came, as they say, from a good family, which is to say nothing about goodness, but only about money. The money was from her mother's side. She was a self-absorbed minor novelist. Her father was an art historian with one of the coldest hearts I have ever encountered. When Christiane was eight they packed her off to a children's home for four years of brutality – partly because she was 'wild', mostly because they were busy. She might have thanked them in the end: the home made her an acute observer, as are all the best actors. She learnt the working-class *Berlinerisch* within days, and she learnt to entertain the tough kids, and the overseers. But her father's cruelty also meant that her standards of decent treatment from a man were way too low to protect her from me.

'I am poison to you!' I told her at the beginning, even as I courted her. *'Caveat emptor!'*

Christiane is the only woman I ever lived with. She saw the worst of it, in London, when I stayed in a dark room for months. My contempt for myself at these times contaminated my feeling for her; it killed the love and replaced it with itself.

A girl from Christiane's background was not expected to cook, but in London she tried, apologising for every meal she boiled or burnt or drowned in butter as I waltzed out the door to a restaurant. Nor could she darn. My socks lay about our Hampstead room like demands. When we were invited to a grand country house, she knew the servants would unpack our bags and check our things for missing buttons or caught threads, then mend them before putting them away. Christiane packed four pairs of my disintegrating socks for a weekend trip, and imagined I'd be pleased at the result. When I saw them all perfectly darned I did not speak to her for three days.

Once, I took her to get a permanent wave. (Did I want her to look older? Shame.) My silken-haired girl sat trusting in the chair while I chatted with the hairdresser, who left the stinking, burning solution on too long. Christiane came out looking, as she said, like a poodle. But she decided to comfort me. 'Not to worry,' she said, 'berets are all the fashion this winter.'

It didn't stop when we got to America. Her talent was obvious to everyone; a big studio offered her a contract that would have made her a star. I forbade her to take it. I also forbade her to tell anyone I had done so. Then she said she wanted a baby, and I forbade that too. I despise myself.

It is not their fault, the spouses who come after, that we do not love them as we loved before. Christiane loved me no matter what I did to her. Because of this, I felt her love like a provocation. (Look at that! Can it be true that I continue to blame her, even now?) She excused all my private cruelties with the idea that I was a great man. I was fighting to save humanity – what matter that I left her alone in London for a three-month book tour in Russia, forgetting, simply forgetting, to give her any money? She was eighteen years old, a refugee and not allowed to work. What matter that when I got back I scolded her for failing to tell me she needed funds, for working illegally so she could eat, and for then starving herself to buy me a short-wave radio I had wanted for my birthday – childish! I said. Irresponsible! Too thin!

Dora said I could be more intimate with thousands than I could be with one.

I move to the small desk by the window and write Christiane a note. It is in part an apology, which I know she'll shoo away with one hand. So I make it mostly of thanks, and genuine – truly – good wishes for her future. I tell her she will be a star. I seal the envelope and resume my chair.

Clara brings across the letters for my signature.

'Oh, and another thing,' she says, slipping the cover over the typewriter, 'I had Mr Kaufman on the phone yesterday. He says MGM will pay your passage, first class. He said it was the least the studio could do.'

I shake my head a little. 'That's nice.'

'Yes, it is,' she says.

'I mean of you. To think of asking him.' She shrugs off my compliment. 'You should go and see Christiane's doctor friend. He treats refugees for free. On East 61st Street.'

'I'm *fine*,' she says, at the door. 'Try sleeping, will you?'

Once Clara is gone, I pick up the note again. I could just walk right out there into the night lights, get a cab across Central Park South and deliver it to her in person. I might surprise her.

I look towards the bathroom. The door is shut. I can leave it; there's a lavatory in the lobby. I collect my Burberry trenchcoat from the closet and put it over my arm. I can't remember the last time I wore it.

My room is five storeys up but I take the stairs. When I get down there, the lobby is a vast acreage of swirly-patterned carpet and potted palms between me and the revolving door to the street. Capped busboys criss-cross with trolleys and people are moving all about, from the door to reception, reception to the lifts, or up the little stairs to the bar. I have a few seconds before my stillness is noticed.

My shirt is sticking to my skin and my mouth is dry. My heart pounds. I want, I really want, to get through that door and into the glittering night. But am not sure my legs will do my bidding. I turn and make it, just, into the men's.

In the mirror an ashen-faced man stares back at me, grey hair spiralling off his forehead. My mother is dead now, but I try to find, here, some remnant of what she loved.

The taps are the same as in my bathroom upstairs, 'H' and 'C' in enamel buttons on them. If I leave the building the wings will make their escape and their blackness will foul this city. Or is it the other way? The wings are a function of me: if I walk out of here will they come with me and contaminate it then? Either way it will be my fault. I have to stop them.

RUTH

Bev is in the doorway, armed with a spraygun and a fluorescent yellow microfibre cloth. It's a stand-off.

'I might go for a walk then,' I say. 'To the library.'

'By yourself? But I was going to get you some lunch, after.' Everything Bev says contains an inbuilt reproach.

'I'll get something at the shops.'

'Suit yourself.' She runs her eyes over me, as if I am doing this purely to thwart her and my comeuppance is nigh, nigh, nigh. 'I'd change my top if I were you,' she says, picking up the biscuits and my cup in her pink rubber hands and turning on her heel.

When she's gone I pull out my cardigan. There's a hand-sized coffee stain under my breasts. I am long past shame; it is the pity of passers-by I don't like. I try to get out of the chair but my arms seem weaker than usual. I can't get up enough momentum to – push – off.

Bev reappears with my crutches and handbag and a fresh cardigan.

'Well, then,' she says from her height. 'Not a lot goin on here.' But she helps me up, and off with the old and on with the new, and as I put the crutches under my arms – the metal jangle of them rings like freedom's bells to me – I bow my head to her and she hangs the handbag over my neck.

When I'm at the gate she can't help herself and darts out to open it.

'You'll be right, will you?' she asks. She reaches up and straightens my wig. Her face is a picture of mock tragedy over what I recognise, with a stab of surprise, as genuine concern.

'I think so,' I say. 'Thanks.'

And then I am free on this glorious day, down the street with its pavement cracked open by the roots of the Port Jackson figs that will not be contained. And the sun close enough to kindle sparkles of response from the bitumen, way down here.

The morning after we hid Toller's cases, trucks woke me before it was light, rumbling over the cobbles of our street, then brakes screaming into the corner. Next to me the bed was untouched. I moved to the window and saw an open vehicle full of uniformed men. It had happened before that Hans, carried away with the night, had not come home. I went to the kitchen and put the coffee on. I could never eat first thing. I heard more trucks.

The door flew open and Hans threw his shoes down hard, one then the other in the hall. He leaned on the doorjamb to the kitchen.

'They're raiding homes!' he panted. He ran his hand through his hair. 'I came as soon as I heard.' I caught his air of vodka and cigarettes.

I stared. 'I've been here,' I said. 'I'm fine.'

'Look at this!' He passed me the *Völkische Beobachter*. The headline was huge: 'Communist Terror Plot: Reichstag Burns!'

'But it's not . . . but they didn't —'

'Of course not,' he said. 'There was no plan to do that.'

I read aloud the Leader's words: '"The German people have been soft too long. Every Communist official must be shot. All friends of the Communists must be locked up. And that goes for the Social Democrats and the Reichsbanner as well!"' I looked up at Hans, who was lighting a cigarette. I read on: '"You are now witnessing the dawn of a great epoch in German history. This fire is the beginning."'

Brakes squealed, right outside this time. We moved to the window. Four of them jumped off the truck. There was nothing to do. Nothing to be done.

Hans opened the door before they knocked. There they were: a plainclothes man and two SA boys in brown with automatic pistols. Plain Clothes nodded at one of the boys, who moved straight past us into the flat. My coffee was burning.

'Gentlemen,' Hans said, standing straighter than sober. I stood behind, pulled my dressing gown closed.

'Herr Wesemann?' The man was tall as Hans. 'Frau Wesemann?'

'Yes,' Hans said.

'You have twenty-four hours, sir. You must be outside the borders of the Reich within twenty-four hours. Or your citizenship will be revoked.'

'I have done nothing illegal,' Hans said. 'I am a decorated veteran. And I am not a member of the Communist Party.'

'Sir.' The man pulled a folded piece of paper from his inside breast pocket and made a show of checking it. 'The order is for Johannes Alois Wesemann and Ruth Wesemann, née Becker. Sir.'

'Whose order?

'Reichsminister Göring's. Sir.'

The boy came back with my red flag from the closet. He handed it to his boss, and the three of them looked at us in silence. Then the little one behind broke it.

'Count yourself lucky,' he piped.

'Lucky?' Hans said.

'You get a warning.' The boy smiled a smile of pure power, the sudden enjoyment any mortal might have at being on the right side of the line.

By the time they got to us that morning, these boys and their fellows had already killed fifty-one people, and arrested more than four thousand. At first they worked from the membership list they'd stolen from the Communist Party headquarters, but then new orders came which were much broader – to capture or kill anyone who had spoken out against them. If they found you in a bar or café or some other public place they took you into custody; if you were at home you could be shot there, 'attempting to escape'. Some they didn't bother taking or shooting. When they found eight Communists hiding in a cellar in Mitte they simply boarded it up. People walking to work heard their calls from the vent at pavement level but no one dared help. It took two weeks for all cries to stop.

Before noon on the 28th of February Hitler presented to Cabinet his Reichstag Fire Decree, 'for the Protection of the People and the State', to counter the 'act of terror'. It permitted arrests without warrant, house searches, postal searches; it closed the newspapers and banned political meetings. In essence, just as Bertie had predicted, it prevented campaigning by any other parties before the election. By the end of that day, thousands of anti-Hitler activists were being held in 'protective custody' in makeshift SA barracks – empty factories, a water tower in Prenzlauer Berg, even a disused brewery. Soon there was not enough room. That was when they set about building the concentration camps.

On the night of the fire, the authorities found a dishevelled Dutch ex-Communist labourer called Marinus van der Lubbe and arrested him. He confessed to the arson, insisting he had acted alone. But Göring's people used the chance to arrest others who were nowhere near the scene – a Communist MP called Torgler and three Bulgarian Communists who were visiting Berlin. We scoffed at the idea that van der Lubbe had done this by himself. He was twenty-four years old, half blind and feeble-minded.

I don't know why they warned us that morning. Perhaps we were protected by Hans's notoriety – they couldn't be seen to be killing well-known journalists, or not at first. Or maybe they were playing with us. We soon heard that lists with names and photographs of people they wanted to catch had been distributed to the railways and all border crossings. Perhaps they would get us in flight. We booked the 18:04 to Paris.

Later we heard our friends' stories. Some had disguised themselves as mental patients or *Fasching* revellers in order to slip across borders, or they'd simply skied off-piste into France. They arrived with no papers, no clothes. Hans and I disguised ourselves too, I suppose, as casual holiday-makers, packing only one large case, and a briefcase each – more would look suspiciously like flight. I took two changes of clothes and filled the rest of the space with my camera and lenses, books and photographs. I couldn't fit the albums, so I chose quickly, ripping pictures out of their corners: our wedding at the Majestic Hotel in Breslau, my parents and Oskar in the garden at Königsdorf, Dora and me as children at the Kleinmachnow fair, Hans asleep on our first night, the sheets rumpled light-and-dark like landscape.

Hans packed his typewriter, his folio and his evening clothes. He came in as I was closing the case. 'Room for this?' He held out his hand. It was the porcelain pâté pot from the TicTacToe. 'For cufflinks,' he said. He must have souvenired it. The knob on its lid was a chubby pink pig lying on his back, laughing regardless.

'You're unbelievable,' I said.

No one on the platform spoke to one another, and no one started conversations in our compartment. When I heard the ticket collector coming down the train corridor, my heart banged in my throat. As he opened the glass door I sat very still. While the others reached quickly into purses and bags for tickets, Hans slid his hand casually into his jacket pocket and pulled out a napkin. Then, corner by corner, he unwrapped it to reveal a single, perfect, hard-boiled egg.

'*Mahlzeit*,' the conductor said. Bavarian for *Guten Appetit*. A round fellow with bushy sideburns, for whom Berlin was, hopefully, a faraway place with faraway problems.

'Thank you,' Hans said.

I didn't trust my voice to come out properly. I passed over our tickets. The conductor punched them, then dropped his puncher back into the pocket of his leather apron.

'You change at Frankfurt for Paris,' he said, as if it were the most ordinary thing. 'Platform two.' He left.

'An egg!' I hissed. 'When did you do that?'

'While you were packing.' Hans smiled, pleased with his magic trick. He had always been good under fire. The others in the compartment chuckled, and started chatting – it turned out every one of us was fleeing. Hans reached into his pocket again and pulled out an egg for me, then a twist of paper with salt in it.

Once over the French border we allowed ourselves the dining car. From Paris we went to Calais, where we got a boat to Dover. Then one more train and we were in London.

Hans and I must have been safely over the border when Dora went back with a duffle bag for the diaries.

It was three o'clock in the afternoon. She snibbed both locks behind her inside the apartment and placed the keys on the little bookshelf. Slipped off her shoes.

The bedroom held no power over her today. The desk was as he'd left it, messy with current business – the white rock from the beach at Rügen sitting on letters to be answered, an open matchbox with a muscled sailor on the lid, undrunk coffee blooming aqua and white in a red china cup. She took the cup to the kitchen, washed out the mould. It made a sound as she placed it on the draining board. Too loud. She froze. A man's cough outside the front door. A knock.

She wasn't here. The kitchen was the first room on the right off the entrance hall. Whoever it was stood listening three metres from her. She did not breathe.

Dora slid out to the hall, edging along the floor so the boards would not creak. She was an animal, or a child – unprotected, elemental. If she could reach the study, she could get out the window to the yard.

Perhaps it was just a delivery? She'd laugh at herself later.

'Open the door please.' A man's voice. The neighbour again? She was halfway down the hallway.

'Frau Fabian! We know you are there, Frau Fabian.'

Them. She flew into the study, slid her desk across the door. She heard thumping, then a gunshot, shocking and unmistakable. The sickening groan of the wood splintering. A flash of her – bizarrely – felt responsible for the damage.

And then a shout. They were inside. *Shot while attempting to escape.* It would be the irony of her life if she proved with her death their truthfulness. How is it that in terror there is time to think this?

She kneed up onto Toller's desk to reach the window. Fist first, then head. From the yard she would get through to Sächsische Strasse – no, they'd have someone there. To the cellar – but the keys were back in the hall.

They were coming, room by room.

'Not here! Sir!'

'All clear!'

To Benesch's apartment then, up the back stairs – a risk, but what choice was there? She shoved away some papers to steady her feet and then she saw the white rock. Yes! She hefted it in her right palm and ripped the thin curtain aside —

Christ, Toller!

Bars. Black iron bars, a hand-width apart.

There was no sound.

They must be outside the door.

They are long, the moments trapped in a room, waiting for the end.

A knock. 'Frau Fabian. Wieland, Ministry of the Interior. I am asking you to open this door.'

Fear can open up silence and make it hum. Revealing, finally, the sound of the universe shifting quietly, making ready to accommodate you.

No answer from the room. The three of them stood outside, the boy holding her shoes and the offsider with his gun in both hands, trained on the floor. The orders were to take her alive.

'Frau Fabian,' Wieland said into the door, 'you have nowhere to go.' He nodded to the marksman. 'Stand back!' he commanded.

A voice from the room. 'Don't shoot!'

When they opened the door, what did they see? A tiny woman, a beaked bird with a glossy black head – was she twenty? Or thirty? Stockinged feet hanging below the desk and a white rock smooth in the cleft of her lap. Trying to strike a match on a box with fingers bitten to the quick.

The man trained the gun on her. The boy held her shoes.

'We have orders to arrest you,' Wieland said. 'On suspicion of treasonous activity against the Reich.'

'I work for Mr Toller.' The voice was husky, low. 'I am doing nothing wrong here.' Black eyes through the smoke.

'It's the law, ma'am.'

'A new law?'

'No, ma'am.'

'New Reich then?' She smiled at him.

'Yes, ma'am.'

She blew out the match. They had no humour, these people.

He nodded at the others to get her.

She put up a palm. 'It's all right, gentlemen.'

The boy held out her shoes by the laces. The scraps of leather and sole were suddenly intimate things, moulded by her body, open and loose-tongued and revealing. The boy gawped as if he had never in his life watched a woman slip her foot into a shoe. She jumped down from the desk.

On the way to the car an Alsatian, his face in a cage, kept to her side. She scratched his ears in consolation, or comfort. 'Inside everyone the ice hounds bark,' she said.

On my crutches in the street people look away from me, a legacy of their mothers hissing 'Don't stare!' when passing puppet-spastics, the violently birthmarked, dirty flashers or dwarves. Or they give me sympathetic smiles, encouraging me in these, they assume, my precious last steps. I could scream at them: 'You have no idea! How – lucky – I – am!' Something in me wants to say 'blessed' but I stop myself. I am not a pitiful old woman hanging on to her mind while her body shuts down. I am a woman on her way to eat cake.

The shops in Bondi Road show the transformation of this place. The older ones have been transplanted straight from Riga or Stettin or Karlovy Vary, but the greengrocer now calls itself a 'Fruitologist' and the butcher is organic. The Hungarian bakery still has the best *Gugelhupf*.

I have loved *Gugelhupf* since I was a child, its heaviness and vanilla scent, the swirls of dark poppy seeds in the thick white cake. I order, then manoeuvre myself onto a stool at the front counter and lean my crutches against the window. When the cake comes it is more friable than usual. I lift the fork carefully from plate to mouth, a distance which has increased with age and is now full of treacherous possibility. The cake drops off just before it reaches my lips. I hope no one is looking. *It is the pity of passers-by I don't like.*

'Dr Becker?' A voice at my ear. 'Dr Becker?' At my age everyone thinks you are deaf, or slow. Already half departed.

I turn as much as I can on the stool and the face looms in to me – I see molars, and smell perfume like an advance guard of verbena.

'Yes,' I say. 'Hello there.' It is a middle-aged woman with rectangular tortoiseshell glasses and streaky-blond bobbed hair. She could be anyone. Every now and again one of these creatures accosts me, sweetly, gratefully.

'Trudy Stephenson,' she says. 'Trudy Winmore I was at school.'

'Oh yes. Trudy.' I have no idea. 'Of course. How are you?' I look closer at the face – kind, deep-set eyes, and a small gap between her front teeth – trying to summon the girl underneath. People say babies look alike, or the very old, all grey and sexless and sunken-skinned. But for me it is the middle-aged women of the eastern suburbs who are so hard to distinguish. They are all neatly, crisply put together, stout-bodied under striped shirts with their collars up, the hair streaked and smoothed to the exact same substance. I taught at the ladies' college for twenty years. So many, many girls. But as I squint longer at this one the years peel off her till she is an earnest, pudgy, sweet-faced girl in my matriculation German class.

'Do you remember?' she is saying.

'Yes,' I say, 'I do.' They like to be remembered.

She chuckles. 'And do you remember my father?'

Oh God. 'I'm afraid . . .' I start.

'You taught us Goethe's love poetry,' she smiles. Is that a blush?

'"*O Mädchen, Mädchen wie lieb' ich dich!*"' I start. O girl, girl how I love you . . .

'"*Wie blickt dein Auge!/Wie liebst du mich!*"' The look in your eye!/How you love me! She takes it up like a long-cherished thing, a mantra she has muttered throughout her life at particular times, never telling anyone about it. '"*Wie ich dich liebe/Mit warmen Blut.*"' How I love you/It heats my blood. She laughs and her eyes are suddenly full of tears. 'We'd never heard anything like it! We didn't think you were allowed to speak those things.'

'*Ach,*' I say. 'Australia in the '50s.' *Those things* – like love, like desire, the most precious – were to remain subterranean for your whole little life. It was as if these Anglos thought the feelings were tainted by the involvement of the bodies needed to express them. I never got used to it.

'My father,' this Trudy starts. And then I do remember. It is all still inside of me. Her father wrote a letter to Miss Blount, the headmistress: 'Who is this fellow Goethe anyway? It would be better for the girls to learn something useful instead of this filth.'

'I remember now!' I say. I am so pleased. '"This filth" he called it, didn't he?'

'I'm afraid so.' Trudy purses her lips mock-ruefully, then smiles again. The tears are gone. 'But we loved it.' She touches my forearm. 'We loved you for it.'

'Thank you, dear.'

She leaves, square-bottomed and tidy as a tug, a box of cakes dangling in a stork's triangle from the plastic bag on her arm.

The girls knew I had been in one of Hitler's prisons for my political activities. I told them about the five-year sentence, three of it in solitary so that I, as a 'political', wouldn't infect the others – abortionists, prostitutes, thieves, poor souls – with ideas of social justice. But at their age the girls were more interested in love, of course. They imagined, because I had been married and unmarried, that I had a scandalous degree of experience. They believed I taught them Goethe's poetry of desire as if I could vouch for it. None of us – teacher or taught – realised how an imagined romantic life can sustain you as a possibility, a hope, and remain just that. Like parallel train tracks, it runs alongside, but will never meet, the life you are living.

The Gestapo had nowhere left to take her. Every possible cell was full. And in any case, they wanted Dora to be alone, to soften her up. So she was put in an ordinary cellar in the old police building – a dirt floor and the vestiges of a pile of coal in the corner. Two buckets in another corner, one with water, one empty. There was no light and the cellar was unheated. She spent her time pacing in the dark to keep warm. She had one army blanket and she shared it with lice.

The arrests were taking place so quickly that there were no arrangements for feeding the prisoners; dear Mathilde Wurm heard that they had her and immediately took in baskets of rolls, wurst, bananas, underwear and cigarettes.

They kept Dora for five days before the interview, which was as long as the law allowed. As the guard undid the padlock she said, 'You would be my Orpheus, come to rescue me?' He stared blankly at her. She apologised. In the light of the yard she saw that her clothes were covered in dirt and her hands were rimmed in black. As they walked to the administrative building the boy motioned to her forehead. 'You might want to . . .' He gestured a rub.

'Thanks,' she smiled back, 'but it's not my filth.'

The bare electric bulb in the interview room hung from a brown cloth-covered cord. Dora blinked after the dimness of the cellar. The interrogating officer was not an ordinary policeman, but one of the newer, black-uniformed ones. His face was shiny, small eyes stuck in deep, like raisins. He asked her what she had to say in her defence.

'So far as I know,' she said, 'I am not on trial here.'

'You have been apprehended on the grounds of lèse-majesté and suspicion of high treason.'

'On account of what?'

He looked at the sheet in front of him. She knew he would have been studying it well in advance.

'On account of membership of the Independent Social Democratic Party and its successor the Socialist Workers Party. And of your editorship of this . . .' He pushed an edition of a pacifist journal across the table. She stared at her name, next to Walter's, on the masthead. 'Not to mention,' the man continued, 'certain writings such as,' he put his finger on another page in front of him, '"the ecstasies of women for the Leader are a sign not of loyalty, but of need. This need will not be satisfied by him, nor the husbands he promises, nor any man."'

He looked at her a long moment, then back at his paper. 'Such utterances are designed to bring the authorities into disrepute and slander the Leader. Membership of the Socialist Workers Party is now an offence —'

'As of?' Her voice might have sounded genuinely curious if you didn't know her.

'Tuesday.' He lowered his eyes to the file.

'Not before then, then?'

He looked up. 'You have continued your membership. You have committed the proscribed act.' The man adjusted the leather belt over his shoulder and around his waist. 'Where are the materials you took from Herr Toller's apartment?' The preliminaries were over.

'I burnt them.' Dora was suddenly afraid, in her filth under the too-bright light, that it didn't matter what she said, and it didn't matter that she'd left the party. The point had been passed where the law could protect her. This argument was a farce, the cat playing with the mouse for the pleasure of smelling its fear.

'I want to speak to your superior,' she said. It was a risk, but she had nothing to lose.

'He's not here.' The man held her gaze.

'I am sure he is.' She smiled a little. 'And I wish to speak with him.'

'I would say, Dr Fabian, that you are not in a position to be making demands.'

She was taken back to the cellar.

The next day they brought her up again.

'What's this for?' she asked the guard. She wondered whether it was to give themselves a new start on a further five days of detention.

'The Director is coming.'

When he walked into the room she felt relief, although she doubted he had come to help. She looked at the familiar pointed moustaches, the perfect bow tie, the pinkie ring.

'Dr Fabian,' he said. So, there would be no familiarity in front of the warder. She would not compromise him. She was here to get out.

'Dr Thomas.'

'You have been told the charges against you.' He put his manila folder on the table and sat. 'I am not sure what help I can be to you now.'

'I am entitled to a lawyer. And,' she took a breath, 'as far as I know, you cannot keep me on remand after five days.' She held his gaze. 'It has been a week.'

Uncle Erwin looked down and squared the papers in front of him. 'Your father would have been proud of you.' Then he started to shake his head, as if, regrettably, the whole situation were out of his hands. 'But the law has been changed.'

'The opposition parties may have been made illegal,' Dora shot back, 'but criminal procedure?'

Thomas glanced at the warder. 'Not yet,' he said. 'But it will be done. The charges are serious. You are here for having, among other things, destroyed evidence wanted in legal proceedings.'

'What proceedings?'

'Proceedings against Mr Toller.'

So now they were criminalising whomever they pleased, impounding all their possessions. She couldn't argue the substance of it. She would have to argue, with Uncle Erwin, a technicality.

'You are obliged . . .' She too glanced at the warder and eased her tone. 'I believe the law requires me to be released after five days to await trial. Or there would be no rule of law here.'

Thomas held his lips together and breathed hard through his nose. 'The first sign of respect for the law I see in you,' he said, standing up. He started to walk to the door. '"A fig leaf over power", as I recall.'

Dora said nothing.

Thomas motioned to the warder. In the doorway he turned his shoulder almost imperceptibly to halt her exit. Spoke down into her left ear. 'A loophole,' he muttered. 'Soon fixed. We will call them the Fabian amendments. In your honour.'

They let her out to await a trial.

She did not go back to her own flat to pack, but to ours, checking that there was no guard outside. When she got in she saw why. They had smashed all our furniture already – dinted the chrome chairs, slashed the mattress in the bedroom; horsehair and feathers everywhere. They'd had fun with the glass (they loved glass, didn't they? Glass, and lists, and fire), destroying the top of a drinks trolley, shattering picture frames and the mirror of the bathroom cabinet. Someone had drawn a lewd cartoon of Hans on the kitchen benchtop and placed the mojito stick upright as a penis.

Dora found a towel to clear the bathtub of glass and showered quickly with the hand-held shower. Then she packed a briefcase with a change of clothes from my cupboard. A suitcase would almost certainly attract a guard's attention. It would have been senseless to try to retrieve Toller's cases from the garden shed. At Friedrichsstrasse station she bought tickets for Switzerland – there were two train changes.

Later she learnt they had been waiting for her at her flat – 'Three cars outside, no less,' she said – to take her straight back in for a new period of remand, while the law was changed. She would never have got out.

Over the years, rumours circulated about her escape from Germany. They were mangled and magnificent, conflated like Chinese whispers until it was herself that Dora had smuggled over the border in the case, along with Toller's papers. This made sense to people because the meaning of a tale is never practical; a story is not a how-to. The meaning of the tale was that she was small, brave and clever. But, as Dora joked, if she had packed herself into the case, 'Who would have carried me?'

When Dora told Toller the rumour he smiled and said, 'But where would you have put my papers?'

On 26 April 1933 Göring passed the first Gestapo law. It placed the political police under his own personal control so that the ordinary rules of criminal procedure did not apply. Uncle Erwin drafted it. It was his 'Fabian amendment'.

TOLLER

Clara has gone to get our coffees for this morning (infinity lasts here – at least in the matter of bottomless cups – only for a single day). Small clouds shadow parts of the park, dappling it like something underwater.

If I can conjure Dora, I think I can get out of this room and deliver that note to Christiane.

While she worked for me, Dora also worked with the calm and stolid Social Democrat Mathilde Wurm. It was Mathilde who wired me at my hotel in Ascona: 'Bird coming. 9.3.33.' The code names were just starting then. So she was Bird.

But when she stepped down from the train Dora was more of a scarecrow figure in Ruth's too-big clothes. Her eyes were set deep in shadowed sockets and her skin pulled thin to translucent over blue veins at her temple. She smiled broadly, swinging a briefcase at her side. Something in me I did not know was taut relaxed; I was home.

We didn't make it back to my room at the hotel, but veered off along the creek and up under a bridge in deep shade. Small fires were burning on the bank, the litter and leaves turning into columns of smoke rising straight in the still air. Sometimes making love is making love and sometimes it is other things, a homecoming and an attack – stabbing to get back into the life that was nearly taken from you. Behind me the stone was cold but I leant into her, my hands under her thighs and her mouth on my ear, lost and found in the heat of her, her quick need. She exhaled. Stayed still a long moment with an arm around my neck, head in my chest.

'Dora?'

When she stood back her eyes were full. She had let herself feel the fear she must have been beating down for days.

'Let's eat,' she said, putting her foot back into a trouser leg.

The light on the promenade by Lake Maggiore was golden and slanted, stretching the shadows to comic proportions even in the morning. Dora stood where the foreshore sloped to the water for boat launching, first on one foot, then the other, dancing and dodging her larger, attached shadow-self and laughing. She threw it punches. 'Come and get me!'

Ducks came up, curious and proprietorial, on the cobbles. Their heads phosphoresced a green and purple so regal we seemed a ragged, loose-limbed species, running from the law and copulating under bridges.

Dora took my arm and we looked for an open restaurant under the arcade across from the water. Most of the shops had their shutters drawn till April. Plane trees in two rows along the promenade were pruned to four or five stubby limbs, like black fists held up at the sky. Through some of them tiny lights were threaded, to be turned on in summer. Without tourists this place was restoring itself.

We ordered coffee and pastries and settled into a corner. Dora's back was to the window and her face to me, in shadow. She started to tell how she had gone to my flat the night the Reichstag burnt and taken out the manuscript of my autobiography.

'It was a hunch of Bertie's,' she said, unwinding her scarf.

'Being there probably saved me from being rounded up. They were waiting for me at my place.' She'd slept two nights in Ruth's shed, she said, with the suitcases of my work. Before going back for my diaries.

I was incapable of thanking her. Thanks would have been pathetic given the risks she'd taken. And I wasn't sure I could get the words out.

'I'm sorry about the diaries,' she said. She paused as the waiter set down coffees and water, sugared croissants.

'I wish you hadn't . . .' I started. It wasn't true. I was upset she had so nearly been caught – she would have been killed. But I was pleased beyond price that my manuscript had been saved. The shame choked me.

'Don't thank me yet,' she said, pulling apart the pastry. She wielded a corner in each hand and waved away my distress. 'I still have to get the cases out of the country.'

'Please don't do anything —'

'Stupid?' She raised her eyebrows. 'I'll try not to.'

Dora didn't want to embarrass me. When she told me how they'd caught her in my study she added quickly, 'And there's me like a film bandit about to get away with it – but of course I'd forgotten about the bars.'

She couldn't have known of the bars. My eyes smarted.

Sometimes I think that the physical peculiarities of a situation bring out the strangest things. If I had been able to see her face clearly, I might not have told her. I wonder, now, about interrogation chambers: why do they think bright light brings the truth out of people? They should try the seduction of shadows, where you cannot watch your words hit their target.

I signalled the waiter for a fresh ashtray and shifted in my chair. I leant in to her. 'I have chosen every flat since prison,' I said slowly, 'for one small room. And I have had bars put on it.'

She said nothing.

'It's a superstition,' I went on. 'To remind me of my most productive time. I need the . . .' I looked down at my hands. My fingers had threaded through one another into a futile arch. 'Containment.'

She nodded, this free bird. Trying hard to understand the need for limits. The liberty they might give a soul like mine with its tendency to dispersal.

'I need it in order to write.' I opened my hands. 'Bad poetry.'

'Not just the poetry,' she said.

I laughed. The light coming in behind her kept her face in the dark.

Her tone changed. 'Is *that* why you refused the offer of clemency?'

I looked at my plate. 'I feel terrible.'

She was shaking her head.

'No – honestly,' I said, 'I was hugely sustained by your campaign to free me. I just . . .' I shifted my shoulders. 'Well, and I wouldn't have left the others in there, of course.'

'I see.' She nodded. 'But I took Hans's *head* off for it. I've never stopped blaming him. For putting you off the outside world.' She laughed. 'You know, with his Great Unbearable Charm. Giving you a taste of the sycophants and social climbers and slobbering attention-seekers that awaited you.'

I looked up at her. 'I didn't think he was so bad.'

'Oh, he's not,' she sighed. 'He's just insufferably lucky. If I'd known you *wanted* to be in there, I wouldn't have . . . Oh God.' She put her forehead into her palm, a cigarette still in two fingers. Then she laughed – that beautiful, wide mouth. 'I'll have to apologise to him now. Damn.'

I wanted her then; I wanted to erase this conversation with a physical act.

We stayed eight days in Ascona and over that time my throat

constricted less when I looked at her in unguarded moments. I tried to catch glimpses of her as others might see her. I watched her chat with the vendors across the market stalls in broken Italian and shameless hand gestures. Or press her face to the wind on the ferry bow; step steaming and unselfconscious out of the shower. When you are in love with someone you cannot see around them, you cannot get their human measure. You cannot see how someone so huge to you, so miraculous and unfathomable, can fit, complete, into that small skin.

Towards the end of our time in the hotel we turned away the maid and went to bed in the afternoons, the room a litter of clothes and papers and plans, shoes muddy from our walks and the air bearing its combined trace of us.

Sleeping was difficult for Dora. Some nights she took Veronal, mixing the bitter powder with coffee. Once I woke to see her standing in a robe on the balcony. The sky was pricked with stars. Below us the lake was a vast black gap, its far shore marked only by a line of tiny, sparkling lights.

I leant over the rail. After a while she spoke.

'I'm an atheist,' she said.

'It's "I'm an atheist *but* . . . " isn't it?' I joked. Water slapped at unseen boats; halyards pinged their masts.

'But I think my father was looking out for me.' Her voice was tight. 'Back there. With Erwin Thomas.'

'Nothing spooky.' I turned to face her but she kept looking straight ahead. 'He taught you the protection of the law of criminal procedure, and you protected yourself with it. Hugo would have been proud of you.'

'He taught it to *him*, too.' She started to cry silently, shaking her head a little.

'Thomas?' I said. 'Well, yes.' I reached for her hand. 'But he won't have much use for those principles any more.'

She turned her face to me, noble and destroyed. 'Do you think they are so easily thrown away?'

On the second-last night I said, 'Let's leave Europe. Go to Africa, India.' Dora's PhD had been about workers' rights in the colonies; now she was planning to translate her English friend Fenner Brockway's book on colonial India.

'You think you can escape politics?' she said. I was sitting on the bed. She stood in front of me and held my head. 'If we left here we'd be abandoning our lives for coconuts.' She let go and sat down, hands open in her lap. 'Our lives are given to us; they are not entirely of our own choosing.'

'Do you love me?' We weren't looking at each other.

'Yes.' Straightforward as a fact. But not enough, not enough.

'I mean, do we belong together?'

'No one "belongs" to anyone any more. Rule number one, remember.' She was smiling, fully aware of the ridiculousness of rules for living.

I would not be deterred. 'What if you got pregnant one of these nights?'

Her smile faded. She turned to me. 'I wouldn't have the baby.'

I searched her face. She tried to explain. 'It doesn't seem part of my life to me.'

'So India and babies are not part of what is given to you?'

'I can take these risks for myself. But not for a child.'

I don't know what I was asking her. Was it as simple as whether she could put me first? Or even herself? I went to the window. The moon had risen. A lone oarsman pulled the water, wrinkling its silver blanket.

When I turned back her resolve had vanished. Her face was a mask of distress.

'I can't . . . leave . . . this.' Her hands fluttered about, over the papers in the room, over Germany, over what had been given to her to do. Her eyes were full and blind and trapped.

I put my hands on her shoulders and breathed in. I would never be hers above all things.

'You should take a leaf from your cousin Ruth's book. Choose beauty!' I joked. 'Choose pleasure!'

She blew her nose, loudly, then looked up. 'I do choose pleasure,' she said, and pulled me down.

In the morning we walked up the hill behind the village, where there was an eleventh-century fort. The tops of the hills here all had forts on them, and closer to the lake squatted all the churches – war and peace at two hundred paces. We went down to the church. It was cold and empty and smelt of stone. From the back pew we watched shafts of light enter through the high windows, feel their way down here.

'How's the little one?' Dora asked, in a tone that implied we were discussing a mutual acquaintance.

'Christiane,' I said. She could never say her name. 'Fine. She just refused to play the lead in a Nazi film about Horst Wessel.'

'Good for her,' Dora said, and we left it at that.

Dora had decided that my attraction to Christiane consisted largely of my basking in her admiration. Dora had also decided, I believe, that this was a fantasy which would be of limited sustenance. Her own idea of me was of a man who did not need such things.

Dora may have been right about why I wanted Christiane. But Christiane had other charms, and not just the obvious. She had no sense that things might end, which is, I suppose, the definition of youth. Everything lay ahead of her on an even plane of wonder: all the cruelties and beauties of a world she took no responsibility for. More than her nymph's body or her faith in me, I wanted what any older man wants: to recapture the anticipation of the unfolding world.

From Ascona we tried to make arrangements to get our things out of Germany, and money too – Dora with her mother, and me with my publishers. We had no idea how the future looked, together or apart, and no idea how to fund it. The economics of whole societies had always seemed more manageable than our own.

Dora left for Paris, then went down to Strasbourg to see her friend Berthold Jacob, and from there to Ruth and Hans in London. I bought three cream Italian silk shirts and continued on my lecture tour to Palestine, untethered now from Germany and looking for a new home.

When Clara opens the door she lets in odd strains of music from the room across the way. Strauss, I think. Starting and stopping. She puts down the coffees and looks at me strangely, welded to my chair. It is a look I know. She is realising that the famous, her elders, are just as flighty and full of foibles as she or anyone else, and that although we do not grow out of this, neither do these things bring us down. The miracle of life indeed. But what frightens me is I can see in her face that instead of breeding contempt for me, this insight makes her fonder. *Don't waste your time!* I want to warn. *I am poison to you, girl.*

But instead I ask, 'Do you dance?'

'I love to dance.'

She is young and beautiful, and stuck here in this room. I do not wish her to fall in love with me. And the surest way to prevent that is to ask her to dance (who would touch such a shrunken Minotaur?). She places one hand on my shoulder, her grazed forehead near my cheek.

'I warn you,' I say, 'you take both our lives in your hands.'

'I'll risk it,' she smiles.

I hold her a little stiffly at first. But as we move to music we can no longer hear I lean into her and my hand settles, gently but proprietorially, in the hollow of her back. She lets herself be to me the warm body I want. She lets me have her back, in this room.

PART II

Spies in the bedroom, spies on the roof,
Spies in the bathroom, we've got proof.
Spies on the lawn where the shadows harden,
Spies behind the gooseberries in the kitchen garden,
Spies at the front door, spies at the back,
And hiding in the coat-stand underneath a mac.
Spies in the cupboard under the stairs,
Spies in the cellar, they've been there for years.

'Spy Song' by W. H. Auden,
from his translation of Ernst Toller's
No More Peace!, *1935*

RUTH

In London Hans and I looked for rooms like itinerants, in this new world of labyrinthine terraces divided into single cells, landladies now mighty over us. At the first house, on Coram Street, Bloomsbury, a woman in a pale green housecoat showed us a room underground. It had a bed, a chair, and a dresser with a one-ring Primus stove on it. The only window was a thin oblong of grey light at pavement level.

While she talked of the rate (a pound a week, bath extra), the conditions (home by ten p.m., quiet from ten-thirty; cooked breakfast between seven and eight, kippers extra), I watched shoes and ankles on their way to work. Hans, in his faltering English, told her, 'We are having only temporary visas, we will —'

'As long as you're not Irish,' she cut him off, 'I don't mind.'

The second room we looked at was on Guilford Street. This woman was square-jawed and skinny, with red-chapped hands and an Irish lilt. When Hans raised the issue of our papers she shook her curls and laughed. 'As long as you're not English,' she said, 'dat's all right wi' me.'

I looked at her face – a lifetime of pasties, skin that sucked the light and reflected nothing back. We could have come from anywhere; we were just 'foreign'.

In the end we took a small flat to ourselves at 12 Great Ormond Street, Bloomsbury. It was a few doors down from the children's hospital and a block away from Coram's Fields, where the foundling home had been. The caretaker had lived there with his wife, but they'd moved to the bigger, basement flat. To get to ours we entered the front door from the street, under a fanlight with an angel's head looking over it. There was a grand staircase that spiralled back on itself, past the large flats on the first three floors. Then the proper staircase ended and a narrow, rickety set of wooden stairs led to our place under the roof.

The ceilings were so low Hans stooped involuntarily going through the doorway. From the entry space, there were two rooms to the right, each with paned windows facing the street. The glass in them was old and uneven; the Georgian terrace houses on the other side wobbled and shuddered as we walked. On the left off the entrance was a kitchen we could eat in, with a door on its far side onto a large bare concrete balcony, which was really the roof of the larger flat below. Tucked away next to the kitchen was a small third bedroom and a bathroom. Straight ahead in the entryway was another door. Hans opened it and pulled the light cord. It was a walk-in cupboard with shelves on three walls.

'We'll need to find ourselves a *teensy* refugee for this one,' he said.

Because my father could send us money from Poland we were relatively well off compared to other exiles, who were prohibited from getting their money out of Germany. Which is to say we were not destitute, begging for money from the refugee-relief and Quaker organisations, like most. Though our flat was small, its great advantage was its three separate rooms. If we ate in the kitchen, there would be room for Bertie, and perhaps Dora.

Unless she stayed with Toller – but we never knew quite what was happening there.

In my parents' villa the maid lived in a room off the kitchen, but Cook and the other staff lived in houses I'd never visited. In Berlin, Hans and I had had a girl, Rosalie, who came every day, but she lived with her parents and brothers in a two-room flat in Neukölln. We had all spent years talking about the working class, but as I looked around this little place with its low, plain ceilings and tiny rooms I realised that we hadn't ever, really, known how they lived.

And though we had talked ourselves blue about workers' rights, it would never have occurred to me to join their ranks in a practical sense. The second week at Great Ormond Street we hired Mrs Allworth, who charred for the elderly couple below us, to clean. Mrs Allworth lived in the East End. She was skinny, snub-nosed and energetic, prone to rashes that started on her neck and bloomed up behind her ears, sometimes across her jawline. I don't think they were caused by embarrassment, just emotions she could not at that minute place and put away.

At the interview I looked into her pale-blue eyes and ignored the pink blooms, but they made me like her. It felt like honesty, to be able to see this life shifting below the surface. Mrs Allworth held her hands together in her lap and looked around her in wonder that this place had existed, tucked up here, all along. I saw it for a moment through her eyes: rickety rooms with mismatched donated furniture. A faded green couch we'd inherited from the caretaker and his wife, a crate with a cloth on it for a bedside table. The walk-in cupboard was stocked with stationery and typewriter ribbon instead of food. She made no comment, but I imagined she lived in better (no doubt neater) circumstances.

Mrs Allworth wore her wavy, faded-auburn hair bunched in a net, a pinny tied at her tailbone and her sleeves rolled up to her biceps. I grew to appreciate her through her language. She used 'elbow grease' and 'went like the clappers' about the flat; things 'tickled her fancy', and people 'rabbited on' or 'made a palaver'. Her 'old man' or 'himself' worked on the docks and they had four sons, and all of them, the whole family, were to be killed in the Blitz. She came Tuesdays and Fridays.

The Reichstag fire and the persecution in its wake had sent fifty-five thousand Germans into exile – some two thousand writers and artists among them. Several hundred of us ended up in Britain. An exiled wit joked that we were the 'Emigrandezza': the educated political opponents of the regime. The mass of Jews came later. There was nothing grand about us, though. Everyone was dislocated and struggling – without our language, often without money, without readership and with no right to work.

Our English visas also stipulated 'no political activities of any kind'. But our lives would only have meaning if we could continue to help the underground in Germany, and try to alert the rest of the world to Hitler's plans for war. We were being offered exile on condition that we were silent about the reason we needed it. The silence chafed; it made us feel we were betraying those we had left behind. The British government was insisting on dealing with Hitler as a reasonable fellow, as if hoping he'd turn into one.

Even receiving mail from Germany could place us under suspicion, which might lead to our visas being revoked. But word leaked out, one way and another, of what was happening at home. With every carefully phrased letter or rumour, the threat of being sent back acquired new colour and terror.

The barbarians started with the revenge they had stored up the longest – against the revolutionaries of 1919. Toller's adjutant, Felix Fechenbach, was 'shot while attempting to escape' at such close range the back of his chest was blown open. When Hitler's men found Erich Mühsam, another of Toller's co-revolutionaries, they branded a swastika on his skull and bashed him to a pulp. Then they made him dig his own grave, but pulled back from killing him at the last minute, giving him just a foretaste of hell. Hans's editor, the renowned pacifist Carl von Ossietzky, had been taken prisoner and there was no news. There was nothing covert about what they were doing: they wanted everyone's fear.

Every three months when we respectfully begged His Majesty the King of England to be allowed to stay, our minds flooded with the things we could not mention in our polite visa application letters, the true reasons we could not go home. It was like submitting to a medical test; you feel fine until the test itself conjures up the possibility, in minute and excruciating detail, of the illness being tested for. Suddenly the symptoms you've been ignoring, the twist of spleen and liver ache, the shooting pain in your upper breast, are proof of the diagnosis any fool but you would know is coming.

London was harder for Hans than for me. I had reasonable English from school, but his was rudimentary. He found reading the newspaper difficult, and he found the fact that his name did not appear in it worse. Hans brought the same honed eye to the British that he had trained on the Germans, but here he had no outlet to tell what he saw. Slowly, he lost his sense of public self, and with it his private one evaporated. For him London was a place where the wind blew litter around red postboxes and the parks were under lock and key. Businessmen in suits and bowler hats dressed to disguise the human underneath, signs of individuality restricted to the pattern or colour of their ties. The houses too were identical, in blank-faced rows with black cast-iron railings, distinguished only by the colours of their doors.

In fact neither of us could get used to the minutiae of differentiation, we couldn't take it seriously. We mistook people's exaggerated politeness and lavish praise for friendliness, when it was meant to keep us at a distance. The manners, Hans quipped, fenced off unassailable and pristine areas, like the parks.

During the daytime, while I busied myself working with the Jewish Refugees Committee and the Quakers and taking pictures, he walked alone to the reading room at the British Museum. He would write himself into a novel.

Those first weeks, I found it a shock not to be recognised for what I had always been seen to be – a German, a bourgeois, a Jew. As socialists we had argued for an international brotherhood of man in which class and race were irrelevant, but I had never stopped to think what that might actually feel like. Here, by the magic of exile, whole categories of my identity were obliterated.

Very soon, though, it became clear that I'd been granted a glorious liberty. It was the liberty of a licensed observer, a tourist – of someone from whom nothing could be expected. As winter turned to spring I spent long, absorbed hours taking photographs around the city – children in bright knitted hats at London Zoo; swift-fingered cardsharps on Oxford Street, all winking, incomprehensible charm; calm-faced women nursing their bags on the top decks of buses. Hans, who was shy speaking to the English, spoke of them as they fitted his preconceptions: a nation of shopkeepers, tea drinkers, lawn clippers. But I came to see them differently. What had seemed a conformist reticence revealed itself, after a time, to be an inbred, ineffable sense of fair play. They didn't need as many external rules as we did because they had internalised the standards of decency.

Which, in an unspoken way, they tried to teach us. A rich and kind Jewess, Mrs Eleanora Franklin, held an open house for refugees every Sunday at her residence at Porchester Terrace in Paddington. Mrs Franklin's earlobes hung heavy with gems and she carried an apparently legless white animal in a bag made of carpet. On the way in to tea she asked whether we would like to wash our hands. Neither Hans nor I had touched the dog, whose head, with its mesmerising underbite, nodded at her elbow.

'No, thank you,' I said.

'My hands are clean, thank you,' Hans said politely.

Mrs Franklin leaned in to him, enunciating clearly. 'I meant, dear, would you like to use the lavatory?'

He shook his head in silence.

The meal was announced as the clock chimed. It was afternoon tea, not a repast we were familiar with. The table was fully laid; there were sandwiches made of white bread on tiered stands, with fillings of cucumber, smoked salmon, egg and mayonnaise, prawn. Other stands held cakes – tiny chocolate squares in ruffled paper, berry tartlets, and pink-and-white coconut fingers. Bowls of jam glistened darkly at each end of the table, next to ones of clotted cream. The maid appeared with platters of warm scones and put them down. We didn't know what order to serve ourselves in. We watched others closely and followed suit: it seemed you could have cake before a sandwich or an asparagus roll, but only one thing on the plate at any time. Our hostess stood and poured tea from a height. There was no lemon for it, but milk instead. A serving girl came round with a tray bearing coupes of champagne.

Hans sat next to me, waiting and watching, in quiet conversation with a middle-aged Quaker with pomaded hair. During a lull I heard the man say, 'That's how you sit, is it, in Germany?'

I looked quickly at Hans. He was sitting perfectly upright, his hands in his lap. Hans said nothing, inclined his head politely. The man stretched out his arms, garnering the attention of the room before placing his wrists ceremonially on the edge of the table. 'In this country,' he said, as if to be kind, 'we sit like so.'

I watched Hans redden and smile weakly. I knew that even if he could think of something to say, he wouldn't trust himself to get it out without stuttering. His silence deepened.

The tea party took a tour of the garden afterwards, a garden like none I'd ever seen: it was carefully, cleverly designed to look wild, its limits concealed with trees and trellises and extraordinary thistles towering prickly in messy beds. The neighbouring houses barely existed. When we came back inside people lounged on sofas and comfortable chairs; the men smoked cigars. Standing by the fireplace, I was startled by a luxuriant snore from the wing-chair at my elbow. It was our hostess. For a tiny instant the room went silent, as if to register something. Then, as though on reflection it had been nothing at all, talk resumed.

At home Hans and I laughed about the snoring, but he still smarted on his own account. He set a fire in the kitchen range and paced. In Berlin he had made himself over from a stuttering country pastor's son into a master of language, of nuance; a smooth, seamless charmer. Here in London he was pushed back to feeling like a small-town nobody who needed to be taught euphemisms for bodily functions and how to sit at table.

'Did she truly think,' he stood with his hands on his hips, staring at the linoleum, 'did she truly think I'd got to this age without being able to excuse myself and ask the maid where the toilet is?' His voice was rising, chipping. 'They infantilise us.'

I was at the table sorting rolls of film and labelling them. I was getting better at deflecting these outbursts of hurt. 'I'm collecting English euphemisms for "toilet",' I said. 'Lavatory, ladies' room, powder room, bathroom, smallest room, loo. Mrs Allworth taught me "crapper" and "spend a penny" but I had to force them out of her. They're shy about it,' I said. 'This is not a culture at ease with the body.'

'It's more than that.' Hans came to the table and started to hack at a soft square loaf with a knife. It was wobbling and crumbling off in unbutterable chunks. 'It's a code. Every conversation has a subtext you're meant to divine. If you do, you're in; if you fail – *shit*.' The knife had torn into his thumb. Blood popped out in a bright bead. He put up a hand to stop me getting up for a bandage. 'I-if you fail,' he continued, finding his handkerchief, 'they relish the opportunity to point out to you how *outré* you are. They stutter that false stutter – I think sometimes just to tease me. They say "With the gr–gr–greatest of respect" when they're about to absolutely demolish you. And they pretend to know nothing about something when they're in fact an expert, in order to trap you as p-pretentious.' He was buttering a shard with one hand. 'Or ridiculous.'

'It's British indirection,' I said. '*Understatement*.' I used the English word. 'They probably find us crude.'

Hans gave up on the bread and fell onto the green couch. He took his notebook from his pocket. 'It's a sneaky culture. All back-handers.' He was thumbing the pages so they fanned. Between those covers he was pouring all the late-imagined retorts, his dislocation and homesickness. They could not contain them.

I knelt on the linoleum between his legs and steadied his hands. His eyes were swimming and lost. It was one thing to reinvent your-self in your own country and your own language, but quite another in a completely foreign place. It required reserves of strength we might not have. I wanted to be enough for him.

'They are trying to teach us to fit in,' I said.

He shook his head. The notebook fell to the ground. 'Why would they assume,' his voice was thin with shame and rage, 'we want to be like them?' He picked up the notebook and went into our room. I sat on the couch, alone. Then I finished sorting my film. When I went in to him he was asleep.

Not long after we'd arrived, I had taken over our correspondence with Bertie because Hans felt he 'had nothing to report'. I enjoyed Bertie's cheery, chatty letters on 'this so-called life I am leading'. He couldn't say anything about his political work in case our mail was being intercepted, so he was forced to write about the texture of his days. Bertie seemed surprised to find that, looked at closely, life outside of work could contain so much, although his sole interactions were with the baker, the barman, the postman. But his spirits were high, and loneliness was making him into a better observer.

'I start to see the little things, like you do,' he wrote, and I knew he didn't mean it as an insult. 'I see corners of beauty and think of your photographs.' Bertie shared small, silly details – about his teeth, 'loose from living on soft crêpes'; the dogs in the park, 'small as birds on leashes'; the beauty of the women, 'who walk always as if they are being watched'. This, he joked, was something he might have to learn.

I thought of him in his life of poverty and work and exile, his wispy hair and untended teeth, the old home-knitted jumpers from when his mother was still living, his neglect of himself somehow a sign of his keen and terrible commitment to the rest of us. While Dora was off somewhere with Toller, and Hans poured his life into his notebooks, it felt intimate to have a friend who let me inside his skin.

TOLLER

'Do you think it is possible to love just one person?'

Clara's eyes flicker away. Her body shrinks into itself and she looks down in her lap.

Idiot! First I dance with her and now I make her afraid I want to love her. The look on her face is one of betrayal: I thought we were friends, the look says, but *this* is what you want; I thought I was a person to you, but see now I am sport. It is these niceties between men and women, especially between older men and younger women, that are such a trap.

'No, no – I am so sorry.' I lean towards her and then think better of it and stay back. 'I am not asking you a personal question. Or any question. Not that I am not interested – please, I just . . .' I pinch my eyebrows together.

Clara relaxes a little. She wants her version of me back: grand and faded, maybe, but not a dirty old man.

'Why did you love as you did?' She pushes back her hair and sits up straight, a nugget of anger in her voice, the residue of a scare.

'I think,' I close my eyes, 'we were trying to live by the new rules of our "freedom", which meant loving . . . widely.' When I open them she is still looking at me.

'But why did you love others when you only really loved Dora?' She is brave, this girl, and she will take it up to me.

'Because,' I stub out the embers of a cigar, 'I did not want her to see me,' I gesture across my knees, at the whole room, this imploded life, 'like this. If I could help it.' I feel hot tears of self-pity rising. I stab them away as I kill that cigar.

Outside sounds filter up: car horns and a paper crier. '*Her-ald Tribuu-une!* Yankees lose Gehrig, beat Red Sox! . . .' In the corridor the soft silver rattle of a laden trolley grows loud then faint, as it passes the room by. And then, instead of calling it a day or giving herself an errand so as to escape, Clara picks up her pencil and pad.

'We don't have so much time,' she says, and from her tone I know I am forgiven, or if not, that concessions have nevertheless been made. 'We should get this down.'

I should have told Dora in Ascona. But sometimes conversation leads away from things in spite of you, like an untrained horse. Asking her if she would have my child was as close to proposing marriage as I had ever come. I didn't think she would accept me. But I needed her to reject the idea, so that when Christiane came to London – she was on holiday with a schoolfriend in St Moritz – we could resume our triangulated life: Christiane as my girlfriend, and Dora as my private love, who had chosen, of her own free will, to stay that way.

In Hampstead I took a flat on Constantine Road, near the heath, in a red-brick terrace with chaste blue stained-glass birds over the front door, and a patch of garden down some steps out the back. It was spring when Dora got there but the garden was still mud, with scrawny things around the edges that might or might not resurrect.

An abandoned concrete bird-feeder down the end. So far as I could tell, the street was entirely inhabited by psychoanalysts.

I was looking out the front window as the cab pulled up. I stayed put a moment to watch. It felt like spying, or theft. She was leaning forward, listening to the driver finish a story. They were both laughing as they got out. After he'd helped with her bags she offered her hand to shake, and I saw the man's back stiffen in surprise, pleasure. When she bent to pick up her luggage her neck stretched, bare and fine and white, out of a red coat.

For me there was no going back from Dora; every other woman was less than real. She gave me access to things my striving nature would not otherwise have let me see; things my vanity would have kept from me. Without her I was only half the man, and half the writer.

I raced down the stairs and gulped my breath and opened the door. She gestured to where the cab had been. 'He was telling me he once had the Duchess of Kent in his cab,' she said. '"Right-on-that-very-seat-you-yourself-are-seated-on-miss-no-less."' Her mimicry was nearly as good in English. She laughed, putting a briefcase and typewriter case down in the blue-lit entry. 'They treat an encounter with the arse of royalty like it's some holy benediction.'

Then, 'Hello you.' She jumped, arms around my neck and her legs clamping my hips.

I carried her up the stairs and when we stopped kissing I let her down. 'What a load!' I said. We smiled at the unspoken charade of carrying someone over the threshold. I went back for her bags.

My three rooms were on the first floor. I'd laid a fire in the grate in the bedroom. As she took her clothes off she said, 'Home sweet home!' It was a small joke about our homelessness, but it was also, I believe, how she felt about me. I shrank inside with the foreknowledge of harm.

'Oh. I nearly forgot.' She opened her suitcase and took out

two expensively wrapped presents. I opened the smaller. It was a heavy silver ashtray from Christofle.

'It's magnificent,' I said, 'but crazy.'

'Perfect for you then.'

I smiled. Dora bought little for herself – not from frugality, more from lack of interest. But she had no moderation in gifts.

The other was a large box of Angelina macaroons. Each pastel ball lay in its own compartment on a bed of soft tissue, like the egg of some exotic bird. She rummaged further in her case, retrieving a dozen packets of Gauloises.

'Stimulants,' she smiled, as she jumped into bed.

Dora and I didn't discuss whether she was staying for a few days, or weeks, or till she was established, or whether we might be setting up a household together.

We had never lived together. Even in her brief, friendly marriage to Walter Fabian, Dora had kept her own apartment in Berlin. Her need was visceral – the space of the only child – but it was also a political position. Dora's view was that working women were trapped by ridiculous domestic expectations which, as she put it, 'link their moral virtue to the state of their flat'.

I remember vividly a socialist congress in Hildesheim where she gave one of her signature addresses, telling the movement it needed to 'liberate half of humanity from the endless trivia of the household'. She paced the stage like a small, clever cat. 'This can be done,' she pushed up her sleeves, 'with technical innovations and communal kitchens.' The women in the audience cheered, the men nodded and shifted their feet. 'Until we free ourselves from the insane idea that communal households and communal cooking "undermine family life", we will never achieve a true family life of free and equal people living together – one of them will always be the doubly burdened slave of the other.'

She waited a moment, then opened her arms in the gesture of

inclusion she used when making a particularly hard-hitting point. 'This individualist irrationality,' she said, 'is swallowing the best energies of women.' There were hoots and whistles. Dora laughed a little too, as if they were all in this together. 'There are higher values than duster and cooker – than the "cosy home", which, despite appearances, makes a *slave* of the woman who has to keep it that way.'

Towards the end the applause for Dora was joyous, unconstrained, intoxicating. Then she stared out into the audience. It seemed she was looking straight at me. The crowd vanished. 'To say nothing,' she cocked her head slightly, 'of a new way for the sexes to live together. Until we change these material expectations, a new valuing of women will remain only a dream and a hope.'

So, naturally, she had no intention of running a household for anyone else. The question of our living arrangements hung in the air of my room; we trod carefully around the unspoken thing. We were thrown together in a bed in a house like a presbytery, in a city that seemed to contain a hundred foreign towns, and there were enough questions for now.

In the bedroom there was only the bed; the suitcases lay open on the floor. When we got up towards evening I said, 'I'd say hang up your things, but there's nowhere to hang them.'

'When is your next trip?' she asked. She was rolling a stocking over her knee to meet the fastener.

'The PEN congress next week,' I said. 'Dubrovnik.' I buckled my belt. 'You can stay here if you like.' She looked up – I hadn't let her assume it. 'Of course,' I added.

She finished the second leg. Placed her palms flat on her thighs. 'Are you angry with me?'

I put my jacket on; the place was always cold, the little grate too small.

'Why would I be?'

'For what I said in Ascona. About a baby.'

I can never tell how much of a conversation is engineered by my subconscious trailing its coat for a fight. I didn't want to have this talk so early. We had work to do together – my speech for the writers' congress, for one thing – but I couldn't not tell her.

'I'm not angry,' I said. I took a breath and looked to the corner of the room. 'Christiane is coming.'

Dora stared straight ahead of her. She seemed smaller.

'Why?' she said finally, her voice high and stretched. 'She doesn't need to . . .' She turned to me. My arms were empty and useless; I couldn't work out where to put my hands.

'I see,' she said. 'You asked her to, to —'

'I asked her nothing,' I said. *It was you I asked!* I wanted to scream. *It was you.*

Like most things, that contained its own lie. If I had truly wanted Dora to stay with me I would not have frightened her away by talking about babies. I would have just talked about us. 'Christiane is coming to be with me.'

Dora's eyes welled with tears, which made her cross. 'I didn't think . . .' she said, and stopped. She put her pullover over her head and yanked it down. Stood to do up the hook and eye of her skirt. 'I'm going out.' She retrieved her coat from under the pile of clothes on the floor. 'For a walk.'

'She does have to leave, actually,' I said to her red back at the door. 'Because of the role she refused. They wanted to see whether Toller's girlfriend would work for them. It's my fault.'

Dora turned around, her voice quiet. 'Stop talking about yourself in the third person.' I couldn't tell whether her anger was directed at me or at herself. 'It's not funny any more. You want to believe in The Great Toller the public figure, so you need a little girlfriend who does too.'

It is true that I enjoyed feeling like the man Christiane thought

I was. I didn't know how long it would last, but if I could keep up the front for a young girl, maybe the black months would stay away.

'Why is it so wrong to want to be . . .' I wanted to say 'better' or 'normal', but couldn't get it out.

'The Great Toller?' She threw her head back. 'Because that's not all you are.'

I followed her to the corridor as she started towards the stairs. Halfway down she turned around, chin up to me, her pale, pointed face floating in the darkness of the stairwell.

'Does the little one know you need bars?'

I heard the front door slam.

I don't know how much later it was that I heard steps. I went to the door. It was a woman coming up the stairs, carrying a string bag bulging with brown-paper packages. I watched the top of her head, blond and neatly parted on the side. A nothing. No one.

I went back inside. I couldn't go near the bed. In the front room was a chair. I pulled it to the window and sat there, still and lost. For over an hour I could not move. I felt the punch of emptiness in my gut, a black hole inside that threatened to open up and swallow me down. Superstitions from my childhood returned: if the third person to come along the street was a woman, the world was in order; if Dora came back by my fifth cigarette, everything would be all right.

If Dora left me, there would be no one to catch me. It is only when your beloved leaves you that you realise the stake is gone, and where they were there is only cold air, with nothing to hold you up.

When she came through the gate the hole in me closed over, a very thin sheath. By way of humbling myself I didn't bother pretending I'd done anything but sit waiting. Her nose was red, sore-looking. She stared at me, hunched and hopeless in the chair. She could see I'd been in freefall. Her eyes grew soft. Our love was like a carpenter's spirit level, each of us holding an end up so hard, fighting to keep that trembling bubble in sight.

Dora had sat watching mad fellows, she told me, diving into the dark from a high springboard. The pond was blacker than the sky. She must have decided that she would weather this like we'd each weathered other relationships before, as symbols of our freedom.

'We have work to do, don't we?' she said, taking off her gloves, one finger at a time.

Clara's hand keeps moving across the paper for a few moments after I've finished speaking. It must be sore. She has flipped over a centimetre of pages on the steno pad, which are stacked now on the underside of the spiral binding.

'Shall we take a break?' I ask.

'I'm fine,' she says, but she has put her pencil down and is gently flexing her right hand open and shut.

'Just a couple of minutes, I think.' I get up from the chair, go to the window.

'I'll get these cases in order then,' she says behind me. Clara is someone who cannot sit and do nothing, who will never be pulled down to nothing. I hear her start to rustle gently through my papers and clothes.

A life in two cases. Clara is taking my travel plans seriously, and I need her to. As for me, I am finding them harder to believe in. Although I have arranged to see Spender about a translation, and have agreed to public appearances in Oxford, London, Leeds and Manchester, I have to beat down the black part of me that sneers, *Who are you kidding?*

I cannot escape it by boat.

The cherry blossom trees across the street are extravagant explosions, pink confetti burst from a can. I scan the park for them now, but it must be over. Their beauty seemed unwarranted, heartbreaking.

'How long will you be gone?' Clara asks.

I am already gone. I turn around. Clara has removed everything from the cases, so as to audit my plans and fit out my future. She is counting shirts and dividing time to come by their number. Her blouse snaffles the light into its deep, magenta folds.

'I'm not sure. Perhaps indefinitely. For the time being.'

She gives me a small nod as if I have made perfect sense, then turns back to her task. 'We'll pack as much as we can, then.'

Even pared down, my life might be hard to carry out of here in two cases. I feel a sudden and terrible pity for this girl who has to deal with me, now.

'I'm a hard case, wouldn't you say?'

She winces and shakes her head at my weak pun.

'Sorry.' I hang my head in mock shame. 'No, truly, I wouldn't worry too much about the packing.'

She looks up sharply.

'Well, I mean they might hold some of my papers in the safe downstairs,' I offer. 'While I'm gone.' I move to her and make as if to touch her arm, but don't. 'How about you finish that later?' I ease myself back in the chair. 'I'm ready to go on.'

I had a lot of work to do in London, and Dora and I set about doing it in the weeks before Christiane arrived. My first plan was to finish the autobiography, but events in Germany forced me to speak out about them instead.

On the 1st of April 1933 Goebbels warned Germans of three things that represented the 'Jewish spirit' which, he said, was undermining the nation: the magazine *Die Weltbühne* (they had imprisoned its editor, Carl von Ossietzky, already), the philosopher Theodor Lessing (now safely in Czechoslovakia) and me. 'Two million German soldiers,' the little hysteric screamed over the radio, 'rise from the graves of Flanders and Holland and condemn the Jew Toller for having written: "the ideal of heroism is the stupidest ideal of all".'

The German chapter of PEN promptly expelled me. And then my books were burned, by eager university students and their craven professors, in towns and cities all over Germany. They made a bonfire party of it, with music from SS and SA marching bands, sausage stands, and ritual incantations as they threw the books into the fire: 'Against decadence and moral corruption, for discipline and decency in family and state, I consign to the flames the works of Heinrich Mann, Lion Feuchtwanger, Erich Kästner, Ernst Toller . . .'

When I got to London, H. G. Wells, who was outraged by what the Nazis were doing, made a point of inviting me to the PEN conference in Dubrovnik as part of the English delegation. I would be the only non-Nazi German there. I felt the weight of it on my shoulders.

While Dora and I drafted I walked the room, or the garden if the day was bright, and she sat over her writing pad, flipping the pages around their coil of wire. People often have to be alone to think or to write, but being with Dora wasn't like being with another person. We rarely made eye contact. I orbited her chair, eyed without seeing how her hair was cut soft into her nape, the gloss of it. To be with Dora was to be relieved of the burden of my self. This is the trick to creative work: it requires a slip-state of being, not unlike love. A state in which you are both most yourself and most alive and yet least sure of your own boundaries, and therefore open to everything and everyone outside of you. The two of us threw ideas and words around until we had carved a new way forward for the world – clearer and surer and nobler than had ever been done before. Then, elated, we went to bed, whatever the time of day.

The German government had silenced writers in Germany, and

now it was trying to silence those of us who'd managed to get abroad. The Nazis were putting pressure on the British government to prevent us addressing public events. They threatened reprisals against publishers in Britain who published our work. It wasn't just about depriving us of a living, it was the first step to silence.

'What about that?' I moved into Dora's line of vision. '"This is the first step to silence."'

She chewed the side of her cheek. 'Sententious,' she said, looking up at me. 'And in your case, unlikely.'

'All right, all right.' Sometimes you just need the tone, the voice of the thing, and then it will come. 'What if I start by telling them that the SS came to my flat the night the Reichstag burnt and that I was not there? That when they got to von Ossietzky's and Mühsam's and Renn's and all the others', those men were there, and now they're in concentration camps. What about "The freedom I have retained by pure chance obligates me to speak for those who no longer can"?'

She nodded, took it down. She said nothing about the fact that it was she who had been in my flat and she who was arrested in my stead – I knew she wouldn't want me to write that.

'I refuse,' I went on, 'to recognise the right to rule of the present rulers in Germany, for they do not represent the noble sentiments and aspirations of the German people.'

When I got up to speak in Dubrovnik there were catcalls and booing from the German, Austrian, Swiss and Dutch delegations, all of whom walked out. But there was cheering too, and when I finished a standing ovation. On the street people in cafés stood to applaud me. My words were reported around the world. I was pleased; I thought some idea of the Other Germany might survive the madness.

I have used the speech we wrote for PEN that day, or versions of it, more than two hundred times in the past six years. But I have to say that the reverence and attention I craved to save me from the solitude of writing was not good for me either. The more causes I supported, the more I wondered what would be left of me to give to the page. I remember Dora once risking a joke about it. 'What must have happened to you,' she asked, 'to need approval on such a global scale?'

At the Hampstead house the mail came morning, mid- and late-afternoon. Dora sorted it, opening all correspondence except that from Christiane, which she'd place apart on my desk, partly out of respect and partly reproach. One day, after my return from Dubrovnik, I came in from my morning walk and caught her moving away from the desk crumpling a letter in her hand.

'Bad news?' I asked.

She nodded, realising there was no way of hiding it from me. She flattened it out. 'DIE JEWISH TRAITOR SCUM,' it read. The letter was in German, typed.

I took the envelope from her other hand. It was addressed to me, dated the day before.

'It's a local postmark,' she said. 'They must be watching the house.'

'Who?'

'I'd say it's the local fascist group trying to feel important,' Dora said. 'They're hotheads, but probably harmless. They meet at the German Club here. People say they inform Scotland Yard about refugees' activities, hoping to get them expelled that way, but that could just be fear talking.' She touched my forearm. 'It won't happen to you,' she said. 'You're The Great Toller and the British love you.' She said this gently and she meant it as a comfort, that my fame might protect me. But an irony had crept into her tone lately.

'What about you?' I said.

'What about me?'

I smiled stupidly. 'Is "scum" singular or plural?'

'Well, it's addressed to you.' She cocked her head to one side. 'But if you're asking me to share your lovely life, I'll think about it.'

The truth was, I had already been receiving hate mail, and I knew I was being followed on the streets.

The day before Christiane was due to arrive, Dora was still staying at the flat. I wasn't sure when she was leaving and I couldn't ask. I came back from my walk early and found her in the bathroom, pulling a hypodermic out of her arm.

'Pain?'

She looked at me and her eyes were brown and huge and pinned and I knew the nothingness had hit her in the gut.

'A little,' she said.

In the afternoon she was gone.

Clara gets up to draw the curtains.

'Please. Leave them. I like to watch the lights at night.'

She reties the green-and-gold curtain rope and turns, putting her things together to leave. Clara does not comment now on how I have loved, but I can tell she does not judge me. I can tell it by the way she thinks to stack the half-packed cases on the floor so that I can use the bed, and by the way, calm and firm, in which she says, 'See you tomorrow, then.' This is a job we are doing together; it is important, and it will be done. I have always been saved by practical people.

RUTH

I pay for my cake and walk from Bondi Junction down through the wildness of the ravine at Trumper Park, its vines and frog noises and overhanging darkness. In summers past I used to beat a stick to warn the snakes off the path, though my crutch does just as well now. I find the worn sandstone steps and go down them sideways, like a spider with four legs. I come out at New South Head Road and get the bus five stops to Rose Bay.

This is the most perfect bay on earth. Pleasure boats bob lightly, tied to buoys. Behind them the seaplane shuttle touches down, pulling a delicate furrow of foam through the water. Further out, the harbour is covered in spinnaker craft, all white sails and pale blue, blown into the same shape and direction, like hope. *Like hope?* My loose, loose mind.

I stand on the promenade, looking out. Across the bay a sleek ferry slides silently into its dock. The world is muted, without those aids in my ears. A bare-chested young man jogs towards me, a tattoo like a spider crawling out of his trunks; could it be a sign of some kind – Celtic? Runic? Come hither, or beware? God knows I was always the last person on earth to tell the difference.

At my feet a gecko moves in staccato bursts. A small boy runs up the ramp from the beach, holding out his hands. I can't hear what he's saying till he's upon me. 'It's a jelly-blubber!' he shouts, happy as if he created it himself. 'Look! Jelly-blubber!' In his palms wobbles a perfectly transparent piece of sea creature. It is so clear I can see the child's little fingers cupped underneath. How can that bear life? I might sit down.

It is all residential here, large old homes or fancy apartments. Except for over on that corner, where there is a pink hotel with tables and chairs out the front under fig trees. I press the button and wait. Beside me a huge, cushiony pelican sits atop a lamppost. I watch the four lanes of traffic, full of the speeding wealthy in German cars.

When the lights change I step out from the pavement but not quite far enough – my built-up heel scrapes the kerb and the other foot cannot find purchase and time – pulls – apart. There is time to breathe in – even, as I move through the air, to wonder what will be broken. There is too much sky the earth slams close my limbs are useless as matches.

I lie smashed on the bitumen. For a moment I am afraid of the traffic. Then I close my eyes.

When I open them I am still here. A woman is standing over me. Her messy blond hair lifts about in the wind. Behind her on the road lies my wig, about to be run over by a four-wheel drive. The tyre clips it and it flips alive, coming to rest again on the white lines in the middle of the road.

I ran white lines once.

I look up at the woman. To one of her hands a child is tethered, a little girl of four, maybe five. The other hand she holds high over me, stopping the cars in this lane.

The little girl watches me, curious and unafraid. She is unafraid of the mess in front of her – a scraggy-pated crone with blood in her eyes and one functioning limb, which, still attached to a metal crutch, flails and scratches at the tarred road. Cars are lining up behind. I'm feeling bad about the traffic jam. Someone gets out and starts speaking to his mobile. Half his shirt has come untucked and it flaps in the breeze from the water.

The woman's lips are moving. 'Can you sit?' she is asking. 'Can I help you up?'

The girl looks on, as sober and distant as if this were just one of numerous, equally unlikely events dished up to her on any given day.

'I . . . I . . .'

When I wake up I am in hospital and they have given me something that makes light of the world. I am unaccountably happy. The nurse is herself a cheery, one-woman party, festooned with lanyards and swipe cards and chinking keys around her neck. She tells me I just have to squeeze a button attached to the drip if I feel I need more.

'More what?' I squeeze before she can answer and the stuff slides cold and welcome into my forearm.

'Pethidine.' She picks up my hand between hers. 'Morphine family. Takes away not only the pain,' she smiles, 'but even the memory of it.'

I look at her sideways. But I am not done with them yet! I am a vessel of memory in a world of forgetting.

When she leaves I look down at my arm. There's a cannula taped on my skin, above the wrist.

Dora used morphine occasionally, discreetly, much as you might have a whisky to unwind. It had started with the abortion before she was married, but she always controlled it. She didn't feel the need to hide the stuff. At Great Ormond Street the glass vials lived in a wooden stand in the bathroom cabinet.

I sat in the kitchen of the flat in Bloomsbury, barely breathing. A fly was making its way around the rim of a teacup, throwing a surreal, leggy shadow into the bowl. I was delicately focusing the camera lens to try to catch it before the shutter noise sent it off. The fly raised its two back legs and rubbed them together, in some kind of dyslexic glee. Hans was at the library.

A ringing broke the air. The fly vanished.

Our phone number was Holborn 7230, but we weren't in the book so you had to be told. I picked up the receiver to nothing but dial tone. Then I realised it was the intercom for the front door that had been installed to call the caretaker down for parcels, or people who'd forgotten their keys.

'Hello?'

'It's me,' she said.

'I'll try this buzzer.' Hans and I had our own keys, so I hadn't used the system before. I started to fiddle with the switches.

'Can't you just come down?'

Dora was standing on the doorstep between a briefcase I recognised as Hans's and a heavy typewriter case. She was wearing trousers and a grey rollneck and what looked like a man's jacket, though it might have just been too big. It was raining.

'I need my own space,' she said. 'Can I stay here?' Her eyes were red and puffy.

'You need to ask?' I hugged her.

Dora hadn't been sleeping. That first night she took Veronal and slept till morning. At breakfast she came into the kitchen in Toller's burgundy pyjamas and poured herself a coffee. She ripped open another sachet of the drug and emptied the powder in, flicking it with her index finger to get it all out. 'I'll be caught up by this evening,' she said, and went back to bed. She knew intricately about dosages – too many grains at once and the sleep would be permanent, so she'd do it in two stages.

In the evening she woke up fresh-faced and sparkling, and left us for a meeting of the International Women's League for Peace and Freedom. Hans and I went to see the new picture *King Kong*; we watched the monster climb to the top of the building and bellow at the world.

From that time on, the three of us lived in the eyrie flat at 12 Great Ormond Street, circling and dodging and loving one another in our own particular ways.

When Dora wasn't sleeping, or with a man, she was working. Her English was fluent – from school, and stays in Britain – so innumerable refugees came to see her at the flat for help. She translated documents to prove who they were to the British authorities, and wrote supplicating letters to the Home Office. Through Fenner Brockway, she got to know other left-leaning members of the House of Lords, one of whom, Lord Marley, who chaired the Relief Committee for the Victims of German Fascism, became a close friend.

Dora was soon the best-connected refugee in the city, the 'go-to girl' with a reputation for being able to fix things with the inscrutable British administration. Under a pseudonym she wrote articles for the *Manchester Guardian* about political prisoners and German rearmament. She worked to help free political prisoners in the Reich and on the Nobel Peace Prize campaign for Carl von Ossietzky. She worked with Toller on his speeches and his vast correspondence. Most of what she did was unpaid, but she managed to scrabble money together from committees, a little from journalism or from work with those few famous refugees, like

Toller, who could still pay. Sometimes she asked me for a cheque to tide things over. It was usually for someone she considered needed it more. Funds circulated through her; she lived on air, crumbs, smoke and hope.

Yet in all this work, with all these people calling on her energy, I never saw her flustered. Like many people who work all the time, she seemed, paradoxically, always to have time. In her presence others became calm, all panic seemed childish, or at least unproductive. I watched desperate and downcast refugees in our kitchen regain a sense of themselves as the activist, politician, poet or journalist they once were, while she heard them out quietly, toes on a chair rung, cigarette between thumb and forefinger. They were restored by a secular faith: her sense that something could always be done.

Dora's busyness put Hans and me to shame. Although I was happy enough exploring the city with my camera and doing bits and pieces for the relief committees, he was cranky and listless. So I suggested we offer to hold the meetings of the Socialist Workers Party-in-Exile at our flat. I thought that might put us, or him at least, more in the centre of things. A few other members of our little party had washed up in London, and they were keen to keep on meeting. We started to gather Tuesday nights in our kitchen, with me taking the minutes on Hans's typewriter. I found I liked being behind the machine almost as much as behind a camera; it gave me a purpose, and a protection.

The first through the door was always Helmut Goldschmidt, a typesetter from Mainz. Helmut was a large man, as friendly and volatile as a bear. He had rust-coloured hair and no-coloured eyelashes and a thick bottom lip that hung loose if he forgot to close it. Before the war he had been an apprentice roof-tiler, but afterwards he developed a passion for books and retrained. During a lull in a meeting he would heft a book like a grenade and quip, 'An idea is a weapon to change the world!'

Hans secretly rolled his eyes to me at such displays of earnestness, but it wasn't as if we could be choosy about our membership. Helmut addressed us always as 'comrade' and took his shoes off when he came in.

Our friend Mathilde Wurm – Dora's old boss – came too, often with cheese and brown bread, herbal teas, and her knitting in a basket. Mathilde had been a stalwart politician, but standing at the door in her sensible shoes and with her basket of supplies, she gave the impression that what our movement most needed now was correct feeding and clothing, after which changing the world would naturally follow. Eugen Brehm, a quiet, bespectacled bookseller from Berlin, was also there, and a short blond boy with waxy skin who was always hungry and whose name I forget.

The leadership of the party had installed itself in Paris. We were an outpost given three tasks. First, to raise money, which the party would send to Germany for members in hiding who needed feeding, or those in prison or concentration camps who needed legal defence. It wasn't clear how we were meant to raise this money, short of standing on a street corner with a tin (for which we'd have been arrested). Our best idea so far had been to produce a bulletin on what was going on in Germany and charge a subscription for it.

Our second task was to try to alert the British public to what was really going on at home. The world needed to understand the threat Hitler posed, not only to Germans, but to the rest of Europe. But this too was an 'activity of a political nature', for which we could be sent back to our deaths. Lobbying members of parliament, publishing articles in British newspapers, even our relationship with our British sister party, the Independent Labour Party, all held the danger of expulsion.

Our third job was to produce leaflets and to somehow smuggle them back into Germany. The boy, especially, had some good ideas for how to do this: we could make tiny-print tissue for the lining of cigar boxes, or print them on wax paper to wrap around packages of English butter, or, more boldly, fold them inside Nazi pamphlets. Hitler might have muzzled the press but we thought that the people, once properly informed, would come to their senses and prefer their freedom. (As it turned out, we underestimated the liberation from selfhood the Nazis offered, the lure of mindless belonging and purpose.)

Each of these tasks – producing a bulletin in order to raise money, alerting the British and making the leaflets – depended on us having sources inside Germany who could get fresh information out to us. We didn't. We relied on new refugees arriving to tell us what they'd heard, and on interpreting what was already in the press. We ended up deciding to repackage this mixture into our bulletin and the leaflets.

At our meetings an undercurrent of fear made us tetchy and indecisive. Squabbles about the past broke out easily; the present and the future were too murky to navigate. We wasted time arguing about which left faction – the Social Democrats, the Communists or our own little party – was more responsible for allowing the Nazis their victory in February. The boy rambled on like a scout about invisible ink and letter-drop boxes and barrels on the collars of dogs. But our main problem remained how to get information out of Germany first. We simply didn't have the contacts. We were stuck. We hadn't even been able to decide, in the past two meetings, on a name for our bulletin.

Dora didn't come to these gatherings. She had left our party in January, before the election, arguing that its very existence would split the left vote against 'the rabid little brute' even further. As usual, she was right.

And by mid-1933 she was involved in something much bigger. Dora referred to it as the counter-trial, but it was officially called the Commission of Inquiry into the Reichstag Fire. This was to be a spectacular event: a mock trial in London before some eminent international judges. It was ostensibly to examine the evidence against poor mad van der Lubbe and the others indicted for arson, so as to discredit their upcoming trial in Germany and hopefully save their lives. But its true purpose was to put the Nazi gang itself in the dock – to show the regime's terrorist beginnings in the fire and the crackdown that followed. Then, we thought, it would be impossible for Britain to continue to ignore or tacitly support Hitler.

Dora couldn't talk about her work, but I knew she was using her underground contacts to help smuggle witnesses from Germany into Britain. Once, she was so thrilled she let slip that she had managed to get the former Berlin President of Police – who had overseen the investigation into the fire – to come. She had been spending her nights translating into English these witnesses' testimonials for the judges.

Through her friendship with Lord Marley, Dora had ensured high-level British support for the trial. Lord Marley was a handsome, serious, stubborn man with large dark eyes, a prominent brow, a jet-black moustache and a significant girth. He had had an illustrious war he never spoke about, after which he had taken up difficult causes as if there were no matter of conscience involved, but simply because 'one mucked in and did what one could'. He was as much a man of deep persistence as deep principle: he had tried five times, unsuccessfully, to be elected to parliament (before he was raised to the peerage) and it took him four visits to the flat before he agreed to stop calling me Dr Wesemann, but only if I would call him Dudley. Because of his work helping refugees, he had recently had to shrug off the title 'Jew-lover' in the papers. 'Not much of an insult,' he said to me over breakfast with a grin, 'now, is it?'

One afternoon in early August Dora said, 'I'm home tonight, so I might just sit in. On your meeting – if that's all right.'

I was pleased, but Hans was annoyed. In Berlin he had known

everyone worth knowing, been *au courant* with news and gossip before it hit the papers. Here, Dora was well connected in a way he could never be. It made him relive the rivalry of those early meetings in Munich. And, worse, the parochial insecurity that had dogged his childhood: the feeling that real life is always elsewhere, and it is going on without you.

'She deigns to come,' he muttered, lacing his shoes in our room. 'How utterly thrilling.'

'Be nice,' I said. 'It can't do us any harm.'

I'd recently noticed that Helmut had begun to get the sunken, grey-skinned look of a man living on 'tea and two slices' – the bread and margarine they doled out at workhouses. There was a kind of pride, even among exiled socialists, and we pretended for Helmut's sake we did not see his hunger. But Hans and I decided our meetings should involve food. Mathilde had brought meatloaf last time, and now it was my turn.

I'd never cooked in my life. Mrs Allworth gave me a 'foolproof' recipe. 'A nice piece of beef in the oven,' she said, 'stoked medium, for forty-five minutes, then leave it to rest for ten. Put the taters in with it. Can't go wrong.'

I did as instructed, and the others arrived to find the flat steamy with a powerful smell new to us: the smell of British beef.

When Helmut came in he had one eye socket the colour of eggplant, marbling into yellow at the edges. The lid was red, barely open.

'Good Lord,' Mathilde said, putting down her knitting.

'Small altercation,' Helmut said, pulling out a chair at the head of the table. A refugee in his boarding-house had accused him of 'turning' and smashed his face into the door handle. 'He looks worse than me now, I can tell you that much,' Helmut went on, taking his papers out of his satchel. 'It's probably him, anyway. The ones who accuse are the most likely to be doing it, aren't they?'

I looked at Dora, who had one knee against the table and was turning a pencil over, top to bottom, again and again. She said nothing. Nor did anyone else. It would have been easy to become paranoid here. Rumours were already rife of refugees who couldn't manage this life of fear and deprivation – and who turned informer for the British. Or worse. We had no proof the Gestapo were already active here, but there was talk.

Then Mathilde placed her plump brown hands one over the other on the table. 'Important, I think,' she said, her voice so calm she might have been discussing the distribution of milk to kindergartens, 'not to let our energies be sapped. By mistrust. Probably ill-founded. And,' she looked pointedly at Helmut over her glasses, 'most certainly damaging.'

So we sat at the table. We might have been in a small, low-ceilinged attic kitchen in a miasma of hot meat, but we would not be derailed. Dora picked at a hangnail. Her presence made all of us – apart from Mathilde, who was imperturbable – feel we had to show what we'd been doing. The boy started to eat bread. Hans smoked. His leg jigged up and down.

I took the dish out of the oven with a mitt I'd bought that had the Tower of London embroidered on it. The meal looked like a meal should look. I lifted out the beef and put the potatoes back in the oven to crisp. When I started carving I noticed the meat had a colour and texture – pinky-red and stringy – I'd never seen before.

Hans winced. 'What happened to that cow?'

Dora looked up. 'That beef,' she said, 'is corned.'

'Ow.' Hans threw me a sympathetic glance. I stared at the steaming burgundy jerky – it was a cut for boiling, not roasting.

'No matter,' Mathilde said firmly, and then it wasn't. I hacked it into threads of meat and served it up.

Helmut declared the meeting open. The first agenda item was the international trades union conference coming up in Brighton. One of us should go, he said, because no German delegation would be allowed to come. Perhaps there might even be a chance to encourage the unions here to help the German unionists, now underground at home. Helmut knew someone in the London Society of Compositors who could get us a ticket. We all agreed that he should be the one to attend.

'So,' he continued, 'agenda item number two: printing of our bulletin.'

'Whatever it's called,' Hans mumbled. I threw him a beseeching look.

It was my turn to report. I told the meeting that the Independent Labour Party had agreed, in principle, to allow us to use their printing machine, but that it was broken at the moment.

'That,' Hans interjected, 'is the least of our worries. Our main problem is that we can't expect to make much of a splash rehashing information that's already out there. We have to find sources of our own.'

'I thought we dealt with this,' Helmut said. 'We don't *have* sources, so we decided to make the bulletin like a digest.' He was looking at Hans, unwilling to go back over old ground. 'Didn't we?'

But Hans was uncomfortable summarising the news instead of breaking it. And particularly so in front of Dora. Helmut kept on talking in his straightforward, carthorse way, as if Hans really hadn't remembered what had been agreed at the previous meeting.

'Second problem, remember,' Helmut was saying, ticking it off on his thick fingers, 'was that our articles for the press would need to be in English. So someone would have to get them translated. And third, we can't put our names to them, obviously, but we decided an anonymous piece wouldn't carry much weight. So —'

'I could help with that.' Dora spoke for the first time, not looking at us, but at the meat on her fork. She was not a group person. Like Hans, she was impatient with quorums and agendas and minutes and firsting and seconding. But unlike him, she could now do things quicker alone.

Hans sat up. 'You have a source inside Germany?'

'Sort of,' she said.

'We could work together then.' Hans's face was bright with sudden purpose. 'Write the articles.'

Dora put the forkful of stringy beef in her mouth. I don't think she ever really tasted food.

'What sort of material is it?' Helmut asked.

'You know,' Dora said, responding to Hans with her mouth full, 'I have to translate it all anyway. By the time I've done that, the article has nearly written itself.'

Hans slouched back in his chair.

'It's reliable,' she nodded, in answer to Helmut. 'I'm getting a lot about the Reich's new air fleet at the moment.' She removed a piece of meat from between her teeth.

The question of where her information was from hung in the air. No one asked. We were learning that though it might have been one for all and all for one, there were among us unspoken hierarchies of knowledge and trust.

'And just on the anonymous issue,' Dora said, 'I agree. We shouldn't publish anonymously if we can avoid it.'

'But we can't —' Helmut began.

'We must find an English person,' Dora continued over him, 'in whose name it can be done. This protects us – and it protects our sources. Also,' she pushed her plate away and patted her jacket pockets, then her trousers, for cigarettes, 'it's easier for the English to trust one of their own.'

'You can say that again,' Hans said under his breath.

She ignored him. 'Think of it as the Trojan Brit. For everything,' she chuckled, striking a match, 'we need to find a Trojan Brit.'

Hans was crushed, though Dora was only being funny and

direct and businesslike as usual. But from this distance, I now see that since she had left Toller's flat, these qualities were no longer the surface manifestations of a deeper tenderness in her. They were more like defences.

At the end of the meeting Dora took Helmut aside, near the balcony. I was clearing plates at that end of the table.

'Just on the TU conference,' I heard her say, a current of authority in her voice. 'Be very careful how you talk about supporting the underground.'

'Of course,' Helmut said. I couldn't tell whether he bridled a little at being told what to do by a sparrow of a woman fifteen years younger than he.

When the others had left, Hans and Dora and I sat in the kitchen among the dishes and ashtrays. The door out to the balcony was open. The sky was the greyish-yellow night-blanket of a coal-burning city, only marginally higher than our own yellow-grey ceiling.

Hans's unhappiness had deepened over the evening. 'It's Bertie, isn't it?' he asked her. His knee was uncontrollable. 'He's sending you material.'

Dora was sitting back in her chair with her ankles crossed. She would be returning to her room to work into the night, roughing out translations and articles. Some refugees we knew had been reported for political activity – betrayed by the noise of their type-writers – so she saved the noisy typing for the daylight hours when the neighbours were at work.

'Yes.' Dora exhaled a rod of smoke.

'Sending it here?' I asked.

'To the ILP offices. And anyway, that's the beauty of him being in Strasbourg,' Dora said. 'A French postmark.'

Hans looked at her sideways from under his brows. 'You didn't trust us with that information? About Bert?'

'It's not you two.' Dora jerked her head to indicate the door the others had left through. 'I barely know those people.'

'Are you serious?' Hans asked. 'Helmut is a typesetter, salt of the earth. Mathilde is your old boss, your friend – isn't she? Eugen is a founding member of the party. What's-his-name is just a boy.'

Dora was silent. The air seemed to go out of Hans; his shoulders narrowed into the green couch. 'So,' he said, 'Bertie chose you, not me.'

'Don't worry about it, my love,' I said. 'Don't take it personally.'

'There's some other way to take it?' His voice was stung. He was bending back matches in the matchfold and flicking them over, igniting them one by one.

'I really wouldn't read too much into it,' Dora said. 'It's just that I'm the obvious choice because of my English.'

Hans pushed up off the couch, towards the door. 'He didn't even tell me,' he said, to no one in particular. He left to smoke and pace on the balcony.

The doorbell rang. Dora moved into the hall and picked up the handset. 'Come on up,' she said, leaning into the wall, one bare foot resting on her knee. When she pivoted back around she was alight.

In one minute Fenner Brockway was at the door, smiling and panting just a little. I saw what she saw: a tall, innocent-looking man, lanky as a folding ruler, with a long face and a thatch of dark hair. His cheeks were flushed, and his eyes keen and bright behind round, rimless glasses. His body was so long he was concave; it looked like his belt was holding him up. Fenner was the leader of the Independent Labour Party and an old friend of Dora's, 'a true English gentleman', she called him. I'd been negotiating with him to use the ILP's printing machine for our bulletin.

'Did I miss something?' Fenner asked, scanning the debris in the kitchen.

'Party meeting,' I said. Hans waved a silent greeting from the doorway and resumed circling outside. 'Also,' I added, 'some rather spectacular beef. Corned *and* roasted.'

Fenner grimaced dramatically, sucking air through his teeth. 'Oh,' he said. 'Oh dear.' He smiled. 'I meant to tell you, Ruth. Those wax plates are fixed. Awfully sorry about all that.'

'Not at all. Thanks. Once we've agreed on a title we'll be ready to print.'

I washed up. Dora made more coffee and they retired to her room. Then I went outside to keep Hans company. He was watching the street over the back. The people under the streetlights could not imagine lives like ours, cornered and chased up here.

'Trojan Brit,' he nodded over his shoulder towards Dora's bedroom. 'More like *they* are inside *her*.'

'Hans!' In our liberated circle we didn't criticise people for the lovers they took.

'You have to remember she's alone here,' I said. 'We have each other.'

'And she has whoever she wants.' His bitterness stunned me.

In our bedroom he kept pacing. His reflection caught in the windowpanes, a pale shape fleeing one square for another. He undressed and slid into bed. Switched off the bedside light and stayed turned away from me.

In this place of silent damp queuing – the bodies evenly, appropriately spaced – of milky tea and bad coffee and bread full of air, there was no way for Hans to feel he existed. He was ploughing his days into a novel, hoping to emerge one day famous and triumphant from between its covers. But in the afternoons he came back from the reading room like someone who had mislaid himself.

I was little comfort in a world that was failing him. Though he never said so, I sensed Hans was scornful that I could find satisfaction and purpose in these mundane meetings, in feeding people, writing cheques – the small inglorious steps of a foot soldier in this battle. His desire left him. When we made love he handled my body like he was servicing a machine. My dreams shocked me. In one I opened my legs and inside me was a huge mouth with a ridged palate and an epiglottis dangling red at the back; a mouth open in a silent scream of want.

Hans sat up in the dark. He took his clothes off a chair and collected his wallet from the bedside table. 'I'm going to see Werner.'

Recently Hans had made a new friend – a German, Werner Hitzemeyer, who called himself Vernon Meyer to fit in with the English. Werner lived with his brother in Golders Green and was Liberty of London's representative for Germany. When Hans told me Werner could still travel freely back and forth to Berlin, I'd said, 'So he's one of Them.' Hans had exploded, shouting that I'd become paranoid, I'd let Them win over me, that the whole world was not politics, that elsewhere other life went on. That other life, I supposed, included a neat blond man with a small moustache and a case full of fabric swatches who went out nights with my husband.

'All right,' I said. He slipped out into the dark.

It hurt, but not enough for me to try to stop him. For all Hans's glamour and success, I had always, deep down, felt the more solid of us, an anchor for his high-flying. I thought he would get through this, and would come back to me. But the price of letting him go was that my own life began to seem second-rate to me, as if I were an understudy in it and someone of effortlessly more charisma and talent would shortly step in. Perhaps he had already.

In the morning Dora came out to make coffee. I was cleaning lenses at the table with a soft cloth and alcohol, preparing to start a new project, photographing the workers at the docks. Mrs Allworth's husband, a foreman there, had arranged entry for me. Dora wore a singlet and pyjama bottoms. It was warm up here already.

'Hans left early?'

'Yes,' I lied. I kept polishing.

'Ruthie?'

I put the lens and cloth down. I'd have to look at her. 'Why can't you include him?' I said. 'Give him something to do?'

'He's writing the Great Novel of Exile, isn't he? That's quite a job.'

'Don't be cruel.'

'I'm not being cruel,' she said, but her voice softened; she knew making fun of him was a cruelty to me as well. She pulled out a chair and straddled it back to front. 'I'm being careful. For all our sakes. Bertie's and mine and both of yours.'

I bit my lip. 'He just wants to be useful.'

'All right,' she said, 'I'll think of something.' And she took her two cups back into the bedroom.

As I was leaving, Dora put her head around her door. One bare, brown shoulder.

'I just remembered. What about *The Other Germany* as a title for your bulletin?'

'Good idea,' I said.

'Not mine,' she replied, 'Toller's.' She eyed my camera gear. 'Don't miss your boat, then.' Her voice contained a lazy singsong, a feeling I could hardly remember. She gave me a captain's salute and slipped back into her room.

Later, she did pass on to Hans some of the material Bertie was sending her, and other information from German publications so we could use it in our bulletin. It was mostly about the setting up of the camps for political prisoners, and the fate of people we knew in them. Ninety-five per cent of the people in the camps were from the political opposition – the time had not yet come for the campaign against the Jews and the others.

But Dora kept for herself the high-level documents, to try to place articles based on them in the British dailies. I presumed they came from Bertie's contacts in armaments factories – they were order forms for parts, invoices to the government. She saw her task as being to get the information into the public eye, and at the same time to protect Bertie, and his sources in turn, from discovery. It was always a balance between these two things: the information, and its possible, terrible price.

It is hard to know when something begins, when the result first becomes possible. And then there is the other point, the point at which there is no pulling back from what you have set in train. *Take this cup from me*, Christ said, didn't he? But by then it was already too late.

TOLLER

It's eight a.m. Two knocks at my door and she comes straight in these days.

Clara's hand is unsteady, holding out the *New York Times*. Her voice is clotted with anxiety. 'Paul's boat has reached Havana harbour but Cuba won't let them dock – the government is demanding huge sums. Where can anyone get that from? I don't —'

I take the paper from her. The headline is 'Refugee Ship on Approach'. She can't wait for me to read it.

'They were meant to stay as tourists in Cuba, awaiting a visa for America.' I can hear her effort to control her voice, to make this a rational matter of entry permits bought and honoured, to convince herself that the world is reasonable and her fears cannot be real. 'Paul has a landing document – my parents paid for it with the ticket – now the Cuban President has cancelled them all. I don't understand —'

'They'll give them visas,' I say. 'Or some kind of permit.'

Clara pinches her nose together, closes her eyes and swallows hard.

'They're hardly going to turn away a whole ship of people,' I say, 'now, are they?'

She smiles a little, as if, yes, what a silly, black thought. Then her face clouds over again. 'There are letters to the editor,' she points at the paper, 'against letting them land here if Cuba turns them away. Saying there are not enough jobs for our own kind —'

'Are there letters in favour too?'

'I think so . . .' She sits, picks at a thread on her sleeve. 'Our own kind,' she repeats.

'You have to ignore that,' I say. 'I'll write a letter too. Let's do it now.'

I scan the article. There is a photograph of the SS *St Louis* in Havana harbour. It looks oddly festive, a string of flags flying from bow to stern. But it is surrounded by a ring of police boats. Behind those are small craft from which relatives and friends already saved wave at their loved ones. The Jewish Joint Distribution Committee, the piece says, is going down there to try to negotiate something for the refugees with the Cuban government. The US government has gone very quiet. The Canadians have rejected the refugees outright. And in Europe, Hitler is making the most of the situation, saying if the whole world is refusing to accept the Jews, how can Germany be blamed for their fate?

We write an open letter to the president, in the name of international brotherhood and our own humanity. I write: 'To be given the chance to save someone and refuse it must be, in any-one's religion, a cardinal sin . . .'

After Clara types it, she calls a boy to deliver it to the paper. When she sits again she takes a deep breath and smooths her skirt over her knees. 'Do you think letters can make a difference?' she asks. Her eyes are riven with pain and hope.

I pull as much power as I can from somewhere inside me, from the actor, the orator, the hope-pedlar and the charlatan. 'Yes,' I say. 'Yes, I do.'

RUTH

This little button, innocuous as an electric-blanket button, delivers the pethidine to me whenever I want it. They don't bother rationing someone as old as I am. *Après moi, le déluge!* as the French say. The stuff sends me in and out of parts of my life as if they were now, more real to me than this room. From what Bev has told me, an addict can lose ten years of their life in a quest for exactly this: the constant present tense. Afterwards, those who do not die wake to a world that has moved on without them: it is as if nothing happened to the fiend in those years, they did not age or grow and they must now pick up – with school, or people they loved – only time has shunted everyone on, elsewhere.

Sometimes I went with Dora on her walks. I would discover from the destination and the pace she set what sort of walk it was. In the mornings it was usually fast, her feet moving along an unseen track – past Coram's Fields and Russell Square, around the British Museum and back through Bloomsbury Square. She wouldn't speak. I knew then she was pacing out some problem of strategy or a piece of writing. I don't think she noticed a single thing we ever passed, not the school children in rows being taken to visit the museum, not the man with his forehead pressed to the glass of the phone box, not the lady cyclist with a full pannier who wobbled and swerved as Dora stepped blindly off the kerb.

Afternoons, when her work was done, we walked arm in arm like sisters, talking of whatever came into our heads, or not at all. These walks were slower, greener – often Hyde Park or Regent's Park. One summer day on Primrose Hill we lay on the grass, our backs curved to the spine of the earth. The sky was pale as a cup. If you pressed your skull to the soft ground and closed your eyes the whole city could fall away. The air above my face was honeyed and heavy with dandelion parts, tiny midges that could not but dance. Sounds reached us divorced from their makers: a woman's laugh, a baby's bleat, an animal groan from the zoo. We felt the planet turn.

Something wet hard-slapped into my armpit – a ball, followed closely by the nose of a floppy blond retriever pup in skin too big for his body.

'Nice catch,' Dora laughed. She propped herself on an elbow. A small voice called, 'Digby, Dig-*by*!' then a girl with fair plaits stood panting before us in sandals. There were gaps in her mouth where her teeth had been, and also in her fringe, where she'd clearly been experimenting with scissors. The girl bent down, holding the pup's collar in one hand and twiddling his ear with the other.

'Sorry!' she said, eyes gauging us. Seeing we were not cross, she added importantly, 'I'm *training* him.'

'I can see that,' I replied. Satisfied, she turned and threw the ball and ran.

'Kids!' I smiled. I clasped my hands over my middle and lay back down. I closed my eyes. The sun exploded inside me, pink, orange, black bloodblossoms careening across the insides of my lids.

Then Dora's hand, low and firm on my abdomen. 'Are you . . . ?'

I opened one eye. She was turned to me, squinting into the sun. Kept her hand there.

'What?'

'Well . . . ?'

It was a question from another world, another life. I looked squarely at her face. She was serious. Hopeful even. I turned back to the blank sky, shocked at how profoundly my future had foreclosed. It was almost beyond comprehension to me, to bring a child into the madness we were living. But suddenly, in this soft afternoon of balls and dogs and toothless girls, the predators, uniformed and not, known and as yet undeclared in the city outside this park, fell away. Why let Them take that, too? Why not allow ourselves some kind of purchase on the future?

Dora maintained the small, sweet pressure on my belly. When I looked back at her, her eyebrows were raised and the corners of her lips turned down in a parody of questioning and I knew two things: that she did not, herself, expect to come out of this, and that she was curious as to what the future would hold without her. I shooed the thought away.

She snorted a little laugh at my silence. 'It's usually, you know, a yes-or-no kind of question.' She took her hand away.

'No,' I said. 'The answer's no then.'

She inhaled deeply, as if tired of a trivial topic. 'This will all be over soon.' She gestured dismissively around her at our situation. 'We'll go home. You can think about it later.'

A bell sounded on an emergency vehicle, getting louder as it came nearer.

'Ambulance?' I wondered aloud. 'Firemen?'

'Some Honourable Member probably forgot his pipe.' She looked down towards the zoo. 'Or a lucky beast has made a break for it.'

*   *   *

Our next party meeting was mid-August. I asked Mrs Allworth, as casually as I could, if she would mind making us a soup.

'Righto then,' she said. She was wiping the iron top of the stove with a grey flannel rag. She looked over her shoulder. 'How was the beef?'

I confessed. She turned around and stared at me open-mouthed, as though her long-held views about the incompetence of the upper classes were now confirmed. But she was a kind woman and here we were, brought low. She got her face under control. 'I can see how that could happen,' she said, the merest trace of disbelief in her voice.

The soup was pea and ham, a rich green perfumed thing. Helmut shook hands all round, his shoulders hunched and his hair a red pelt. The skin around his eye had turned a paler yellow-green. Eugen came, and the boy, and Mathilde, swishing through the door in a black gabardine dress, a big tin of cream biscuits under her arm. We weren't expecting Dora.

We had just sat down to the soup when the front door slammed and she ran into the kitchen. Her pullover was on inside out.

'Look at this.' She pulled a telegram from her briefcase and put it on the table. 'They're denationalising people.'

'Wha-at?' the boy asked. I didn't understand either.

'It's a list of thirty-three people Berlin is making stateless by decree. Because of political opposition or,' she looked down at the telegram, 'for having "violated the duty of loyalty to the realm and the people, as well as damaging German interests".' She flung out her arms; her voice was fractured. 'They're taking everything – houses, flats, cars – stripping people of their qualifications, impounding their bank accounts, cancelling passports. They are making us legally cease to exist.' Her hands were shaking. She gripped the back of a chair. 'Toller and Bertie are on it.'

What happens to you if you are declared by the powers that be to no longer exist, but persist in doing so?

Hans picked up the telegram. 'Is everyone listed here out?' he asked.

'Yes.' Dora watched him scan the names. 'You're not on it,' she added.

Hans looked up quickly, then recovered himself with a wry smile. 'Don't know what I did wrong there.'

Dora explained to the others that our friend Bertie, in exile in Strasbourg, would now have his small income from Germany confiscated. The party, from this room, would need to send him money.

'Easier said than done,' Mathilde replied. 'It's not as if we're making pots of it.' Mathilde had the no-nonsense manner of an old nanny. 'He should come here to be with us. He has more chance of finding support here than all alone over there in France.'

Dora looked at her blankly. 'I don't think that's such a good idea,' she said. 'Anyway his passport has expired. He can't get in or out of anywhere.'

What Dora couldn't say was that if he came here he'd be too far away to get information from across the German border. The best weapon against the Nazis would be silenced.

There were always points at which we had to decide whether the danger someone was in was worth the work they did for the cause. We became responsible for the peril we let each other assume. There should be a syndrome name for this too.

In the West End a group of expatriate Germans had formed a club for local Nazis and patriots. Its leader, Otto Bene, was a hair-tonic salesman who had come to Britain in 1927. After the list of thirty-three came out, the group pinned up photos of each person on it along their wall. Over the photos – Toller's, Bertie's, and the rest – they hung a huge banner, painted with dripping red letters:

'IF YOU MEET ONE OF THESE MEN, KILL HIM! IF HE'S A JEW, MAKE HIM SUFFER FIRST!'

For some reason it is harder to fear what you can see in front of you – boys in uniform led by a rabid brilliantine vendor. Fear thrives better on the unseen, because we do not want to think we are afraid of something we also find laughable.

What would that make us?

Blind.

I was on a wharf at the docks one morning, watching men shoulder sacks of blue asbestos heavier than themselves off a boat from Wittenoom, on the other side of the planet. When the sacks whacked their necks the men grunted, their feet fighting for purchase on the ground. The air around them bent into waves as dust belched from the hessian. I crouched with my camera to catch it all against the light – skin and sweat, sinew and particle and air. Each morning, kind Mr Allworth let me onto the wharf. Over the past weeks the men had ceased to notice me.

I knew when I saw Hans come running that there was something wrong. He ran the length of the wharf without stopping. When he reached me he was gulping for breath.

'They've – killed – Lessing,' he panted.

Theodor Lessing, writer and philosopher and iconoclast, was famous in Weimar Germany. He and his wife Ada were friends of Dora's family. 'Shot by two agents.' Hans bent over with his hands on his knees. 'At his home.'

I froze. 'But he'd left! He was in . . .' My mind went blank.

'Marienbad. Czechoslovakia.'

I led Hans off the wharf. I felt we should be moving, we should be anywhere but still.

When we reached the street, a woman with a glass-eyed fox biting its tail around her neck asked us politely for directions to Redman's haberdashery, but we couldn't help. I apologised into her little brown eyes, beady as the animal's. I could have touched her gloved arm, she and I could have gone off to buy ribbons, drink tea, become friends. We could grow to swap stories of pedestrian disorientation and bedroom disappointment and taxidermy and I would never, ever be as safe as she.

In our childhoods during the war we had lived through the catastrophes of belief: in God, in the nation, in our leaders. It had been Theodor Lessing, a generation older than us, who had torn the veil from them, showing us whose interests they served. Famously, he'd called religion 'an advertisement for death'. More recently he had been examining the lure of the irrational in political life, focusing pointedly on fascism. For this, even more than his ridicule of God, the Nazis hated him. He and Ada had fled to Czechoslovakia when the Nazis came to power.

A few weeks before Lessing's murder, the German papers had announced an 80 000-Reichsmark reward for anyone who could kidnap him and bring him back to Germany. Dora had laughed, showing us his letter to her about it. Lessing's response was typically dry. He said he'd suffered derogatory comments about his head all his life – egghead, nutcase, contrary-minded – and had barely been able to earn a living from it. 'Who would have guessed,' he wrote, 'that it would, in the end, be valued so highly?'

When we got home Dora's bedroom door was open. I could see the usual papers in piles around the bed and at the foot of her desk, and could hear her moving around in there. Hans and I looked at each other. Neither of us knew what to say.

Dora came out under an armful of papers. Tears were running down her face.

'It's so awful,' I said. 'I'm sorry —'

'This is just the beginning.' She moved past us and turned her keys in the hall cupboard. She'd moved our stationery supply to the kitchen cabinet and started using the hall cupboard, which locked, for documents. She yanked it open and put the papers away, banging them down on the shelves. Some fell to the floor.

'The beginning,' Hans repeated in a vague voice as he crouched down to help her pick them up. Then he stopped. 'The Czech government might do something about it? Make an international outcry?'

'I doubt it,' Dora said, taking the papers from him. 'And what would Hitler care about a Czech protest? They're putting it about that it was some leftist internecine murder.'

Hans picked another stray paper up off the floor. It was the list of those made stateless. 'Lessing wasn't even on this,' he said, almost to himself.

Dora's voice came bitter from the back of the cupboard. 'I'd say they have another list for *this*, wouldn't you?'

Hans's eyes widened. His pride had been wounded at not receiving the 'honour' of expatriation, but he was terrified now that he too could be on a hidden hit list. I saw him shake the thought away. Dora seemed always to catch him thinking of himself.

'We have to get Bertie away now,' Hans said, 'or he'll be next.'

'You think I haven't thought of that?' It was a shriek. Hans and I looked at each other, deciding without speaking to leave this discussion for later.

More news of Lessing's murder filtered out to us over the next days from friends in exile in Prague. The assassination had been professional. A 'Bible salesman' had called at the house to scout it out; a 'former acquaintance' Lessing didn't recognise, with a Hamburg accent, had accosted him in a coffee shop, presumably to check he'd know his quarry when the time came. After dinner Lessing was in his study on the first floor at the rear of his villa. Two shots were fired from different pistols through the windows. The next morning an eight-metre ladder was found against the wall. Ada was downstairs the whole time.

The murderers left him bleeding to death over his desk and ran out to the woods, where, in the hunt the next day, the dogs lost their scent. The men must have had a car waiting to take them back over the German border to their party bosses.

I can't even remember the names of the nurses here now, and am always grateful for the badges they wear. But I do remember the names of Lessing's assassins: Eckert and Zischka. They had been sent by Ernst Röhm, head of Hitler's political police, the SA. After the war they found Eckert and put him on trial. He said they had been trying to kidnap the philosopher, 'but something kept getting in the way, so the plan changed'. The amended order for murder had come directly from Berlin.

The morning after we got the news Dora was up uncharacteristically early, boiling eggs. Her eyes were red. A man I hadn't seen before sat reading at the kitchen table.

'Good morning,' he said and went back to his book. After a moment he appeared to think better of that and closed it. Without quite meeting my eye he straightened the cutlery in front of him to make it symmetrical, adjusted the salt and pepper shakers to be equidistant between his place setting and mine. When his egg came he tapped it cautiously.

'Usually,' he announced, when he saw the yolk was solid, 'I like a three-minute egg.'

'I'll bear that in mind,' Dora said calmly.

After hearing about Lessing, Dora had called Fenner, who couldn't come over. Then she called this man, the professor. No doubt for Dora it was desire, but it had nothing to do with romance. It had to do with staying close to life.

I'd heard of Wolfram Wolf back home, but the man in front of me was not what I'd expected. He had a long face like an Irishman's and a dark moustache trimmed neatly under his nose. He wore a pale-green mohair cardigan, buttoned to the top, and pants pulled up high over a bottom that spread out to cover the chair. Wolf had been a legal academic before gaining some small fame as Minister for Justice in the brief Communist–Independents coalition government in Thuringia in 1923, before the army was sent in from Berlin to wrest power away from the left. Perhaps this dramatic end to his one foray into politics had sent him scurrying back to the university, under the grey bedclothes of theory. His wife, a prominent educator, was in Denmark setting up a progressive school. He was about fifty.

'And you are a *photographer*, Dora tells me.' Wolf put his spoon down and smiled a millisecond smile over his half-glasses. I heard in his question a hidden challenge to call myself a photographer, as if that would require the presumption of an awareness of form and aesthetics I could not possibly have.

'Not really,' I said. 'I trained as a teacher. Photography is a habit – I mean, you know, a hobby.' I was flustered despite myself. 'Something I can do while we're here. I'll teach when we go back.'

'Indeed,' Wolf said. He was so softly spoken you were obliged to lean in to him, as if in deference to the delicate pearls of wisdom that might issue, in their own good time, from his lips. I looked to Dora for solidarity, or maybe a laugh, but she was studying the paper.

As I got to know him – for more and more frequently it was Wolfram Wolf at the breakfast table – his superiority acquired form and shape. We could have pulled up an extra chair for it. He made us feel that the inexorable grand march of history could scarcely be affected by leafleting, or raising money, or writing articles. In fact, his theory left our reality so far behind as to make the lives we were living already passé.

I saw his condescension as an attempt to leach the courage from our actions, so as not to have to account for his own timidity. To be writing but never publishing here, to be supported by his wife in Denmark – he was running no risks at all! I believe it took all the nerve he could muster to spend nights at our flat in the company of activists who were illegal not only in the Reich, but here too.

The next time I saw him at breakfast he held forth on the 'failing courage of the socialist leadership'. I wondered how he dared, considering small beads of perspiration appeared on his hairline at the mention of Mrs Wolf.

When he left I started to scrape the plates. He'd eaten every skerrick of his egg and three pieces of toast.

'I get it now,' I said into the sink. 'In *theory* the professor loves all humanity. It's just that we individual specimens can be so damn disappointing.'

'Leave the man alone,' Hans said mildly. He was putting on his coat to go to the library. 'He's just trying to get by like the rest of us.'

Dora grinned and put her newspaper down. She had come to the conclusion that in some obscure way I was jealous, so she was being exaggeratedly patient with me. I was not jealous. I just didn't want her to be someone who was so easily fooled.

'It is true,' she said, 'that while Wolfram sees the general, he is very particular.'

When the front door closed behind Hans Dora lowered her voice to the jokey whisper she sometimes used to cajole me out of a bad temper. 'Very particular indeed. He wipes his penis after sex.' She raised the newspaper again. 'From base to tip.'

You can't be mad with love for someone if you say that about them, can you? After that sordid fact I no longer felt the need for tact.

'Well,' I shook my head a little over the sink, 'what *is* it about him then?'

Dora put the paper down again and her voice turned respectful and serious. Wolf's *magnum opus*, she explained, had reinterpreted communist theory for Germany so that we did not need to blindly follow Moscow; so that a local, autonomous variant of a more just society might take root on German soil. The Russians were running a nation of peasants, and doing it with a whip. But Germany was the most advanced country in Europe – we needed a more sophisticated, inclusive version of socialism. In Wolf's view fascism and bolshevism were both deceivers of the working class, and educating the masses the only protection against them. His was a work of genius, Dora said, and of great feeling for the people. But Moscow had punished his apostasy by forcing him out of the party.

'He's a lone dog now,' she said, 'like me.'

The thrill of having someone explain the world anew to you was ingrained in Dora from her brilliant, patient father. Her most basic pattern of loving involved intellectual exploration: new worlds revealed, this one changed by thinking it different. I wanted to scream at her, But you are not alone!

But then, who can compete with lights going on inside you?

TOLLER

'Shall we keep working?' I ask. Clara's shoulders are sunk. She seems uncharacteristically lost. 'I understand if you'd rather be with Joseph right now,' I add.

She shakes her head. Clara will manage to put her concern for her brother away, for the time being, and keep going. What else is there to do?

'The next time I saw Dora was after Lessing was killed,' I continue. I explain how Hitler, after making us stateless and poor by decree, then began sending hit squads outside the country. She is shocked; another thing she didn't know.

'Not your fault,' I say. 'It was barely reported, and then only in the émigré press.'

Lessing was assassinated in August '33. The next day Dora was on our stoop. Christiane opened the door. When I heard Dora's voice my heart sped; I tucked myself in and straightened the papers in front of me.

Christiane showed her in, then left us. She understood that Dora worked with the underground, and that for those who didn't, it was safer not to know. Also, while my private cruelties may have seemed boundless, they did not extend to torturing Christiane with my love for Dora.

It was the first time I'd seen her since she'd left to live with her cousin. She was tanned; her hair was shorter, mussed at the back from how she'd slept, and one side of her collar was tucked under. She was pacing the room, rubbing one hand in the other and speaking quickly, not looking at me.

'You're on that list,' she said. 'And Goebbels' speech – he named you. They've got von Ossietzky in Oranienburg, they got Lessing and, and . . .'

I stood up to move to her, steady her, but she wouldn't come into my arms. I stepped back to the bay window. 'Look out there.' I tapped the glass. 'I have my own tail. Chasing me.'

'Very funny.' But she came over to see the fellow, a short man in a hat, propping his behind on the low brick wall across the road, a quartered newspaper in one hand. After I reported the hate mail, Scotland Yard had given me a policeman to follow me around. He seemed both dogged and useless. I was starting to feel a little sorry for him.

'Doesn't look like much,' Dora said. And then, her face to me, 'Ernst, I think they are sending us threats. In the speeches. I'm so —'

'They wouldn't dare do it in England.' I put my arms over her shoulders.

'No,' she said. 'I suppose not.' She was blinking, her chin shuddering. 'But I'm finding it harder and harder to believe there are limits to what they will do. Sometimes,' she looked at me hard and pressed her lips together, 'I think there aren't.' The light from the window caught her at temple, cheekbone, chin.

'Well – I *am* The Great Toller, as you say. They love me.'

She cupped my face roughly. 'If you would only believe it.'

RUTH

The S-Bahn carriage is empty. The windows are open and the wind is trapped in here with us, wild and trying to get out. Dora is here!

Why haven't I seen her for such a long time? For decades? And we are just girls – I am thirteen, so she must be eighteen. She holds on to the pole and spins.

Things are distilled, clearer than life. It's hot. As she spins, Dora's hair comes loose from its inadequate plait; there's a wet strand in her mouth; her black eyes are huge. At Schlachtensee station we run down the steps, coming out at the lake. It is rimmed by spindly, eager trees bending to the water. With a piece of my reason, I know that in the many hollows and bowers other people must be picnicking and reading and stepping off to bathe, but I see none of them. In a bower of our own Dora and I hang our dresses and underthings on branches. These ghosts of us flutter and wait while we, naked flesh-and-breath creatures, step out on underwater roots and part the lake.

It is still hot, so hot when we come out. We lie on the ground, limbs sleek-shiny as fish. Dora places a wet palm, low and firm, on my abdomen.

'It's locked?'

I can't speak. I sink into the earth and into her hand; I become the melted lake, an open, aching universe of rivulet and stone, animal and flower, and – no! no! —

An emergency bell is sounding. It must be from the boat hire, or an air-raid, or a ship's horn, or a car alarm, or the anxiety of church bells —

An alarm has gone off in the hospital somewhere, and there's knocking at my door. I open my eyes. It's the cheery nurse.

'Good morning, Ruth,' she says. She wears a white coat and sensible shoes which make little sucks on the floor, some syncopation happening now with the keys and cards that jingle around her neck. *Suck suck jingle, suck suck jingle.*

'Good morning,' I say. I didn't know it was. The nurse – her badge says MARGARET PEARCE – presses a button and the torso half of my bed rises up. The Risen Ruth. I hope I didn't say that out loud.

She opens the curtains. 'Sleep well?' she asks over her shoulder.

'Yes. Thank you.' I can barely tell the difference now. The sleep is more alive than the waking.

She looks at my chart. I can't help feeling that there might be information on it about myself that could be useful, all things considered, for *me* to know. I might see progress plotted there. Or time elapsed. Time to go. But they like to keep it to themselves.

Nurses in this country are highly trained. There are universities for them and extension courses and a career path with promotions and pay rises and conferences at salmon-coloured resorts. Not like the well-bred, good-willed amateurs of my youth. But these women also have something that cannot be taught, something the doctors rarely attain. There is nothing they have not seen, no soiled pan or suppuration or botched attempt at words they do not know.

Unlike the doctors, for whom I am a bundle of symptoms to be managed, the nurses are on my side against the depredations of my body – this time a fractured hip and wrist, a damaged head bandaged right round over one eye – and of my mind. We are together in this – whatever you might call what is going on in this bed. And it is exactly the businesslike, professional nature of their thousand tendernesses that is the magical thing: their respectful, first-name ministrations restore my dignity, though I am now barely more than bones and skin hung together.

MARGARET PEARCE has wiry hair in curls that must once have been red spiralling out from her head, and half-glasses that sit down her nose. She holds my wrist between her thumb and two fingers and looks at her watch as she feels my pulse. Scratches the biro into that chart. 'You are due for an increased dose of this, Ruth.' She holds the drip tube. 'But only if you feel you need it.'

I nod for yes, and then she leaves me, safe to dream.

One morning in the kitchen, Hans and I heard Dora arguing with Wolf in her room. Her voice was insistent, and rising. I caught 'solidarity' and 'money where your mouth is'. Wolf's responses were a low, controlled rumble, the words indiscernible. When Dora came out she left the door to fly open. She was red-eyed and scratching her forearms and made straight for the coffee pot. Behind her the professor slipped by and let himself out.

'I don't give a damn that he won't be seen with me in public,' Dora said, plonking her cup down on the table so roughly it spilt over. 'He can pretend we've never met, for all I care.' Her voice was incredulous. 'But he won't even *come*.'

For months Dora had been working to make the Commission of Inquiry into the Reichstag Fire a success. Every German refugee in London would be there, and every British politician, committee member, churchman and concerned citizen who supported us. Except, it seemed, the professor.

No one but Dora could have got the witnesses into Britain. The Home Office had not been keen to admit 'foreign leftist elements, including many Israelites, seeking to upset relations with the Reich'. Through her friendship with Lord Marley and his old school contacts in the Foreign Office, Dora had circumvented the Home Office altogether and managed to get temporary visas issued for people who would testify against the regime. Some of them were even in false names, where the repercussions for the witness and their family in Germany would be too severe.

I remember Dora laughing and hugging her ribs when she got off the phone from Lord Marley. 'With true British restraint,' she beamed, 'the FO has told the Germans that "it possesses no legal power to prevent such purely private proceedings". This will be the most *public* event we can make it.' She stretched her arms out. 'Worldwide publicity! What a lesson to Berlin from a place where the government knows its limits! It's absolutely brilliant.'

Göring and Goebbels planned to use their own trial to justify to the world the Nazis' seizure of power, and to fix in the public mind the Nazi story – that the Communists had set fire to the Reichstag as a signal to their cells across Germany to start burning down all essential government buildings before moving to take over the country. Hitler had got his extra powers to lock up every stripe of suspect and 'keep the people safe'. Guillotining poor van der Lubbe and the others would terrify anyone else who had it in mind to oppose the new regime.

The counter-trial had been carefully planned for the week before the Nazis' trial. It was a Thursday morning in mid-September when Hans and I caught the tube to Chancery Lane. The counter-trial was being held in the courtroom of the Law Society in Carey Street. A throng buzzed and milled outside. Women adjusted the handbags under their arms and men cupped pipes to flames in the breeze. A fellow in a brown felt cap wheeled a gaily painted coffee cart into the crowd.

In the excitement of the days leading up to this, Dora seemed to have recovered her equilibrium about Wolf, or at least quarantined her expectations of him. She wasn't about to let his cowardice spoil her big event. I fingered the tickets she had given me in my pocket.

The courtroom was not huge but it was nevertheless grand, with a dark-panelled dado and a podium at the front. There were so many of us there, emerged from our tiny flats and boarding-house warrens, that we squashed in shoulder to shoulder, lining the walls and spilling into the aisles. As Hans and I walked to the front we passed famous faces of the Emigrandezza, noble creatures in fedoras and mended coats greeting one another as at a bar mitzvah. We saw Otto Lehmann-Russbüldt, Kurt Rosenfeld, Mathilde. Hans acknowledged former colleagues from *Die Welt am Montag* and *Die Weltbühne*. Fenner Brockway was there, and Lord Marley, the suffragette Sylvia Pankhurst, and old Mrs Franklin.

And the place swarmed with British and international press. Dora had warned us not to speak with anyone whose accreditation we didn't carefully examine first – there could be spies among the journalists as well as the refugees, people recruited either for Scotland Yard or for Berlin. But that day I was incapable of fear. I was swept up already into something public, protective, and British.

We found our seats three rows from the front. As I took out my camera a tipstaff banged his rod on the ground. The crowd shuffled and went silent, like a single, hopeful creature.

The judges filed in from a side door, magnificent in black robes with white jabots at their chin. They had come from the United States, France, Sweden, Britain, Denmark and Belgium, and there was a woman judge from the Netherlands. The room exploded with flashes. It might have been only a 'mock' trial or, as the Nazis were putting about, 'a Marxist propaganda front', but as these eminences mounted the podium and took their places, I saw that in the hands of the British the proceedings had a dignity that would be hard for the world to discount.

The famous English barrister Sir Stafford Cripps KC held up his hand. We were welcome, he told us, to photograph members of the bench. But then, if we pleased, the cameras were to be put away. He held up a copy of the *Völkische Beobachter*, its headline screaming about 'overseas traitors'.

'Newspapers in Germany,' Cripps said, 'are calling for the death penalty for any witness who appears here on behalf of the defence. It is clear that in such an atmosphere no proper defence of the accused will be possible in that country.'

Hans put his arm around my waist and squeezed, like old times.

My memories of the four days that followed are like the memories of a day at a fair, or a wedding. Or perhaps a trip on a ship, where you see all the same people each morning at breakfast. I glimpsed a future in which these months of exile would be a small, strange phase in our lives. The world would soon come to its senses. It would withdraw support for Hitler and we could go home.

On the second day, Toller took his place in the witness box. The room quietened as for a movie star, or a prince. He wore a fine English herringbone jacket, and took his time. Without a word he garnered the attention of the room; his eyes seemed to catch every one of us.

'I am not,' he began in his magnificent baritone, 'a member of the Communist Party. Nor any party. I have striven to do what I consider my duty as a writer in the cause of social justice.' He leaned forward, his hands on the box. 'On the day after the fire Stormtroopers entered my apartment to arrest me . . .'

I looked at Dora. She was watching him unblinking, hands abandoned in her lap.

'They also visited the houses of other well-known writers,' Toller went on, 'such as Carl von Ossietzky, Ludwig Renn and Erich Mühsam, and arrested them. The National Socialists wished to bring them into connection with the fire and to defame their reputations.' He opened out his arms to the crowd, 'I believe,' he said, very softly, 'the fire was a prearranged plan.' Then he paused.

There was not a rustle or cough. Toller drew breath. 'I do not know with what I was to be charged. There are thousands of people in concentration camps today who have no idea what they are charged with. I refuse,' his voice was magisterial now, 'to recognise the right of the present rulers in Germany to rule, for they do not represent the noble sentiments and aspirations of the German people.'

The room erupted into applause. Some people stood up, clapping their hands wildly in front of them. By the end we were all standing. I saw then why people had followed him into death in the war and into revolution at Dachau. And as I watched Dora watching him, I could see why, for her, no one else came close.

Dora's own coup came on the last day. In typical style, it was one that would never be attributable to her. A large, older man, very upright, with a balding head and protruding eyes under bushy eyebrows, lumbered up to the stand. This was Albert Grzesinski, the former President of Police in Berlin. Grzesinski spoke in the deep rumble of a seasoned political operator. He told the court that after the Nazis had raided the offices of the Communist Party on Karl-Liebknecht-Strasse, they used the membership list they'd stolen to draw up arrest warrants for the four thousand people on it. The warrants, complete with addresses and, in most cases, photographs, were ready and signed the day *before* the fire; only the date of the action remained to be inserted.

Then Grzesinski told us he could confirm, from his own personal knowledge, 'There is an underground tunnel directly connecting the Reichstag with Minister Göring's residence.'

There was a moment of shock and then heated murmuring started. There remained no doubt in anyone's mind.

At the end, the commission could find no evidence against the four co-accused. The chairman announced that because those who lit the fire probably came through the tunnel from Göring's house, and because the fire greatly benefited the Nazis, 'grave grounds existed for suspecting that the Reichstag was set on fire by, or on behalf of, leading personalities of the National Socialist Party'.

People whooped and cheered, threw off their hats. Tears of relief welled in my eyes as I hugged Hans. I had been more afraid than I'd known.

Back in Germany Hitler fumed. Later we listened to his address to the Reichstag on the wireless, because we wanted to see what effect the counter-trial had had on him. 'An army of emigrants is active against Germany,' the Leader thundered. 'Courts are being established in full public view overseas in an attempt to influence the German justice system . . . revolutionary German newspapers are continually being printed and smuggled into Germany. They contain open calls to acts of violence.' He paused, then added, 'So-called "black radio" programs made abroad are broadcast into Germany calling for assassinations.'

We hadn't known about the resistance radio stations, but as for the counter-trial and the newspapers, we took this as a bullseye, a sign that our work was hitting home. We were not frightened.

The Nazis still went ahead and executed poor, destitute van der Lubbe, their scapegoat for the fire. But the parliamentarian Torgler and the three Bulgarian Communists alleged to have helped him got off – it simply wasn't possible, in the face of the global publicity our London trial had generated, to execute them all.

Afterwards, we felt as if our situation itself had changed, though no law about our status had been altered. Newspaper reports from London to Paris to New York acknowledged that our homeland had been taken over by a regime of terror. Our flight was seen as legitimate. We hoped that the restrictions on us here would soon be eased, so we could talk freely about what was happening in Germany, and maybe even work openly against the regime.

As we milled on the steps outside the court someone wanted to take a photo. We stood close together, a motley group of exiles. Dora and Toller were a step below me, to my left.

'Good speech,' I heard her say, looking straight ahead.

'Thank *you*,' Toller replied, as if he meant it. She looked at him.

'No, really. All your doing,' she smiled. And then he turned and kissed her squarely on the lips. It was the only time I ever saw anything in public between them. Somewhere, there must be a picture.

Dora went off with Toller and the other organisers to dine with the judges. Hans and I walked with Mathilde and Eugen Brehm to a pub near the law courts. We felt we could take up more room on the pavement, speak louder now. The pub was dim and smoky even at lunchtime and the tables nearly full. Hans's friend Werner was already there, waiting for us. We ordered pints of beer and vodka shots, bowls of nuts.

Hans was regaling the table with jokes about Göring's cocaine-fuelled dress-up games – the bearskins with medals hanging off them, his prettyboys; how the vain giant played tennis in a hairnet. Well, not jokes really, because it was all true, but we laughed and slapped the table. Werner shrieked and shook his head. As usual, ridicule made us feel safer. Hans was enjoying the lasciviousness of his tales and the attention. After a punchline he ran his hand up my thigh and squeezed the top, hard as punctuation.

I spied Helmut coming through the crowd, side-forging his way through the dim air to our table. When he reached us he stood there with his cap in both hands. He was hollow and grey-skinned again. The others stopped chuckling.

'Seventy-two hours,' he said in a small voice. 'I have to report to the German embassy in seventy-two hours. Scotland Yard has given me over.'

The victory was over. I burst into tears. The others scrabbled to make room for him to sit down. Mathilde found me a clean handkerchief. Helmut perched on the bench seat as if he were about to be dragged by the elbows from here, or as if he could barely decide, in his last days of freedom, where to spend each of their minutes. His eyes had a yellow cast, he was talking so fast spittle collected at the corners of his mouth.

At the trades union conference, incensed by Lessing's assassination and thinking himself among friends, he'd been unable to stop himself, he said. He had stood up in the plenary and announced that Nazi Germany was a threat not only to those within its borders, but those outside. 'All I said was that the international trades union movement,' he raised his fist as he told us, 'must support *all* its members, no matter where they find themselves. That's all.' He stared into the middle of the table.

In the foyer of the conference building a Scotland Yard officer in mufti had politely introduced himself and asked to see Helmut's identity papers and residence permit. The officer copied out his address and wished Helmut a good afternoon. Three days later his residency was cancelled. Now they were handing him back to Hitler.

We knew there was no way, without a passport, of getting Helmut out of the country. He was almost certainly being followed. Anyone who helped him would be thrown out with him. I caught Hans's eye. They were probably here, in the pub. They would, of course, have been watching our flat.

Helmut downed two vodkas. He kept running his hands through his hair. He didn't know which camp it would be, he told us wryly. 'But I'm sure there'll be plenty of comrades in there.'

I felt a swift black chasm open up right under the beer-ringed table, between those who might survive and this man who probably would not.

When Helmut got to Oranienburg they broke his nose and jaw. They had a close friend of his from the typesetters' union do the rest. The friend cried bitterly but lashed Helmut all the same, until his skin lifted off. The last we heard of him, Helmut had cholera and was cleaning the camp latrines.

When Hans and I got home from the pub Toller's jacket was hanging over a chair in the kitchen. Hans was pacing the room, unable to sit down.

'Come to bed,' I said.

He couldn't stop moving. 'We can't stay here!' he cried. His hands were stiff-fingered and open wide. 'We're sitting ducks up here.' The whites of his eyes were veined. He looked like he might break something. 'War I can do!' he cried, steadying himself on the arm of the green couch. 'I can do mud, dark – the blood and the fighting and the dying. But this – this invisible stuff, this waiting . . .' His voice was high, he sat down heavily. 'We are useless. Refugees are weak. And useless.'

I moved closer, then thought better of it and sat on a chair at the table. Hans was normally a benign if occasionally sardonic drunk, his face crumpling easily to laughter at his own jokes. Other times he swung between self-pity and self-hatred. But tonight was different. Fear makes a person more alone than they have ever been. Picked out by death's steely finger, they are separated from their peers and shown their own personal end-time, the card with their number on it raised in their face.

He sprang up. 'Our efforts are pathetic,' he exploded, lurching into the hall and rattling the door of the file cupboard. It was locked, as usual. 'See? She doesn't even trust us!'

'Don't.' I went to hold him but he shook me off.

'Or should I say *me*.' His eyes were slits. 'She doesn't trust *me*. Whatever the fuck it is in here,' he thumped the cupboard door with the side of his fist, 'is making us targets – all of us.' He formed a two-finger pistol and put it to my head, then back to his. 'You, me, Dora – *pfaff!* – all targets.'

'Come outside.' I pulled his sleeve. 'Please, you'll wake them.'

On the balcony he stood facing out, his back to me. I took a chair. After some time the air around him changed. He came and turned my chin up to him, gently.

'Aren't *you* afraid?' He searched my face, as if I might be hiding my fear somewhere in order to leave him the more alone.

'I am.' I moved my head out of his hands. I should have given him more comfort. But that is not what I did. 'We can't not do this,' I said. 'There's nothing else for us to be doing.'

He squatted in front of me with his forearms on his knees, looking down at the ground. 'You're so . . .' His teeth were gritted and his head was shaking. I flinched. '. . . *good*.' Then his knees hit the concrete and he heaved up a terrible animal noise, in uneven spasms. His face ran shiny with mucus and his eyes were small, hot holes. He let me hold him. After some minutes he drew breath enough to say something.

'What?' I asked. His head was in my chest.

'I – am – no one.'

Inside he poured a whisky and then another and smoked in the kitchen. When we went to bed he calmed his breathing by force, pretended to sleep. He wouldn't be touched. Eventually I slept before he did, the brittle, lonely sleep of half a bed.

TOLLER

I wasn't sure how much the Scotland Yard boy was there to protect me and how much to report back on my 'political' activities. One day I doubled back quickly and grabbed his elbow in the street. He had blue eyes and black lashes and looked terrified – less of me, I think, than that he would be found not to be doing his job properly. 'You should look out for the German team,' I said, 'they've been on my tail for weeks.' He just blinked.

'You know,' I added, 'if you pooled resources you could probably have every second day off.' He didn't even break a smile.

On the morning I went to address the counter-trial I tipped my hat to him. Then I left him outside the court building, milling with refugees and reporters. And no doubt others, uniformed and not, German and English, who were keeping an eye on us all.

The counter-trial was a triumph. I hadn't actually been in Berlin when the Reichstag burnt, but Dora had told me all she knew, and I would, of course, lend myself to her efforts wherever I could. My performance seems ridiculous to me now, because she had been arrested in my stead. If she was a backroom girl, what does that make me – her frontman?

Afterwards the maître d' at Claridge's recognised me and gave us my favourite table. We dined like kings: foie gras and beef and French wine and cigars. At the end of dinner, a refugee I didn't know approached our table and bent to Dora's ear. All joy drained from her face, like a light going out. Scotland Yard was expelling one of the Socialist Workers Party members here, on account of his political activity. Dora wanted to go home immediately.

The double bed at the flat took up most of her room, there was nowhere else to sit or stand. Papers were stacked along the wall under the window, and to the side of the door, in what she referred to, ironically, as her 'filing system'. She often worked on the bed.

Dora sat on the edge of the bed and faced the windows, picking at her fingers in a fury. She'd warned Helmut to be careful, she said. But she seemed more angry with herself than anyone else, as if by some act of impossible intelligence and foresight she might have prevented what happened. I stood at the window. It was dark and raining. A sorry-looking fellow I hadn't seen before was walking from one end of the block opposite to the other, his coat collar up under his hat.

'My Scotland Yard shadow forgot his umbrella today,' I said.

'That's just it,' she cried, flinging a hand towards the window. 'They don't even need to send the Gestapo here. Whitehall is doing Hitler's work for him.'

Hers was the kind of anger close to tears. I wasn't sure what to do. Sometimes I was in awe around her, like a child tiptoeing their way around the mood of a parent. I moved a manila folder off the bed and sat down. To touch, or not. In the end we chose touch, found comfort in these minutes, this threadbare flesh.

I lay with my head on the pillow while she sat up and smoked. The ceiling of the little room was crazed and uneven as a living thing, the palm of a pale hand hovering over us. I turned on my side. Small notes were pinned on the wall next to the bed – reminders to herself, lists, quotes, a photograph of her father on skis. I recognised part of a speech we'd written together and slipped it from under its thumbtack.

'"Fear is the psychological foundation of dictatorship,"' I read out. '"The dictator knows only that the man who has overcome fear lives beyond his power and is his sole dangerous enemy. For whoever has conquered fear has conquered death."' I looked back at the ceiling. 'Not bad,' I said. 'If I say so myself.'

Dora blew a smoke ring. 'I don't see much conquering of fear going on around here,' she said. 'Nor of death, for that matter.' She was sitting against the headboard with an arm across her belly and her other elbow resting on its wrist. A small mole sat just above her nipple, a perfect black dot. She looked down at me. 'To be honest, I never really understood that one.' The hardness was gone from her voice.

Dora thought I sometimes got carried away by my own rhetoric, the sound of the words generating more of themselves with no effort of mind behind them, like the parthenogenesis of self-reproducing creatures, their rousing, hortatory qualities overcoming any parsable sense. It was her job to rein me in. This hadn't been one of those times.

I turned on one hip, my chin in my palm. Her eyes were black, watchful. 'I don't mean we can conquer death in any literal way,' I said. 'What I mean is that if we are not afraid to die, Hitler cannot hold us to ransom. He cannot bribe us with our lives to make us stop.'

She nodded. Then she stubbed out the cigarette in the jam-jar lid she used as an ashtray and slipped down the covers to face me. Put a hand to the side of my head. 'You aren't afraid to die?' She was looking at me, from one eye into the other.

'I don't want to,' I said, 'but I am not afraid.' We heard the front door open and close, Hans's and Ruth's voices in the flat. Her chapped lips parted to speak. I put two fingers to her mouth. 'Sometimes, though, it is hard not to want it.'

She didn't get up and exhort me to action, to proof corrections, to just one more practical thing. She didn't fill the awkward air with words for false comfort. That was her courage: to see what was there. And that was when I knew she understood the black times. I took my fingers from her mouth and the words tumbled out.

'Don't leave me,' she said.

After that it was tender again, love for love's sake. When we finished we heard a man's sobs, wretched and unpredictable, coming from the kitchen.

RUTH

I woke first. I could tell by the light in the room it would be a good day for the docks. Then the night – Helmut – came back to me like a blow. I didn't move, waiting for Hans to stir. I hoped sleep had solved something, that the darkness had closed over his terrors. But when he sat up on the bed away from me, the weight of it was still there in his shoulders.

We were eating toast with marmalade when Dora emerged from her room. She put some documents in the hall cupboard, then came in for coffee. She didn't look rested.

'Quite a night,' she said. 'You two all right?'

I nodded. Hans put his fork down.

'Helmut brought it on himself, really,' Dora said, pouring beans into the grinder. 'Though that's no consolation to anyone. He shouldn't have opened his mouth like that in public.' She sounded factual, even callous, but I could tell she was upset.

'Like that made a difference,' Hans mumbled. 'They were probably on to him before.'

Dora's tone stayed even. 'I doubt it,' she said. It was her calm that infuriated him most.

'They will be coming for us now!' Hans jumped up, his chair clattering onto the floor and his hands waving in the air.

'Settle down,' Dora said. 'It's not going to happen.' She turned around to put the percolator on the stove. 'Not to you, anyway.'

I cringed. She always went too far.

Hans bit. His voice lowered. 'What? You think I'm not a target?' He was ready at any minute to be insulted for not doing enough against Them, and then to blame her for his inability to do so – for not sharing the more important information from Germany.

'No,' Dora said, turning back around to face him. She spoke in a controlled tone, as if to a child having a tantrum. 'I just mean I think you live under a lucky star, Hansi, and it won't happen to you.'

His eyes turned to slits. 'And you're such a hero?'

'Relax. It won't happen to *any* of us,' Dora said. She made an open gesture with her hands. 'Look. There's not much we can do about it in any event. If we think about ourselves, the fear will win. We need to think about the work.'

'What work?' Hans shouted, going into the hall.

Dora raised her shoulders at me as if to say, What did I say?

I examined the lino, a small, cross-hatched pattern in green on white.

The flat was silent. Then a scuffling noise, a shuffling in the hall. Hans was in the cupboard, ripping papers off the shelves. Dora must have forgotten to lock it up. He was turning and turning like a man in a snow dome. Stacks toppled and fell, manila folders disgorged their contents. Blue carbons floated lightly down.

Dora darted towards him, 'Don't! Don't you dare —' She stopped before making contact; something had gone off inside him. He twisted and turned till the shelves were empty and the floor had disappeared.

Dora switched to me. 'You watch him,' she ordered. 'I have to clear out the courtroom this morning. I'll deal with this,' she gestured at the mess, 'later.' She collected her cups of coffee from the kitchen and went back into her room.

Hans walked past me without speaking and closed the door to our room. I went in anyway.

He was sitting on the bed with his head in his hands, adrift.

'She does it to me every time.' His voice was quieter now, but angry to the point of tears.

'She was trying to reassure you,' I said, though I knew that wasn't all of it.

He ignored me. 'She can't help twisting the knife,' he said.

Hans spent a long time in the bathroom. Dora and Toller left without eating.

I washed after him. As I came out of the bathroom he was sitting in the cupboard in his dressing gown sorting through the piles of papers, though he could not possibly have known how Dora had filed them. He stood up. 'I'm s-sorry,' he said, hands fluttering hopelessly at his sides. Some papers, folded, poked out of his dressing-gown pocket.

'Leave them,' I said. 'I'll do it.' He moved to pass me. I pointed to his pocket. 'Those too.'

He looked down, as if surprised. 'I was just trying to find a spot for them,' he said, removing them carefully and placing them back on the floor. But I could see one, folded, still in there.

'That too.' I pointed.

He put his hand over his pocket. 'It's mine.'

We looked at each other. Tears welled hot in my eyes. 'Show me.'

'No.'

How did I get here, policing my own husband? 'If you don't,' I said, 'I'll have to tell her.' I hated myself.

'It's mine.' His face contorted. I had the sudden, sick feeling that he was speaking the truth. I put my head in my hands. I heard him take the paper out. He offered it to me, his eyes streaming.

It was a page ripped from his notebook, dog-eared and worn as if he'd had it in his wallet, fingered it like a talisman. It was covered with writing. But when I looked closer I saw it was the same four words, again and again, line after line. *All will be well. All will be well. All will be well. All will be well . . .*

'I'm so sorry,' I said. He had nowhere to go but our room.

When Hans came out I noticed he'd dressed more carefully even than usual, perhaps by way of making himself feel better. He had a handkerchief in the breast pocket of his better suit; his hair was parted perfectly. Fixing things from the outside in. He left saying he was going to 'walk it off', then go to the library in the afternoon. He wouldn't be meeting me for lunch.

I was used to him dressing carefully. We'd talked about the whiff of desperation given off by our friends on the edge of poverty – the too-hearty thanks as a refugee pumped the hand of a potential editor or benefactor, eyes glimmering with hope for just one translation, one article commissioned. Men betrayed themselves with scuffed cuffs and shiny knees, shoes gaping at the toes and a collar turned to hide the fraying: telltale signs you were doing it hand-to-mouth. We were not poor, but Hans felt that for others to have confidence in him he had to prevent his need from showing at all costs. 'Look the part,' he used to say to himself. 'I must look the part.'

Hans had confided occasionally – at night in bed, or if he joined me for lunch at the tearoom – his dreams for the future. I realised from their intricacy that these scenarios had been sculpted and treasured a long time; they were like reels he could play in his head at will, to lift his spirits. When all this was over he would edit his own colour magazine, a *Time* for a new Germany. He would be a player, wield influence over a fresh dawn in Berlin; politicians and celebrities would court his good opinion. We would have a villa by the Grunewald, five uniformed staff and a car. We would have holidays on yachts. We would see the Pyramids. I didn't long for a villa, staff, or a yacht, but I said nothing. I could see he needed a picture of the future, and I wouldn't take it away from him.

Over time, though, his daydreams became worn and diminished in efficacy. The more outrages the Nazis perpetrated, and the longer no foreign country protested, the more it seemed to Hans that history would rob him of his rightful life. A gap opened up between his dreams and the days at Great Ormond Street larger than he had ever had to bridge before. It was larger than the gap between the vicarage at Nienburg and our life in Berlin, between returned soldier and renowned journalist, between stutterer and sweet-talker, Aryan and Jew. It was a gap that, if he slipped into a dream one afternoon, threatened by evening to make this life seem paltry to him, turn to dust in his mouth. I knew from the way the door slammed, the satchel was thrown, that to come back up here was to come back to an existence he felt unworthy of him.

But that day after the counter-trial, something changed. Hans came home early, just before lunch. I was still there, doing my best with the filing. He burst in the door.

'I've got it!' he said. His shirt was damp, his face shiny and his hair mussed. 'I can go to see Bertie – that's the one thing I can do.' He was walking around and around the tiny hall outside the cupboard where I sat, not looking at me. His speech was rapid-fire, the plans already made. When I caught them I saw his eyes were livelier than they'd been in a long time – tiny flames of hope blown back into them. He would stop work on the novel immediately, he said. Bertie was even less protected than Lessing had been, and Hans thought he should go to Strasbourg to keep him company and cheer him up.

'And then maybe I can place articles from his *Independent Press*

Service here, and send him back the money.' If that went well, he said, he might be able to make a go of helping more émigrés by placing their work in British publications. 'What do you think?' he asked finally. 'If I can't write my own pieces, I can at least be a middleman.'

It didn't make a lot of sense to me, but I understood that Hans wanted to be out of the flat. I suspected he might want to get some information of his own from Bertie, so as to stop relying on Dora to pass him material. And I understood that by my lack of faith I had let him down. That's as far as my thinking went. *Gezwungene Liebe tut Gott weh.* No one can force anyone to love them.

He was gone within a week.

The day of my twenty-eighth birthday, Hans was still in France. Mrs Allworth came with a basket covered in a check cloth. Something was moving underneath it.

'For you,' she said.

I pulled back the tea towel to find a small ball of black-and-white fur. The kitten was still blue-eyed, a tiny perfect life. I burst into tears.

'Dear, dear,' Mrs Allworth said, 'I just thought —'

'No. It's lovely,' I said. I was not used to ordinary kindnesses any more; to beauty in a basket.

I called him Nepo, for John of Nepomuk, who refused to divulge a queen's secrets. He grew into a quirky, friendly lap-cat and I told him everything.

'I'll tell you everything,' I say to the nurse.

'That's good,' she says. This one I haven't seen before; she must just do the nights. She's dark-skinned, a night angel with a gemstone in her nose. 'That's very good, Ruth.'

TOLLER

The photograph in the paper shows the SS *St Louis* lit up at night like a Christmas tree in Havana harbour, by searchlights from police boats and lamps dangling from its decks to stop people jumping. I also read my own letter, demanding that 'this nation founded by those fleeing persecution accept now these refugees fleeing from a barbarism that seeks to make war against us all'.

Same old story. What did Auden say? He could no longer believe in our better nature. The blue-eyed rabbi in our village at Samotschin used to talk to me as though I were a grown person, even when I was just a boy. We must believe in God, he told me, because if we don't we will have to believe in man, and then we will only be disappointed.

When she comes in she's wearing the same clothes, though I know it's a new day. Her face is lightly powdered; the red scrape on her forehead has faded. She is very pale. She puts my ticket down on the table.

'They're saying at the shipping office there have been suicides on the boat,' she says, just holding it in. 'I can't get a telegram to Paul, they won't let them have any contact with relatives, so we can't know —'

I get up and take her elbow, guide her to the other comfortable chair. 'Have you seen today's *New York Times*?'

'No.'

'There's a new plan. To let them land at the Isle of Pines. Maybe to make a Jewish colony there.' I can see relief and hope tumbling in her, then a backwash of despair. 'It's hard that he is so close.' She nods. 'But,' I touch her shoulder, 'it might just turn out okay.'

'Okay,' she echoes. She turns automatically to her bag for her pad and pencil.

'Mail today?'

'Oh. I forgot. I'll go now.'

When she returns – still no news from my sister – we resume.

After the British sent back that typesetter to the concentration camp, panic spread among the London refugees. Rumours flew that there were informers in our ranks. Dora said some misguided souls thought that informing for the British might help you get a visa, and that informing for the Germans might protect you from Them. In her view there was nothing much you could do about it; you just had to keep your information close.

Hans Wesemann came to see me not long after the counter-trial. He was full of flattery and winning self-deprecation. We talked about his visit to me in prison – more than ten years ago by then. He joked, saying I'd been a 'captive audience', then he apologised, quite sincerely, for having asked me to betray my fellow revolutionaries. He said that he was, unfortunately, the kind of person who thinks of saving himself – *'Sauve qui peut,'* he said with a wry smile – and who forgets that others have broader priorities.

As he talked I looked at his fine face, so ridiculously handsome you could get lost in it. As if he were what the eugenicists would have our species look like, the rest of us just dummy runs.

Wesemann had come offering to place manuscripts of mine with British publishers, for a small percentage fee. When I explained that I had direct dealings with my publishers already, he intimated that I needed, perhaps, 'fresh material' and offered a trip with him to see Berthold Jacob in Strasbourg. He said that with Jacob's information and my profile I could write something 'perfectly devastating' about Germany for the widest possible public here. 'More effect than *anyone* else,' he cooed. I said I'd think about it.

Dora rolled her eyes when I told her. 'He's desperate, poor man,' she said. 'Looking for another coup-by-association with you. It's not his fault, in a way,' she added. 'This is no place for a satirist. Our circumstances are beyond mockery.'

When he wrote to me about it a week later, I declined.

After my speech at the counter-trial was reported around the world, my publisher decided to expedite the publication of some of my essays.

Dora helped me correct the English proofs. We worked in separate rooms because I couldn't stand to hear her pencil moving over the paper. Her corrections were usually good cuts – she made my thoughts clearer and the expression of myself less egotistical. But like a squeamish patient, I didn't want to hear the incisions. Once, she came in holding a double page. Eraser crumbs clung across her chest, and her feet were masked things in their stockings.

'I'm just wondering whether this is what you mean here.' She glanced at me before starting to read. '"There comes to man sometimes a sickness, psychic or spiritual, which robs him of all will and purpose and sets him aimlessly adrift in a longing for death, a longing which lures him irresistibly to destruction, to a mad plunge into chaos."' She looked up, her face neutral.

'Well?' I asked. It is much easier to write something than to speak about it.

'Well, this,' she turned back to the sheet, 'is what comes next —'

'I know what comes next.'

She read it out anyway. '"The old Europe suffered from this dreadful sickness, and with the war she hurled herself into the abyss of suicide."'

I said nothing. I made her say it.

'I'm not sure . . .' Her eyes flicked to the window, then back to me. She breathed in. 'I'm not sure it makes sense to give a continent your psychology.'

I was ready. 'It's not my psychology.'

'Well.' She had a way of speaking to me as if it were understood between us that every word I had written was worthwhile; it might just need to be disentangled. This is the gift of a great editor. She spoke gently, as if only figuring it all out for herself right now, showing me she was not far ahead – in fact, I may have led her there. 'The war,' she said calmly, 'was not caused by Germany drifting aimlessly and longing for death, but acting purposefully and longing for power and colonies.'

'You're right,' I said. 'As ever.' I ran my fingers over the corners of my mouth. 'But I think we should leave it.'

She nodded, slowly. She understood that I wanted to have this said. And that I would never say it, publicly, of myself.

I had known her to be unhappy; I had at times made her unhappy. But I do not believe she ever had that particular sickness, the one that robs you of all will and purpose. I do not believe it.

RUTH

A woman in a headscarf like a Madonna brings the newspapers around the ward every morning, on a trolley. *Give us this day our daily news* . . . Twenty years at the Methodist college and all my references have become Christian. I take the two broadsheets, though I never get through them.

One day, lying on the grass at Regent's Park, Dora rummaged in her big bag and passed me *The Times*. 'Look at this,' she said.

'"Fred Perry: 'I have more Wimbledons in me'",' I read out from the back page.

'Having an affair with Marlene Dietrich, apparently,' Dora said. 'But that's not it. Page three.'

I opened to page three. The headline was 'Versailles Outfoxed'. The byline was a British journalist along with 'first-rate German sources'.

'Mine,' she beamed.

'You first-rate source, you,' I said. She laughed that great, head-thrown laugh of hers. I looked back down at the paper. The article was about how, although the regular German army was limited by the Treaty of Versailles to a hundred thousand men, the paramilitary organisations under Hitler's personal control numbered in the millions. The SA alone now had 2.5 million members who brawled in the streets with impunity.

'So many men,' I wondered aloud. 'He'll have to find something for them to do.'

'It's called a war.' Dora was sitting cross-legged, pulling up single strands of grass and stroking them idly against her palm, then tossing them aside. Ernst Röhm, she said, wanted Hitler to allow the SA to swallow the whole of the regular army, so it would become just a small training arm of the Brownshirts. In its own defence, the army was threatening to declare martial law. 'Which would be the end of Hitler,' Dora said. 'However it plays out,' she tapped the newspaper, 'Versailles is a joke.'

We celebrated her coup at the Marquis of Granby with half-crown meals and wine. We stayed out late, didn't worry about looking over our shoulders at the pub, or in the street. At the end of the evening we walked home arm in arm, our steps in time. The moon was a hole punched in the sky, the light still on behind.

Dora skipped up the few steps to our front door, checked the basket behind it for mail. There was a letter from her mother, one from Bertie to me, and an invitation to the Liberty sale for Hans.

'Nothing sinister in that,' she said.

'I'm not so sure,' I replied. She laughed.

We raced, still elated, up the stairs. I was behind her; she was humming some latest English hit, making time with her steps: '"When my baby/comes to me/we will sit in the —"'

Our door hung open. The lock smashed off the jamb. Inside, the world was white, sharded and broken up. Paper all over the floor. The hall cupboard door in front of us jemmied open too – documents spewed off the shelves. I saw the grey half-print on one of a shoe.

Dora motioned me to silence. Slipped slowly into each room, checking they were gone. Then without a word she went to the cupboard and started to pick up her papers. I looked down where I stood and saw a document from the textile works at Zeulenroda; another typed and signed 'S.A. Black Bear'.

I went into Hans's and my bedroom. Every drawer was pulled open. Underwear, trinkets, my Dutch cap – on the floor. The bed was stripped, strewn with our clothes, the pockets pulled out from trousers and jackets and dresses. The cardboard box I kept my photographs in had been tipped over the floor. I walked out.

In the kitchen the mess was brutal. Drawers had been pulled loose and the cupboards were all open, ashes dumped from the stove and trodden through the flat like a taunt: they knew we couldn't call the police. An egg had been smashed on the counter and Nepo sat lapping at it, calm and neat as ever. *What did you see, puss?* They'd pulled my rolls of film from the ice chest and exposed the reels, which hung now in bizarrely festive curls over the table.

I went back to our bedroom. Books lay pulled open and broken-backed over the rug; the scrolled curtain-rod ends had been unscrewed, as if they might hold something. They lay oddly on the ground like severed ears, or question marks.

Dora was in the doorway, still not speaking.

I looked up. 'They took their time.'

'Or knew where we were.' She was holding a document. 'If this is still here I doubt there's anything missing.' Her hand was shaking. The document was from Bertie, via his source inside the army. It was what Dora had used for the *Times* article.

She gestured around us at the papers everywhere. 'They might have photographed some of this though. Left it all here as evidence to get us with later.'

I understood her words but I couldn't string their sense together. 'Who's they?'

We glanced back at the front door, which we could no longer close, let alone lock.

'Could be either,' she said. She was tapping her lips with her fingers.

I didn't want to sleep in the flat. What if they returned? But Dora said we couldn't go; we couldn't leave all this material here with the door open. For the neighbours, or anyone else, to find. She called Professor Wolf. He came around from his room in Boswell Street, in his hairy cardigan and carrying his briefcase, as if to convince himself he was here on business, or perhaps to give a special, one-off, night-time tutorial. He looked more frightened than we were.

I wedged a chair under the remnants of the lock to keep the front door closed. Then I put a trunk full of books behind it. Dora and Wolf went to bed. I couldn't lie down alone, so I spent the night putting away all the exposed and fingered things in my room. When daylight came I spread fresh sheets on the bed and tried to sleep.

Before Hans got back from France we had a new lock put on the front door, and a thick bolt and chain added across the top. We also had Yale locks fitted on all the internal doors: living room, kitchen, bedrooms, and replaced the one on the hall cupboard. We carried rings of keys and became our own warders.

Dora negotiated with the other tenants in the building to have the fanlight above the entrance door boarded up. She told them we'd suffered a burglary and had money and jewellery taken; she mentioned a 'spate' of thieving in Bloomsbury.

Mr Donovan, the nice retired insurance salesman who lived in the flat underneath us, was used to minutely assessing risk. He said, 'But they didn't get in through the fanlight, did they?'

'No,' Dora replied, 'someone opened the door to them, or they picked the lock.'

'Just to put them off then, is it?' Mr Donovan said, but he didn't object.

I don't think we knew ourselves why we wanted the fanlight boarded up. It doesn't make much sense. Perhaps we were already beyond reason and dealing now in omens and signs, battling an unseen enemy fierce as God.

Dora worked more furiously, if anything, after the break-in. I ran errands for her, delivered messages by hand to other refugees, one or two to Westminster. I bought stationery, cigarettes, groceries. We had a few more desultory party meetings at the flat, at which I took the minutes. But mostly I wanted to be out of there. I worked in the ILP offices on the next edition of *The Other Germany*. And I went to the docks as often as I could.

Late one afternoon Dora came into the kitchen with a piece she was typing. I was washing up.

'Listen to this for me, will you?' She had it in her hand. 'It's Toller. "There comes to man sometimes a sickness, psychic or spiritual, which robs him of all will and purpose and sets him aimlessly adrift in a longing for death, a longing which lures him irresistibly to destruction, to a mad plunge into chaos."'

She looked at me. 'You can't write that if you haven't felt it,' she said. 'Can you?'

I didn't know whether her question was rhetorical or not. 'No,' I said. 'It probably wouldn't occur to you.'

'That's what I tell him.' She sat down. 'I say his insight comes from that dark part of him. If he denies that, he'll be cut off from what feeds his writing.' Her face was as open as I had ever seen it. 'Do you think if you love someone there are parts of them you should pretend are not there?'

I turned around, holding my wet hands out from my sides. I thought of Hans out all night with Edgar, or examining paisley swatches with Werner Hitzemeyer, aka Vernon Meyer. I had told myself that each of us must maintain some small private life, even in a marriage. I did not believe, despite one's best efforts, that the whole world could be made visible. I stared at the table, my eyes hot and full. 'You're asking me?'

'Oh Ruthie,' she said. 'I'm sorry.' She got up and put her arms around me and kissed my shoulder softly. 'I'm not good at this.'

I suppose she meant she was not good at leaving anything tacit. Her bare feet padded back across the lino into her room. The typewriter started up again.

That night I undressed before I remembered to draw the curtains. As I lifted my arms to pull the nightgown over my head I caught my reflection in the black window, the rack of my ribs a cage to hold my heart. I thought of one of my first dates with Hans.

We had gone to the *Rummel*, the local fair. In his caravan on a mock throne sat Agosta the Winged Man. His ribcage was inverted, wings of bone were pushing out the skin of his chest. A single rogue cell division in the gamete and a life is reversed, becomes something to display in order to make the rest of us feel normal. At his feet sat Rasha, an African woman from America, with her chest bared and shells strung around her throat. The shells had gently frilled lips which nearly met but not quite; they were tiny, porcelain-white vulvas, enfolding the darkness inside them. Rasha held no interest for Hans, but Agosta fascinated him, with his fine poet's eyes, his perfect mouth.

Outside the caravan a man in an ape suit approached us. Breath floated out of the mouth-hole in his costume. How little it takes – some fur, a couple of glass eyes, a rubber navel – to make someone into something else. We scratched the ape playfully – *Oo oo ahh ahh* – though we would never have so touched a stranger. Freud was in vogue then, and Hans made a remark about our true inner beast being on display: we wait to see the creature scratch its bottom or pick its ears in public so that we feel more civilised, though deep down we know we are not.

But as I patted the poor fellow in the suit I did not think that we were all bestial inside, waiting only for the opportunity to gratify ourselves, covering with effort and sublimation all our animal desires. I wondered whether it wasn't the other way around; whether inside all of us there might just be a cleaner, purer, more hairless version too naked for the world.

I am aware from his cough of a male nurse who has come in and taken my hand to check my vital signs and scratch them into the all-knowing tablet at the foot of the bed. I keep my one uncovered eye closed. As he finishes I open it to catch him leaving. His hip clips the bunch of keys someone has left in the cabinet by the door. They chinkle and swing.

The keys were hanging on the outside of Dora's bedroom door. I was just home from the docks, mid-afternoon, ten days after the break-in. Nepo jumped up to paw the keyring.

'Dora?' I said softly.

No answer, so I went into the kitchen and made coffee. Her big bag lay on the couch. There was no typewriter clatter. Maybe she had company.

I turned on a lamp and started to sort slides, holding them up to its shade. The flat was very quiet.

A couple of hours later I knocked on her door again – it would be odd for her to sleep during the day. Unwanted thoughts of too much Veronal, too much morphine. Though of course she was the world's expert in these things.

'Dora?' No answer.

Was it locked?

I turned the handle. It felt wrong – what if she wasn't alone? – but

I kept pushing. The *shhhh* of papers moving behind the door, one of the many stacks – a whole city of paper, crooked skyscrapers covering the floor, and I come as the wrecker.

She was lying on the bed fully clothed. Alone.

'Dee?'

Her eyes were open.

'Dora?' I heard the catch in my voice.

She moved her eyes to me and smiled without warmth, without lifting her head. 'Come here.'

I approached the bed. 'What is it? Are you all right?'

'I'm fine,' she said. 'Lie down.' She patted the covers beside her.

I lay down and looked up and it was like being on Primrose Hill again. In our tower I felt the earth's spin. She rolled an arm over me and put her forehead to my shoulder.

'Sometimes, if I am still too long, I freeze,' she said, her words muffling into my body. I knew it wasn't from cold.

I started to talk, to fill the room with sound, painting word-pictures, concrete and contained and, most of all, of things that were alive. I told her that if you look up through the bare twigs of a plane tree against a white sky you can see that the seed pods hang down straight, festive as Christmas decorations. I told her Nepo holds his tail with both paws to clean it. I told her that her ear is a pink cup to catch notes.

She breathed in and out slowly, holding me. 'Don't you leave.'

I suppose she thought that I might also go to France. 'I won't,' I said.

I hadn't written to Hans about the burglary, because there was nothing he could do but worry. As it was, he telegraphed me that he was coming home early. 'All OK here,' it said.

I ran downstairs to meet him. He'd grown a narrow moustache and looked, suddenly, very French. He gestured to the crudely hammered boards above the door, his face twisted into a question. I blurted out then and there about the break-in. His hand flipped to his mouth. For a moment I thought he might not come in.

'We might as well put a red mark on the lintel,' he said.

I hoped for a joke, that he still could. 'To advertise us Reds in here?'

'No.' He shook his head, biting the inside of his top lip. 'To hope we are passed over.'

Hans's account and Bertie's were the same.

Each afternoon the two of them had walked out of Strasbourg proper, along the River Ill. The days were getting shorter, the ground held the sog and feel of winter. Boys out of school played football in a field of unsprung grass. They set the goals at the ends with their satchels, the boundaries of the pitch with pullovers at each corner. There were three on each team, brothers and friends probably, a little one of about nine, and the others twelve or thirteen. On the fourth day the eldest called the two men over into the game.

Hans and Bertie left their coats on the side of the road and joined opposite teams. They had not run for a long time, or felt the air in their lungs and the joy of kicking a ball. Hans had enough French to chat.

'Real leather,' he said, spinning the ball on one finger.

'Birthday present,' the littlest one replied, proud as if he'd sewn it himself.

'Nice,' said Hans. 'I learnt with a rag ball. This is much better!'

Hans was a good kick when the ball got to him, but Bertie was surprisingly nimble, dodging between the others to get it down his team's end so a boy with big knees could kick it between the satchels. 'Yesss!' The boys danced and punched the air, pleased with their new recruit. Bertie beamed, and took off his waistcoat.

'Not bad,' Hans said. He rubbed his hands together, smiled at his team. 'Now let's get serious.'

'Don't listen to him, *mes p'tits*,' Bertie countered. 'We're up, and we're staying up.'

They were still kicking, running and laughing, streaked with mud, when the sun began to set. They could smell wood smoke from the evening fires.

'Don't you boys have homes to go to?' Hans called, panting, from one end of the pitch.

'Nah,' the big one said, 'not till supper time.'

'All right then.' Hans shook his head in mock apology for the slaughter he was about to inflict. 'You asked for it.'

Play was at Bertie's end, but a skinny, determined kid on Hans's team got in and pushed the ball out through the scrum of legs to him. Hans mothered it down the pitch ankle to ankle, trying to stay ahead of the little legs around him. Probably too soon he gave an almighty kick. His leg overstretched and he fell backwards; the ball careened off course, not between the goals at all but way over them, beyond the pitch to the other side of the river. Hans fell groaning to the ground.

'Sorry,' he called. 'Your kick.' He stayed put. 'I think I've done my ankle.'

The boys looked uncertain. The little one was trying not to cry. His brother put his arm around him. They started packing up their things.

'What's the problem?' Bertie asked. 'We'll get it back.'

'We're not allowed,' the brother said. 'The river's the border.'

'It's guarded?' Bertie asked.

'Not here,' the boy said, 'but further down.'

'Righto then,' Bertie said, 'I'll go.' He looked at Hans. 'You all right?'

Hans was packing mud on his ankle. 'I'll be fine in a minute,' he said, not looking up.

Bertie left the pitch and slipped down the embankment to the river, where he found an arrangement of new-looking planks across it. The water was shallow but fast-flowing. He walked in the direction of the kick through a couple of willows. Sky, grass, trees, stones were fading into one another. Still, he should be able to see it, a round, whitish ball. On the other side of the river there was a ridge with a dirt road along the top. It must have come to rest here, over the lip. He scrambled up.

A car, waiting. One in the driver's seat and another standing outside. Holding the ball. Smiling.

Bertie, puffed, smiled back, started to approach. '*Bonsoir*,' he said. The man kept smiling.

And then he knew and turned and bolted, his head white with it, his body so noisy – his chest, feet – he couldn't hear if they were coming behind him. He slid-scattered down the embankment, his back open as a target. He felt nothing, not his feet, not the water.

When he reached the others he couldn't speak.

The boys were gathered around Hans, who was still on the ground holding his ankle. Bertie hid behind them and bent over, wet and struggling for air. 'You – hear – a car?' was the first thing he got out. His eyes were staring, wild. 'You —?'

Hans looked up. 'What?'

'A car.'

Hans understood then. The boys looked at Bertie's empty hands. The little one wiped his face on his sleeve.

'I'll go,' said Hans.

'No!' said Bertie. 'It's just a ball.'

Hans stood gingerly on his foot. 'They're not here for me,' he said.

The worst part, Bertie wrote to me, was not when he'd seen the men. The worst thing was waiting for Hans to return.

It was almost dark when Hans limped back with the ball under one arm. 'Spoke perfect French,' he said to Bertie, in German.

'*Pardonnez-nous ce drame.*' He smiled at the boys as he handed the little one back his football.

The boys ran home, no doubt with stories of panicky, paranoid Germans for their parents.

Bertie put Hans's arm over his shoulder to help him walk towards the lights of town. Both of them aware that the car had not yet put its headlights on, nor turned on its motor.

'Perfect French doesn't mean much,' Bertie mumbled. 'Might still be Them.'

'We need to get you away from the border,' Hans said.

Bertie nodded as he walked and was glad Hans couldn't see his face.

Bertie had a wireless in his attic. 'Listen to this,' he said to Hans on their last afternoon, turning the dial. There were snatches of French, Dutch, Swiss German. When he got to the official Hitler channel he muttered, 'Uh-huh.'

Hans thought he must have wanted to listen to some propaganda, to mine it for what they were covering up. But Bertie kept turning the tiniest bit further. 'Here we are,' he said, sitting down.

It was a single voice, no musical jingles, no announcement of the time, nor the station. 'This channel broadcasts right next to the Hitler channel, hoping people will find it,' Bertie explained. He shook his head a little. 'See if you can pick who it is.'

A male voice was saying, 'How can we allow this pudgy, cake-scoffing homosexual, this flatulent nailbiter, to represent Germany? But seriously, they say that the Leader is a teetotaller, a bachelor, a non-smoking vegetarian, as if he were a man removed from our normal, base desires, uninterested in satisfying himself.

Concerned only with the wellbeing of the German nation. But we say he fulfils his bloodlust in other ways. You do not have to read Dr Freud to know that desire denied does not go away of its own accord. It warps and moves like a river denied its course, it flows on to drown other things. And in the case of Adolf Hitler, those things are us.'

Hans listened intently. Ten minutes later the voice said, 'And I leave you, friends, till 18:00 GMT or 19:00 Berlin time tomorrow.'

Bertie's face broke into a grin, half-clown and half-cemetery, with his crazy hair and crooked, tombstone teeth. 'So, can you guess?'

'Couldn't have put it better myself.' Hans was shaking his head, smiling. 'Is it from inside Germany? That would be out-and-out suicide.'

Bert shook his head.

'The voice is familiar somehow.' Hans smoothed his tiny moustache. 'I give up.'

'Rudi Formis!'

Rudi had staged one 'technical difficulty' too many at the state radio station in Berlin and the Nazis had come after him. He escaped over the border into Czechoslovakia and immediately started assembling a secret radio transmitter in the roof of an inn at Slapy, smuggling in antenna parts and everything else in his suitcase. And from there he had started broadcasting anti-Hitler messages.

Bertie leant back with his hands behind his head. 'Unbelievable, eh?' he said.

'The man is a genius,' Hans said. His eyes were bright. 'He must need people – we could write for him?'

'No.' Bertie's tone was definite. 'He's being very careful. Won't tell anyone where he is. I'm one of the very few who know.'

He couldn't help the pride in his voice. 'Sometimes I send him information, but it's through an intermediary in Prague.'

'Priceless,' Hans said.

'Yoo-hoo.' There's a curtain on a rail that runs inside the door of my room, to give me privacy, and so people don't get a fright, opening straight onto a spectacle such as *moi*. But you can't be protected from everything. A hand and some pinkish fuzz appear on one side of it.

'You right for visitors?' Bev's voice is businesslike and caring at once – so she knows the drill too?

'Come in.'

'Well then,' she says. She pushes aside the curtain with a swoosh and there she is, a huffing and puffing reminder of my other life, the outside one with biscuits and banter and sunshine walks. Bev is wearing a long white T-shirt which hangs down over her pillowy body, and leggings underneath. Around the neck of the T-shirt there are coloured sequins, and for an instant I can think of nothing but a life-size vanilla ice-cream cone with sprinkles. She bustles about, finding a chair and pulling it over, plopping a bulging supermarket bag on her lap.

'What's goin on here, then?'

'Not a lot,' I smile at her.

She smiles back. 'I brought you some things from home.' She takes my toiletries bag out. 'Shampoo and a toothbrush and baby powder and this.' She puts my hearing aid in a ziplock baggie down on the night-table. 'And I got you today's paper.' She hands over the horrible tabloid I do not read, all the junk advertising in its guts spilling out. 'And,' she reaches down to the top of her handbag, 'these.' Bev holds out a little wicker basket. Inside are four of the most luscious purple-green figs I have ever seen, resting in some kind of hay.

'Out of season,' Bev sniffs, 'four dollars *each*.' This is as close to a declaration of love as I have had in a long time.

'Exquisite,' I say. 'Thank you very much.' Bev knows how I love fruit, even if she laughs at me for sometimes eating it with a knife and fork. I touch them. The precious, soft-skinned figs bring their pregnant beauty into this sterile place. They have cost her nearly an hour's pay.

'They are just perfect,' I say, and I see she is chuffed. To deflect her pleasure she picks up the newspaper.

'Them tree killers are at it again over in Woollahra,' she says, whacking the paper with the back of a hand. Woollahra is a grand suburb, where developers have been known to sneak out in the dead of night to poison 150-year-old Moreton Bay figs so that their flats will boast broader harbour views. Like many things here, it is only evident in the perpetrators' denial. '*Disgusting*,' Bev tuts.

I look at the paper and recognise the spot where the magnificent tree used to be. The underside of the fecundity of this place is its avidity: for sex, for money. This town is all about getting away with it. If I close my eyes I can see Seven Shillings Beach below where the tree was, a strip of white sand looking across the water to the city, with an aqua boathouse at one end. A small sign on a cyclone gate declares it to be a private beach belonging to the mansions behind it, from the high-tide mark up. But the gate is always open and everyone, mansion owners and public alike, completely ignore this rule. We are all dazzled by beauty here; it is a prelapsarian world where people kill for the view but everything is always, already forgiven.

'Pardon?' I say. Bev is saying something.

'How about a hand massage then?' She leans into her bag for a tube of cream. 'Oh yes,' she says, 'and here's your mail.' She puts the letters on the bedside stand, all of them uninteresting window-envelopes I know I won't open. I see now, that it has come down to Bev and me. She will have to do so much for me.

Bev takes her rings off and starts to massage my left hand. It feels surprisingly lovely, the freesia smell, the touch.

'Am I one of your old ducks now?'

She laughs. 'Nah.' She is kneading along the sinew behind each knuckle. 'You're too tough.'

I look down at my gnarly old hand. 'You're right about that.' She is working it, her head bent so I can't see her face, just her bright hair as it goes, sparse and strange, into her waxy white scalp. She is pummelling my palm, then pulling finger by finger. She catches her breath.

'You're,' she pulls, 'my,' she pulls again, 'eagle.'

It was around then, in the spring of 1934, that we started getting hate mail at Great Ormond Street. It was always locally postmarked, usually a phrase typed in the middle of the page, addressed to each of us individually. You couldn't call it inventive, but it was effective. 'PREPARE TO DIE BITCH' was one of Dora's. I got 'JEW CUNTS WILL DIE' and Hans 'YOU *CHOSE* THIS.' There were others. We showed them to each other and then burnt them in the stove.

After a couple of months there were calls in the night too. You'd answer the phone to emptiness, not even audible breath. The first few times I screamed, 'Who's there? Who's there?' into the handpiece. Dora put her finger on the lever to cut off the call. 'Don't give them the pleasure,' she said. Hans simply didn't pick up.

One day, I stood at the kerb on Farringdon Road, momentarily stuck, the flow of life on the pavement opening and closing around me like a stream around a rock. I wondered if fifteen paces back someone tailing me had stalled too. In this place our fates were being determined by forces which occasionally revealed themselves – in an unsigned threat, a shadow, a silent call, a plague of white paper in the flat. I felt like a bear in the Colosseum thinking that the situation he sees before him – overwhelming as it is – is the world to be dealt with, yet below him a thousand slaves on pulleys are changing every scene and the end is predetermined by forces greater than the greatest strength he might muster.

A traffic policeman stood on a podium in the road, arms moving from the elbows like a puppet. A scarlet bus careened into the kerb, disgorging its passengers, all of them with somewhere to go. They filed past a street-sweeper in a soft cap with a long-handled dustpan, they wove as if of a single understanding around a group of children being walked out of school. All around me life moved but I could not grasp it.

Although I knew then that there were real forces bearing down on us, this feeling has remained with me all my life, whether in the bustle of London or the beauty of Sydney, on water or land: that there is complex machinery at work, there are invisible roads in the sea, and there is a meaning to all this which I cannot, for the life of me, uncover.

But we were better off in London than in Germany. That last week of June 1934, home was a slaughterhouse. Most of the murders were made public. They trumpeted them about, so we didn't even need to rely on party sources in Germany. The Nazis called it the Röhm Putsch, as if their actions had been in response to a coup attempt. We saw it for the meticulously planned massacre it was and called it the Night of the Long Knives.

On 30 June, before dawn, Hitler had flown from Berlin to Munich. He'd called a meeting with Ernst Röhm, at Röhm's hotel by the lake at Bad Wiessee. Röhm may have thought the Leader was coming, finally, to offer him control of the army. He and the leaders of the SA were sleeping off hangovers. Hitler, his chauffeur and some armed SS men ran through the corridors of the Hanselbauer Hotel, bursting open doors, screaming at the groggy men to wake up, get dressed, get out. When some were found in bed together Hitler pretended outrage and ordered them to be shot immediately in the hotel's grounds, though he had long known of Röhm's penchant for young recruits. Others were bundled into cars, taken to Stadelheim Prison in Munich and shot there in the yard.

When Hitler got to Röhm's door he had the guards open it without knocking. He told Röhm to put his clothes on. Röhm mumbled a sleepy *'Heil, mein Führer,'* and went downstairs and found himself an armchair in the lobby. He ordered coffee from a waiter. Then they put him into a car for Stadelheim too.

But this was broader than Hitler's annihilation of a too-powerful paramilitary. He and Göring had already drawn up a List of Unwanted Persons. When the killing in Munich was done, Hitler phoned Göring in Berlin and gave the order for SS cells in towns all over Germany to open their sealed lists of names, their slices of the master list of the unwanted. Then the local Nazis got to work.

General Kurt von Schleicher, the former Chancellor, they shot in the study of his villa, along with his wife, who tried to protect him. They shot the leader of Catholic Action, Erich Klausener, at his desk in the Transport Ministry because he'd spoken out against Nazi violence. They shot Father Bernhard Stempfle, a priest who had helped Hitler write *Mein Kampf* while he was in prison and knew too much about him. They shot Karl Ernst, a Berlin SA leader who may have been involved in the burning of the Reichstag and needed silencing. By nightfall on 1 July more than two hundred associates, acolytes and committed Nazis, as well as independents, conservatives, military men and political leaders, had been slaughtered. Over a thousand more were under arrest.

But Berlin, we heard, celebrated. Hitler declared the next day, 2 July, to be a flag-waving holiday. In a speech to the nation he declared himself above the law.

It is a mystery to me how people can believe they are being made safer when events clearly show that it is no safer to be a friend than an enemy, and that you might be switched from one column to the other on a whim.

Some saw it, though, for what it was: the consolidation of a killer's state. And within that state one, at least, was turned.

They have added something to the drip. It is collapsing time. I see things I have imagined so many times that they are fact to me. And other things I have known without seeing.

The problem with life is that you can only live it blindly, in one direction. Memory has its own ideas; it snatches elements of story from whenever, tries to put them together. It comes back at you from all angles, with all that you later knew, and it gives you the news.

I knew him once. His hair is receding and his glasses have no rims. His suit is fine and on his little finger he wears a signet ring with the family crest. His new office is large; heavy curtains in red and gold frame the windows in the Berlin Ministry of the Interior. The rich carpet muffles his footfalls as he walks the room. Erwin Thomas is in too much pain to sit. Yesterday they killed his dear friend and mentor Kurt von Schleicher. The thought of Kurt and Ada slumped over the desk at their villa in Neubabelsberg with bullets in their brains makes his jaw clench and his fists curl till his nails bite the palms. It is partly anger, and partly to hold his resolve.

The phone rings.

'Yes,' he says. 'It is drafted.' He listens to the receiver for a moment. 'It is a single article.' He is looking at the paper on his desk. 'No sir, I do not foresee any difficulties there. Sir. Heil Hitler.'

He resumes pacing. His secretary knocks and comes in to remind him of a lunch appointment. He tells her to cancel.

'Your ulcer?' she asks.

'That will do.' She is a fine girl.

He picks up the phone again and puts it down. On his desk

lies the law he has drafted, at Göring's personal request, to justify the killings this week. Though it is but a single article, it is enough to undo all his faith and training. He reads it once more, still standing.

3 July 1934
Law Regarding Measures of State Self-Defence

The measures taken to put down the seditious and treasonous attacks of 30 June and 1 and 2 July 1934 are hereby declared lawful as ones of state self-defence.

Thomas knows there is no such thing as state self-defence. There is only political murder. But he did what he was told. Again.

He sits and takes fresh letterhead from the desk drawer. He is a man in command of language, argument. He is one of the best educated, he is the epitome of culture and loyalty. Look where that has got him. He picks up a fountain pen. Puts it down. Taps a cigarette on his silver case and lights it.

And then it comes to him: the one thing she will recognise. He starts to write. The note is very short. He seals it in an envelope which he does not address, slides it inside his breast pocket. He collects his coat and hat from the stand near the door, shoots his cuffs without thinking and walks into the July heat of Wilhelmstrasse, in the direction of the Foreign Office.

The flat at Great Ormond Street had come to seem like a place besieged, by phone calls and mail and eyes under hat brims in the street. We tried not to think about it too much; we would have gone mad if we had.

I found myself more and more often at the docks. The boats

came in and went out to all the untouched places of the world: to Monrovia and Singapore and Fremantle. Through Mr Allworth I became friendly with a manager, Mr Brent, who let me go wherever I wanted, as long as I looked out for myself. I was making a series of prints about the work in the dry dock, starting with the *Muscatine*, a huge, anvil-bellied ship, magnificent as a building. It rested on wooden blocks, each the size of an automobile. At the front its anchor chain spewed down, hundreds of metres long, and lay coiled on the ground as if it were the intestine of a majestic beast. Men in overalls and caps checked the links, pecking over them like tiny, cleansing birds.

One morning a worker came to tell me that a lady was waiting for me in the site office. When I got there Dora stood up, pale as if she'd been punched.

'Is there somewhere we can go?' she asked. I took her to my favourite teashop nearby.

A letter had come this morning, after I'd left the flat. She passed it to me across the table. It wasn't in a plain envelope, like the others. This one had the crest of the Reich Foreign Office on it.

'Open it,' she said. Inside was another envelope, with 'Ministry of the Interior' embossed on the left-hand side.

'The —'

'Just read it,' she snapped.

The note was very short, handwritten, unsigned. *It is finished, this being a fig leaf over power. Please call First Secretary Jaeger at Whitehall 7230.*

Fear was like static in my brain. I knew the expression 'fig leaf over power' from my childhood but I couldn't make sense of the note.

Dora slid her forearms across the table and took the letter back. She folded it and slipped it into her bag between other documents. I waited for her to speak. When she did, her voice had the clipped, businesslike tone it got when she was afraid.

'Is this what Helmut got? An invitation to call the German embassy?'

'No,' I said. 'He had his papers cancelled by the Home Office here – it was all done through the English. After that he had to report to the German embassy, because they said he'd be illegally on British soil.'

'Right. Right.' Dora breathed in. Chewed her cheek under her hand. She looked around. People were eating soup, or sandwiches cut in perfect triangles, drinking tea with their meal.

'It might be a trap,' I said. The idea of something happening to Dora was a worse terror than something happening to me. My mind raced. What could they possibly want with an exiled opposition journalist other than to do something harmful? They were singling her out. Unless it had to do with her mother back in Berlin – oh God, what could they be doing to Else? We knew other refugees whose family members had been taken hostage and put into camps in order to force home those who'd left.

'Yes,' she said. She started to pick and tear at the ragged skin around her thumbnail with her index finger, then put it to her teeth. She put her hand down crossly.

'You might not come out,' I continued despite myself, my voice high with the effort not to cause a scene. 'They might send you —'

She reached for my hands. 'Shhh. I'm not going in there. We can agree on it, second it and minute it.' She forced a smile. Her fear seemed to have transferred itself onto me; being the comforter made her stronger again. I blew my nose. She let go of me and started spinning the sugar bowl around between her hands. 'It's just that . . .' She looked over my shoulder. The waitress had appeared. We ordered ham sandwiches and tea and the girl cleared the table.

'It's just that what?' I asked as the waitress left.

'I know who the letter is from,' Dora said. She put the sugar bowl back.

'Who?'

She didn't answer me, but spoke as if to herself. 'Which is not to say it isn't still a trap.' She wouldn't be drawn further.

Dora didn't burn the letter, but she didn't respond to it either.

Two weeks later another one came, in the same two envelopes. This time it was an offer to meet in a public place of her choice. She called the embassy number and said she'd come in.

I went with her. The embassy was in St James's, a grand corner building on Carlton House Terrace. Inside, long corridors led off an atrium. Dora and I sat on a carved wooden bench. I had come because she wanted me to, because we both thought – completely irrationally – that if they were going to make her disappear it might be harder with two of us.

The assistant who came to get Dora wore an enamel swastika brooch on her lapel. The woman ignored me.

'Shall I wait here then?' I asked her.

'If you like,' the woman said to the space above my head.

'How long will they be?'

'Impossible to say.'

I started to choke, to battle for air. Dora leaned into my ear as she stood up. 'Don't let them see it,' she whispered.

Waiting makes your mind roll forward, uncontrolling all the waking dreams. I tried to focus on small things: the lion's paw leg of the bench opposite, the zigzag pattern of the floor tiles, the heavy frosted lights hanging from chains at intervals along the ceiling. I watched the doors in the corridor open and shut, releasing sometimes the bleat of a phone, sometimes a person. Secretaries in neat suits and stockings walked past me, their hair coiffed and mouths painted, interchangeable assistants. They looked capable of reducing anything to an administrative decision, a memo in sub-numbered paragraphs. I felt dishevelled, scrappy, undeserving of a place in this lacquered, decided world, even though I'd taken some care this morning: my one skirt suit, spare underwear in my bag. I couldn't have told you if I'd dressed and packed for detention or to ward it off.

After a time I ceased to think. I counted doors. I blurred my eyes in and out of focus. *She will come back to me.* Part hope and part anxiety, this dumb lay prayer would keep her safe. *She will come back to me.*

One of the doors further down the corridor opened. It was a man. Disappointed, I kept watching so as to take my mind with him, step by lanky step away from here. He passed a secretary, who nodded at him familiarly. He was walking towards the other end of the corridor where there was a window, and as his knees bent a diamond of light formed and unformed between them. A clench in my stomach: I knew that walk. I knew from its long-legged laxness it was Hans.

I believe I would have let him go.

In front of him another door opened. Dora came out.

They stood at twenty paces from one another, a moment of recognition. And then I was up, running to them. Hans turned to watch me come, the third wheel spinning.

'What are you doing here?' Dora was asking as I reached them.

'Dora,' he said, calmly. He was in his good suit. 'Fancy seeing you here.' He turned to me. 'Ruthie.' He kissed me ceremonially on the cheek then drew a fine paisley-print handkerchief from his pocket. He dabbed his forehead. 'I am here,' he said in a low voice, 'to try to help Bertie. With a passport.' He smiled, a little sheepishly, I thought. 'Wasn't going to tell you till it worked.' Then he tilted his chin at Dora. 'Though I might ask you the same question.' The smile was still there, but his eyes were steady, unflickering.

It was the only time I ever saw her pause for an answer, look unconvinced of herself. She cleared her throat.

'Same,' she said. 'Me too.'

After we got home Hans went out to the shops for beer and

chips. Dora couldn't stop smiling, couldn't sit down. She told me she now had a source from very high up – a legal adviser to Göring, no less. It was a chink in the great machine; it was *unbelievable*. She couldn't tell me who it was, of course, that would endanger him. And me as well, if They thought I knew.

But in the relief of her coming out of there safe and sound my mind had unfrozen and it had come back to me. I remembered being a child watching a jaw flex in anger through a crack in the door, and I remembered her fig-leaf quip. I knew who the source was.

We heard Hans's footfalls on the wooden steps. Dora lowered her tone and put her hands on my forearms. 'Don't get upset,' she said. I sensed what was coming. In that instant all joy from this little victory drained from me. 'You can't tell Hans. At all.'

'That's not fair,' I said. 'You leave him out all the time. It makes him worse.'

'Look,' she said, 'we don't know what he was doing at the embassy.' She wouldn't voice her suspicions, whatever they were.

'Same as you, remember?'

She let go of me. Her look changed from one of a tiny Napoleon to a sympathetic friend. 'It's not even that. Really, it's just that the fewer people who know anything of this at all, the less likely our source will be exposed. I know it's hard, but you have to go along with me on this.'

I'd never been able to disobey her.

The three of us celebrated that night over steaming chips rolled out in newspaper. We toasted Bertie's future and told ourselves we were closer to getting him out. 'Great minds,' Hans said to Dora as they chinked glasses.

In my memory I have a fisheye lens and I see us from a high corner in that little kitchen. I watch the lithe dark one who speaks with her hands, fiddles with cigarettes and matches, chews her fingernails while someone else is talking. Her shoes are off and one knee is bent up to the table. I see the stiller, quieter me, smiling and torn. And I see Hans, drinking and joking like a man saved, like one who has found his god or been admitted to a longed-for club. It looks like we are together, we three, in the picture.

That was our life then, a sequence of celebration and despair, as if the whole world were on drugs.

As Hans and I got ready for bed I couldn't help it. I'd bottled it up all day. 'Why didn't you tell me what you were going to do?' I blurted.

He was sitting half undressed, his bare torso soft in the light, something so known to me, so dear. I sat down beside him.

'I just wanted to pull a rabbit out of a hat.' His face was sorrowful. He kissed me. 'I don't even know if it'll work.' He looked at the floor. 'I can't have another failure.' He meant in front of Dora.

I put my hand on his knee. 'Next time, you tell me,' I said. 'I hate this feeling.'

He nodded. 'I'm sorry,' he said. 'I know.'

TOLLER

The bell rang at my Hampstead flat. I looked out the window. There she was again, standing on the stoop, black hair twisting the sun inside itself, pale summer dress. I had not seen her for a month. Next to her was a suitcase, a dun-coloured rectangle with a horn handle that looked vaguely familiar.

Christiane was out buying groceries. She would likely come back before going to lunch with her new friends from the theatre group.

I opened the door to a moment of adjustment; Dora's face no longer fitted the picture I had been quietly nursing. Was she taller? Paler? The sockets around her eyes were darker. A nicotine stain on her eyetooth that wasn't there before. The mind makes a shoddy likeness – oh, why can't we hold on to them properly? But in less than a second the mistaken memory-picture was obliterated by the breathing, smiling reality of her: she is here.

'I have something for you.' The voice was the same, airy and sure.

I looked down at the case. It was, indeed, one of mine.

'Come in, come in.' She moved to step over the threshold

but I didn't give her any room and leant in instead, kissed her full like a homecoming. She tasted of mint and smoke and something in me was stronger. I put my hand on the small of her back and pressed her into me.

'Nice to see you too,' she smiled, pulling away. 'Can you bring it up?'

The case was heavy. In my room I opened the straps and pulled its hinges apart and saw my own words, typed and bound with metal-clasped elastic. *I Was a German* on the top, and *Look Through the Bars* underneath it. There were poems and a sheaf of notes from my bedside table stuffed in the sides. Thoughts I did not remember having and would never have again. Though it was my past it felt like my future: I was restored to myself. My eyes filled.

'How . . . ?' I dreaded to think it had cost her, or someone close to her, something awful.

She moved from one foot to the other and I noticed she was wearing evening shoes, midnight-blue velvet and completely out of character. She was beaming. Her happiness was always someone else's.

'Uncle Erwin Thomas!' she said. 'The other case is coming soon.'

She was alight. She kicked off her shoes and tucked her legs beneath her on the bed.

Two weeks before, she said, she had been summoned to the German embassy on Carlton House Terrace. She was terrified that because German law applied there she might go in and not come out. But it helped to go with Ruth. 'She was more frightened than I was,' she said, adjusting the pillow behind her back. 'So I had to keep my wits. The whole place was very *graaand*, but it still smelt like boiled potatoes.' Which is to say, she smiled, of Germany.

'So I concentrated on that for a while, till I was taken in to meet with First Secretary Jaeger. Tall, fair-haired, in his mid-forties with duelling scars. He handed me a sealed letter. The first thing I saw was the signature. When I looked up I couldn't tell from this Jaeger person's face if it was some kind of a test, or a trap. So I said, "Old family friend," thinking I might need a reason to be receiving mail from the legal division of the inner sanctum of Göring's office. Then Jaeger told me he'd brought it by hand from Thomas, and that he shared his concerns. "We are not,' he said, "all Nazis here yet."'

Dora tried hard, she told me, to imagine the well-fed moral anguish trapped under that fine suit and silk cravat. The difficulty must have showed in her face, because then Jaeger offered, 'Tell us how we can prove ourselves to you.'

She took my face in her hands. 'So, Mr Public Enemy Number One,' she said, 'I told them I wanted this case, intact and unopened, to be brought from the garden shed at the Bornholmer Strasse allotments to me. The other one is coming later.'

I looked down. It was an ordinary case. She had risked her life twice now for it.

'And one other thing.' She rummaged in her bag between manila folders and index cards with rubber bands around them and folded newspapers. 'This.' She pulled out an envelope and passed it to me. Inside was the blue carbon of a memorandum addressed to Minister Göring. It listed the numbers of warplanes secretly being put at the disposal of the Reich.

'How on earth . . . ?'

'I didn't even ask for this,' she said. 'Uncle Erwin wants to be my source now. To save his own dear soul.'

She wanted me to keep the carbon, and his three letters to her. In case they came searching the flat again.

We made love in the bed and Christiane did not come home. She might have – I trailed my coat again for fate to make the decision for me – but she didn't.

'Nice shoes,' I said as she reached down for them.

'Ruth gave them to me. Too small for her.' She was suddenly, uncharacteristically self-conscious. Her ears reddened. She stayed bent over. 'Thought you might like them.'

'They're evening shoes, Dee.' She raised her head and sat up.

'Does it matter?' It wasn't a reproach, but a genuine question.

She slipped her feet, sinewy and fine, into the velvet, did up some buttons at the front of her dress. I watched her leave from the window. She wore no slip and as she walked from the house the dress floated around her knees, caught the curve of her arse.

RUTH

It was a Sunday. Early February, 1935. Dora burst through the door, flushed from running up the stairs.

'Front page this time!' She threw the newspaper on the table.

The *Sunday Referee* headline was 'Troops, Tanks and 'Planes'. The byline read 'From an anonymous correspondent'.

Hans looked over my shoulder as we scanned the article. It detailed Germany's secret build-up of troops, the importation of materials and parts for tanks, and, in extraordinary detail, the construction program of the Reich's military air fleet, including the exact numbers and types of aircraft the Germans were making, the weapons they could carry, the range they were capable of flying, even the locations of their hangars. Most incredibly, the correspondent said, documents made available to the newspaper showed that these warplanes would be ready for deployment within three months. The article concluded: 'This clearly demonstrates that the intention of Herr Hitler's government is to wage a war in which the targets are civilians in the great cities of Britain and France. There is no other reason for such an amassing of aerial power.'

We were ecstatic. Hans gave Dora a spontaneous hug. It looked as if her risks were paying off; as if the world would be warned and saved, and us along with it.

Dora was right to be so happy. Two days later Seymour Cocks, a Labour member, stood up in the House of Commons brandishing a document which, he said, 'gives an elaborate and detailed account of the present air organisation in Germany'. Cocks begged the house to pay attention to what Herr Hitler was doing. And then Winston Churchill, a backbencher for the Conservatives, also used Dora's information in a speech to parliament. 'The mighty Germans,' he said, 'that most technologically advanced nation, mean to have a war and we will be in it.' He pleaded for Britain to take the threat seriously, to arm herself instead of indulging in 'pacific dreams'.

The morning after Dora's article appeared, I woke to a knock at our door. Hans's side of the bed was empty.

They hadn't buzzed from downstairs, so I suppose someone must have let them into the building. There were two of them. A tall one in a uniform, double-breasted with brass buttons, and a short detective in a brown suit. I couldn't think. Plainclothes man spoke before I could.

'Scotland Yard,' he said, opening a leather wallet and flashing a shiny identification badge. 'Alien Registration Division.'

Fear trawled through me like cold.

'We have a warrant to search these premises for evidence of activities incompatible with your residency status.'

I'd stepped back automatically and they were inside the flat already, holding their hats in front of them. Dora was still in her room. The little detective was dark as a Cornish miner, the tall one in uniform blond and upright. It's finished, I thought. Every cupboard and drawer of the flat was filled with papers that could only mean we were doing political work. Not to mention those all over the floor of Dora's room.

She emerged, pulling the door closed behind her. 'Good morning,' she said. She was dressed but her face was puffy from sleep. She had socks on her feet.

She extended her hand to the men. 'Could I see that warrant? If you don't mind.'

'Of course, ma'am.' The short fellow nodded to the uniformed man, who handed her a typed piece of paper. I saw the letterhead over her shoulder: 'New Scotland Yard'. When Dora passed it back her hand was shaking.

She spoke in German. 'They're Germans,' she said to me.

Something was making it hard for me to breathe.

'Do you wish us to call an interpreter, ma'am?' the detective asked, friendly enough. His English was flawless.

Dora continued in German, her voice icy. 'That won't be necessary.'

My mind raced. Was this a delaying tactic? If they went to fetch an interpreter we'd have time to move the most sensitive material. At least the documents that would deliver Bertie and Uncle Erwin straight to them.

'I'd like to meet your boss,' Dora went on in her cut-glass German.

Saliva pooled in my mouth.

'I am sorry, ma'am,' the detective said, enunciating very slowly and clearly. 'I don't speak German. Would you speak in English, please? As you began?'

Dora had a thread of scorn in her voice I had never heard. 'Why don't I call your office right now?' She looked down at the warrant in his hand. 'The number must be here, no?'

The detective glanced at his underling, who shrugged. I blurted, in English, 'There is nothing illegal in this flat, sirs, we have in fact ourselves been burgled —'

'They know that!' Dora hissed, still in German. Then, in a

voice so calm, so full of hatred: '*Sie wollen deine Furcht.*' They want your fear.

She moved to face the tall one. 'Nice uniform. But then your kind like dressing up – don't like yourselves much, do you? Bet you've got lovely big boots at home.' She turned to the little one, who was not much taller than she. Tapped her nose. 'What happened to you? Worried you might be mistaken for a Jew?'

The men stood there, blank-faced.

'They don't understand —' I started.

'Shut *up.*'

'Dee, please —'

'Ruth, that's *enough.*' She was looking from one man to the other now. 'You know, boys, the education you so resent has its uses.' She snatched the warrant back from the tall one and held it up.

'Fucking amateurs. No Englishman signs his name *Lord* Trenchard. You take this back to Berlin and tell them from me: a peer uses one word only. Trenchard.'

The smaller man had his back against the door now, which hadn't been shut after they came in. He was blinking.

'Get out,' Dora told them.

'*Hure,*' the tall one muttered as she shut the door behind them. Whore.

She turned the key in the lock. Their footsteps thudded down the wooden stairs and then were absorbed by the carpet. My heart beat so hard I could hear the blood in my ears. I went to the bathroom and threw up.

When I came out she was at the kitchen table. 'I'm sorry.' My voice was tangled, my eyes stinging. 'I didn't realise —'

'How could you know?' She wasn't angry any more. 'It's one of those class foibles. And only the case in writing. I know it from Dudley, I suppose.' She moved a hand to her mouth in an unconscious gesture of comfort. Then waved it away. 'It doesn't matter.'

But I saw her hand was trembling and her arms too, shoulders, teeth. I lowered myself into the chair opposite.

'Probably better that Prinz-Albrecht-Strasse come after us than the real Scotland Yard, anyway,' she said, thinking aloud.

'Really?'

'Well,' she steadied her hands on the table and looked at me squarely, 'they can't send us home.'

'No. I suppose not,' I said. 'Golly gosh, I feel a whole lot better now.'

Dora smiled fleetingly. Then she leant forward and took hold of my wrists. Her palms were damp. 'I don't want you to tell Hans.'

It was an order, an entreaty, and an invitation to betrayal, all at once. I shifted back in my chair, away from her eyes. Her hands slipped down to hold both of mine.

'I mean it, Ruthie.' She was gripping me. 'I want you to swear it.'

'You're wrong about him.'

'I hope so.' Her fear came out like anger. 'Just swear it.'

The command in her voice riled me. 'I *know* you're wrong!' I cried. I had mistrusted him once; now I would make good by defending him. I pulled my hands away. 'I can't stand all these secrets, I —'

'Where is he now?' There was no bitterness in her voice and she was looking at me squarely.

'He said he had a meeting about an article. Dee, please – don't make me shut him out. It's hard enough for him.'

'For *all* of us.' She meant it. 'You swear it to me.'

Afterwards she went to the bathroom cabinet and got what she needed. And I told myself that I was protecting Hans by not telling him, not adding to his terror.

*   *   *

Rudi's murder did not rate a mention in any London paper. Why would it, the murder in February '35 of an obscure German radio technician exiled in Czechoslovakia? Some people from our party went out from Prague to the inn near Slapy, where Rudi had been living under the name of Otto Fenech. They pieced together what happened from talking with the publican, the maid and the Czech police.

Rudi had been in the hotel for six months. The staff considered him a quiet fellow who liked to chat but spent most days in his room. By midwinter he was the only guest.

One Tuesday a young German couple came to dine at the inn. They got into conversation with Rudi because he was the only other person there. On the Saturday they returned, bringing another friend. The friend remained up in his room, while the three others dined together. After the meal the girl fought with her boyfriend, who excused himself and went upstairs, saying he'd drunk too much. 'Good riddance,' the girl said.

The publican described this girl as exquisite, fair and slim and fine. It looked, he said, like she might have drunk too much as well. Once her boyfriend had left, she nestled in close to Rudi.

Rudi was upstairs escorting her back to her room when the third man appeared in the bar, the maid ahead of him at gunpoint, her hair in papers. As she and the publican were herded down into the cellar they heard two shots, followed some moments later by a third.

When the meat delivery man let them out the next day they went up and found Rudi in the corridor. He had been shot in the chest and also, the *coup de grâce*, in the forehead. There were nail streaks on his wrist.

A trail of blood led down the stairs and outside to where the visitors' car had been parked. Afterwards, Bertie learnt from sources in the government that the girl had been wounded – one of the shots must have clipped her as she stood with Rudi. She was Edith

Sander, hired by the Gestapo to accompany its agents Naujocks and Schoenemann. The men carried her to their car and raced to Germany. A policeman who stopped them for speeding said he'd seen no girl, only a pile of blankets in the back. When they went to take her out at the Leipzig hospital she was dead.

Strangely, Rudi's transmitter, so lovingly installed in the roof, had not been disturbed. Bertie heard that Göring was pleased with the success of the mission. The 'boyfriend', Naujocks, was promoted.

Rudi's murder racked me more than Lessing's, and not just because I'd known him. What I hated most, after the fact of his death, was the interval between the last shots – the time he must have lain breathing his own blood on the floor, aware it was the end.

And I was distressed, too, by the slow ebbing of the girl's life in the speeding car, even though she was one of Them. It was the knowing what was coming, the fatal black curtain, that got to me. Did she think, And that was it? That was *me*? I started to wake with night terrors, often in a half-empty bed.

Hans, though, seemed to be managing better. He was busy finding publications for articles by refugees and taking solace in his nights on the town. As I winnowed out my feelings about Rudi's killing, I realised it was also the elaborate, theatrical effort they had gone to that troubled me. The first, innocent visit of the lovers to the inn, and the later ruse of their drunkenness and spat. Their Czech number plate. The speeding back over the border to backslapping and beer and the awarding of breastpins. And a dead girl written off as matériel on their ledger.

'Do you think they rehearsed it?' I wondered aloud to Hans. We were walking under the plane trees near the British Museum. 'I mean, how do you think they plan these things?' I had my camera gear in a backpack. My hands were fluttering loosely in front of me, shaping messy questions in the air. 'Does someone —'

'Shhh,' he said, eyes to the pavement. 'Keep your voice down.'

I lowered my voice. 'I want to know,' I said. I had to get this fear out of me. 'Do you think they sit in their offices in Prinz-Albrecht-Strasse and one bright spark comes up with the plan, another with the dialogue, a third with the costumes —'

'Honestly, Ruthie.' His voice was scornful, sharp. He was shaking his head and breathing heavily, concentrating on his tread on the pavement. Our most common ground, our most uniting activity, had always been to make something ridiculous. Or at least to see, together, the ridiculous in our own situation.

Why wouldn't he play the game, our game, any more? It was a refusal of intimacy, the in-joke of our marriage.

Perhaps he was too afraid to talk about it, I told myself. Though the way he went about each day as if nothing had happened, it was hard to tell. I didn't know if his was true insouciance or a front. I let it drop. On the one hand I didn't want to increase his fear, and on the other, if I was wrong, I couldn't begrudge him for managing better, under fire, than the rest of us.

It was worst of all for Bertie. Rudi's murder shattered him. Whatever equilibrium he had managed to recover after the football incident – mainly just by allowing day upon day to accumulate between him and it – left him. The courage to continue in Strasbourg rested on the belief that he would be all right, and he simply couldn't summon that up any more in a place where the Gestapo could kidnap him on an afternoon drive. Hans had had no luck obtaining a passport from the embassy, where the officials told him all passports had to be issued from Berlin.

And Bertie was poorer than a church mouse. Hans and I did what we could. Once, we sent him a pair of boots. We tried to sell subscriptions to his *Independent Press Service* bulletin in Britain, but we had few takers. Bertie sent Hans chapters of the book he was writing on the Reichstag fire, called *Who? Inside the Arsonists' Arsenal* – in which he attributed responsibility to a clique close to Göring – hoping Hans might place them in journals. We sent him money occasionally, telling him it was from selling his material and enclosing a copy of an article from a British newspaper or magazine that covered similar topics – a report from an unnamed political prisoner, the training methods of the SS. Mostly though, it was money of mine.

One afternoon, Hans came back uncharacteristically happy.

'Dora home?' he asked.

'No.'

'Sit down, Ruthie.' He had an idea. His face was bright with it. His friend Werner, he said, knew a graphic designer in Switzerland who was now forging passports. If we could just get Bertie to him, along with fifty pounds, this man could make him a perfect passport.

'Well?' he beamed. Hans looked as happy as if he were saving himself.

'But how does Bertie get into Switzerland, without a passport?' I asked. I didn't know quite how to believe in such a plan.

Hans grabbed my shoulders. 'They barely check from France,' he said. 'Look, I know it's risky – but he could be snatched from Strasbourg now, as it is!' He squeezed me. 'This fellow has done lots of passports before. None have been found out. It's Bertie's only chance.'

I felt an uneasy lurch – I couldn't tell if it was hope or fear.

'Have you told him?'

'Not yet.' He kissed my forehead. 'And another thing,' he said, 'you can't tell a soul.'

'Of course not.'

'Not even Dora,' he said. He looked at me tenderly, his eyes bluer than blue. 'I'm telling you because I promised you I would.'

I nodded, slowly. I could see he wanted to do something useful, pull his rabbit out of the hat. 'Bertie won't be telling a soul either,' he added.

For several weeks I put by what I could from my father's money. We needed to pay the forger, Hans's travel costs to Switzerland, his and Bertie's living expenses there and tickets back here. In the end I sold a ring and got my father to send more. We told Dora that Werner had offered to take Hans hiking in Switzerland. This opened up another crack of deceit in my life at Great Ormond Street. I developed a permanent knot in my stomach.

As his departure grew nearer it became clear to me that I wouldn't be able to stay in the flat when Hans was gone, eating breakfast and dinner with Dora while keeping his scheme from her.

Dora noticed my withdrawal. One day, walking home along Theobalds Road, she said, 'Look, I wouldn't have asked you to keep it from him if it wasn't important. And it really doesn't do him any harm not to know.'

I realised she thought I resented her for making me promise not to tell Hans about the visit from 'Scotland Yard'.

'It's not that,' I said.

'Well, what then?'

And then I was completely stuck. I could hear children over the wall of the schoolgrounds skipping rope to a sing-song chant.

'I think I need to go away for a while,' I said. 'Get out of the flat.'

Dora looked relieved, put her arm through mine. 'I know how you feel,' she said.

'But then Hans and I will both be gone and you'll be there . . .'

'Don't worry about that,' she said. 'Why don't you go and work with Walter for a bit?'

Dora's ex-husband had recently, narrowly, escaped the Gestapo, and was running the headquarters of the Socialist Workers Party-in-Exile in Paris.

'I'll think about it,' I said.

I might not have gone, except it turned out that Mathilde needed a room, so she would stay with Dora while I was away. And once Hans was back here with Bertie, the need for secrets would dissolve and we could all be together again.

'Knock, knock.'

Who's there? I want to say. It's the only answer, isn't it? But I don't because they are sending a hospital counsellor to assess me, and at my age the line between dry and deranged can be hard, even for trained professionals, to see. The woman is tall and slim, with a blond ponytail and honey-coloured glasses.

'Come in, come in,' I say instead.

'I'm Hannah,' she says. 'I'm a counsellor in this hospital.'

'Not religious?' I ask.

'No,' she smiles. 'Would that be a problem?'

'Not my problem.' I smile right back.

'You won't recognise me,' Hannah says as she sits down next to the bed, 'but I saw your accident. I was walking with my daughter near the water and we saw you fall.'

'I don't, really . . .'

'No. You wouldn't.' Her voice is calm, her face open. 'We live in the flats near there, because it's close to the hospital. Still, it is a coincidence, isn't it?' She opens her clipboard and takes something out. 'Sarah wanted me to give you this.'

She passes me a crayon drawing in bright colours where everything is on the same plane: sun and moon together in an aqua sky which meets dark-blue water in a perfect straight line, lots of triangular sails and a rosy-beaked pelican bigger than a yacht. In the foreground there's a road. The drawing is painstakingly done; the bold crayon strokes make each thing moving, alive. Except for a stick figure in a red-triangle dress lying flat on the road. Cars with headlights like eyes bear down on her. But a little-girl stick figure stands by her. She has a large hand, fingers like five spokes of a wheel, and with it she holds the hand of the one on the ground.

'Thank you,' I say after a while. 'I am very sorry she saw, your daughter saw . . .'

'She's fine.' Hannah passes me a tissue from the bedside table.

An orderly comes in to empty the bin. He is an old Vietnamese man and he smiles at us, as at grandmother and granddaughter.

'The doctor comes every day,' I tell her as the man leaves.

'That wasn't the doctor.' There's a softness to her voice, but a firmness too.

'I know that.' I must make more of an effort if I want to go home, and not into some sort of compulsory assisted cell for the weepy and confused. 'I was just saying, the doctor comes to *each* cell *every* day.'

Hannah looks at me closely. I realise what I've said.

'Well, you know – compartment.'

She nods. 'They tell me you were a teacher of literature.'

'Yes. French and German.'

'Would you like me to bring you something to read?' Hannah is looking at my bedside table – the high, hospital thing – which is suddenly, incriminatingly, naked of decent reading material.

'You know,' I say, in my best teacher's tone, 'I've been rather busy.' The grey eyes widen, just a little.

'Remembering,' I explain. She nods again. 'It's all starting to make sense to me,' I add. The nods get slower, the look closer. 'Which can't be a good sign, can it?' I laugh and then Hannah does too. She is relieved, I think, to find me sane.

'Do you understand what is happening here?' she asks then. I look at her and see that her job is hard.

'In terms of "time elapsed and time to go"?'

She nods once more. Picks up my hand.

'Dear,' I say, 'you don't need to worry about me.'

And then we just sit, this stranger holding my hand. In the expanding silence I wish to reassure her: the end is no problem for me. I willed it once, and I can face it now. It is what happened in my personal three-ring circus – the cat's-paw sleight of hand, the balls under cups and the trick pony, the man in the gorilla suit and the note in a pocket, the girl in the lake and the cities blown to dust – that waits for me now. But I say nothing, lest I seem mad. And who, after all, would believe it? We don't understand one another, we may not ever give each other just what we need. All that remains is kindness.

When she leaves she stops at the nurses' station. I hear one of them tell her, 'You know, she was in prison under Hitler. In the resistance.'

'Yes,' Hannah says, a small clip in her voice. 'And let's not send her back there, shall we?'

TOLLER

This morning it's pelting down outside, early summer rain. When Clara walks in, her hair wet, clothes wet, it takes me a moment to register that she is crying.

'The *St Louis* is going back to Europe.' Her arms are flung loose, dark strands plastered to her forehead. 'The coastguard fired a shot —' She chokes. 'Off Florida.'

There has been nothing but silence from President Roosevelt.

'Paul was so close, and now, and now . . .' She sits and weeps, head hung over her lap. I lean forward and place my hands on hers till they too are wet, and she gets a handkerchief from her bag.

'The captain seems like a good man,' I say. 'He will try to dock in Antwerp or Lisbon or somewhere. It won't be straight back to Germany.'

Hope-pedlar, snake-oil merchant – who am I to know? I can't remember how anyone gives comfort any more. Clara looks up, sniffs. She believes me, because the alternative is unthinkable. She wipes her eyes while I nod, pants on fire.

RUTH

The week before Hans left, we were invited, along with Dora and Professor Wolf, to a costume ball at Mrs Franklin's in Paddington.

'I'm afraid,' Wolf had announced at breakfast when we'd talked about it, 'on that evening I am not available.' As if juggling competing ball invitations were the bane of his London life. Dora didn't care; she had plenty of friends to see at Mrs Franklin's, and business there to conduct. But I saw then that everyone thought her so independent as to have no needs, or at least none that they, single-handedly, could meet. This is the curse of the capable; it leaves them prone to pockets of aloneness, sudden elephant traps in the ground.

Hans and I dressed together at home. He wore his beloved tails and fashioned a baton from a coathanger. I put on my best dress – a long cream silk thing – and took a piece of sheet music: we were a conductor and his singer. Dora marked her cheeks with three dark stripes of my lipstick, grabbed a feather I'd been photographing from the mantelpiece and stuck it in a headband.

We were on time, which is to say, too early, and were let in by the butler. The three of us shuffled to one side of the marble entrance hall and stood with our hands behind our backs, expectant as staff. But tonight the house had lost the stuffy formality of afternoon tea and clocks. Furniture had been cleared for dancing. Side tables held vast, round-bellied vases of flowers, hydrangeas and gladioli, peonies and roses in arrangements so gloriously abundant they looked thrown together by some careless, generous-spirited giant. In a back room someone barked last-minute instructions, as before a live performance. The string quartet on the other side of the hall chinned their instruments.

The music must have alerted our hostess. Mrs Franklin appeared at the top of the massive red-carpeted staircase, a cross between a battleship and a giant Fabergé egg.

'Hulloooo, dears,' she waved, chins wobbling and the dog-in-a-bag under her left arm.

She smiled and nodded and began her descent. Her emerald-green skirt, a massive, bone-segmented thing, moved all of a piece. As her foot peeped out to find the stair, I gasped to see it clad in a faded brown, rubber-soled house slipper. By the time she reached us I had understood that Mrs Franklin was dressed as some kind of courtesan, albeit one whose comfort, in her own home, would not be compromised.

'How lovely, how utterly lovely.' She kissed me and Dora on both cheeks and took Hans's hand between her soft little paws. 'That you could come. I thought of you with all that, that terrible Herr Goldschmidt business. I feel I ought to have done more. Really, so much more.' Her body was overflowing its corset, blossoming from a dark wrinkle of cleavage up to her heavily powdered face. A large black mole had been enthusiastically pencilled above her lip.

'But not at all, Eleanora,' Dora cooed. 'Your open Sundays are a wonderful thing. Very much appreciated by all of us. As they were by Helmut too.'

I looked at Hans, who was collecting a champagne coupe from

a waiter's tray. Then he turned, smiling down into Mrs Franklin's
eyes. He took her hand and raised it to his lips. 'And you would be
Madame . . . ?' The sheer beauty of him could be disconcerting at
close quarters. Mrs Franklin laughed like a girl.

'Mme de Staël,' she said, her teeth yellowing mildly under the
carmine lipstick. 'Though I don't really suppose anyone will recognise me.' She laughed again.

In that instant I saw the eccentricity and generosity and ever-
so-slight wariness of the English that I'd grown to love, the luxury
of Mrs Franklin's class being an insouciance about how one is per-
ceived. At home in Silesia at such a ball, the flowers would have
been arranged in a classical, symmetrical order; the carpets would
never be allowed to fray so nobly, and no hostess would greet her
guests with messy lipstick and tender insecurity and in slippers.
I felt how far we had come since our first encounter in this house,
when our lostness had made us trigger-quick to take offence. If Hans
recollected being slighted here, he showed no sign. He seemed in
his element.

Mrs Franklin sailed off to greet a black-faced, white-lipped
minstrel with a banjo under one arm who was coming through
the door. Behind him a veiled Mata Hari with a bared navel was
taking off her coat. Girls in black uniforms and unmade faces bore
trays of champagne and gin; oyster flesh swayed in china spoons.

Hans had been scanning the rooms to each side of the entrance
hall for faces he knew. His colour was high and his lips slightly
open. When someone started playing the latest Noël Coward hit
on a piano we followed the music into the room on the left. Toller
was near the fireplace, turned away from us, but his head was
unmistakable. He was moving his hands like a conductor, a cigar
for a baton. People had gathered in a semicircle around him,
enthralled. Christiane, willowy and taller, was dressed in a man's
suit as Chaplin's Little Tramp.

Dora peeled off in the opposite direction. I took a glass of champagne from a passing tray.

In the back corner of the large room an elderly German in a green loden suit and high collar stood alone under a potted palm, both hands on his cane. It was Otto Lehmann-Russbüldt, the pacifist and human-rights activist. In exile, he had become a kind of uncle to us younger refugees. A gently smiling melancholic, he managed to give us the impression that things as they were, although so unprecedented in our lives and, after all, so unlikely, had predictable outcomes nevertheless. Without ever saying so, he gave us to understand that we would, one day, go home. I was always pleased to see him.

Hans and he were quickly deep in conversation about the questions that Cocks and Churchill had raised in parliament. Hans was pressing Otto to see if he knew the source. 'It's got to be one of us,' Hans smiled. 'Who's not standing up to take the credit?'

I gulped my drink. Otto shrugged his shoulders. 'The truth will out,' the old man said, 'one way or another.'

'Aha!' Hans exclaimed. 'Here's someone who might enlighten us.' Lord Marley was striding our way, no doubt looking for Dora. He was his tall, calm and magnificent self. I couldn't tell who he was dressed as – he wore a short red jacket and long dark boots. He stood with his feet together in front of us, his eyes bright, waiting.

Hans moved to introduce them. Facing Lord Marley, he opened one arm to encompass the older German, who, leaning forward, offered his good ear. Palm fronds reached and dipped, unnoticed, over his head.

'May I present,' Hans addressed the Englishman, 'Otto Lehmann-Russbüldt. You perhaps know him, at least by reputation?' Otto made a little bow.

Hans turned, gesturing now to the other, 'And this,' he said, 'is Marley.'

The Englishman gave a slight start, of the kind I would not have noticed before we came here. It was the subtle shock-and-bemusement reaction to a faux pas and it froze for a split second the air between them.

Then Lord Marley smiled and proffered a hand. 'Dudley will do fine,' he said.

The elderly German noticed nothing. 'Very pleased to meet you, Dudley.'

I felt a thrumming of blood in my brain. I excused myself and placed my glass on a small chiffonier. The floor listed. Snippets of conversation, a high tinkle-laugh, floated towards me as I walked. People an obstacle course.

In the room opposite I found a wing chair near a fire. My mind had gone blank. It was a sensation like wind, like a vacuum. I could think of only one place where Hans, in his assiduousness to master the manners of this country, could have learnt that a lord should be referred to by one word alone – the same place where the people wouldn't have known that this was only the case when writing.

The horror of it crept up on me. The fire leapt and licked. I hoped he would not come over. I had to find Dora. My legs felt flimsy. To my right a flamenco dancer in a backless dress and red shoes danced loosely with a mummy, or a victim of some kind.

Staring at the fire, I recalled the ember on my mother's carpet. Surely this matter of titles was something Hans could have learnt anywhere, and as easily mislearnt? Perhaps I was as paranoid as Hans had been telling me lately, my brain reduced to a rat's thing of instinct and survival so I saw only treachery and threat everywhere.

A pair of shined shoes with fine rounded toes dented the silver pile of the rug. Hans placed one hand on the back of my chair and smiled down, the small solicitous smile of an attentive but not overly concerned husband to his wife in front of a ballroom crowd.

'Ruthie?' His voice said, Nothing can be wrong. It said, This is innocence and your thoughts are unworthy.

'Dance?' Hans asked. 'Or are you . . . ?' I realised he thought I was suffering from period pain, or the ache I sometimes got in my hip when it rained.

'No – yes, yes.'

The trick of dancing is that it allows extreme physical closeness, of touch and breath, at the same time as it is possible to have an entire conversation without eye contact. This is why it is so popular for risky, initial intimacies. For questions.

I affected a lightness that surprised me. 'You *have* been mixing in exalted circles,' I said to his lapel. 'How on earth did you know to introduce Dudley as Marley, instead of Lord Marley?'

Hans nodded over my shoulder at an acquaintance I did not recognise, a fair-haired man with a small moustache in a jockey's silks and cap. 'No idea,' he said. 'Common knowledge, I suppose.' He turned me, deftly. I glimpsed Dora deep in conversation with Fenner Brockway, his wide forehead half covered by a pirate's hat made from newspaper. Fenner was leaning back, laughing hard at something Dora was saying and wiping his eyes. 'It's an old-boy public-school thing, isn't it?' Hans mused. 'Or perhaps from the army – I know they just use one name, anyhow.'

I nodded. He seemed so calm and sure and I wanted to credit him with an honest mistake.

I said nothing to Dora. But that night, for the first time in my life, I got so drunk that later I could not remember how I got home. I drank to obliterate the night, to require Hans to be solicitous, to force him to come home with me and put me to bed, even if I did not see him do it.

Dora spent the next two nights at Professor Wolf's. When Mrs Allworth came on the Tuesday I asked her, as casually as I could, about the use of surnames and titles in schools and the army, and she said she knew it to be so from her time working in a big house. When I told her that Lord Marley had seemed surprised to be called Marley, she smiled. She explained that, no, a lord would usually be introduced as Lord So-and-So, though his school friends and army buddies and, occasionally, his wife might use his surname or title alone.

By the time I saw Dora again I had decided that the incident was exactly what it had seemed, a small slip-up entirely of Hans's own making, understandable given the intricacies of the English class system, the different terms of address, verbal and written. Hans left the next week for Bertie and Switzerland, and I packed for Paris.

Dora came to see me off at the station, something I later wondered about. Sentimental scenes of arrival and leavetaking were not her forte. She was businesslike until the last minute, checking she had my Paris address, making sure I had the money she had scraped together for Walter, and handing me a sealed letter for Bertie she wanted posted from Paris. We walked along the platform till we found my carriage and stood in front of its steps. The train steamed impatience; a dyad of red lights flashed alternately at the outgoing end of the platform. Dora put a gloved hand up to my cheek.

'I'll miss you,' she said, as if the idea were just occurring to her. Then, 'When I see you again it'll be nearly summer.'

I nodded. We had plans to go walking in the Lake District in June. I took the keys to the Great Ormond Street flat out of my coat pocket. I had had another set cut for Mathilde (so many! – one for each internal door, like a secret, or a cell) so I could take mine with me. I held them up and dangled them.

'I'm not leaving you,' I said.

She put the back of her hand to her forehead in mock histrionics, to forestall a scene. '*Quel drame.*'

I hugged her for a long moment, till she pulled away. 'Better get on then,' she said. 'Have a kir for me at La Coupole.' She shifted her weight from foot to foot, clapping her hands together against the cold: the muffled sound of wool on wool. 'Righto.'

I pushed my case up the steps. When I turned round she was already gone – halfway back along the carriage, walking briskly, shoulders hunched. Then she turned sideways and disappeared, a red coat swallowed by a grey crowd.

In Paris I took a flat by myself in Neuilly. There were many more of us refugees in Paris than in London, and I felt less conspicuous in France. Perhaps because of my darker colouring, or perhaps because it is possible for us Germans to speak virtually unaccented French, whereas in English we can never lose the trace of our mother tongue altogether. I worked in the office of the party, helping out as best I could. Walter directed my days.

In Dora's first letter she wrote that Mathilde had made the flat into a home, with 'massive good cheer and moderate housewifery'. Mathilde and her late husband had had staff to run their grand house in Berlin but she could still, by some personal alchemy, make corners of order herself. Small bunches of jonquils appeared in drinking glasses, and she ingeniously hung kitchen implements from a rack she had the caretaker drill into the bricks behind the stove, so that now even the dresser drawers could be filled with papers. Mrs Allworth was delighted, Dora wrote, and Nepo, after two days curled in mourning on my bed, was slowly coming round. The changes to the flat didn't bother me; I had no love for those walls and floors. The main thing was that Dora wasn't there alone. I had not abandoned her.

There's a man at my door. The light is off here and he is face-less and silhouetted, pausing to look. He sways a little, touches something on his chest. I close my one eye and slyly press my finger-button for him to go away, for more ice inside of me.

He's still here. It's Walter. The concierge must have let him in to my Paris building and he is standing in the doorway. I say, 'Come in,' but he speaks before he moves. He was always sweet to me. Sweet and tactical. His eyes are small and hooded and grey-blue and his hair is pushed back, thinning. In another age he would have been a loyal Frankish warrior protecting his tribe, routing out traitors. He wears a dark coat, torso sliced into diagonals by his satchel strap. He takes off his gloves. He is not smiling. He is not coming in.

'They've got Bertie,' he says.

Ice will creep into your veins and stop your heart.

He moves his gloves into one hand, watching my face. 'I thought you should know.'

No. *No* —

'Mrs Becker? Mrs Becker?'

I open my eye. The doctor is about twenty years old. I must seem prehistoric to him. At least a hundred and fifty; a heavy-lidded tortoise, an evolutionary relic long since surpassed, washed up by some freak disaster, coughed out of the earth and into this modern hospital bed.

I crane my neck from the pillow and know it wobbles loosely; it is reptilian, criss-crossed with deep dry crevasses. Around his own smooth neck the boy doctor has a stethoscope with a yellow plastic stem. A toy. Sideburns creep improbably across his babycheeks.

'You seemed distressed in your sleep,' he says. 'You were calling out. I came earlier, but you were asleep then too.' He unhooks my chart and examines it, not pausing for answers. 'I'm finishing up now, wanted to check on you before I leave. You sleeping well?'

I wonder if he listens to himself, let alone to anyone else.

'Any pain?' He looks at me, pen poised, like a doctor on day-time TV, an underage actor cast to suspend disbelief. Next they'll require me to believe in my own recovery, walk out of here as the credits roll for the century just passed, ready to combat the return season of terror in a world that never learns.

'None I can't account for.'

'Pardon?' He hangs the chart back.

'I'm fine. Vivid dreams, that's all.'

'Let me see.' The hairy infant picks up the chart again. 'Sometimes with more . . . senior patients, we recommend a mild antipsychotic along with the pain relief.'

'I am not hallucinating.'

'No. No, well. It's entirely up to you.'

But that's the thing, boyo, it's *not*. This vast life – the real, interior one in which we remain linked to the dead (because the dream inside us ignores trivialities like breath, or absence) – this vast life is *not* under our control. Everything we have seen and everyone we have known goes into us and constitutes us, whether we like it or not. We are linked together in a pattern we cannot see and whose effects we cannot know. One slub here, a dropped stitch there, a bump encounter in that place, and the whole fabric will be different once it is woven.

I look into his clear, caramel eyes. Who knows what trace I might leave inside of you, boy?

'They are all so real to me,' is all I say. I still have a modicum of control.

He looks at me quizzically. There's an indentation in his left ear where he's taken an earring out. As he leans over me I allow myself to wonder about tattoos insinuating themselves across the soft inside of his upper arm, perhaps a bull's head and horns in the sweet hollow of his back where his shirt tucks in. The mind is a curious thing, spooling and unspooling.

'May I?' he says as he pulls down my bottom eyelid without waiting for my answer. 'What about some B12 then? I'll arrange for it tomorrow.'

I couldn't really care. What he cannot yet know – oh, why are we taught so little? and it is such a basic, basic thing – is that one does not remember one's own pain. It is the suffering of others that undoes us.

I lift myself onto one elbow, which is the most emphasis my ruined body will allow. 'I'd like to go home.'

He looks at me as if the idea had never occurred to him as a possible clinical outcome, as if it were an ambition above my station. He folds his lips together.

'I'll discuss it with the team,' he says. 'We'll get back to you on that, Mrs Becker.' As he tucks his pen into the pocket of his gown he holds my gaze, and then he smiles, lips still closed. It is a sympathetic look: he is wondering whether I know what he knows. And then he pats the bed twice, a brisk parting coda, and walks out the door.

'Doctor Becker, actually,' I mutter to his crisp white back.

Eventually, it all came out. The pieces were filled in, reported, documented in a court case and in letters that flew all over Europe. Memory cobbles together what I knew then with what came later. Standing in my Paris doorway, Walter Fabian, the philandering, charismatic, balding, hardworking, ex-underground ex-husband, was trying to read in my face what I knew then.

'Bertie!' My mind was racing and my mouth flapping with it. 'Is he . . . ?'

'Alive as far as we know. They have him at Prinz-Albrecht-Strasse.'

My thoughts flew to the football game with Hans at the border, the waiting car. 'They lured him over the border? They trapped him —?' I must have been shrieking; my hands like panicked birds in the doorway. Walter grabbed one of them.

'Just a minute, Ruth. You need to sit down.'

He helped me along the hallway and sat me down on the sofa. I held my stomach. He disappeared into the kitchen. Outside the clouds hung, bruised and inert over slate roofs. Walter came back with whisky in two glasses. Its colour was the only colour in the room.

'Let's start from the beginning,' he said. He hitched his trousers to sit, opening a gap of white shin between sock and cuff.

I realised – not a neural process at all, but one in the body, a creeping freeze – that this was an interrogation.

'You and Hans had been sending Bert money,' he said slowly, watching my face for something, perhaps surprise, feigned or real. Or recognition. I felt none of those things. I was walking along the black and charred lip of a crater: if Bertie does not live I will be drawn into it and burned to dust.

'Yes. We were.'

'To get a passport?'

'Yes. And to live.' The whisky was fire down my throat. 'Hans and Dora both tried to get him a passport. But even the non-Nazis left in the embassy in London could do nothing. They are all issued from Berlin, so, so . . .'

Walter leant forward with his elbows on his knees. I saw he wore a mint-green shirt and his new wedding band. He was a snappy dresser, in a careless, flamboyant way.

'But you know this already,' I added.

'Yes,' he said. He shifted a little in his seat. 'We'll get back to that. Let me tell you what else we know.'

I bit my lip. Walter watched my face. 'A German acquaintance of Bert's,' he said, 'a man he trusted, lured him into a trap.'

There are things in that black hole. Waiting for me.

'Bertie was taken in a car from a restaurant meeting with a so-called passport forger in Basel straight over the border. Gestapo had come from Berlin.'

He sat back. 'That's all we know for now. All our sources can tell us.' He threw back his head to finish his drink, then placed the glass carefully down on the coffee table in front of him.

'Does Dora know?' I am trying to think of more questions, there are more questions to steer this —

'Yes.' He turned to me. 'She asked me to come to you. Ruthie —'

'But he – they – were always so wary.' I am picking my way round that black, steaming place, dread weaselling in my gut.

'Ruthie.' Walter took the glass out of my hand and set it down. 'The friend was Hans.'

And then I fall. It is dark and hot and silent. There is breath in my ear, a heated rhythm I need to get away from. I stagger down the hall to the bathroom and retch. The whisky burns and stinks again. I check in the cabinet, then close it, holding on to the basin.

When I came out I saw Walter sitting in his mint-coloured shirt on the sofa, more innocent than I would ever be.

He watched me sit down.

'I'm sorry,' he said, 'but I need to ask you this.' He had an activist's grief-and-anger and he had come to show it to me, to get as close to the culprit as possible. I couldn't blame him. 'You said Hans went to the German embassy in London?'

'For a passp—'

'You saw him there.'

I nodded. My stomach turned again.

'He was getting his instructions,' Walter said slowly, articulating what we both knew. 'And delivering Bertie up to them as proof of his turning.' Walter rubbed his eyes with the heels of his hands. 'Also Rudi Formis – we think.'

I was screaming, but nothing was coming out. After a minute Walter put a hand on my shoulder.

'Is there anything else,' he said more gently, 'you think we should know?'

I shook my head. The question hurt.

'Are you sure?'

There was nothing left. We sat for a few minutes in silence.

'They will want Bertie's sources,' I said, trying to pull myself together, to show some inkling of the strategic thinking I so clearly lacked. 'But he barely has any. He gets all his information from —'

Walter cut me off. 'It's his *outlets* they want. They want the link between Bert and the British papers.'

It was as if a rifle sight were trained on her.

'Bert will never give Dora to them,' I said.

Walter breathed in sharply, running both hands over his head with his eyes closed. 'They don't need him to.' He got his voice under control. 'They have Hans for that.'

After a few moments he put his arm around me and squeezed my shoulder. He must have decided that my guilt, all that I saw but refused to see, would punish me without any help from him.

He stood, retrieved his coat from the back of a chair.

'Dora will need to change the locks,' I said.

Walter nodded, but we both knew that our world – Dora's and mine and who knows who else's – had been blown open to Them, locks now a gesture as futile as the boards over the fanlight.

'Nothing you want to ask me?' He was putting his satchel strap over his head.

I looked up. I couldn't say his name.

'Well,' he said. 'I'll tell you what we know. Hans ran off from the Gestapo car at Weil am Rhein. They made a play of shooting him but no body has been produced. My guess is he's either back in Berlin with his masters or gone to ground somewhere.' He placed a hand on my shoulder. 'I want you to promise me something, Ruth,' he said. 'If he contacts you, you let me know.'

I nodded, humiliated to have to be told to do the right thing.

In the hall Walter said, more kindly, 'I don't feel right leaving you alone.' But he went anyway.

The whisky bottle was on the kitchen bench, under cabinets of a soft, unnatural green with turned-bone handles. I poured another. The plumbing flushed loudly from the communal toilet on the stairwell.

In the bathroom cabinet there were two sachets of sleeping powder in the box. I had never taken it before. I didn't know if two would be enough. I considered the question at a distance, like a hypothetical, even as I stood there at the basin with the box in my hands. Extraordinary, really, to have the means of escape in every sleepless refugee's cabinet: a small box with 'Veronal: Good Nights' written on it in cursive script. So many of us, then and later, took this way out, each into their own good night – Zweig and Hasenclever, Tucholsky and Benjamin. I needed a glass from the kitchen. But as I examined the grey face in the mirror, I failed even to have a sense of my own life as tragic enough for the gesture.

And I would not leave Dora.

Just as she would not have left me. Though it is the hardest thing, to work out one's weight and heft in the world, to whittle down all that I am and give it a value.

I washed my face and left for the post office, to telegraph her that I was coming, and then to book a train. I walked along the median strip between the plane trees separating opposing streams of traffic. Women in suits and seamed stockings were leading dogs, taking children to run about in the *bois*. A boy on roller skates tumbled into me to brake, the mother so kind, apologetic, as if, God knows, we were all in this together, and how could she control it? *Pardon, Madame, je suis desolée. Desolée.* We are all desolated here.

There were no seats available on the ferry for two days. When I got back to the flat in Neuilly I pulled the blinds and went to bed.

In the afternoon her reply came, slipped under my door by the concierge. 'All well here LX,' Dora wrote. 'Swiss investigator coming. Using your room 1 week for interviews. Please come after. Waiting for you Thurs am.'

That she called me Loquax was either a gesture of forgiveness or a sign she'd never expected much from me in the first place. I got out of bed and made myself a bowl of instant soup. I'd do as she said, and leave in a week.

The next morning, a postcard arrived from Switzerland, dated before the kidnapping. '*Gruss aus Ascona*' printed in red over a photograph of the lake. 'BJ in good spirits,' Hans had written in his perfect hand. I felt his betrayal rip right through my life. I called Walter. I hoped the Swiss would catch him soon.

TOLLER

That last week I saw Dora twice. Once, when I was ostensibly at one of my morning sessions at the psychiatrist's. We took a walk on Hampstead Heath. Dora was incandescent with rage and hope together; she had the concentrated glow of a hunter approaching her quarry. There was no pull to anything else.

Spring was late, just a softening of the greyscape. We moved at a clip to stay warm, our boots crunching in time on the gravel. Dora talked the whole time, stopping only to cup a hand to light another cigarette. Her nails were massacred and there were reminders, names and numbers, inked into her skin; layers of them, some recent and some faded by a wash or two.

She was consumed by Berthold Jacob's kidnapping. They had got him drunk, she told me, bundled him into a car 'to go to finish the business at the "forger's" house' and sped him across the German border. The simplicity of the plan was offensive, given all Bert's and her caution during these two years of second-guessing the Gestapo. But this case was a far cry from those of Lessing and Formis, Dora said, where the Czechs, cowed by German threats, did not protest.

The Swiss were outraged about Gestapo activity on their soil. They had threatened to cut diplomatic ties with Berlin and had protested to the League of Nations. And they'd sent a public prosecutor to investigate the case properly in London.

'Here?' I stopped. 'Why London?'

Her eyes squinted coolly at me. 'It was Hans.' It could have been the sun, or the smoke from her cigarette, but in her face I read also disgust – with him of course, but also with herself for not having foreseen it. 'Our Hansi lured his best friend into a trap.'

'He turned?' A stupid question, blurted in one of those moments of shock when one becomes iterative, grasping with a dumb word which one does not wish to be true. She didn't bother answering.

'You're not safe now,' I said.

'The Swiss have arrested him.' She touched my arm with one hand. 'In a restaurant by the lake at Ascona, of all places.'

The Swiss investigator, Roy Ganz, had already arrived in London. Scotland Yard was being deliberately uncooperative, Dora said, not providing anywhere for him to conduct interviews, or any information they might have on Nazi activities in Britain.

'It's outrageous.' She stamped out the cigarette under her boot as if it held some of the blame. 'So I'm organising for Roy to do his interviewing at the flat instead. I've called everyone in – and I mean *everyone* – to tell him what they know about Hans, and everything we suspect about what that lot have been doing here in London. Ganz will go back *fully* armed.' She extended her hands as if to hold something big. 'We can connect Hans directly with the German embassy in London – Ruth and I saw him there with our own eyes, for Christ's sake. That's enough to place the Nazis on British soil, planning this kidnapping. And God knows what else. It will be impossible for this government to keep turning a blind eye.' She stopped and touched my forearm again. 'We'll get Bertie out too.'

There was a quiet ecstasy under her fury, her hand-waving and chain-smoking. For a long time she and They had been waging a tactician's war, each camouflaged and concealed, the only proof of their existence being mysterious epiphenomena – violent deaths, articles in newspapers, questions in parliament. Now the waiting was over, and they were coming out to face one another.

She slipped her arm through mine. 'It'll be a coup for us in the end, I'm sure,' she said.

This wasn't a hope she was cajoling herself into. Her confidence was genuine. Bertie was now a lure on a long red thread, and when she and this Ganz fellow reeled him back into the light of international scrutiny, they'd beach the beast. I didn't want to think about Ganz.

'How's Mathilde?'

'Fine. Unflappable, as it turns out. Makes good tea cake. Reigns calmly knitting over everything. Though nothing escapes her, at all.'

She took a strand of hair out of her mouth where the wind had blown it. 'Ruth's coming next week, so that'll be three of us. It's funny, but she's never left me before.' She laughed a little.

'I don't see how that makes you safer.'

'Actually,' she said, 'it's the safest I could possibly be for the moment. Ganz is staying with me. My own private investigator.'

It slipped out before I could think. 'Is he, are you —?'

What on earth was I asking her? Whether she was in love? I had no right.

She put her hands in her pockets. 'He's very . . . nice,' she said, in a tone by which we both understood perfectly the limitations of the thing. 'Look, they're hardly going to dare do anything to us while he's in the flat. The British would have no choice then but to protest as loudly as the Swiss about something done under their noses.'

'And when he goes back?'

She turned her head on the side, looking up to me. 'Thought I might turn up on your doorstep. With a suitcase.' She smiled a close-lipped smile. 'Again.'

I looked at the ground. Sometimes your life feels like a pile of wrong decisions.

'I'm kidding!' she laughed. She took the inside of my arm again, just above the elbow. We started walking. 'Mathilde and I are thinking of going up to Dudley's country house. We'll take Ruth. There are always options.'

I couldn't tell if she was rallying me or herself.

We walked in silence, till we reached the pond she had visited the night I'd told her Christiane was coming and she had left me to sit watching men leap through the dark into the black water. We both knew that refuge in some baron's country house was just a way of stalling for time. There was no place on earth she could go and not be in their reach.

We sat on a bench. I thought of the carp I used to glimpse sometimes in my mother's pond, blurs of gold under the ice, like something half remembered or yet to come, déjà vu or a promise. I looked at the water here, the ground around it dirty and naked. A few daffodils bobbed surprised, oversized heads out of the earth, lonely for colour in a dun world. My breath got shorter. There seemed a terrible inevitability about it. I studied the space between my legs.

'Stop it.' She put two fingers to my chin, turning me to her. I let myself be kissed. When we drew apart she put her forehead to mine. 'Ernst. We made this decision a long time ago.'

'Did we?' I pulled away. I was holding back sobs. 'Did we? I don't remember.'

A duck came from nowhere and launched herself on the black water. Two early-born ducklings followed, eyes only for their mother. Dora put her hand on my chest. 'You did for yourself.'

She breathed in sharply. 'And I did for me.' She removed her hand. 'I'm not stupid. I know it's quite possible they'll get me.' She turned to face the water. 'But I am not —' Her voice too started to crack. She patted herself crossly for cigarettes, found them. Lit one. I saw she was gulping it back, the thing she couldn't think about, that would take her over if she let it. She threw her head back to shake it off. 'I am *not* making it easy for them.'

We sat not touching. After a few minutes I took out my handkerchief and wiped my face. 'What about India? Africa?' I said without hope.

She shook her head slowly. 'I wouldn't be me.'

And then a fury rose inside me, white behind my eyes. I wanted to take her tiny stubborn shoulders and shake them, wanted to drag her off, imprison her in a tower. I could not bear this foreknowledge, I could not bear that she also knew. I wanted to scream at her that if they got her she wouldn't be her precious self then either. But that would have been cheap. And anyway, of course, there was still hope. I said nothing at all.

The last time I saw her was at the Great Ormond Street flat on the Friday. I'd dropped by to have my own session with the Swiss investigator. Wolf the academic was just leaving. Dora propped the door open with her body, one hand covering the mouthpiece of the phone. 'I'll bring you back your keys then,' I heard Wolf say to her, raising his hand in wordless salute. When he turned he was startled to find me there. His face was blotchy and pinched behind his trim moustache. He touched his hat and fled.

I took off my coat while she finished her call.

'He seemed in a hurry,' I said, gesturing to the door.

'You won't believe this.' Dora was smiling, shaking her head. She told me when Wolf had arrived that morning and realised Ganz was already in the flat he bolted into Mathilde's bedroom and shut the door. 'He stayed holed up in there the whole morning.'

The Swiss investigator was now out for a walk so Wolf had made his getaway. Dora rolled her eyes.

'Actually,' she said, 'it's a permanent getaway.' Wolf had told her 'she had gone way, way too far', inviting attention with all this interviewing and 'public agitating' against the Reich. Having Ganz stay overnight with her was absolutely the last straw. 'He told me things were stretched between us beyond repair.' Dora shrugged at the mysteries of male pride, which I doubt were mysteries to her at all. 'How can you break up,' she said, 'if you were never really together?'

Dora didn't love Wolf. She knew full well the narrowness of his appeal, the fragile constructions of grey breath and thought that were his theories for changing the world without setting foot in it. He was the worst kind of armchair revolutionary: supercilious and cautious to the point of cowardice; international and theoretical to the point of irrelevance. He had been precisely nowhere during our *real* revolution. What the men Dora took as lovers understood – indeed, what made her so attractive to them – was her independence. She did not want more from them. She certainly did not want more from Wolf.

We were still drinking our coffee when Ganz returned. He was a tall blond fellow with an even, open face, perfect as a mannequin, and as forgettable. When he started speaking it was clear he was fair-minded, decent and intelligent and I could not have liked him less. In our interview I told him how I was being followed in London, about the death threats in the post, about Hans proposing a trip with me to Strasbourg, and his wanting to see what I was writing.

When I left, Dora was already greeting the next interviewee at the door. I placed one hand on the small of her back, half-caress and half-goodbye, and she nodded at me. Our thing was always continuing.

RUTH

When I arrived at Great Ormond Street from Paris I left my case in the entrance and ran upstairs. The building smelt like it always did, a warm combination of piny cleaning fluid and toast. I hadn't heard anything from Dora since her telegram, but I didn't expect to. I knew she'd have been consumed by the investigation.

I reached the wooden stairs and caught my breath. They might still be interviewing. I'd prepared my confession over the past seven days for whoever would hear it, the tale of all I had failed to see. Of football and the embassy and Hans in the document cupboard, of the Gestapo impersonating Scotland Yard and how Hans knew to introduce a lord by one name. The passport plan. I would tell it and tell it. I smoothed my skirt and knocked.

No response.

I took out my ring of keys. I didn't have much hope that the old one would work but I tried anyway. It didn't even fit in the opening. I knocked again. Put my ear to the door. Nothing.

Then Nepo crying.

I went downstairs and sat on my case. I probably sat there for an hour. I wasn't thinking. I was hoping that the situation itself would take over from me, that Dora or Mathilde would walk in before I had to make a decision. Nepo was there; they couldn't be far. Then I thought to look in the letterbox. There was three days' uncollected mail.

A key turned in the front door and opened out my heart. But it was the retired insurance executive, Mr Donovan, coming home. I told him I was back from France but had no key. He said he thought the ladies had gone away. They had had a great many visitors the past week, he said, but he hadn't seen them at all since the weekend. It was Thursday.

Mr Donovan let me use his telephone. There was only one person I could think to call. Christiane picked up, and I introduced myself. 'I know who you are,' she said, not unkindly, and passed me to Toller. He suggested that Dora and Mathilde may have gone to Lord Marley's house in Sussex. Toller said he didn't have the new key, or any key for that matter.

When Mr Donovan came back into the room he was wearing a dressing gown over his clothes. He offered me tea and went into the kitchen. I sat still, on his sofa.

Dora knew I was coming today, this morning. She would never have met me at the station but I could not imagine she would not be here when I was due.

I called Toller again. 'She knew I was coming,' I said.

He was at our building within the hour, his movements fast and fidgety, dark circles the whole way around his eyes. We walked to the police station on Gray's Inn Road, Toller talking all the while. We just needed to check inside the flat, he said, we could have any damage to the door repaired before they got home. He thought the local police would probably have nothing to do with Scotland Yard, and it shouldn't be too hard to keep them away from the cupboard. We just needed to check. I didn't speak – there was a pit of anxiety in my stomach.

Police Constable Hall came back to Great Ormond Street with us. The three of us stood on the doorstep under the angel's head and the boarded-up fanlight. The policeman rang the doorbell for the top flat. We waited out the silence of its wake. Then I let us into the building with my key.

Upstairs, PC Hall knocked on the door of the flat and opened his case. Fear crawled cold over my skull – for what we would find, for the violence of finding it. He barely waited for an answer before jemmying the door.

The wood barked and flew open. Both locks stuck whole in the jamb as the door splintered away from it.

Nepo sprang out of the kitchen, so alive, so grateful, circling through my legs. I picked him up. The flat was silent, neat and clean. There was milk and food in his bowls in the kitchen. It was fresh: they couldn't be far. Toller and the policeman moved through the other rooms. Nepo roared like an engine in my arms.

PC Hall came back and stood in the kitchen. 'That one is locked.' He pointed across the entryway.

Toller was very quiet. He seemed to be deferring to me. I suppose it was my home.

'That's Dora's room.' I put Nepo down.

The moments of greatest intensity in my life have taken on automatic qualities, as if soundless, underwater. One thing leads to another and you break down a door, sit on a chair, drink tea, scald your mouth, freeze your heart. Then a powder to sleep – desperate for oblivion, but sad too, at each night that takes her further from you – you going into an unshared future. The soul who has gone leaves your own lonelier and small, shrunken inside a body that is now a shell for loss. PC Hall picked up his jemmy again.

They lay in the bed facing one another, the covers drawn up to their chins. Toller leapt to her, fingers on her throat, then

Mathilde's. He backed off like he'd been burned, slid down the wall. PC Hall stayed away.

Her forehead was cold on my lips. Her mouth was greyish blue, parted. Eyes closed, deep in their sockets.

Mathilde looked weary. A crust ran from her nose and mouth to the pillow.

I threw back the sheet. Dora was in the old cream pyjamas I'd given her, coffee stains down the front. Mathilde was fully dressed – a black silk dress, stockings, but shoeless. Their hands were clasped together, heads bent close.

Did one go first, the other watching, waiting for her time all alone?

There was nothing to do. She was gone. She was here still. A small, cold bird. PC Hall didn't stop me. I put one arm under her body and the other around her. I pressed my cheek to her forehead and I rocked and held my brave girl, my wild dead love. The policeman looked away. It was the loss of the world.

What had I thought I would grow into? I was grown. Why had I thought I might, still, become something else? It was over.

PART III

You, a writer, were missing as we buried them in a hideous Jewish cemetery in East Ham. A pitiful bunch of mourners, Toller giving interviews all the while. You would have seen what it is, emigration . . . the glorious middle section of a grim novel that no one will write.

*One friend of Dora's writing
to another, 24 May 1935*

TOLLER

I sat for two days in the chair by the bay window, where I had waited for her the night she went out to the heath. I have seen a lot of death. I willed myself to acknowledge hers. But the heart will not be told. I was desperate for sleep to take me but if I closed my eyes my mind would leap to imagining she might be here at any minute, come stomping cold and cross through that door.

'It must have been hard for Christiane,' Clara says. 'To see your heart broken by someone else.' She is closing the first of my cases, with a firm snap. She is right to think of Christiane.

Christiane ministered to me quietly those days, I tell Clara. She brought me toast, coffee. I barely saw her, though, until the afternoon of the second day when I noticed her watching me, crying, in the doorway. She wasn't crying for Dora. She was crying for me.

It is possible for grief to transmute itself to anger, and for that anger to keep you alive. The inquest came the next week, and my fury about it has kept me going these past four years. While there was an injustice to be resolved, I would hang on to fight for it.

'It's still unresolved.' Clara is sitting near me now. Her eyes are huge, the furrow has reappeared between her brows.

'That's true.' I nod as if to say it's all right, it really is. But the other thing I left for myself to do was to write her into existence. And that part is done.

Outside the coroner's court some people had brought folding stools, as for the races. I held the fury inside me. They probably had sandwiches and thermoses in their satchels as well. The day was clear and bright, an outrage. It was ten to eleven.

But when I got closer I saw that there was nothing festive about most of those filing in to fill the seats. They were refugees, grey-gulleted and swivel-eyed and hoping for protection. In the six days since Dora and Mathilde were discovered the newspapers had been full of 'The Bloomsbury Deaths'. Two single foreign women poisoned in a bed together in the heart of London: it sold copies. Tabloid headlines screamed 'Hitler Henchmen Among Us!' More sober papers in the first days simply declared the deaths to be 'in mysterious circumstances'. They quoted 'friends who preferred to remain anonymous' on the break-ins at the flat where nothing had been stolen, on the death threats in letters. The best reports made the link between Dora's activities in helping uncover Wesemann's Nazi connections in London and the dangers faced by outspoken refugees like Berthold Jacob and herself, outside the Reich.

Theories flew around. Like most theories, they were as much about the prejudices of those who held them as about the situation they described. There were ridiculous intimations that Dora and Mathilde had been 'intimate friends' (as if lesbians, by nature, court simultaneous assassination). According to others, Dora had been deceived by an Englishman who had promised to marry her and so was driven to suicide, taking her friend with her. (Why is it that with women, some kink, some vulnerability of the sex, is always presumed to lie at the heart of things – as if they have no other life, no relevance as important as that which they have for us men? How she would have hated that theory.)

On the fourth day, rumours of a suicide note surfaced. I'd certainly not seen one in the flat, nor had Ruth. I didn't take the talk seriously. But from then on the tabloids ran openly with a new theory of romantic suicide. The 'unnamed friends' started to waver, conceding that even if political intrigue could not be proved, the cause of death should still be attributed to the Hitlerites. Without their bloody regime the women would not be in exile, said the unnamed; they would not be in financial insecurity, frightened of having their visas cancelled and being sent back to Germany; they would not have been driven to *this*. To my relief most of the better papers remained steadfast, intimating foul play by 'the Wesemann-Göring Gang'.

On the way in to the court on the tube I'd overheard two women discussing the 'Bloomsbury murder-suicide pact', along with the 'high-strung nature' of our race. They felt entitled to their salacious tut-tutting, as if someone else's tragedy confirmed the deep pleasure of their unwagered lives. The truth had dislodged itself from any connection to Dora and become a matter for open debate, in which any idiot could express an opinion. And today, the meaning of her life would be toted up by a committee of jurors, on the basis of 'reasonable probability'. Which standard, in my view, had long ceased to apply to us.

Members of the Wesemann-Göring Gang were no doubt here at the coroner's court, mingling among the crowd, dressed as embassy officials, reporters, refugees. Come to gloat, to see the terrorising effect of their murder on the community of exiles. I saw Dora's prominent friends – Lord Marley with his wife, Fenner Brockway pale as a plate, Sylvia Pankhurst, Churchill, and some other parliamentarians I recognised but couldn't name. There were a lot of press – men in Homburgs juggling cameras with saucer-flashes.

I spotted Ruth on a bench at the front. She was holding her bag on her lap with both hands and staring rigidly ahead of her, flanked by strangers. I had a sudden need to sit with her. But there was no room, so I found a place four rows behind. I watched her straight back, the curls escaping beneath her green hat. Over the past few days she had come into focus for me in a way that made me ashamed not to have ever, really, seen her before.

After the ambulance had come to take them to the morgue, Constable Hall had escorted us both to the station, to be interviewed by his superiors. Pain is as selfish as love. It takes over the body and the mind and supplants them with itself: you become the element incarnate – there is no 'you' left to think of anyone else. But when I looked at Ruth walking beside me, my own suffering was dislodged. She was a picture of ruin, ashen and collapsed. I don't think she noticed how she got from the flat to the police station; I don't think she could imagine herself into any action at all, any future.

They took us into separate rooms. My interrogation room was small and bare, a fire-drill map on the back of the door. They – there were two of them – began by asking me what might have been making the women unhappy. I told them categorically that they were *not* unhappy. I said I knew for a fact that Dora had been in high spirits on Friday, though of course well aware that they might kill her. They asked me who 'they' were and I said the same people – agents of Hitler – who killed Lessing and Formis, who kidnapped Bertie.

The men went quiet for a moment, concentrated on taking notes. I saw that this story, so familiar to us as the basis for our current lives, sounded cloak-and-dagger outlandish to these ordinary, sensible policemen. I should have gone slower, back to the beginning to account for it. I should have gone back to the war, the revolution, the tender spirit of pacifism and freedom in Germany and the nationalist force that had now risen to kill it. When I looked at their young, blank faces I felt hopeless.

They asked, politely, whether my same theory applied to Mrs Wurm.

I didn't like 'theory': I was giving them the solution to the crime on a plate. But I kept my cool. I told them Mathilde was a former Social Democrat MP, and that while I considered Dora to have been the main target, Mathilde was supporting the work her flatmate was doing, and would have had to be assassinated too, like so many wives or assistants of other targets who got in the bullet's way. I told them that as late as Friday, Mathilde had been unflappable.

But it didn't seem to matter what I said; their questions came to revolve more and more around the easy, feminine solution of suicide.

'How do you account, sir,' they asked, 'for the room being locked from the *inside*? The key left on the shelf?'

At that point I could think of no other way to answer: I admitted to them my own area of shameful expertise. 'Sirs,' I said, 'I am familiar with the black pull to death.' My voice was rising but I got it under control. 'And I can tell you that Dr Dora Fabian did not have it.'

They looked at me. Everything I had ever accomplished fell away. I was what they saw: a dark-looking foreigner, a Jew, a hysteric from a former enemy nation. They took neat notes and thanked me politely.

I waited over an hour for Ruth on a bench in the entrance of the police station. The rotating door spat out people going about their business as on an ordinary day. When she emerged from the other end of the hall her eyes seemed smaller, her lips grey. She lowered herself onto the bench by my side.

Ruth was taller than Dora, long-bodied, with legs ungainly as a foal's. Her fingers were fine and tapered, no wedding band. Ruth was never the first person you would notice in a room, probably not even the second or third. But as she sat there trying to gather herself I felt her humility, her gentle watchfulness. She was a woman with no pretensions of any kind – to beauty or talent – no claim on public attention. This freed her, I believe, to have a true sense of another person. Which is a rare thing.

She started to rock forward and back, holding her arms across her body. 'I told them Dora would never have left me to find her like that,' she said. 'She would never have done it without a note to me.'

'No,' I said. Nor to me, I thought. Ruth fumbled in her bag for a handkerchief.

'They kept saying that the room was locked from the inside, that it seemed a pretty clear case. I told them she'd been investigating Hans's activities in London for the Gestapo —'

Ruth broke off to put her hand to her face. 'There is so much I didn't see.' She hunched over. When she spoke again her voice was a tight howl. 'I could have warned her.'

I put my arm around her. 'Dora didn't see Hans turning. Neither did Bertie. You're too hard on yourself.'

Her voice, when it came, was terrible. 'I was closer.'

'Sometimes,' I stilled her flighty hands in mine, 'that makes it more difficult.'

She started to weep. Her words came in a flurry. Something about seeing her husband at the embassy, about him engineering a practice run at kidnapping Bert at the French border. Then after the counter-trial he'd suddenly become happier, behaved like a man saved.

'You can say it all at the inquest.' I stood and held out my hand. 'We should leave now.'

It was as if she didn't hear me. Then she said something I didn't catch. I bent to her, cupped my hand under her elbow. She turned her eyes to me, blurred with pain, and repeated, 'It should have been me. With her.'

I didn't think she would be able to get up. 'You should stay with me and Christiane tonight.'

She shook her head. She would go back to the flat. They were not even treating it as a crime scene.

'But the door is smashed open,' I protested. 'You'll be scared.'

Her response came from some far place. 'They won't be back,' she said. 'I need to empty the cupboard. They will have photographed what they wanted, and left it now for Scotland Yard to find and use against people.' When she looked at me I saw something solidify behind her eyes, some decision quietly made. 'Besides, we've done it before. A chair against the door.'

At the coroner's court a jury had been empanelled in rows on the right-hand side of the room. When the coroner came in we all stood. S. Ingleby Oddie was a silver-haired man in his sixties with a narrow, lined face and dark circumflex eyebrows: a face set in permanent surprise, so as never to reveal any. He took his papers from a briefcase and laid them on the desk. In front of him was a table for counsel: Mathilde's family had hired a barrister. No one represented Dora. Her mother, Else, I heard later, had been taken off to a camp, as they often did with relatives of their victims.

I watched the back of Ruth's head. It occurred to me that perhaps the benches up the front had been reserved for witnesses. But surely I would be called, because I had been there to discover them, because I knew Dora so well, and because, well, I had so much to say.

Constable Hall was the first witness in the box. He had his helmet off; his pale-brown hair had been trimmed since Thursday and his ears were newly prominent, pinkish. I felt I'd had some intimate experience with the man as in a war, though I knew him not at all. PC Hall described forcing the door of the flat, and then the locked door of the bedroom. He said the women were lying on the bed, facing one another and holding hands. The covers were drawn up over them and they were 'no longer alive'. He had taken a cup with a dark liquid in it from the bedside table as evidence, and called an ambulance. There was no disorder in the room, the constable said, though two cases lay half packed next to the wardrobe. The key to the room, he said, was placed 'neatly' on a shelf beside the inside of the door. I hated that he allowed himself the flourish of an adverb.

'Thank you, Constable,' the coroner said.

A tightness fizzed and curled in my sternum. Everything Dora had been trying to do could happen in this room. In this room – as much as in the newspapers or in parliament – the public could be warned of the danger and the vicious reach of the Hitlerites. She would have proved it with her life. When I closed my eyes I saw her on the park bench, her neck stretched back and her eyes blinking away the fear. Now that fine body I knew so well lay in a box in the cemetery mortuary at East Ham, waiting to go into the ground this afternoon. I looked at the coroner, this representative of world-famous British justice. He cleared his throat.

'You say, Constable, that all the inside doors were fitted with Yale locks.'

'Yes, Your Honour.'

'And the room in which the women died was locked from the inside.'

'Yes.'

'Have you formed a view as to why there were locks on every door?'

'Refugees, sir, I would say.' Hall moved his weight from one leg to the other, the light catching the double row of buttons on his uniform. 'Sharing a house. Perhaps they let the rooms singly —'

'Not so!' someone cried. The room rustled. Ruth raised herself in the front row, clutching her bag. The coroner remained steady as a surgeon, looking down from the bench.

'Your name, madam?'

'Ruth,' she said. Then more softly, 'Wesemann, sir.'

He trailed a pencil over the paper in front of him. 'You are named as a witness, Dr Wesemann. I would ask you to hold your contribution until that time.'

Ruth's hand searched the air behind her for the bench's edge and I saw in its fumbling what it had cost her to speak out. I hoped I was on that list.

The next witness was Dr Taylor, a pathologist with a soft voice and a spray of acne scars. He had conducted the autopsy and he gave the cause of death as respiratory failure due to Veronal poisoning. The drug had been mixed with coffee, he said. The difference between a lethal and a non-lethal dose was a matter of some twenty grains, which was not very many.

'And in this case, Doctor?' the coroner asked.

'The concentration in the cup was very high. I would venture the opinion, Your Honour, that it was an intentionally fatal dosage.'

The coroner put down his pencil and inclined his head slightly towards the witness. 'And in your view, Doctor, would this Veronal be evident by taste?'

'Oh yes, Your Honour. At such a concentration the coffee would be very bitter, granular. Not mistakable for coffee in any event.'

'Do you have the cup here, in evidence?'

'No, Your Honour.' The coroner waited. 'Inadvertently destroyed, I'm afraid.' The pathologist looked down at his hands. 'Cleaners, sir.'

'I see.' The coroner made a note.

The doctor then told the court that the women had, in his view, been dead since the Sunday evening or the Monday before they were discovered.

You feel things before you can think them. A narrative was being drawn here from selected facts – the easy story. And I was in a waking dream of drowning, a puppy in a tin bucket, silent bubbles coming out of my mouth, floating uselessly to the surface. Every time I want to protest I take in water.

Mrs Allworth the charwoman climbed into the witness box. She wore a pale grey suit I'd seen before on Ruth. It hung from her shoulders. Her knuckles moved like jackbones under the skin of her hands, gripping the wood. Her words had a second-hand quality, as if she had been practising them.

'On Tuesday,' she told the room, 'I went to the flat as usual, to clean. I was surprised to find, when I let myself in, that the ladies were gone away. They always left me a note when they went away, telling me how long for, and asking me to drop by on the days I didn't clean to feed Nepo. They paid me for that, of course,' she added, unscripted. 'The ladies were very fair.' A red blush started from behind an ear, leaking its hot way across her face. 'Nepo is the cat – sorry.' She took a deep breath. She'd lost her place.

'Take all the time you need, madam,' the coroner said.

It was most unusual, Mrs Allworth said again, that the ladies did not leave a note. But she decided they must have gone away. 'I could see no other explanation, sir.' So she had started to clean. She cleaned the kitchen and the bathroom, Mrs Wurm's room and the spare room. 'I did not go into Dr Fabian's room as I found it was locked,' she said. 'This was a most unusual thing also, as she'd never locked the bedroom before. However, after I done my work I left the flat, at about twelve-thirty p.m.'

The coroner nodded.

'Oh,' she added, 'and I fed Nepo. Of course.' Her face crumpled like a paper in fire. 'And all that time the ladies, the ladies —'

'Thank you, thank you . . .' He glanced down at his paper. 'Mrs Allworth. I have only one question.' He waited while she silently blew her nose. 'Apart from the door of Dr Fabian's bedroom being locked, you say you saw nothing unusual, no disorder of any kind, in the flat?'

The woman's face and neck were glowing puce. 'No, sir. No disorder. Sir.'

'Thank you, Mrs Allworth.' The coroner looked at Mathilde's counsel. 'Your witness.'

The man asked Mrs Allworth a few questions I do not remember. Then she stood down.

The clerk stood. 'The court calls Professor Wolfram Wolf,' he announced.

Wolf stood from the front row. Why on earth had *he* been called? What could he possibly know that I might not? The turkey wore a three-piece suit, his neck angling forward out of a trim white collar, as if to duck whatever was coming. The idea that a man so relentlessly trivial, so nasal and pernickety, could stand up there and speak of Dora while I sat mute sent my blood roiling. I was furious at her for dying, but probably more so for having ever been with him.

The coroner asked Wolf to describe his relationship with Dora. The professor's voice was adenoidal, barely audible.

'We were close friends.'

'I see. Professor Wolf, can you tell us whether you spent any of the days or nights last week or the week before at the flat on Great Ormond Street?'

Wolf's answer was muffled, his eyes to the floor. The coroner watched him a moment, and then seemed to understand something.

'Are you a married man, Professor?'

'Yes.' There was a slight stirring, a human breeze in the court.

'Very well, I won't press you,' the coroner said, 'but I was wondering whether you had spent a night at 12 Great Ormond Street in the last fortnight.'

Wolf started to speak in long, disarticulated sentences. If I were casting him in a play he'd be a comic character, a ridiculous wordy Polonius, an i-dotting and t-crossing windbag rival. But there he was, talking, and I was not. He was saying that sometimes it was the case that he and Dora talked into the evening, that she was frightfully busy always, that she was forever working through the night as well as the day, and that, occasionally, he did end up, when it was late, staying over. He couldn't say exactly when had been the last time this happened.

The coroner waited until Wolf had exhausted all possible circumlocution. 'I have no wish to embarrass you, Professor Wolf,' he said. 'I desire only to lay before the jury the reason why it was you, as I take it, who received the deceased's suicide note.'

The hairs on my arms stood up. The air in the room went static.

'Can you tell us when you received it?' the coroner asked.

Wolf looked down at his hands. 'Monday morning. By the Monday morning post.'

'And would you be so kind as to read it for the court?'

The jurors' heads were all turned to look at him. Wolf took from his suit pocket a folded piece of paper. He coughed into his fist and started to read:

I have failed too much, caused too much pain to you. I don't find any way back, neither to you, to myself nor to life. Do not think that my death is the consequence of the last days, even if you had come back I would not have continued to live. I have been too fond of you. I am sorry. Goodbye. I take with me the only person for whom my life meant anything.

The silence deepened. We paused, collectively, to take this in, the words of the dead woman, the last words one might choose. Then racking, solitary sobs from the front bench.

My heart had stopped but my mind was clear. The falsity of the note was patent.

'That cannot be!' I found myself standing, shouting. 'It's a lie!'

Two guards disengaged themselves from the wall. The coroner held up a hand to halt them.

'Sir,' he addressed me calmly, 'I understand that some of the evidence presented here is of a distressing nature. But I would ask you to refrain from interrupting the proceedings or you will be ejected.'

'I want to give evidence!'

'Your name?'

'Ernst Toller.'

He nodded, then examined his list. 'I'm afraid, Herr Toller, that your name does not appear on my list. You will understand, I'm sure, that we have had to restrict witnesses to those directly connected with the deceased.'

'But I am . . . We were . . .' Christiane was in Hull at a repertory theatre, but the room was full of press and I couldn't do it to her. 'Old friends.'

'I'm sorry, Herr Toller, but we will be hearing from close associates of the deceased women only.' He looked again at his list. 'From, ah, Dr Wesemann, I believe.' As he shuffled his papers I looked at Ruth. She had turned to look at me, along with everyone else.

'You gave a statement to the police,' the coroner continued, holding a document he'd found, 'and on that basis it has been decided whose evidence to put before the jury. You can be assured, Herr Toller, that your evidence has received due consideration. I would ask you, now, to resume your seat.'

The guards retreated to the wall. I sat. The coroner pulled his half-glasses down his nose and turned his attention back to Wolf, whose face was a picture of relief. I could have strangled the bastard.

'When Dr Fabian writes of "the consequence of the last days",' the coroner said, 'what do you take that to mean?'

Wolf coughed again. 'We had had an argument, Your

Honour. Dor— Dr Fabian wished . . .' He pulled his suit jacket down. 'I had decided, sir, to break off my relations with Dr Fabian. She was distraught about it. She was frightened. She feared her political activity would bring her to the attention of the authorities here. She had wished for me to move into the spare room of the flat. She was, I have to say, quite hysterical when I told her that I would not do so.'

'Not true!' It came out of me like a cry of pain.

The coroner's tone was quiet, practised. 'I must warn you, Herr Toller. For the last time.' He turned back to Wolf. 'And were you surprised to receive this note?'

'Sir, I have to say that Dora had threatened to commit suicide before. If I left her. Sometimes I believe that all the work, and not sleeping, and the morphine took their toll —'

A ripple of understanding went through the crowd, as if she'd been a fiend, as if something were being explained here. I was drowning in air, trying to catch Ruth's eye, willing her to turn around to me again.

'And what did you do when you received this note on Monday morning?'

'I telephoned the flat. When there was no answer I went around there. No one answered the bell either. I walked about for half an hour and came back again, but there was still no answer.'

'Why, given you had received this note, a suicide note as you took it, did you not then call the police?'

Wolf looked a little green, fingered his tie. But he was prepared for the question. 'I was almost sure that she had gone from London either to Sussex or somewhere else, and I did not want to interfere and show the police her residence and everything in it, and perhaps cause some harm to her.'

'Indeed,' the coroner said. 'I wish now to return to the suicide note. May I see it?'

The note was passed from Wolf to the clerk, who handed it up to the coroner.

And then things started to move in slow motion.

'This is in English.'

'Yes, sir.'

'Where is the original?'

Wolf looked at the ground. 'I believe it is no longer available, sir. It was given by Scotland Yard to the German embassy for translation. I am told it was inadvertently destroyed by embassy staff after the translation was made.'

There were murmurs in the court.

'I see. Well, from memory then, Professor Wolf, did you recognise Dr Fabian's handwriting in the note to you?'

'The note was in shorthand. Sir.'

Another, louder rustle of shock went through the courtroom. Wolf spoke of his own accord to quell it. 'We usually corresponded in shorthand.'

This was too much even for the coroner. 'For something so brief, so important, as her suicide note, do you not think she would have used words?'

'No, sir. It was our habit.'

'And the envelope, did it show her handwriting?'

'It was typed. As I recollect.'

'So,' the coroner spoke slowly, 'she had no time to write a three-line suicide note in longhand, but time to put an envelope in the typewriter for the address?'

Wolf was quiet, one hand clasping the other in front of him. 'I'm not sure, sir. Perhaps it was habit – she was always so busy.'

It was beyond bearing. I rose again. I could feel the room with me this time. 'What kind of love is that?' I shouted. I had nothing to lose – thrown out or sitting here, I'd be silenced either way. I held out my hands, my voice not quite under control. 'Dora was in *high* spirits! She was doing her life's work! She was uncovering the Hitlerite activities here!'

The coroner nodded at the guards again. I had seconds. I was pointing at Wolf now. 'Why didn't he call for help? Why didn't he try to find them as I did? Because . . .' I knew I would manage to say it now, so I slowed down for effect, 'he knew they were already dead!'

I kept my eyes on Wolf as I felt them take me under the arms, one each, and pull me into the aisle. I turned my neck to look for Ruth. It will all depend on you now, I wanted her to know, it's all up to you.

RUTH

A trolley with someone on it goes past in the corridor, but by the time I look up I see only the feet sticking out of the sheet.

I can't remember how they took them out of the flat.

The next time I saw Toller was at the inquest. His feet lifted a little off the ground as they took him down the aisle, his head swivelled around to find me. I knew what he wanted.

And I would do it. I had practised what I was going to say for the Swiss investigator and I hadn't had my chance to say it. I had held back with the police because I did not want them to get to the cupboard before I cleared it. On the Saturday I'd given all the documents that could implicate anyone here, or in Germany, to Otto Lehmann-Russbüldt. Now I could say everything. I did not care if they sent me back. I would tell this court, the press, the world, of Germany's preparations for war. I would tell them about the death threats and the flat being ransacked. I would tell them Dora was killed because they wanted to silence her. I left my bag on the bench.

As I lowered my hand from taking the oath I saw only a sea of skin and hair and eyes. I could not put the features together. The room swayed a little, in a blur of unknown flesh.

'Could you state your relationship to the deceased, please, Dr Wesemann?'

'I was Dora's cousin, sir. Our fathers are brothers. Mathilde I knew as an acquaintance. From Berlin.'

'And you lived at 12 Great Ormond Street, Bloomsbury?'

'Yes, sir. Though I had gone temporarily to France. I was just coming back when —'

'We will come to that. Can you tell the court why you were in France, Dr Wesemann?'

'I . . .' I breathed again to start properly. 'My husband, sir. He had gone and I – I needed a change. It was temporary.'

'I see.'

'My husband was working for them, for the German government, and he, I didn't see it —'

The coroner's voice was suddenly authoritative. 'I feel I must make it clear at the outset, Dr Wesemann, that we cannot have politics introduced into this court.'

My blood ran cold. It was all about politics – the life, and the death.

'Not matters concerning another sovereign power, and especially ones that may be *sub judice* between other nations at this moment. I would ask you therefore to confine your contribution to the matter at hand, that is to say, to the deaths of Dr Fabian and Mrs Wurm in the flat at Great Ormond Street.' He paused briefly, examining me over his spectacles. 'I would like to start, actually,' he continued, 'with the matter of the locked room. Were there locks on the internal doors when you and your husband took the flat?'

'No, sir. We had them put on. We were broken into and – and nothing was taken. They were looking for documents we had from Germany, documents which proved Hitler's plans for —'

'Dr Wesemann,' his tone was icy, 'I say again: I will not have politics introduced into my court. And I do not need to warn you of the consequences for refugees in this country who continue to engage in the political agitations, whatever those may be, of their home country.'

'I'm sorry,' I said automatically.

But he had picked the wrong threat for me. And then I glimpsed a face in the crowd that I could put together: Fenner! About halfway down the aisle, on the end. Fenner had told the newspapers this week that Dora was 'the bravest person' he had known. I had no other worth than to keep speaking here. There would be no other time. I cleared my throat.

'It is that very fear, sir, of being sent back that motivated my husband to work for them, to turn over Berthold Jacob and to betray Dora as his outlet —'

The coroner banged a gavel on his desk and the room was shocked. His voice came out with a studied calm. 'I have warned you, Dr Wesemann, that in this country we do not permit the courts to become fora for unsubstantiated political innuendo. I am asking you about the locked room. Specifically. And I would be grateful if you would confine your answer to this matter alone. Now, can you tell me, if you would, who else had a key, or keys, to the flat?'

This is a question I wanted. 'I had keys. Dora and Mathilde of course. And Professor Wolf.'

There were cries of outrage in the room. The associate banged his own gavel.

'Thank you, Dr Wesemann,' the coroner said when the noise subsided. 'You may stand down now.'

But I had not finished. I held on to the edge of the stand. 'But Your Honour, we had death threats before this happened! Letters and phone calls —'

'Now, Dr Wesemann.' His tone was curt, as to a misbehaving child. 'Thank you.'

The orderlies or watchmen or whatever they were moved towards me. I stood down before they could complete my humiliation.

Wolf was recalled. He flatly denied having keys to the flat.

It was 1.15 p.m. when the coroner summed up: two lives were worth precisely an hour and forty minutes of his time. He told the jury that Dora's shorthand note – 'if she wrote the note, and if it was correctly translated' – indicated that she had committed suicide because of 'unrequited love'. The fact that the door to the room was locked from the inside – a room on the top level of the building, inaccessible by any other means – was one that the jury needed to take into account in their deliberations. He said the situation in the case of Mathilde was 'far less clear', because it was unlikely a woman of her age and character would be dominated by her younger flatmate. It was possible, though, that Mathilde was suffering 'the imbalance of mind known as depression', to which many refugees were vulnerable in this country. He said that Dr Fabian may have administered the poison to Mrs Wurm before drinking it herself, though 'of course this is a matter of fact for you to decide'.

The decision took twenty minutes. The foreman came back in and we rose.

'We find that in both cases,' the man read, 'the deceased committed suicide whilst of unsound mind, by means of self-administered narcotic poisoning.'

The room was still. Then there were noises, but no uproar. The people were infected by the terror of what had happened to Dora and Mathilde, a terror magnified by what had just taken place in this room: there was no earthly authority to turn to, no one who would believe them and keep them safe.

The coroner left through a side door, the jury through one on the opposite wall. I remained seated as the room emptied. The world was closing over her. She wouldn't leave a trace.

TOLLER

I stood outside the court smoking, walking up and down like a schoolboy on detention. I watched as they all spilled out onto the steps. The mood was worse than at a funeral, fear being more awful than sadness. Ruth didn't come out.

I went in. The room was empty. Had they taken her away? And then I noticed the curve of a back, just visible in the front row. Bent over and rocking. When I reached her I saw that her mouth was open in a silent cry. She registered me.

'I tried . . .'

I helped her up. The funeral was in one hour, at three o'clock. We had to catch the underground, then a bus out to the Jewish cemetery at East Ham.

They were plain wooden boxes, each covered in dark cloth. I'd say there were a dozen of us all told, gathered up the front of the synagogue. The service was short. Ruth sat sunk into a pew, sobbing. When I hoisted one corner of Dora's coffin onto my shoulder it was horribly light. The rabbi led the way. The sky was low, rain falling on my face. Two fresh pits had been dug next to one another at the back of the cemetery.

'Thou shalt not be afraid of the terror by night nor of the arrow that flies by day,' the rabbi intoned. Ruth swayed beneath an umbrella but held herself upright. 'He shall cover thee with His feathers and under His wings shalt thou take refuge.'

Fenner, Lord Marley and I took up shovels as they lowered the coffins. It is the turning away, the walking off to tea, that is the hardest part.

Outside the iron gates journalists had gathered, from *News Chronicle*, *Daily Express*, *News of the World* and *Jewish Daily Post*. I mounted the running-board of the hearse. Someone held an umbrella over me and I began.

'We have buried here today a brave woman,' I said. 'She died fighting for us all – for the people of Germany who suffer under the tyrant, and for the peoples of Europe against whom he is determined to go to war.' I was speaking over a huddle of black umbrellas. 'I, personally, owe Dora a huge debt of gratitude . . .'

The umbrellas parted. Between their black-boned segments, something bent and white was pushing. I kept talking.

'It was Dora Fabian who smuggled out of Germany, at risk of her life, my manuscripts . . .' My mouth kept moving but Ruth had all my attention. 'And I tell you today, categorically, that there can be no connection between this alleged note to Professor Wolf and her death . . .'

Ruth had taken off her jacket and dropped her bag; her white shirt was stuck to her torso and her red skirt stained dark with streaks of water. She walked to the cemetery gates. When she reached them I watched her face into the sheeting rain, turning each way down the street. She could not know the area, which direction to take. She walked halfway across the street, stopping at the white lines in the middle. Took off her shoes. The rain was pelting now, the sky had broken its moorings. She started running. Cars had their lights on, honked at the racing woman to get off the road. Curtains in houses parted to see: a picture of lopsided grief, a bull in the ring trying to outrun its pain.

RUTH

The funeral does not bear remembering.

Afterwards Toller cruised the streets in a cab with my hand-bag and shoes. When he found me, he took me back to Great Ormond Street. We sat on the edge of her bed together; there was nowhere else to be. I hadn't touched it. The pillows still had their hollows in them. We stared out the window, me soaked and him holding my bag. Grief was making of us a club of two.

'You'll be all right?' he asked, after a time.

He was asking this of himself, as much as of me. Whatever strength he'd found to address the journalists had deserted him. He started to weep. Then he turned and put a hand to the pillow where her head had been, and moved as if to place his cheek in the indentation. Something in me snapped.

'You should go home. To Christiane.'

I sank into her bed where she had been. I planned it there.

I don't remember telling anyone what I was going to do, but

that doesn't mean I didn't let it slip. I was heedless, desperate. Three weeks after the funeral I went to visit my parents in Poland. When she saw me my mother said, 'You are not in your right mind.' She assumed it was grief. I had no faith that my mind had been right before at all.

My plan was to go back into the Reich, up to Berlin. I would retrieve Toller's other suitcase from the garden shed on Bornholmer Strasse. No one else knew where it was, apart from Uncle Erwin, and he would never risk sending it directly to Toller. It seemed to be the one part of Dora's work I might be competent to finish. While I was doing it I could maintain my connection to her, to our common project. And if they got me, I deserved it.

I took with me *The Other Germany* leaflets we'd printed. One hundred and fifty of them, on tissue paper pressed flat against my stomach, crossways under my navel. I borrowed the Polish passport of a school friend who resembled me and got the tram to the station.

They were waiting for me there. Two Gestapo agents, and a woman to do the body search. She asked me to undress and took the leaflets. I suppose they'd been watching me. They put me on the same train to Berlin I had a ticket for, keeping guard outside the compartment door. That arrest has provided me with the one heroic act I have retold my whole life, and in which I cannot, of course, believe. Having failed to do it myself, I was now getting Them to do the punishing for me.

In a cellar at Prinz-Albrecht-Strasse they splayed me like a starfish on the wall and shot around me clockwise, the bullets spitting plaster between my legs and hands and onto my hair. They wore earmuffs, as for target practice. The interrogator wanted information about our party meetings in London; he wanted to know Dora's source for the documents from Göring's office. After the last shot he said, 'The next one goes into you.' When

I turned my head to look at him he saw that I did not care, so he would not give me the satisfaction.

My father hired the best Nazi lawyer he could find. The judges – twelve of them, no less – were all in Nazi uniforms, but when Father came into the courtroom, an old Jew with a war injury and his medals jangling on his chest, they stood to honour him. At that early stage, they still loved the war more than they hated the Jews. The prosecution wanted to put me away for twelve years. If that had happened I would have been killed in the camps like all the others. But money will buy you many things. I only got five.

I spent most of them in solitary. Alone in my cell I was required to make 144 fake chrysanthemums every day, scraping a metal implement over wax paper to curl each petal. My fists cramped in pain. Such idiotic work, making decorations for the salons of the Berlin bourgeoisie, that if the other prisoners didn't have political ideas when they came in I thought they'd develop them quick enough. My own thoughts turned mostly in a small personal circle, around all I did not see, and all I did not say. They turned around Hans and Bertie and Dora and me.

When my father's heart failed in the third year of my term, my mother offered to pay for a private police escort of six armed men so I could attend the funeral. Permission was denied.

I was released in October 1939. War had broken out. Some have found it strange – another piece of undeserved good luck, their veiled looks say – that I was released at all, and not simply sent to be gassed and burnt like all the rest. But unlike the rest I had the benefit of a sentence imposed by the law, and it required, at its end, that I be set free.

The Nazis duly stuck to the letter of it, but added a creative ultimatum. At the prison gate I was given twenty-four hours to leave the Reich: if found on German soil after that time, I would be sent to a concentration camp. I was a grouse, being set into flight before hunters. I thought back to when Hans and I had been given twenty-four hours to leave. This time they weighted the stakes in their favour by confiscating my passport.

I boarded a train to my mother's villa in Königsdorf. When the ticket collector came I hid in the toilet, and when the military police did their sweep I stood on the outside platform behind the last carriage. My brother had left for Switzerland, so Cook had moved into the house to keep Mother company. When I came in Cook held my face in two hands, tears leaking silently. In the entrance hall a letter with my name on it sat on a silver salver, postmarked three years before.

'I knew you would come to get it,' Mother said. That small sentence carried the freight of a lifetime's undeclared love.

I need to go home. They are waiting for me in my front room.

I hope I didn't say that aloud.

I tell the nice nurse MARGARET PEARCE I want to leave. She says she'll see what she can do. When she comes back she tells me the doctor isn't happy about it, but, as she reminded him – and her tone implies that these child doctors need corralling – 'We have a new policy of letting people go home, so long as palliative care can be arranged.' It's the first time anyone has said 'palliative care' to me.

Do I have anyone to care for me? she asks, jangling and smiling behind her half-glasses. This is clearly a step-by-step procedure. Nothing to worry about, all quite by the book.

Bev picks me up from the hospital. She opens the drawers next to the bed without asking, packs my things into my toilet bag. I submit to this invasion of privacy because at my age one needs mothering, again. And again, I think, as she clatters about and I look at the hospital triangle hanging above me where once hung a butcher's rig, one must accept the mothering however it comes.

My head is bandaged this time as well. I am reduced to an eye on the world, a single aperture.

I watch Bev work with a brusque kindness I know will turn into a story in her own honour later. Her spotted hands are covered in cheap gold rings. I wonder if she would eat her own fist to make me laugh.

In my kitchen Bev gives me instant noodles and puts my pills into a lurid fluorescent container she has bought specially, as she tells me. It has compartments for every day of the week, morning, noon and night. The pills sit in there in their colours and shapes ready to push me, in plastic-coated increments, into my future. She holds my hand in hers before she leaves. She says, 'Dear. Dear.' She is crying.

After the war I came to this sunstruck place. It is a glorious country, which aspires to no kind of glory. Its people aim for something both more basic and more difficult: decency. I couldn't see it at first, but now it is all around me, quiet and fundamental. It is in the hydrotherapy angel and the smiling Melnikoff, in Trudy Stephenson my pupil and the scrap-haired woman holding the traffic at bay, in the nurses and the baby doctor. It is, I would hazard a guess, in Bev.

The letter on my mother's salver was from Bertie. I have kept it with me through all that came afterwards. I must have read it a hundred times. It is five pages long. The last page, with his best wishes and blessing, hangs framed in my kitchen. I take it down now and place it on the bench next to the pills.

The Swiss government's protest worked: the Nazis set Bert free after six months in custody. He went back to France, while Hans languished in a cell in Basel. Though Hans begged the German government to make the same kinds of protests on his behalf to get him back, the Nazis left him there to rot.

Bert wanted me to know that he too hadn't seen what was

coming. He wanted me to know how it happened. Bertie wrote that he'd met Hans at the restaurant in Basel. Hans was at a table with two others, a man he introduced as Mattern, and the forger. Bertie hadn't been expecting anyone else, but Hans explained that both men worked together. Bert produced the photo he had brought for the passport, and the forger wrote down his date of birth, height and eye colour on a piece of paper. Without asking, the man wrote 'Religion: Jewish' in his notes.

They drank fairly solidly for an hour and a half. Then the forger said that 'for the money part' he would prefer them to come to his flat in Riehen. Bert said he looked at Hans, who nodded calmly: it must have been part of the plan. Downstairs a car was waiting. 'What self-respecting forger doesn't have a car with a chauffeur?' Bertie wrote.

Bert and Hans got in the back of the car, Mattern and the forger sat in the front next to the driver. Bert didn't know where the district of Riehen was. They passed a train station on the edge of town, then drove into the night where there was nothing. The car was going fast. He looked at Hans, who shrugged his shoulders as if to say, Who knows how these things are done? There was enough alcohol in Bert's system to be second-guessing his first responses, telling himself to calm down.

Until they got to a guard's hut with the Swiss flag hanging from it. The border! Instead of slowing as the sentry stepped out, the car accelerated. The man had to leap clear to save himself. Bertie cried out then, and Hans too. Mattern and the forger snapped around to rest the stubby snouts of Mausers on the back of their seat.

'Gestapo swine!' Hans shouted. Mattern pistol-whipped him, hard, across the face. When the car reached the German boomgate, it was already raised.

At Weil am Rhein they sped down Adolf-Hitler-Strasse to the police station, pulling up around the back. Men were coming out of the building, shouting. Hans was hunched on his side, one hand holding the door handle. Bert was cowering too, but in all the movement and noise he felt oddly calm. After all, he wrote, some kind of end is not unexpected, not unimagined: so this was it. And Hans was with him.

Then, without speaking, Hans turned away and opened the door. In seconds he was a white shirt disappearing into the dark. 'He didn't say a single thing to me.'

Mattern took his time aiming and shooting a single bullet. 'Shot while attempting to escape,' someone said. There were snickers. The choreography of the scene gave them away. 'I wasn't even angry at first,' Bert wrote. 'It was more an emptiness, as if my soul had been removed.'

Bert asked to see Hans's body; of course they refused to produce it. The interrogation in the provincial police station lasted till after midnight. Then they put him, under guard, on a train for Berlin.

Bertie said that Dora had died trying to save him. He said we were tied together like climbers on a mountain and if they picked one off the rest would fall. And about Hans he wrote, 'I was fooled to the end, so how could you not be?'

But Bert had not known all that I knew. I have kept his letter hung up in my kitchen to remind me at what price my survival has come.

Bertie added a postscript about Wolfram Wolf. The British, he said, though availing themselves of Wolf's story so as to avoid any conflict with Berlin, didn't believe it themselves. Shortly after the inquest they expelled him from the country. Wolf wasn't politically active in any way, but they knew he was the cover guy for the Nazi action. A cover they themselves had made use of.

*   *   *

My mother had two identical dresses made for me from the blue-and-white curtains in the vestibule at home. She stayed there until, after their invasion, the Germans requisitioned the villa as their headquarters for our region. Then she fled east, my poor, proud mother. I heard that she suicided under a train in Warsaw, before it took off for the camps.

From Königsdorf I managed to get a train to Genoa, where the docks were filled with Germans and Poles, Romanians and Estonians – every spectrum of humanity fleeing the coming cataclysm. At the ticket window I paid for passage in steerage to Shanghai, the only port that would accept refugees without passports. People slept about the docks. Children dozed on bags or wriggled in their mother's arms; men sat on the ground playing cards for matches. I had three days to wait.

The morning of my departure I was washing my alternate dress in a tub on a ramp near the water when I saw him. There were still boats that accommodated first-class passengers. Well-dressed people with decent luggage and papers boarded in a leisurely, ceremonial way, with the staff lined up in greeting and a bugler, bugling. In full view of us human detritus. I dropped the dress.

Hans – it was him, surely – was in a pale suit with a gold cravat at his neck. I started slowly, then broke into a run. People skittered out of my way. I tripped on a coiled rope or a bag or a person. When I reached the ship the ticket collector moved his body to block the gangway.

'*Biglietto, Signora?*'

'Where . . .?' was all I could think to say, trying to look behind him. '*Dove* —?'

'Venezuela,' he said. '*Biglietto?*'

The man knew I wouldn't have one; I was undernourished and had no luggage, my dress was wet and my wrists grazed red. I craned to see. Now turned away, Hans was pressing his right hand into a fur coat worn by a woman with dark hair up in a chignon. They vanished into the crowd on the lower deck.

I have seen him numerous times since then, in the way you might glimpse someone you once loved, or someone who died, in the shape of the back of a head on the ferry, or a distant, lax-legged walk. It brings the same sick lurch in the stomach, though it is not from love. I feel thrown away. Other times he has shown his face in my dreams. Then I feel fury. Sometimes something worse: wanting. Wanting his good opinion, wanting him. I wake disgusted that I have not been able to shake the power over me I ceded to him at eighteen, and get myself back, complete.

In Shanghai we foreigners lived under Japanese occupation. Because Germany was an ally the Japanese didn't intern us, but we were crammed into a closed area, under curfew. I shared a partitioned room with a female tram driver from Berlin and I nearly starved. I fell pregnant to a self-taught Polish philosopher in exile. The doctor said if I could barely feed myself, there was no hope for carrying a child. I paid him for the abortion with a large tin of Nescafé, worth more than money on the black market. All my hair fell out. When it grew again it was still dark but thin, leaving white gaps of scalp when I pulled it back. The sorrow I felt from the abortion has gotten worse, not better, with time.

The news didn't come to me until 1944. Fenner sent his letter care of the Shanghai Baptist College, where I was teaching by then. I took it to the park at lunchtime and sat on an ironwork seat around a tree. It was hot. Somewhere the toothless old man played his two-stringed erhu. Birds hung in cages in the trees, where people had brought them out to taste the air. In the part of the city where I lived there were no birds, they had all been eaten.

The Nazis never made the connection between Uncle Erwin and Dora. They never could account for how information about their secret air force got from Göring's desk into the British parliament, and into the papers. They satisfied themselves with the thought that Bertie had somehow, through his arcane sources, given the facts to Dora.

After she was killed, Fenner kept in contact with Bertie, who was living in Paris. When the Germans invaded France Bertie was interned, but Fenner's Independent Labour Party helped him escape to neutral Portugal. They installed him in a flat above a pet shop on Lisbon's Rua Ouro while they tried to procure him an American visa. There was no guard, Fenner wrote, but the party was looking out for him. Their people warned him not to go for walks on the street, in fact not to leave the flat. They arranged for a woman to deliver food. It must have seemed to Bertie, though, so unlikely that he'd be followed here, from the internment camp at Le Vernet, over the Pyrenees to the backstreets of Lisbon. All he wanted was the newspaper. He could see the kiosk from his window. It would take five minutes.

The limousine had three men in it. Bertie was nabbed off the street and driven to Berlin, put in a cell on Prinz-Albrecht-Strasse. There, over months that turned into years, the other prisoners watched him get thinner and sicker. But he remained their unfailing source of hope because he never wavered: he was utterly convinced of an Allied victory. 'Hold your head high,' he told one of them, 'don't let the pigs see how beat you are.'

At the start of 1942 Bert had to have his teeth removed. Fenner believed the Germans were keeping him alive thinking he might have some exchange value for the Allies. In February, after a beating, he was taken to the prison hospital to die. He weighed thirty-two kilograms. The cause of death was recorded as tuberculosis.

Fenner wrote that he was saddened and very sorry. 'I have failed you all,' he said.

That was it then. Dora was gone, and Toller had been dragged under too, just before the war. Now Bertie.

Somewhere, though, Hans was at large in a land of mojito sticks and quietly available boys, probably still in the pay of the Germans. I did not want to share survival with him.

By 1947 I had enough money for passage to Australia. In Sydney I worked in a trouser factory in a suburb where trees would not grow, where the weather forecasters always had it a degree or two hotter.

Sometimes I would give Dora another life, one with a different ending. The human brain cannot encompass total absence. Like infinity, it is simply not something that the organ runs to. The space someone leaves must be filled, so we dream forever of those who are no longer here. Our minds make them live again. They try, God bless them, to account for the gap which the brain itself cannot fathom.

She goes on working from London after the war breaks out. Mathilde buys the stationery as usual from Cohn's and Dora finishes her book about the psychological attraction of fascism for women, forgetting to eat the meals Mathilde has prepared and pacing the balcony trailing smoke. In her book Dora writes that women are taught to want an ideal man, a model from whom reality always falls short, so they are vulnerable to a leader who says he knows them and who promises to be 'true'. He can remain ideal, their lives can continue to fall short, and in the space between, the women live with desire itself, which is a pleasure all of its own quite apart from its fulfilment. Dora's book is celebrated. She is a German de Beauvoir: less sex, but more political. She stops seeing Wolfram Wolf, but continues to love others as a pastime, a benign diversion. Her victory is in decoupling the female fantasy from the instant pleasures called Fenner Brockway, Lord Marley, and then others – English, American, a Czech in exile. She stays in contact with Toller, who, despite her best efforts, has taken up permanent residence in a chamber of her heart, forbidding all others entry there.

Maybe he too survives. These things being contagious.

After the war she covers the Nuremberg Trials for the *Manchester Guardian*, compiles a book from these pieces and dedicates it to Bert. She calls it *What We Knew*. She shares a literary prize in America with Hannah Arendt, who only came to these things afterwards.

Then Eleanor Roosevelt invites her to America at Toller's suggestion. She becomes provost of an elite women's college, she publishes in *The Nation* and decries Korea, Vietnam. She goes on Johnny Carson's TV show wearing lipstick someone must have put on her. It gets in her teeth.

I like to think of Dora, but at the same time it is also true that I take little pleasure in these imaginings. I do it as a way of trying to measure the dimensions of loss. As if it might, one day, be finite.

In 1952 a box of my things arrived in Bondi Junction. It had been packaged up by the Social Democrats-in-Exile and stored in London. The box contained two photo albums, my camera, the pink porcelain pig pot (of all things to follow me!) and my PhD certificate. Finally I could prove my qualifications from Germany and be accepted into a high school to teach languages. Slowly, I started to photograph this place, which made me see it better.

That same year I received the letter from Jaeger – Dora's German embassy man in London – looking for Ruth Wesemann. I had long since resumed my maiden name. I wrote back, and we had a small correspondence.

Six months after Dora died Jaeger's London posting had

ended. He returned to Berlin, where he remained in the Foreign Office through the years building up to the war, then for the war and its aftermath. Passing information between Erwin Thomas in Berlin and Dora in London, he wrote, though it had not even been his initiative, was the single shred of evidence he had of his own decency. When it was all over he had requested, in some kind of atonement, to be transferred to the Reparations Payments Department in the Treasury of the Federal Republic of Germany.

This man Jaeger, whom I never met, wanted to make sure I received my pension for the time I'd spent in prison. I accepted, of course, because a teacher's salary was meagre and my parents' villa and everything in it had been lost behind the Iron Curtain. Jaeger was also, gently, tying up loose ends. 'You will know,' he wrote, 'the fate of my esteemed colleague Erwin Thomas.' I had no idea. He said Thomas never forgot Dora. The day Jaeger returned to Berlin Thomas visited him in his office. 'I was the only colleague he could come to.' Thomas remembered a girl, he told Jaeger, standing on a red carpet giving him a lecture. He wept.

Uncle Erwin had no other contacts in the resistance. He survived for years deep in Göring's ministry. To leave would have invited suspicion. In 1944 his chance came when von Stauffenberg and other senior insiders planned the bomb-in-the-briefcase assassination of Hitler. Erwin Thomas was their contact man high up in the Ministry of the Interior; he would be issuing the interim orders in Göring's place once the Leader was dead. After the bomb went off, for the afternoon of a single day when the plotters thought Hitler had died, Thomas stood tall, gave the orders, started to undo his years of closely watched criminality. At four o'clock the news came that Hitler was still alive. The following afternoon Uncle Erwin was taken with von Stauffenberg and the others to the back of army headquarters and shot.

Jaeger thought I was also entitled to be told what the Foreign

Office had known of Hans. He said, politely, that of course I may know this already. I did not. Apart from in dreams, Hans had been lost to me.

In Venezuela, Hans had tried to curry favour with the German embassy in Caracas by reporting on other émigrés. This had prompted the embassy people to keep tabs on him. Hans had married a wealthy woman and begun to breed a local species of water rat for their pelts. When he contracted malaria, thinking himself on his deathbed, he converted to Catholicism. The marriage did not last and the business failed. Desperate for funds, he tried to turn in the priest who had nursed and converted him, for spying. Still the Germans would have nothing to do with him, so he left for the United States.

Hans was in Texas when America joined the war. The Americans interned him as an enemy alien. When the war ended, the Socialist Workers Party members who went back to Germany sought to have him extradited to face trial for his crimes against them. Hans hired a small-time New York immigration lawyer on the Lower East Side and successfully evaded their demands. There were no further reports from that time.

Jaeger enclosed a copy of the very first report on Hans from the German embassy in London to the Foreign Office in Berlin. Dated 21 September 1933, it was typed on letterhead and marked 'Top Clearance Only'.

From: Rüter, German Embassy, London
To: F.O.
CC: Reichsmarschall Göring

A Hans Wesemann, formerly a journalist in Berlin, came in today without an appointment, demanding an audience with the Ambassador. Herr Wesemann appeared to be in a state of high agitation, if not outright anxiety. He spoke with a pronounced stammer. He was brought in to me.

Herr Wesemann's name will be familiar to you perhaps as it was to me: he is a member of the Socialist Workers Party and the journalist who penned the slanderous attacks on both the Führer and Herr Dr Goebbels.

Herr Wesemann led me to understand that it was now clear to him from the distance of exile that the agitations of his former self and of his former and current colleagues and associates both in the Reich and now in Britain were distasteful acts against the Fatherland. He expressed the view that one's connection to one's country is not severable by distance, and may even be made the stronger for it. This he has only come to realise, he says, when separated from Germany. He said he feared, were he not able to receive some support from us, that he would be drawn back into that world of treason.

In return for our protection and some payment (see below), Herr Wesemann alleges he has information and connections, from his association with Socialist Workers Party-in-Exile, which might prove useful in protecting the Fatherland. Wesemann mentioned in particular that he had the trust of Berthold Jacob and of Ernst Toller. Furthermore, he alleged that his wife's cousin, one Dr Dora Fabian, formerly secretary to Herr Toller, is Jacob's conduit for smuggling classified information from the Reich Government into Britain and arranging for its publication in the press.

In support of his claims Wesemann produced a document, allegedly from the office of Reichsmarschall Göring, outlining the air capabilities of the Reich (encl.). If this paper is genuine it would appear to indicate a leak from the Reichsmarschall's office, perhaps via Jacob or another source, to Dr Fabian in Britain. Please confirm:

1. Origin and authenticity of the document and;

2. What action to be taken re Herr Wesemann, B. Jacob and
   Dr Fabian.

Herr Wesemann says that he is supported by funds from
his wife's father in Silesia, but that he is looking for an alternative source of income. Proposing payment of a weekly retainer
for services and information offered. I gave him £10; request
approval for instating more permanent honorarium.

Heil Hitler
Rüter
First Secretary

Seeing it in black and white, the sale of us for money and
protection, comes always, every time I read it, like a stab.

Later, I heard other things from Jaeger's successor. In 1956 a tall
European man was arrested in Oaxaca, Mexico, for a crime against
the morals of a minor. He gave his name as Ernst Toller, but within
a week Interpol revealed him to be Hans Wesemann, born 1895.

Then the details got sketchier. Hans tried to make the fugitive Nazis
in Mexico his friends, but even they did not trust him. The last report
was from 1961. Hans bought dried rabbit meat from a woman at the
covered market in Ciudad Juárez, telling her he was setting off into
the Chihuahuan Desert with a donkey and supplies. He was going to
peddle the meat to villages close to the US border and make a killing.

I hope I have outlived him.

TOLLER

This hotel chair is low, I can lie right back. I am a small man, bigger inside – I liked to think – than my frame could reasonably be expected to bear. My chest lifts and falls of its own accord. I look over my belly and hips, groin and legs, feet. Those feet embarrassed me all my childhood, dangling from chairs and never touching the ground. But really this body has served me well, been faithful in pleasure and done its best in pain. I hold up my hands. I know every word they have written, gun they held, caress they've given.

After she died London was empty for me. Christiane and I left for the New World. Hollywood didn't want me, but I hope this place will be kinder to Christiane.

I close my eyes. I am tired. But there is work to do – she always says it is about the work, not about me. *Grossly exaggerated*, she says, sand squeaking under her elbow. Bells outside. A peal of life, shunting the hours of the day. Who would have thought? Her hair has grown longer, but it is the very same hair, in luscious black waves. The very same neck. How ridiculous to have been so sad for so long when here she is, right in front of me! And there's so much to explain. All the things she's missed out on, all the work we have to do. For which I suddenly, mysteriously, have the energy. I won't ask where she's been, she'll only laugh at me. Her *freedom*, remember. Main thing is, she's here, feet on the rungs of that chair, tanned forearms hovering, bitten fingers edging the steno pad. Only do *not* turn! That hair I have run my hands through, tight at moments of communion.

Do *not* turn around.

And these four years lived with a hole in my heart and the wind soughing through it – for what? She's right. *Monstrous waste of time.* We must get down to it now. The world needs us; together we can do it – find some way around Franco. His stupid victory parade two days ago. I wonder if she knows Berthold Jacob is safe and in France? We can do it with him!

And I am filled, now, with something else – something that makes the sorrow inside me ridiculous and small, a personal indulgence in a world I had come unstuck from. No. It is more, even, than that. Suddenly I am a different man. It runs through me and I hover above the world; I have breached a membrane that keeps us from seeing, and from pity, and I am filled, filled in this chair to the brim with the calm, visceral certainty of us all being forgivable. And all, ultimately, saved. It is a peace that spreads through me like warmth. It is a gift, a final, unaccountable joy. If I were a religious man I would call it grace. The black-winged reproaches are laughable compared to this truth. I laugh.

She turns. This girl who is not her.

The room is small, cream coloured. I am empty. The act of remembering Dora did bring her back. But, as it turns out, it was better to live with the idea that I would get to her one day. Now that I have summoned her up and written her down she is more dead than before. Am I the only person to carry her with me? Will the world forget we tried so hard to save it?

I wonder if her cousin still lives.

Clara is standing there, a question on her face. She must have asked me something.

'Sorry?' I say. And I am. Clara's kindness is my all.

'The usual for you today?' There is no impatience in her voice. She has lived with me through these weeks and this morning, through my reckoning and tears, and just waited, unafraid, for the story to come. She knew not to comfort me or the spell of my girl would be broken. And, now that it is over, she knows – how does someone so young know this? – that my girl is gone. It is to practical things that we must turn. In this case, bagels.

'I think I'll have rye today. Instead. Please.'

'Okay.'

'Oh, and would you deliver this to Christiane for me?' I pass her the note.

'Sure.'

But she makes no move to the door.

'Anything else? Coffee?'

'Yes. Coffee. Thank you.' I smile up at her as if everything's all right, she can go now.

She does not believe me. 'Why don't you come too?' She pulls some hair out from under her jacket collar. 'Stretch your legs.'

'I just want to sit.'

And then the unexpected. She, I think, as surprised as I am. Clara places one hand on the arm of the green-and-gold chair, bends to my cheek and kisses me softly, quite long. My eyes close.

'You did well,' she says into my ear. It is finished.

I can't speak.

At the door she turns. 'I'll be half an hour, at the most. All right? Just . . .' She's stuck for words. 'Just wait.'

The door closes behind her. One minute there is life in the room, the next it goes out. I am nothing. I am an eye with nothing behind it, an eye on the closed steno pad on the desk with my love inside it, and next to it the photographs of the dead children of Spain whom I also failed. The newspaper still folded: somewhere deep inside it the beginnings of this war we have not prevented, and a ship of Jews being sent back into it. And the curtains behind the desk – I notice for the first time there's a flower pattern running over (or is it under?) the stripes, like embossing. Christiane's cord tying them back.

I used to make my wife pack a length of rope in my suitcases. Oh God oh God – fetid bird-stink, the bluesteel flash of beak. That beast will have me, it will not leave here until it gets what it wants. There is a hook on the back of the bathroom door. If it will hold.

I get up to write a note for Ruth. If she lives she is the first audience for my efforts, the one who also loved yet failed her. She should have this before any publisher. The one thing she always had, that kind, lopsided listener, was the ability to imagine herself into another's skin. I think it distracted her, really. Clara will find her.

My hand trembles over the paper. There is no neat cover note for passing this life – Dora's life – from one person to another. I find I am out of words. So I just write 'For Ruth Wesemann' and put the note on top of Clara's steno pad, which lies on the book. The parts she has already typed Clara has inserted into it. I go to the window and untie the cord. A puppy downstairs has wound its lead around a parking meter; two young Negro women in pastel hats, one green, one violet, walk under the fringed entrance canopy and emerge, as expected, on the other side. The cord runs coolly through my fingers, will slip nicely. I will not fail this time.

In the bathroom there is nothing, just a flickering light. There is no time for thinking; for once no point coming up with words to recreate this later: there is no later! The idea is a relief to me. This, too, is a practical matter. I tie a slipknot firmly around the hook on the door, and make another, wider one for my head. My poor hands shake their protest but I get the cord over me, turn my back to the door.

I feel the exact same feeling – hesitation and blind purpose – as before jumping into a cold pool. The fall off the block.

Nothing more —

RUTH

When Bev is gone I get out of bed and make my way down the hall to the front room. My balance is slightly out and I trail my fingertips along the wall. I flick the switch in the room. But the darkness has come inside! The ceiling is black – it is moulting and velvety. Bev must have left a window open; the bogong moths have come in on their migration and lined the place. The room shimmers with brief, misdirected life.

I am a vessel of memory in a world of forgetting.

I sit under the canopy of moths. It is deep dark outside. Everything out there, every squat, sun-bleached house and frangipani tree, the domed synagogue and brick school, the rag-tag shops, the cliffs with the ocean behind them, has vanished. The world has shrunk to a small area of light from the streetlamp. Lines of rain slash through its bright cone. The bogongs are welcome here.

I pick up Ernst. It occurs to me only now: he must have thought of me in his last hours in that hotel.

Toller was always kind to me, but it was clear he inhabited a different sphere. I was neither beautiful nor important enough to occupy a place in his world. But he did not send me this life of his with Dora put back in because I am her cousin. He has sent it because we had her in common. We were the two for whom she was the sun. We moved in her orbit and the force of her kept us going.

His book opens in my hands to this: 'Most people have no imagination. If they could imagine the sufferings of others, they would not make them suffer so.'

This is what we all believed. It is what he believed, I suppose, till he could no longer.

Imagining the life of another is an act of compassion as holy as any. We drafted the leaflets, cyclostyled the truth. We told the stories on butter paper, in cigar canisters, smuggled them back into Germany. We risked our lives to help our fellows – there and in London – imagine. They did not imagine it. But Toller, great as he was, is not right. It is not that people lack an imagination. It is that they stop themselves using it. Because once you have imagined such suffering, how can you still do nothing?

Now, at a distance of seventy years, it is safe to imagine, because no one can be called on to act. No one held to account. The costume party will not be interrupted. Of course, for me, the failure runs deeper. I failed to imagine the need inside Hans, and I failed to see his turning.

And here I am, in a week when a manuscript was delivered, I swam, I went for cake and fell, they patched me up and sent me home. But in truth I have been with them all along. I can imagine what it is like to be another till I float in and out of them, till the imagining sets like memory. How else can we know anyone, love anyone, but by imagining ourselves inside their skin?

I see the room as clearly as my own. As clearly as when I found it.

They were armed when they entered, bulges at their hips, but not uniformed. Five of them, with hats on. Slipping quietly into the building using the keys copied from the set Wolfram Wolf handed over. Their people had been watching the flat, waiting until the Swiss investigator was gone and the two women were alone. They had to wait a week. It was Sunday evening.

The action had been discussed in Berlin and London. It would have been simplest to shoot them of course, as they had Lessing and Rudi. There was no need to kidnap Dora because they had her source already. She just needed silencing. But a shooting in Bloomsbury would have upset the English, and the English were upset enough. Also, she had contacts in high places. So shooting was ruled out, and they would need five men, two on each woman and one to give the order.

They'd approached Wolf in a bakery, when he was buying his morning rolls. He'd looked at them as if at the sudden incarnation of all his fears. They escorted him to a seat in Russell Square to discuss a proposition. It was hardly much to ask, they said: lend them some keys, write a letter, barely anything at all. Wolf stammered something about it not being possible; at the inevitable inquest his relationship with Dora would become known and his wife would find out. Then they mentioned his daughter, in Denmark, how convenient it was for her that she could walk to school. They spoke of other relatives in Germany who were still free; they terrified him with what might, in certain as yet undefined circumstances, happen to them. When he worried about having to imitate her handwriting they knew they had him. They were in a position, they said, to ensure that Scotland Yard would hand the note over to the German embassy for translation and graphology. It would be 'taken care of'. Wolf came up with the idea of using shorthand himself, as an extra protection.

He wrote the suicide note on Sunday morning, typed his own address on the envelope. He dropped it through the letterbox around the corner from 12 Great Ormond Street, then walked swiftly past the children's hospital with his collar up and hat pulled low, lest one of the women come out, slowing only once he got to the corner.

They knew from their previous visits to the flat how much Veronal was likely to be in the bathroom cabinet, but they hadn't been in there while the Swiss was staying so they brought their own just in case, along with a bolt-cutter. It was evening. They let themselves in with the keys; the door was not chained. They found Dora in her pyjamas, Mathilde still dressed. The flat smelled of coffee. There was no discussion, no fanfare about it. This was a plan devised and approved at the highest level, rehearsed, and now to be implemented. They kept their gloves on.

They gagged each woman and tied her to a chair in the kitchen. Dora counted while they emptied three sachets into each cup. So this was how she would go. Tailor-made.

The boss man used this time to visit the famed hall cupboard he'd read about in the reports. When he came back into the kitchen he nodded at one of the men standing next to Mathilde, who placed the muzzle of his gun cold against her temple. He addressed Dora. They would shoot Mathilde if she did not drink. And quietly. Understand?

Mathilde moved her eyes, her head, almost imperceptibly, to indicate no. Dora should not drink. It was nonsensical to think that Mathilde would be let go after this. When they took Dora's gag off for her to drink she screamed. A glove slammed over her mouth and nose; the gag was retied, tighter. So they would make her watch instead.

They removed Mathilde's gag. She kept her eyes firmly on Dora: the two of them were still there, together. Mathilde opened her mouth when they told her to. Dora knew the taste, bitter, granular. It took Mathilde three swallows. They put the gag back on. There was no fear in her eyes. She was still Mathilde, for the time it would take. Dora's eyes filled.

'Look what you've done now,' the boss man said.

Where do they get these calm killers from? He nodded at the one standing to Dora's left, who yanked her head back by the hair and pinched her nose together. The other untied the gag and her jaw fell open. They poured the bitter stuff into her. Drops spilled onto her pyjamas.

They kept them tied to the chairs. The women watched each other, their eyes all they had. All the life in the world in them. An eternity of looking condensed here, into not being alone in this. Mathilde lost consciousness first. After fifteen minutes her head sank to her chest. Dora still held her in her gaze. Would not look at them. Would not give them the pleasure of the eyes of their prey in the intimate moments of death.

When Dora's head fell they moved them to the bedroom. Pulled the covers back and put the bodies, still breathing, on the bed. They took off Mathilde's shoes, placed them neatly against the wall. Turned them to face one another in a last embrace, entwined the fingers of Dora's left hand and Mathilde's right in a mock scene of sorrow. Then they pulled the covers back over them. How else, for God's sake, could the covers have been so firmly up to their necks? No two people ever lie so neatly, die so neatly, covers firmly tucked up.

They placed Dora's key on the shelf next to the bedroom door, locked it with their own behind them. Straightened the kitchen chairs. A tabby cat watched from the corner near the stove, its white tail-tip twitching. They locked the front door behind them, pocketed their gloves. If the neighbours saw anything, it was nothing they hadn't seen before: five Germans coming down from a meeting in the attic flat.

Toller is still open in my hands. I close the book.

It is time for me to sleep. My tongue is dry as a lizard's. I think I'll just stay here.

When Bev comes at nine Ruth is still in her chair in the front room. A few moths cling to the ceiling, but most lie motionless on the floor, a thick, dusty-black carpet. Bev doesn't speak to her but leans in and touches her hand – then her own flies to her mouth. As she calms herself, an old book and some yellowed papers slide off Ruth's lap and make a mess on the floor. She'll clean that up later. Slowly, Bev leans in again. She picks up the hand, holds it in both of hers.

Afterwards she walks down the hall to the kitchen and boils the kettle for a cup of coffee. Sniffs at the milk in the fridge, because Ruth always leaves it there too long.

Perched on a stool Bev surveys the cheap trinkets and keepsakes and practical things in the room. She realises she hasn't just sat here since she applied for the job, three years ago. That day the old woman had gestured with her still-magnificent hands at the mess and creeping dust around her and said, 'As you can see, I can't do this alone.'

'I can see that all right,' Bev had said.

On the windowsill above the sink a velvet-leaved violet survives by catching steam. A small porcelain pig lying on its back is very happy with himself, looking down on his curly tail and anatomically detailed – over-detailed, she thinks now – penis. Bet that's not Australian. On the table is a faded photograph of two girls at a fair, and on the fridge an appointment card for Professor Melnikoff. Below it there's a magnet the same as the one on Bev's fridge, with a Crime Stoppers number to call if she sees anyone she doesn't like the look of, like that Portuguese woman. These objects made sense only to Ruth; Ruth held them together in a constellation of story: the violet, the pig, the photo, the card and the magnet. Now they are junk.

Bev tips the half-cup of black fluid down the sink. She pulls the phone from its cradle in the wall, dials the necessary number and starts to clean.

Acknowledgements

My most profound debt is to my friend Ruth Blatt (1906–2001), whose humour and humility I admired almost as much as her courage. I am also grateful to Charmian Brinson, Richard Dove and John Spalek for discussions with me. The plot of this novel, the relationships between the characters and their interior lives are all invented. But many of the events depicted actually happened. For material on these and others, I am indebted to *I Was a German: The Autobiography of Ernst Toller*, William Morrow, New York, 1934; and Toller's *Look Through the Bars: Letters from Prison, Poems, and a New Version of 'The Swallow Book'*, translated by R. Ellis Roberts, Farrar & Rinehart, New York, 1937; *The Strange Case of Dora Fabian and Mathilde Wurm: A Study of German Political Exiles in London During the 1930s* by Charmian Brinson, Peter Lang, Bern, 1996; *He Was a German: A Biography of Ernst Toller* by Richard Dove, Libris, London, 1990; *Die Göttin und ihr Sozialist: Christiane Grautoff – ihr Leben mit Ernst Toller*, edited by Werner Fuld and Albert Ostermaeier, Weidle Verlag, Bonn, 1996; *Der Fall Jacob-Wesemann (1935/1936): Ein Beitrag sur Geschichte der Schweiz in der Zwischenkriegszeit* by J. N. Willi, Peter Lang, Bern/Frankfurt a.M., 1972; and *Nazi Refugee Turned Gestapo Spy: The Life of Hans Wesemann, 1895–1971* by James J. Barnes and Patience P. Barnes, Greenwood Publishing Group, 2001.

On a personal note, I am indebted to the Rockefeller Foundation, the Australia Council and the University of Technology, Sydney. The book has benefited hugely from the close and kind attention of its editors, Venetia Butterfield of Penguin UK, Terry Karten of Harper-Collins USA and Ben Ball of Penguin Australia. My agent, Sarah Chalfant, has been the most wonderful source of strength for many years. My children, Imogen, Polly and Max, have been more patient, and more inspiring, than they yet know. My greatest thanks go to my husband, Craig Allchin, whose wisdom and insight sustain the life and the work.

About the Author

Anna Funder is an Australian writer who grew up in Melbourne. She has worked as an international lawyer specializing in human rights and constitutional law. She is the prizewinning author of *Stasiland: Stories from Behind the Berlin Wall*, which has been published in twenty countries and translated into sixteen languages. In 2004 *Stasiland* won the BBC Samuel Johnson Prize, the most prestigious nonfiction award in the United Kingdom. *All That I Am* is her first novel. Anna Funder lives in Brooklyn with her husband and children.

Sources

When Hitler came to power on 30 January 1933 my friend Ruth and her friends fled into exile. From there, they tried to bring him down. This is their story, or what I have made of it. It is reconstructed from fossil fragments, much as you might draw skin and feathers over an assembly of dinosaur bones, to fully see the beast. These are the bones I found.

Most characters' names are genuine, others have been changed. Toller's secretary in New York City was Ilse Herzfeld; my character Uncle Erwin Thomas, who suffered qualms of conscience from within the Nazi elite, is largely based on Erwin Planck, son of the Nobel Prize-winning physicist Max Planck. Erwin Planck was killed in January 1945 for his role in the von Stauffenberg plot to assassinate Hitler. Jaeger's equivalent at the German embassy in London was the (non-Nazi) diplomat Herr zu Putlitz. Wolfram Wolf is an invented name.

For Dora's life I have relied on *The Strange Case of Dora Fabian and Mathilde Wurm: A Study of German Political Exiles in London During the 1930s* by Charmian Brinson, Peter Lang, Bern, 1996. Dora's speech on the need to 'liberate half of humanity from the endless trivia of the household' comes substantially from Brinson p. 111, quoting Dora's articles in *Jungsozialistische Blätter*, 5, No. 5, May 1926, p. 156; and *Kulturwille*, 3, No. 9, 1 September 1926, p. 179 (my translations). On Dora being lifted into the air by an SS man at a Hitler rally, see Brinson p. 120, n. 76, quoting a letter to her from Pieter Siemsen,

Berlin, 9 January 1991.

Dora said that the desperate women in the crowd at the Hitler rally were subject to 'chiliastic enchantment' in an article published in the *Sozialistische Arbeiterzeitung*, 14 April 1932 (Brinson pp. 119–20 and n. 75, 76).

On the 'burglaries' at the flat, especially following Seymour Cocks's revelations in parliament, see the report after Dora and Mathilde's deaths in the *Manchester Guardian*, 6 April 1935 (Brinson p. 103, n. 239). And Dora is alleged to have said to her friend Ellen Wilkinson, 'The greatest asset the Nazi agents have is that no one, neither police nor one's friends, will *believe* that anyone can do the things here that we have proof they do.' (Brinson pp. 131–32, n. 150, italics are in original.) On Seymour Cocks's address to the parliament, see *Hansard*, 5th Series, Parliamentary Debates, House of Commons, vol. 285, cols 1019 ff., Brinson pp. 130–31. Dora is reported to have said to Roy Ganz, 'I suppose that one day I shall meet the same sort of end as those who have been working in different parts of the Continent.' (Brinson pp. 168–69, quoting *Evening Standard*, 'Refugees' Death Premonition', 5 April 1935, pp. 1, 5.)

The inquest proceedings are no longer to be found in the National Archives at Kew. There is a gutted file containing only a few pieces of paper and a passport-sized photograph of Dora's friend, who cannot be named for legal reasons. References on the front of the file indicate there were other volumes, most likely destroyed. For Mrs Allworth's testimony, see Brinson p. 164, n. 54: Public Records Office Kew, MEPOL 3/871, 3G, p. 1. On Dora's 'suicide note', see Brinson p. 160, n. 36, as given in Public Records Office Kew, MEPOL, 3/871, 3A, p. 4. Brinson quotes the coroner as directing the jury that '"if she wrote the note, and if it was correctly translated", it indicated that she had committed suicide because of unrequited love' (p. 181). The coroner was so quoted in 'Tragedy of German Woman's Unrequited Love', *Daily Mail*, 11 April 1935, p. 21 (Brinson, p. 181, n. 151).

Brinson describes contemporary accounts of the funeral on pp. 182–83. The epigraph to Part III of *All That I Am*, 'You, a writer, were missing . . .' is from Rudolf Olden's letter to G. Tergit, 24 May 1935 (Brinson p. 183, n. 165, my translation). Fenner Brockway is quoted as telling the media Dora was 'one of the most courageous persons I have known' in *New Leader*, 12 April 1935, p. 3 (Brinson p. 120).

For Toller's life I have relied mainly on his own accounts in *I Was a German: The Autobiography of Ernst Toller*, William Morrow, New York, 1934, and *Look Through the Bars: Letters from Prison, Poems, and a New Version of 'The Swallow Book'*, translated by R. Ellis Roberts, Farrar & Rinehart, New York, 1937, from which comes the dedication to Dora ('I call to mind a woman, to whose courageous act . . .'), p. xv. On Dr Lipp's papal and carnation madness, see Toller's account in *I Was a German* (pp. 161–63). I have relied also on R. Dove's, *He Was a German: A Biography of Ernst Toller*, Libris, London, 1990, including for the quote from Toller's speech to the Paris Writers Congress: 'Fear is the psychological foundation of dictatorship . . .' (p. 245); for Goebbels on Toller (p. 200); and for bringing to my attention Auden's 'Spy Song' (p. 227) and 'In Memory of Ernst Toller' (p. 265). *Die Göttin und ihr Sozialist: Christiane Grautoff – ihr Leben mit Ernst Toller*, edited by Werner Fuld and Albert Ostermaeier, Weidle Verlag, Bonn, 1996, was important for insights into Toller's private world.

For Berthold Jacob's life and work I have relied mostly on *Der Fall Jacob-Wesemann (1935/1936): Ein Beitrag sur Geschichte der Schweiz in der Zwischenkriegszeit* by J. N. Willi, Herbert Lang, Bern Peter, Lang Frankfurt/M 1972.

For Hans Wesemann's life, see *Nazi Refugee Turned Gestapo Spy: The Life of Hans Wesemann, 1895–1971* by James J. Barnes and Patience P. Barnes, Greenwood Publishing Group, 2001, and specifically: Hans's visit to Toller (p. 6); his 'visit' to Hitler (*Die Welt am Montag*, 19 November 1928, Barnes p. 14); Goebbels' attack on his 'sick brain' (*Der Angriff*, 10 March 1931, p. 1, Barnes p. 18); his 'visit' to Goebbels' godmother (*Die Welt am Montag*, 20 October 1930, Barnes pp. 17–18). Also Charmian Brinson, 'The Gestapo and the German Political Exiles in Britain During the 1930s: The Case of Hans Wesemann and Others', *German Life and Letters*, vol. 51, no. 1, 1998, pp. 43–64.

More generally, but still profoundly, I am indebted to Richard J. Evans's *The Coming of the Third Reich*, Penguin, London, 2004, most especially for his noting of the marchers going in circles the night Hitler was appointed (p. 310), and the intellectuals caving in (p. 424). Ian Buruma's essay 'Faces of the Weimar Republic', in the catalogue *Glitter and Doom: German Portraits from the 1920s* (from the Metropolitan Museum of Art), edited by Sabine Rewald, Yale University Press, 2006, was my source for descriptions of Berlin prostitutes. The portrait *Agosta the 'Winged One' and Rasha the 'Black Dove'* by Christian Schad (1929) is reproduced in the same catalogue.

The first epigraph on page vii is from 'In Memory of Ernst Toller' by W.H. Auden, Copyright Ó 1976, 1991, The Estate of W.H. Auden; the quote on page 159 is also reproduced by permission of The Estate of W.H. Auden. The second epigraph on page vii is reproduced by permission of Mute Song; the third is Simon Leys' translation of Antoine de Rivarol in *Other People's Thoughts*, Black Inc., Melbourne, 2007, p.11.

Insights,
Interviews
& More...

Interview with Anna Funder

Interviewer: Boris Kelly
Date: November 21, 2011
Publication: Overland magazine,
www.overland.org.au

ANNA FUNDER is an internationally acclaimed bestselling Australian author whose debut, *Stasiland*, recounted the personal stories of people who worked for the East German secret police and those whose lives were affected and even destroyed by their covert activities. The book won a swag of international prizes. The manuscript of her follow-up first novel, *All That I Am*, created a sensation at the 2010 Frankfurt Book Fair. [**Note:** The novel has, since this interview, been published internationally to huge critical and popular acclaim. It was a number-one bestseller in Australia and was on the bestseller list for more than a year. It has also won many awards, including the most prestigious national prize for fiction in Australia, the Miles Franklin Award.] The novel derives from real events in the lives of activists, intellectuals, and artists in pre–World War II Germany. *All That I Am* begins with this:

'When Hitler came to power I was in the bath. . . . The wireless in the living room was turned up loud . . . , but all that drifted down to me were waves of happy cheering, like a football match.'

Overland's Boris Kelly corresponded with Anna Funder.

BK: *Both of your books deal with the politics and, to some extent, the logistics of covert surveillance. What is it about spying that fascinates you?*

AF: To secretly gain information about people and use it against them is a form of power, often illicit. It is done everywhere—by political parties, by secret services, by news organizations, by Internet giants, by corporations trying to sell us something. I think it is a kind of voyeurism and theft combined, and I think we need to be wary. Of course, that is also what writers do, so the ethical entanglements of it are personal, not theoretical, to me.

BK: *The central characters in* All That I Am *are German émigrés forced out of the country after the burning of the Reichstag and Hitler's ascent to power. Although they are Jewish, their persecution by the National Socialists is primarily a consequence of their political activities, not their religion or ethnicity. What was it about this particular moment in history and the lives of these characters, most of whom are based on real people, that drew your attention?*

AF: I like the dramatic tension of telling a story about prescience and courage. These people were the bell-ringers in a world that would not listen. The action takes place between 1933 and 1935, which is a long time before the war and the better-known stories from that time. In the beginning—though, of course, the Nazis were by nature ▶

Interview with Anna Funder *(continued)*

anti-Semitic—their first priority was to eliminate or expel the educated, the outspoken, and the cultural elite. Hence the expulsions as soon as they came to power. Later came the extraordinary and little-known extraterritorial assassination squads that were sent out. But I never saw myself as drawn to a period. I was drawn to write about the characters themselves. I am interested in courage and its flip side, terror. I am interested in how we can be braver than is good for us, or, on the other side, we can let ourselves and everyone else around us down.

BK: *Historical novels can, and perhaps should, resonate in the present. Did you have any thought of contemporary parallels when writing the book? I am especially interested in your thoughts on Australia.*

AF: I don't think this is a historical novel—it does not set out to represent an era for its own sake. It is, however, one that makes the past firmly present. The situations the characters find themselves in—speaking out against unjust and outrageous governmental power—are utterly contemporary. I could have written the same book about characters in China, or Libya, or Burma, or Russia and set it in the present. The idea that things can be known as facts, and yet not be fully apprehended in the hearts and minds of people or the body politic, is something that fascinates me because it speaks to the fact that humans are only in the second instance rational beings—we apprehend things by emotion first, hence the force of the novel form in our culture.

As for specifics, well, there are many resonances. For instance, Clara's brother is on a ship of Jews fleeing Hitler that is off the coast of Florida, but it is turned away by the U.S., Canadian, and Cuban administrations and sent back to Europe. That is the kind of thing happening off the Australian coast now.

More important, I think the relationships between the characters in the novel are ones I see all around— mistaken loves that are nevertheless permanent and passionate; true loves that don't turn into practical, everyday lives lived together; the difference between what we want and what we need and how, try as we might, we just can't see it.

BK: *There are moments in the novel that contain highly significant but very subtle plot and character details that, on a first reading, are likely to be missed. On a second reading their weight is more apparent. How important are such fine details to the craft and technique of the writer?*

AF: I think they are hugely important. Underneath the suspense story there are several others. The book is in one way about what we don't see— what an individual can miss; what a society can miss—the rise of Hitler, the boats off the coast . . . The details need to be there ▶

for the story, but also for the reader to experience the missing, and then the satisfaction of finally 'seeing'.

BK: *To take that point further: The novel is narrated in part by Ruth Becker, a ninety-four-year-old woman living in Bondi Junction in 2001. Ruth reflects on the years she spent in Germany and then London with her cousin Dora, her own journalist husband, Hans Wesemann, and the celebrated revolutionary playwright Ernst Toller. At one point Ruth says this: 'In my experience, it is entirely possible to watch something happen and not see it at all.'*

It is an observation that reflects on both her personal life, especially her marriage, and on wider social and political circumstances. How do you regard this tension between the personal and the political? Was this a challenge in writing the novel?

AF: I loved writing about what we see and what we don't. I'm interested in blindness of all kinds—the necessary ones in marriage, in life; and the devastating ones, in politics and in the limits of public compassion. For instance, I think some marriages, perhaps many, survive by selective blindness to foibles that would otherwise drive us crazy. And yet this too can lead to serious consequences. On the political plane, the blindness of appeasement in the case of the British government—and of course the Menzies government in

Australia, too, though that wasn't my subject in *All That I Am*—while understandable in some ways was also devastating, in the first instance for some of my characters, and then later for everyone. I don't draw any glib equivalence between individual human souls and the shifting movements of public consciousness, but I think one thing a novel can and should do is explore both.

BK: *Dora is the pivotal character in the book. Your characterisation is drawn from accounts of the life of Dora Fabian, a pacifist, leftist political exile active in London who was hunted by the Nazis. She is the most politically driven character in the novel. If she had lived on, do you think Dora would have returned to East or West Germany after the war?*

AF: I think she would have gone to West Germany. She had left the Socialist Workers Party a long time before. Or she might have gone to the United States, like Hannah Arendt did. Her ex-husband, Walter, went back to West Germany.

BK: *Do you write by hand at any point in the process of drafting?*

AF: I have a notebook that I write things in—scraps, observations, ideas, pre-sleep insights. I never draft longhand, though sometimes the notes in the notebook are sentences or paragraphs that come out ▶

of nowhere and that I need to get down. When I look at the long-ago *Stasiland* notebooks—and there are ten of them—I can see the beginnings of paragraphs that were then fixed and honed for the book. Some come pristine, though. For *Stasiland* I had the final paragraph of the book—'children on swings and roundabouts I never noticed were there'—long before it was written. For *All That I Am* I had the last scene with Bev, and the last line where she 'starts to clean' also for a long, long time before I was done. These things are strange. It is as if I have an ending to write to, a point of hiatus or upswing or unfinished business that I nevertheless know is the final note of the book.

BK: *Are you a meticulous note-taker during the research phase?*

AF: I don't know that *meticulous* is the right word. It implies too much straight diligence. I do take lots of notes that I carry around with me. But they are bowerbird notes—bits of bright things that strike my mind.

BK: *I'm interested to know whether you might at some point write something closer to home, something with an explicitly Australian theme. Would you mind telling me what you are currently working on?*

AF: I'm working on a novel. It's set in contemporary times and it's not very political. Or not at the moment, at any rate.

BK: *Given the acceleration of social and political volatility in the world today and the reactivation of the Left, do you think there is a place for the overtly political novel?*

AF: I think there is always room for good novels. If they deal with political issues, so much the better. But to be good, they have to be about what it is that makes us human, and not, in the first instance, about prescriptions for living.

BK: *Why the title* All That I Am?

AF: When Toller first sees Dora she's holding an audience entranced with a speech. She extends her hand and he sees she is someone who holds her own life in her palm, to do with as she wishes. My characters are people who, like many activists, have to assess the value of their lives when powerful, possibly fatal forces are arrayed against them. Is it worth it to them to give up their lives? And on the other hand, for instance for Hans, he falls short of his ideas of himself. We all do this. When we do, we comfort ourselves with the idea that 'we're only human.' I wanted the title to encompass the extraordinariness, the hugeness, the miracle of a single human being, and at the same time the smallness of a single soul. ෴

Behind the Book

I SPENT FIVE YEARS working on *All That I Am*, including a summer in London in 2006 as part of the research and time in New York and Berlin. The novel was the first thing I thought of in the morning, I worked on it all day, and it was the last thing I thought of before I went to sleep. Other things happened in my real life during that time—some of them quite momentous. My little daughters grew and started school; my son was born. But the whole time, I lived and breathed this book, like some vast, secret, inner parallel life. It took five years to write, but really, this novel has been brewing all my adult life.

I met the real Ruth, who is the genesis of Ruth Becker in *All That I Am*, when I was nineteen. She was exactly sixty years older than me, but so alive, so present in the moment that it was as if history itself had collapsed. The twentieth century concertina-ed back on itself. Having a friend so much older made life seem long, but at the same time it made history seem short. In fact, the stories that Ruth told of her anti-Hitler activities stopped being history and started to be something that a very brave, very humble friend of mine had had the presence of mind and the courage to do.

In conversation Ruth would move from criticising Hitler to criticising our own (Australian, conservative, and anti-refugee) government at the time. Her behavior made it clear to me that whatever the political regime one may be living under, there will always be people who see things for what they are (whether that's dire or just moderately unpalatable) and who choose to speak out. It is this kind of courage, along with the moral compass underlying it, that has always fascinated me.

In the late 1980s I studied in Berlin, and then returned to live there several times through the 1990s. Ruth and I wrote to each other every time I was away. What I knew of my friend's personal history was always with me in that city. I could walk the streets and see the bullet holes in the buildings from street fights between the communists and the right-wing, proto-Nazi groups in the 1920s, or from when the Russians came at the end of the war, and I could put Ruth's life in some kind of physical perspective. I had known for a long time, for instance, her story of being put up against the wall by the Gestapo in starfish position and 'shot all around'. It is another thing entirely to run your finger over a wall and feel how deep a gouge a bullet makes.

All good writing comes out of love of some kind. You can tell a book that hasn't come from this passionate source; it refuses to live. I did a lot of the writing for *Stasiland* in Berlin. To me, that city, and others in the former East Germany, were not places overrun by Nazis and then by the Stasi. They were, instead, full of the courage of people who refused to collaborate with these unjust regimes— wry, funny, self-effacing, and hugely brave people who would not let ▶

Behind the Book *(continued)*

themselves be compromised, who would not betray their fellows. *Stasiland* was, if anything, an homage to these extraordinary people, who were being forgotten in the new, unified Germany. When I came to write *All That I Am*, at least part of the impetus was to honour a group of hugely brave, largely forgotten people: those who resisted the Nazi regime in the mid-1930s. They were examples of what is best in human nature—the kind of conscience that seems naturally to take the well-being of others into account and place it as one's own moral core—people who refused to collaborate with an unjust regime and to let themselves be compromised, and who put themselves in danger for the greater good. Wrapped up in storytelling, in bringing to light true and forgotten heroes, still the aim of any good novel remains to give us an insight into the unseen machinations of the soul. ∽

Also by Anna Funder

STASILAND

Truth can be stranger—and more fascinating—than fiction. When the Berlin Wall fell in 1989, it revealed to a shocked world one of the most pernicious surveillance states of all time: East Germany. Anna Funder's international bestseller *Stasiland* is a lyrical, at times funny account of the courage some people found to resist the communist dictatorship, and the consequences for those who collaborated. Funder meets Miriam, the sixteen-year-old accused by the regime of trying to start World War III, and Frau Paul, who was separated from her baby the night the Berlin Wall went up. She visits the regime's cartographer, obsessed to this day with the Berlin Wall, and gets drunk with the legendary 'Mik Jegger' of the Eastern Bloc, once declared by the authorities—to his face—to 'no longer exist'. And Funder finds ex-Stasi men themselves, still proud of their surveillance methods, loyal to 'the Firm', and waiting for the next revolution.

Published in twenty countries, Anna Funder's powerful account of a brutal world and the survival of human decency in it has become a contemporary classic.

Read on

Also by Anna Funder *(continued)*

'A masterpiece.'

—*Sunday Times* (London)

'A heartbreaking, beautifully written book. A classic for sure.'

—Guardian Books of the Year

'Meticulous and compassionate . . . a heroic act of listening.'

—*London Review of Books*

'Humane and sensitive.' —J. M. Coetzee

'Your book struck me like no other in the last five years. It is fascinating, entertaining, hilarious, horrifying, and very important.' —Tom Hanks

Winner:
Samuel Johnson Prize

Finalist:
Age Book of the Year Awards
    (Nonfiction)
Guardian First Book Award
Queensland Premier's Literary Awards
Award for Innovation in Writing,
    Adelaide Festival
Index Freedom of Expression Award
W. H. Heinemann Award

Don't miss the next book by your favorite author. Sign up now for AuthorTracker by visiting www.AuthorTracker.com.